SKIP SCHOOL, MAKE DRAGONS

RICHARD ROBERTS

MYSTIQUE PRESS

Without bothering to unhook the cord still scattered across the cement, I took hold of the pendant in both hands. Gem side out. Fingers touching the jewel on either side, but with my hands and arms not touching each other anywhere. The current had to run through me. As far as the dragon was concerned, right now I was the soul forge that had made it.

"Sit!" I yelled.

The dragon screeched, head snapping back.

"Land! Sit!" I ordered at the top of my lungs, louder because all the movement caused the scarf to fall away from my face.

The dragon let out its distorted, warbly, predatory bird scream again. Its head and wings flailed, fighting for control of its own body. Flapping furiously, it reared up, and instead of landing it shot up into the air and leveled off to look at me.

Then it opened its mouth and breathed fire at me.

No, not quite. Steam. That approaching mass of white was fresh, concentrated steam. It would still boil me alive.

The sheriff, less a mage and more a man of action who actually had some common sense, yanked me off my feet and out of the way. My view spun for a second and I wasn't sure which way I was pointing or what was going on, but I wasn't dead, and that knowledge hit like a spike of relief.

I squealed in shock, "It shouldn't be able to do that!"

ChapterOne

"This will never fly."

"Of course it will fly, it's a dragon," I snapped.

I was too busy to be polite, okay? This was my first time making a dragon all by myself, and my uncle's soul forge was way different than my dad's. I had to double check everything and be very careful not to wake up the sleeping pigeon. I was pretty sure my uncle's sleeping potions had been out of date.

Chain of serpent essence symbols that go *past* the tail. Fire invocation goes here. Air invocations here, quarter sized. Better double up on the wing sigils to be safe. No, triple. My orange hair flopped forward over my eyes, and when a quick puff upwards didn't help, I put my stylus down and pulled my hair back with my hands, loosening the rubber band scrunchie and then fastening it back again to keep my hair back in a ponytail where it belonged and out of my face.

Now, one last little touch. I'd upped the flying sigils, so added a few extra lines and symbols my dad had discovered to make sure the dragon would be able to handle any amount of extra power.

Hands clasped behind her head, lost in hair that the sunlight made flicker exactly like flame, Lisa gave me a literally diabolical smirk and corrected, "No, I mean the town will never let a little girl run the soul forge."

I rolled my eyes, and tapped the symbols around the splayed out, unconscious pigeon in order, making sure I'd gotten them all. I'd drawn the most advanced containment I knew to make sure this didn't fail. "Of course they will. Who else can operate it? Do they want to run Goblita without a bioengineer? Are they going to bring in a thermal engineer to try and operate the forge? Or a tablet scribe? Those think they can do everything. I'd love to watch them try, especially if I have a bowl of popcorn. Besides, you said it's legally mine."

Lisa nodded her head, her glowing, slit-pupiled pink eyes closing for a moment and her curving black horns... not doing anything, really, except catching my attention. Her thin, spade-tipped tail flicked to one side, then the other, swishing her short, lavender dress. Her little red mouth pursed tight, then smiled, then parted in a fangy grin. "That's what Leo told me, and that's what the will says. Your family gets the house and belongings, you specifically get the soul forge."

Me, I scowled some more and gave the whole arrangement one last lookover. It all seemed right. "And I'm the only member of the family here, so the house is mine until Dad decides what to do, which will be weeks at least. When he finds out I'm running the forge, I bet he'll let me keep going. He trusts me. I'm a prodigy!"

"So you've mentioned," she snickered, kicking a hoof in the dust.

I stuck my tongue out at the thirteen-year-old demoness. She was about to see.

Opening the hatches on either side, I reached in, took hold of the green, shiny, uncomfortably hot, fist-sized soul fragment in the center, and lifted it up to touch the leads.

Exhaustion hit me like a hammer. I dropped the crystal from numb fingers, letting it float back to the center of its containment chamber. Pulling an arm out, I propped my elbow against the top of the forge, and wheezed.

Seconds later, a long tail with a crest of spikes and a fan of iridescent feathers around the sides flicked past my face. Oops. I'd missed watching the transformation!

The newly forged dragon sat up on the altar (Dad and I hated that mystical-sounding word, but it was official terminology) and cocked its head from side to side, looking around the forge chamber.

Lisa leaned back against a tool rack, trying to sneer condescendingly, but her glowing eyes were fixed on the dragon. Oh, yeah, she was impressed. Sarcasm mixed with cautious awe as the little demon asked, "Isn't it supposed to be pigeon-sized?"

"I overdesigned. Prodigies don't do anything halfway," I replied airily, as if I'd planned this.

I had definitely overdesigned. No question there. The dragon was as big as me. Of course I was exhausted, if I'd supplied the power to build that with only a pigeon's puny soul fragment. If I didn't have the magic capacity of a whole squad of regular adult mages the spell would have failed and I'd have hurt myself.

Still trying to pretend this was deliberate, I lurched over to the study table. I kept my back to Lisa to hide my pulling the rolled-up letter out of the collar I'd had waiting, and slipping it into a much bigger collar. Then, grandly and hopefully not wobbling in front of my ex-uncle's sardonic house guest, I strolled up to the dragon and fastened the collar around its neck.

"You know how to find my dad, right? Our house up at the lake? You've delivered messages before?" I asked the long-nosed, sharp-toothed, half-reptile half-bird.

It made a deep, stuttering coo noise, and nodded. The intelligence boost had worked perfectly! The dragon was a success. Just, um… an *extra* success.

I gave Lisa a glance. For all her sassy wordplay, she didn't hesitate a second to actually help, unlocking the window and sliding it up and open. My brand new dragon hopped off the altar, flapped wings wide enough they knocked a dozen small tools off of shelves in the process, and glided over to the window ledge. It had to tuck in its wings tight and wriggle through the gap to get out, but as soon as it succeeded, it leaped upwards and out of sight into the sky.

I wiped perspiration off my forehead with the back of my wrist. When that just left both wrist and forehead wet, I picked up an old, stiff rag stained with who knew what and mopped my forehead with that.

Lisa pulled her tablet out of her wristband, and rubbed her thumb over one of the lines near the top. The dots and dashes lit up, and as she waved the tablet around, the tools my dragon had knocked over floated back to their original places.

"Thanks," I told her. My strength was coming back, but I definitely wanted to lean against this writing table for another minute.

She shrugged languidly. "I have to give my new host a reason to keep me here."

"I wouldn't kick you out. If Uncle Leonard wanted you to stay, you can stay," I promised.

Lisa frowned. Her mouth twitched to the left. It twitched to the right. She stared at me, head slightly tilted. Slowly, nose pinched up and voice gravely with confusion, she said, "You're... a... nice person and I like you, Artifact."

"Just call me Art, please," I begged.

"Humans need liquid after working hard. Let me go get you some orange juice," the demoness offered.

Smiling, I admitted, "That sounds like a super great—"

A knock on the door interrupted me. A loud knock.

"That's the business door, not the front door," noted Lisa. She hooked her tablet back onto her wrist, gave her hair a little flick, tugged at her skirt, and stood poised with one tiny hoof in front of the other, instantly perfect. I'd known her all of twenty-four hours, but was there something stiff about all that? Like this was training, not natural pride?

Abandoning all hope of liquid refreshment, I headed for the door into the office. My soul forge, my office, right? This was what I'd wanted!

And I did. With every step a little fizz came back. My first customer as a bioengineer!

Lisa swept past me. No, strutted, chin held high, passing through the dim office and reaching the door to the street several paces ahead of me. As formal as a butler, she took hold of the latch and gave me a questioning look.

I nodded.

Lisa opened the door.

Chapter Two

The glare of another bright, sunshiny day in Goblita poured in, nearly blinding me. On the sidewalk, framed in that golden glow, stood a teenage witch.

Had to be a witch. *Had* to be. She was maybe two years older than me, maybe, in a single piece, ankle-length black dress. Shiny black, tied at the wrists, with little charms and pouches hanging from what might technically be a rope belt, but was also a shiny black, a choice of style rather than poverty. Tied up in fancy braids, her burgundy hair went right down to the roots, and since she probably hadn't been bioengineered at her age, that meant high-quality hair care potions.

She was pretty, a round-cheeked pretty rather than Lisa's inhuman heart-shaped face, and knew it. The burgundy-haired stranger looked down at me with a haughty scowl, and managed to carry the huge black satchel at her side with regal ease. "I'm here to see the bioengineer. Fetch him, please," she ordered.

Lisa's butler formality melted into natural insouciance. She shrugged a shoulder, spilling her dress off of it and giving me a peek at the black, jaggedly pointed magic circle tattooed on her back. Pointing a thumb at me, she told the stranger, "That's her.

You saw the dragon, right? She made it."

I nodded, grinning with pride. The stranger and Lisa might have all the attitude, but I got results.

The burgundy-haired girl looked me over, really fully noticing me for the first time. She looked at Lisa, and then back at me.

My pride fizzled into embarrassment. I knew exactly what I had to look like right now. For starters, I was filthy with dust. My supposedly strawberry-blonde but actually orange hair would be matted, curly, and escaping the pigtail in individual spirals. My overalls were old, worn, and stained, and the simple white undershirt underneath blotchy with sweat. I had on sandals, and while so did the girl at the door, mine were crude and worn, and hers were laced up her ankles in spirals of golden thread. Oh, and I hadn't taken off my goggles.

So I was very, very surprised when the girl was the one who suddenly flashed an awkward smile. Setting down her huge, rectangular satchel in the doorway, she used that as an excuse to turn her face away and mumble, "Sorry. It's just, this is a really big day for me. I'm here to get my familiar."

Yep. I knew it. Witch!

Still, a familiar… I mean, whew. That was a lot more than a messenger dragon, or even upgrading somebody's livestock. I knew how to do it, but… honesty forced me to say, "This will be my first time making a familiar. I'll understand if you want to go down to Lady Angel instead."

The girl's eyes went wide, and she exclaimed in a hurry, "No! I'd rather it be done today. I'm sure you can do it. I did see the dragon, and I'm impressed."

She started to give me a glowing, admiring smile, only to interrupt it with a little jerk and another hurried exclamation. "Oh, and my name is Rhubella. Please, call me Ruby."

Who doesn't like praise and being admired? I grinned up at her, and held out my hand. "Call me Art."

"I'll be happy to," she assured me. Taking my hand in hers, which felt calloused despite the faint slickness of skin care lotion, she lifted my knuckles to her lips and gave them a quick kiss.

A very quick kiss. Downright absentminded, an act of formality hurried through, honoring some witch rules I would never understand. Still, I hurriedly brought the subject back to business. "Did you bring a soul fragment?"

"I did," she promised. Reaching into the neckline of her dress, she pulled out a necklace and fairy-shaped locket. Opening the locket to reveal its padded interior, she drew out a tiny green crystal shard, and held it out to me.

All of which was a wise and responsible way to protect and deliver something as valuable as a soul shard. Especially one like this. My eyes went wide looking at the thing in my palm. It was a good half the size of my pinkie fingernail. That was almost as big as a soul shard from a human! If she'd bought it, it had cost a fortune. If she'd harvested it… well, all the candidates were seriously magical creatures.

Ruby wasn't done, either. Kneeling down, she pushed down the fabric sides of her satchel with, if anything, more care than she handled the soul shard. Out of it she pulled a wickerwork box lined on the inside with burgundy cushions.

On the cushions slept a fluffy black cat.

I threw up my hands. "Professional responsibility requires me to warn you that turning a pet into your familiar is something most people regret. The animal keeps its memories and personality, and what is charming in a pet can be counterproductive and downright annoying in an assistant. Do you really want to give your cat the ability to open its own food containers and rely on it to use your tablet for you?"

"Yes," she answered emphatically, voice a touch hoarse and face turned away, looking into the cat carrier. She fiddled with the locket, and to my surprise it opened up on the other face as well. I couldn't even see what she pulled out until she held it up in one hand for me. "And I brought this."

A tiny green sequin sat in her palm, twinkling with its own internal light.

Holy smokes, that was a piece of her own soul fragment.

I wheezed in shock. "That's black magic!"

Calm, distant, still looking at the cat and not at me, Ruby said, "Not if it's my soul and I give it to you of my own choice."

How did she even get a piece of her own soul fragment??? Okay, no. Back to Earth, Artifact. Back to being a professional bioengineer.

Professional bioengineerly, I warned her, "You are aware of all the consequences? You will affect each other's health. Your familiar's life will be extended drastically. If you regret this decision, you'll be stuck with it for decades. It's actually possible the cat will outlive you."

"I hope so," Ruby murmured.

That made me bend down and look in the carrier. The fluff had made me miss it, but the cat was so thin as to be almost skeletal, with patchy fur around the face and loose skin that puddled around it. This was an old, old cat. So old that it might not survive a trip down to Lady Angel to find a regular bioengineer who might refuse to do this not-quite-black-magic anyway.

My heart melted. "Bring her into the forge," I instructed. Plucking the glittery little piece of Ruby's soul fragment from her hand, I placed it and the larger, dead soul fragment in Lisa's hand. "Hold these please, assistant."

Lisa tilted her face down a couple of inches so she could give me a sardonic Look, but at least it was an amused and friendly sardonic Look. She cupped her other hand over the little shards of life with all the care I could ask for, and carried them from the dark office into the workshop.

Ruby scooped out the cat with exquisite tenderness, holding the drugged and sleeping feline to her chest as she stepped inside. She blinked, and said automatically, "It's hot in here."

I snapped my fingers. Uncle Leo had liked magical lamps. They all turned on. A hiss sounded from somewhere inside the house, as an ice elemental hurrying to catch up with the heat stirred the air with a faint but so very welcome chill breeze. Somewhere upstairs, music started to play. I hadn't tried to aim the spell.

It was actually the only spell I knew, that I could cast personally and spontaneously without equipment like a tablet or soul forge. Spontaneous magic tended to, um, overcharge when I used it. It wasn't a fancy spell, either. That wasn't the point. The point was that I had just supplied the power for every appliance in the house personally, and showed no sign of feeling the strain.

Ruby noticed. Ruby was impressed. Her back straightened a little with new confidence, and she followed Lisa into the forge.

That left me to nudge Ruby's satchel inside and close the door, but I tried to do it professionally. It gave me a few extra seconds to enjoy the air conditioning. I'd deliberately left that off thinking I might need all the strength I had today, but… I guess I'd just felt like showing off.

When I got into the forge, Lisa was disappearing through the door into the house, but she'd left the soul shard and living soul speck in the secure, covered bowls on the bench where they belonged.

Me, I got busy. Starting with an actual living animal instead of making one from scratch would make this much easier, but I still could not afford even one mistake. I checked the soul forge, twiddling its cage layers, rubbing my thumb over spots on the sigils, made sure the wires were firmly connected. I refreshed all the reagents in their holders on the altar. I got my pen and made a lot of rough sketches of how I could go about this, then copied a few of those onto the altar itself with my stylus.

Retrieving the larger soul shard from the jar, I laid the little green glass-like flake in its depression in the center of the altar, and patted it. "Place the cat here."

Like pouring the world's most precious oil into a bowl, the burgundy-haired teenage witch slid her fluffy black cat out of her arms and onto the stone surface of the altar. Barely audible, she whispered, "You'll feel better soon, Sophie."

Fast asleep, no doubt from a potion Ruby had made herself with love, the cat lay completely still. Only the subtle movements of its chest confirmed for me that it was alive.

Ruby stroked the cat's ears once, then stood back up straight, and gave me a weak, curious smile. "I guess you're new in town?"

What could I say to that? The truth? That my parents had sent me to Goblita to live with my dad's favorite brother Uncle Leonard, because I could get a much better education in the city? That I'd shown up yesterday at Uncle Leonard's door only to have it opened by a demoness my age, who informed me that Uncle Leonard had died two days before and left me everything in his will?

It would have helped if I had any idea who Lisa was, why she had been living with my Uncle Leonard, or indeed if anyone had ever breathed a word to me about Lisa's existence.

At least I barely knew Uncle Leonard. Writing the letter to Dad that his brother was gone had not been fun to do. Now it was on its way. At least it would arrive with word that his prodigy daughter was safe and sound and finally doing bioengineering for real.

I settled for an honest, "Yeah, but I'm Goblita's new bioengineer from now on. It's exciting and nerve-racking at the same time."

"I'm glad you're here," Ruby said, subdued but sure sounding sincere.

The door into the house flipped open. Lisa skipped in, hooves clicking on the hard floor, holding a glass of orange juice in both hands, which she held out to me.

A chilled glass, I found out as I picked it up. "Oh, bless you," I told her before taking a long, long drink.

Lisa just grinned as I chugged.

When the glass was completely empty I handed it back, wiped my mouth on my sleeve, and with renewed energy declared, "Let's do this."

With all the lights on, the workshop looked... still dusty, but a lot more technical. Dozens of curiously shaped tools hanging on racks or sitting on shelves. Bottles of cleaning fluid and oils. Lead balls and a heating stick to use in repairing or modifying the soul forge. Lots and lots of papers from the notes of previous creations, mostly bound into book covers and stacked on shelves of their own. And the gleaming cage of bronze, silver, and copper that was the soul forge, a cage not of bars but of very precisely shaped metal symbols, all surrounding the cavity that a honking big soul fragment floated in. You couldn't harvest fragments this big. You couldn't make an animal big enough, powerful enough, to have a fragment anywhere near soul forge quality. You could only find them, usually in dungeons, or in the rubble after an earthmover attack.

I took up my stylus again, and drew symbols. Lots of symbols. Sophie didn't need to be bigger, but she needed to be smarter, with human intelligence and usable hands. That latter took great precision, but I had that design memorized and checked my uncle's notes three times to be sure. She would need magic of her own, as well as linked to Ruby's. I laid out a whole network to make sure that vitality would never overflow, but mix back and forth depending on how much each of them could handle.

"I don't recognize these," commented Lisa, tapping a symbol I used several times.

"Because only three people in the world know them. Me. My dad who developed them. The Dollmaker, who consults my dad for research," I answered distantly. Dad always said I would be Dollmaker someday, but now was not the time to get distracted.

I kept writing. I checked notes. That was embarrassing, since I wanted to seem like I knew what I was doing for a job this important, but being competent was more important than looking competent.

Finally. There were only two steps left. I very cautiously opened the cat Sophie's mouth, and with a fingertip stuck the shining speck from Ruby's soul fragment onto the back of the cat's tongue.

Then I reached into the soul forge, lifted up its own fist-sized fragment, and touched it to the contact points.

Oof. I might not be supplying new mass, but making a familiar was not easy. My heart was suddenly pounding, I breathed hard and started sweating again from effort I couldn't feel but my body suffered anyway. Keeping my grip firm and precise, I touched the fragment to the contact points in a careful order, then went back and did it again, lingering when I didn't like what I felt.

On the altar, Sophie wriggled. She writhed. She yawned, lifting her legs and flailing them around. The symbols I'd written over the altar lifted into the air as she changed position, then sank into her. Little hands, really paws with thumbs and more flexible toes, made grasping motions. Other than that, not a lot of drama. This wasn't a major physical alteration.

A faint vibration told me I'd reached the finishing point, and I yanked the soul fragment back into the center of the cage, then let it float. Job done.

Sophie sat up, stretched like a cat with forelegs extended forward, and gave her whole body a shake.

Black fur flew everywhere, in a whole cloud. As it settled, it revealed a pink, wrinkly, hairless animal.

Oh, um. Oops.

Ruby let out an ear-splitting squeal. She swooped down on her defurred pet, scooping it up off the altar to cuddle it against her chest. As the pink thing struggled in her arms, she wailed, "Sophie! Sophie, are you okay?"

Sophie, voice a little yowly but entirely clear, shouted back, "My god, woman, put me down and let me demand you pick me up!"

Ruby sniffled, rubbing her face against Sophie's side, which was well filled out now and no longer skeletal. The motion did drag kitty skin around in big folds, and smeared Ruby's elegant makeup. Tears poured from the previously regal girl's eyes, leaving tracks in the mess as she sobbed, "Sophie, I was so scared. Now we'll be together forever."

The hairless familiar stopped flailing its skinny legs, and asked cautiously, "If I consent to this demeaning relationship, will you give me some of that fish dish you and your family eat? With the spices?"

"Every day," Ruby promised, voice hoarse, rocking the rejuvenated cat from side to side in her arms.

A moment of silence passed, or at least a moment broken only by Ruby's sniffing and snorting. Finally, Sophie declared, "Your terms are acceptable, at least as a start. Take me home and pet me, please."

Black dress swirling, Ruby turned around and rushed into the office. While Sophie grumbled, the burgundy-haired teen witch tucked her back into the carrier. Rummaging around in the satchel, Ruby pulled out a little velvet bag.

Then she pounced, turning and lunging at me. She wrapped her arms around my shoulders, hoisted me up off the ground, and shook me from side to side, squealing, "Thank you thank you thank you!"

"Um," I explained.

Still sniffing, but also smiling with beatific relief, Ruby set me down on the floor, and pushed the bag into my hands. The contents felt like coins. Lots of coins. Clasping my hands in both of hers, Ruby leaned down to gush at me, "If it's not enough, you can tell me when I come back tomorrow. I'll be back tomorrow. You are such a wonder. I want to see you again. Tomorrow, okay?"

"Um," I repeated.

Folding up the satchel, Ruby picked up the wicker cat carrier by its handle in her other hand. She gave Lisa a beaming smile when the demoness held open the street door, and then giggled when Lisa held her tablet up to her ear, mimed swiping across it with her thumb and pointing at me, then did it again.

I rolled my eyes and tried not to look embarrassed. I was also really glad that psychology was illegal. That gesture might mean now that Ruby should ask me out on a date later, but I knew its original meaning was that a love spell should be used on the desired date. Having a demoness like me was going to be a distinctly mixed blessing, I could tell that already.

With the door closed, Lisa turned and leaned against it, ankles crossed and one hoof in front of the other. With only a hint of slyness, she asked me, "So, how much of that went wrong?"

"Hopefully, only the fur," I said. Sophie was intelligent, had superficially appeared healthy, and I was sure she was able to use magic. Those were the crucial traits for a familiar, who had to pick up the slack for a witch dazed by handling toxic plants and whose own magic was all invested in her potions.

"I'm going to come out and say it. You just might be right about the prodigy thing," Lisa came out and said.

I flashed her a tired, lopsided grin, and tried a glimmer of sass of my own. "Told you."

Pushing herself up, Lisa messed with the door handle,

sliding what might be a Closed sign into place and definitely locking the door. She stroked a finger down the plate next to the door, shutting off the office lights again, and then strolled over to loop her arms around my shoulders and pull me back through the workshop towards the main house. "But, prodigy or not, I'm declaring that enough for your first day on the job. I don't care if you're a powerhouse who gets her strength back in ten minutes. Goblita can go without a bioengineer for another day. If someone super urgently needs their dog to breathe fire, that's just too bad."

She steered me into the living room, where the air had now turned exquisitely cool. I lifted my goggles, rubbed my eyes, and enjoyed the feeling of getting ever so slowly less sweaty. Yes, I'd be fine after a breather, but a break sounded very good. I inquired, "I don't suppose you cook?"

Lisa nodded her horned head, and grinned a fangy grin. "Sure do. Anything you want charred into a black and rock-hard mass, I'm your girl."

I made a pffft sound.

Lisa added cheerfully, "I'll get you another drink and make you a sandwich, at—oh, Hell's bells, seriously?"

Because someone had just knocked on the front door. The house's front door, this time.

Taking a deep breath, I banished thoughts of lazying around in a plush chair, and prepared to be dignified and act like an adult.

Lisa wasn't having any of that. She pulled her arms free slowly, but clenched and unclenched her fists, which from the length of her pointy fingernails must hurt. Very, very flat, she asked me, "Killing people isn't allowed in your world, right?"

Chapter Three

In case that was a serious question, I answered solemnly, "Only if someone is trying to kill you, and even then it's the last option."

My breath back, I took a step towards the door. Lisa shouldered me aside, yanked the door open herself, and glared up at the man standing outside. Back to that ankle-crossed, back-arched, demonic posing position, Lisa flipped her hair back and sneered. "I should have known. Sorry, old man, I'm busy taking care of Artifact Forge. You know, the owner of this building? The inheritor?"

The man in question wasn't that old. Maybe, maybe, I could see a hint of grey in his beard. He looked like a town official, or a priest, with a long coat he wore even in this heat, and a fancy white collar. The beard and his dark hair were both neatly trimmed. He held a couple of books in his arms, but didn't seem inclined to do anything with them. Looking past Lisa, he addressed me, "Is that correct?"

"Call me Art. I'm Goblita's new bioengineer," I answered, pawing at my own hair, pulling it back and beginning to very carefully strip off the rubber band scrunchie without causing myself too much pain.

Lisa sneered up at the guy, and raised her middle finger. I was getting the impression she didn't like him. She drawled with evil glee over the words as she told him, "So, suck it, old man! I'm still a legitimate guest of the house owner and your dreams of banishing me back to Hell are as stale as you are."

Um. Lisa was burning a bridge behind me that I hadn't even known I was on. I sure wasn't going to scold her for it in front of whoever this is. I settled for, "I'm thinking of employing her as my assistant. Either way, as far as I'm concerned, Lisa isn't just a guest. She lives here."

Lisa laughed. It was a crazed, evil laugh, all "Ha ha ha ha ha ha ha ha ha!" She slammed the door shut in the guy's face, and locked it with a ferocious, triumphant grin. Her tail wagged behind her with such furious glee that her skirt spun wildly.

Who was that? What had I just been signed up for? Was there any way to stop Lisa from getting me run out of town? Did that guy maybe deserve every bit of Lisa's scorn and more? Was Lisa seriously in danger of banishment? Well, it's not like demons hanging around was normal. It wasn't like they didn't exist, either.

I latched onto the question I wanted answered most. Raising a finger, I asked, "Why are you staying here?"

The laughter died. Lisa tilted her head to one side, and gave me a long, curious look. Hands at her side, tail still high and twitching at the tip, she shrugged and said in a calm, frank tone, "I don't know. I mean, I do, but it seems kind of dumb. My mom thinks that growing up in Hell is bad for me, and I'll be better off here. Leo was a guy she knew from visiting the mortal world, so she sent me to live with him. Didn't tell him ahead of time, either, but he was a good guy. He took me in anyway."

I let out a sigh, and then a weak laugh of my own. Rubber band finally completely free, I shook out my hair and chuckled, "I was worried, I mean, that Uncle Leo…"

I didn't have to explain. Lisa's eyes widened, and she clasped her hands over her mouth, which did not hide the giggle behind them. "Oh, Hells, no! Are you kidding? He might have been my father!"

Spreading my hands helplessly, I stammered, "Look, demons! People think you're, you know... corrupt. You might not be as young as you look, even. I didn't—wait, we're cousins!?"

Lisa let out a little snorting laugh. Spreading her own hands, she gave me a red-lipped smirk. "Who knows? My father was human—"

"You're half-human?" I barked.

Lisa's smirk turned to exasperation. Propping her fists on her hips, she gave me a hard, scolding stare. "No. I'm a demon. Demon breeds true."

"Right, right. I know that," I mumbled, rubbing my damp hair bashfully. I did. No matter how many humans were in the bloodline, it never had any effect. If Lisa looked mostly human, it would be because her mother did, not because of any resemblance to her human father.

Lisa waved a hand in a fast circle, dismissing that and getting back to the point. "So, yeah, Mom knew Leo, I think he might have been my father, Mom sent me here because a mortal environment is better for me or something, and Leo took me in. He was a good guy. Kinda goofy, but really hospitable. I see why Mom liked him. He dropped dead, now you're here." She added another shrug. "Mom was right about one thing. Demons don't have kids much. It's nice having people my own age around. Speaking of which, that should have been enough time. Come on."

Still reeling over the whole "cousins" thing, which had successfully pushed aside "oh wow, I made a familiar" for today's most amazing revelation, I followed Lisa's clip-clopping footsteps to the... other side of the living room. It was a pretty big living room, and Uncle Leonard has packed it with plush-cushioned furniture.

Lisa squeezed behind a ragged blue couch and pushed it a couple of feet farther from the wall with her couch. She peeked through the curtains of the window behind it, then whipped the curtains open and pulled the window open. Beckoning with a pale hand and scarlet, pointy fingernails, she called, "Hey, Artifact! Come meet my boyfriend, Joe."

A boyish voice on the other side of the window, presumably Joe, barked a laugh. "I wish."

I squeezed around the couch, and looked out the window. A boy stood in the narrow stretch of yard belonging to my uncle— belonging to me, now, I guess. A wolf boy. Grey fur, muzzle, sharp teeth, tail. He had to be a teenager, but I had no clue how to read age on a wolf.

I hadn't known there were any furries in Goblita. I hadn't seen any until now. Of course, I'd only arrived yesterday, and I hadn't set foot outside yet today. I hadn't seen any gobbos either, and the town had to be called "Goblita" for a reason, right?

Geez, he was big. I'd heard furries tended to be. If you get yourself bioengineered, might as well go all the way, right? But... well, he was big. In every way. When he smiled down at me, "down" was the operative word.

Part of that was my fault. We had some gobbos in my family somewhere. I might have normal skin color, but I'd already heard every short joke in the English language. Mom insisted that I just hadn't hit my growth spurt yet, but if I hadn't, when would I?

Joe had so much muscle. He had enough muscle that it showed even with all that dark grey fur over it. It showed because he didn't wear a shirt, just a pair of ragged-edged shorts he was rapidly outgrowing. Dirt and dust smeared his fur here and there, and he stood with a tense, rough-edged swagger, like danger might strike at any moment but he was ready to handle it. Somehow, I didn't think this boy had gotten himself transformed. He couldn't afford it.

There was no reason to think the change wasn't generations ago, hundreds of years, even. It took, what, fifty years after the Breach for humanity to master soul forges? The golden age had barely been ending. I had to remind myself that I wasn't living out in the middle of nowhere with my recluse parents anymore. Altered humans were going to be normal from now on.

Subtly tense or not, even despite the mouth full of sharp teeth, Joe had a friendly smile. He offered it to me, and his hand with it. "I'm Joe. You're Artifact? Pleased to meet you."

I put my hand in his, and to my relief he merely shook it. His hands were as big as the rest of him. It absolutely engulfed mine.

The responsibility of figuring out an introduction was taken away as Lisa pushed her shoulder up against mine, and demanded, "Did you get it, Joe?"

"I got it," he confirmed, with a satisfied nod. With his long wolf face, he could really nod.

"Yessssss!" Lisa hissed in glee, bunching up her fist. That disappeared like someone swiping a spell. She hooked an arm around my shoulders, and told Joe, "Artifact here is a prodigy. Did you see that big dragon flying around? She made it."

I opened my mouth. Eh. I was never one for false modesty. I shrugged, and put on a smirk of my own. "I am. I did."

Joe hadn't actually let go of my hand. He gave it an approving squeeze. This close, he smelled like... sand. Joe was a very outdoors kind of boy. My arm extended through the window also reminded me that it wasn't that hot outside. The sun might bake this building if I let it, but the ocean breeze kept the air outside merely warm. So he didn't smell like sweat, just sand.

His voice warmer than the air, Joe said, "I missed it, but I'm impressed she made anything. We need more smart girls around here. I wish I had time to hear the story."

"Right right. Loot. Gimme gimme," said Lisa, extending her arms out the window and making flapping, beckoning hand motions.

Leaning down, the big, grey-furred wolf boy opened up a sack he'd left sitting below the window. Out of it, he pulled a metal object as long as my forearm, and set it in Lisa's waiting arms. She only sagged a little under the weight.

The object looked like a key. In a sense, it was a key. It was a breach detonator. I'd never seen one in person, but my parents had plenty of technical manuals for non-bio magics. Bioengineering was just the family tradition.

Pulling it inside and cradling it against her chest, Lisa let out a long, low hiss of satisfaction. Not friendly satisfaction. The tip of her tail curled up, making the pointy spade tip resemble a scorpion stinger. Her staring pink eyes had a hard, vicious edge, and her tight smile emphasized her slightly oversized canines.

"Let's see the old fart try to banish me without this," she whispered.

And then the nastiness disappeared. My demon cousin gave Joe a sweet, lopsided smile, still holding the detonator like a precious baby, and asked him, "What do I owe you for this service?"

He gave his head an easy shake. Reaching down, he grabbed the neck of the bag and gave it a couple of tugs. It clonked. "Nothing. I took a few other choice items to cover up what I was there for. You distracted him and gave me the chance. Once I go sell these, we're even."

Um... was I suddenly an accomplice to burglary? Or was I suddenly an accomplice to heroically preventing some jerk with a particularly obnoxious god from sending a merely mischievous girl literally to Hell? Or both?

My thoughts must have shown in my face. I realized Joe and Lisa were both giving me concerned stares.

Suddenly all gentleness again, Lisa put one slim arm around my shoulders, and let the key merely hang from the other hand by her side. Equally softly, she said, "Hey, Joe? Sorry to push you off, but Artifact here is kind of a responsible, magic brains type girl, you know? Things were pretty wild before you got here. I think she's had more excitement in the last hour than the whole of her life up until now, and she needs a break."

"Sure," he agreed, easily. Just as easily as he hoisted the sack of loot up over his shoulder. "I'll see you girls soon. I'm looking forward to getting to know you, Artifact. Don't think you have to be a chaos gremlin like Lisa, here, to be my friend."

He ran off. He had wolf legs, with big paws and an extra bend in the leg rather than human feet. His tail wasn't very long, but it was very waggy.

Lisa shut the window, closed the drapes, turned me around to face the living room, and instructed, "Deep breaths."

I took a few deep breaths, heavy and slow, and at the third realized I wasn't confused. I was tired. Incredibly tired. I'd never admit it, but I'd overdone the magic.

My eyes wandered around my uncle's crowded, wood-paneled living room. *My* crowded, wood-paneled living room. My parents certainly weren't going to move in, and they would probably let me stay, especially if I was a successful bioengineer already. This was my house. I owned it. I lived here.

My demoness cousin nodded slowly. "Better. Better. Listen, let's draw you a lukewarm bath, and while you soak I'll try to burn a sandwich for you as little as possible. Then after lunch we'll see. Maybe we'll just stay in and do nothing today. You don't have to be a prodigy all the time."

I let out my breath in one more heavy, heavy sigh. My shoulders slumped. "Thank you. I like this plan."

Her arm still hooked around me like I was a fragile eggshell, my red-haired, black-horned, black-hooved, spade-tailed cousin Lisa led me through my living room, past the forge where I had successfully and professionally created a witch's familiar, towards the stairs leading up to the second floor of my house and the bathtub chamber.

My parents might let me stay, but one thing was for sure.

This was not the kind of education they'd sent me here for.

ChapterFour

A soak in cool but not cold water was nice, relaxing and
energizing at the same time. Leo's wooden bathtub was
deep, wide, and long enough for me to stretch out and even float
a little, with my eyes closed, enjoying not being hot and sweaty.

Eventually even that much water goes lukewarm. I had a
cooling spell on my tablet, which I needed professionally as
well as for household use. I could chill the water again, right
up to the edge of discomfort, and go back to soaking in blissful
peace.

Except that would be dumb. The whole point of the bath
was to stop spending magic and let my body recover.

I opened my eyes and looked around the room. This was
such a nice house. The tub wasn't just big, it was shiny and
carved with fancy curves around the rim and little claw feet.
Lots of glass windows, one of which filled the bathroom with
sunlight. A glass mirror. Ceramic surfacing on a flush toilet and
running water sink. A rug, a hamper for clothes, a closet lined
with shelves and drawers, a towel rack jammed with towels, a
hundred bottles of who knew what… and this was one of the
least fancy and crowded rooms. Plus smooth, lacquered walls

and ceiling, and a little vent for cool air from the ice elemental to get in.

What it wasn't was clean. The whole building had a major dust problem. The towels weren't dirty, but they had that ragged, subtly mottled look of towels that had been used more than once.

Frowning, if only a little, I pulled myself up over the edge of the tub and groped at my clothing until I scooped up my tablet. Sliding my finger over the cleaning spell, I waved it at the nearest towels until they looked fluffy and monocolor again. Then I waved it over the soap shelf, vanishing the dust in sweeping strokes, revealing gleaming, purple-red wood. Boy, what a nice house.

Buuuuut, a few inches at a time would be a ridiculously slow way to clean the house, and dangerously inefficient.

I sighed.

With the soap shelf clean, I examined the shampoo bottle, and saw only a smear at the bottom. I could get that refilled by the nearest witch, but it left my hair a gunky mess of sweat right now, and I had a lot of hair.

Well, the solution to that was easy and obvious, if I was careful. First, I sat up, scooped up my hair that had been hanging over the edge of the tub, and dunked it and my whole head under the water. When I was sure I'd gotten all my hair soaked, I reared back up into the air. Holding my now-heavy rope of hair up with the forearm of my left hand, I activated the cleaning spell on my tablet again and waved it over the mass.

One quick wave. That's it. Brevity was more important than getting every inch. I'd bleached my hair blonde twice before doing this, thanks to my overpowered magic. That wasn't the worst risk, either. Even the magically weak could evaporate hair by focusing a cleaning spell on it too long. "Too long" for me was a few seconds.

Blinking water out of my eyes, I looked around again. I would have to do something about all this dust. Hire a maid? Bad idea. An adult would try to be in charge. Anyway, I could make my own answer.

Lisa walked in, carrying a plate.

Water splashed as I kicked my legs in surprise, pushing a little more upright. The plate wasn't the problem.

"Where are your clothes!?" I exclaimed.

The demoness gave me a lopsided stare like I was the stupidest person in the world, and those glowing eyes could really stare. Voice flat with scorn, she responded, "It's a bath. You're not wearing clothes either. Mortals don't wear clothes in the bath. Nobody wears clothes in the bath."

"This tub isn't big enough for two people!" I argued, trying to sound less hysterical. The tub had seemed huge a minute ago. Now, not so much.

Her naturally cherry-red lips pursed in disapproval, and her voice took on a more disapproving edge. "In Hell we would never waste drinkable water like this for one person's bath."

I screwed up my nose in disgust. "Ew. We don't drink bath water!"

Lisa stared for another second, then visibly untensed. Her expression flickered with the brave tolerance of someone dealing with prudish barbarians, then settled into cousinly concern and a gentle smile. "At least let me give you a massage. My mother taught me how, and you need one."

I pointed at the door, arm dripping water. "Go put some clothes on and I'll talk to you when I'm done."

Lisa stomped one hoof on the carpet. She perched her free hand into a fist and perched it on her bare hip. Rolling her eyes in utter exasperation, she complained, "Is this a family thing? You are just like Leo. Fine. Here's your meal. Sorry, there wasn't anything else."

She set the plate down on the counter by the sink and stormed out, tail tip jabbing behind her like an angry scorpion. Now the plate was low enough for me to see over the edge, and it contained one orange and a crust of bread. Not a thin crust of bread, at least. It was technically a meal.

"I'm going to have to inspect the whole house, aren't I?" I asked the empty bathroom.

Climbing out of the bath, I grabbed a newly clean towel and dried myself off. Should I clean my clothes the same way? No. If this was all the food we had, I'd be going out this afternoon and get them sweaty all over again, and I really needed to go easy for a few hours. I hadn't realized just how much power it took to give a familiar a human-level regenerating magic supply, and the dragon had been worse. I'd upgraded it to ten times its original size purely with my own magic, without a soul fragment or hooking it to the soul forge, because I hadn't expected to need either.

I grabbed the orange and the bread, and wolfed them down as I stumped down the stairs to the kitchen.

Again, the kitchen itself was great. A pantry and lots of cabinets in that beautiful purple-tinged wood. Multiple appliances, including a multi-box refrigerator, and a magical rather than wood-burning stove. The lines of spells running down them showed that both were adjustable. Expensive. Then again, for Leo they'd be one-time costs. He wouldn't have to pay to keep them charged. Like me, he could do that himself.

The clip-clop of hooves on a wooden floor signaled Lisa entering the kitchen, and she watched me with her arms folded over her soft purple dress as I continued my inspection. The refrigerator and stove were about half-full of magic. Fine, I could refill those later. The refrigerator could probably run a week on that anyway. The dishes were mostly clean, which meant Lisa had been cleaning up after herself. The cabinets had all kinds of different dishes and tableware and cooking implements.

What they didn't have was food. We had some cooking ingredients, like spices and a jar of wheat flour, although not many. Pantry, cabinets, and refrigerator all together contained half a bottle of orange juice as the only food that could be made edible without a great deal of time and effort. Bland, unleavened bread that I was guaranteed to cook wrong anyway was all I could imagine with time and effort.

Desperate need for groceries confirmed, I headed for the soul forge. On the way, in the little hall between living room, kitchen, dining room, and stairs, I checked on the ice elemental cooling the house. The little crystal not-quite-creature hovered in its box blowing cold air into the vents, and looked happy and healthy. The box's power gauge was almost empty. Basically, what I'd fed it earlier. Refilling it wouldn't be a big deal, but again, I put that off so as not to strain myself.

Flicking the lights on as I entered the soul forge, I circled the room examining my new working conditions. Lisa trailed after me.

One thing stood out, the same way it did everywhere. Drawing a fingertip over the work bench, I peered at and then rubbed with my thumb the grey film I'd scooped off.

Tail flicking, arms folded, with only a hint of sulk now, Lisa said, "This building gets dusty so fast. It's crazy. Is that a side effect of the soul forge?"

I shook my head. "No, I think some houses are just like that. I've got an idea for keeping it clean, but I'll do it later. I need to do a safety inspection now."

Turning to face the room, I drew myself up straight and focused. Tools. Well, I had plenty of them, enough that I couldn't think of anything I'd need and didn't have. Mostly iron, simple but good quality, but a little grungy and all dusty. At least I didn't see any rust, and everything was laid out in organized rows on the shelves. I wasn't going to have a chisel break or a mana inscriber go dull or not be able to find one just when I needed it.

The supply shelves looked okay. Quartz, bottles of fine sand and ash, some petroleum, some vegetable oil, powdered metals, a big pumice stone, a row of jars and boxes containing everything from cow horn to castor beans to beetle shells. I had a big, tightly sealed, nearly full jar of purified water, and two backup chunks of obsidian. So, Uncle Leonard had left me well supplied.

The floor was absolutely filthy, tramped down dust turned into dirt that smudged most of the smooth cement surface. That covered most of the spell marks not already hidden by furniture, but they looked intact.

Okay, time to safety inspect the soul forge itself. I fastened my hair back in a pony tail, crouched down next to it and—

"Holy snot," I whispered, a chill running up my spine. I was suddenly very, very grateful for those protective formulas, and I desperately hoped they'd worked. Cleaning the floor shot up in priority, because I needed to see how many of those formulas had burned off.

Why?

Two of the rubber stops on the legs of the soul forge were completely gone.

One of those legs was propped up on a piece of wood. Wood! Okay, fresh wood, at least. Dented, but not discolored. The other dangled in the air, uninsulated. If that had touched the floor while I was working this morning... an earthmover would have been here and eaten us already. So it couldn't have happened.

Still, I shuddered.

The remaining two legs were properly insulated and fine. The leg propped up on wood had definitely been leaking power, because the recursion plate was warped. Only slightly. It needed replacement soon, but if I fixed the legs and the wires were tight—

I checked the wires. They were not tight. Two of them wobbled a little when I prodded them. Okay, I was definitely going to have to lead seal those in place. Hmmm. Before or after I went out and bought new rubber stops?

Fingers slid into my hair above the ponytail and closed into a fist. Gently but firmly, Lisa pulled me back up to standing.

Staring at me hard, mouth flat and voice flatter, she said, "I know that look. You're going to do one quick chore. Then another quick chore. Then another quick chore. Then you'll realize that something else needs to be done, and it will be bedtime, but if you stay up just a little late you can get it all finished."

"Um...," was all I could say, because she was right.

Glowing, slit-pupiled eyes made her compassionately frustrated stare vaguely threatening. The red-and-white demoness let out an aggrieved sigh. "You are a *lot* like Leo. Sleep. Go nap. Now."

She didn't take "no" for an answer. She didn't take an answer, period. Turning me with her fist in my hair, she marched me out of the forge and up the stairs towards the house's bedrooms.

Along the way, I whined, "Okay, okay, but while I'm out, make up a grocery list and write down anything else you think we need. We got paid for the familiar job, so we have cash. I know, you can't guess all the stuff I want, but it will be a start."

"I'll do it if you take care of yourself and get some rest," she answered. Tossing her hair suddenly, its red and orange stripes doing that flame-like flicker as she passed through a sunbeam, she muttered, "I swear it's like Leo never left. At least you're small enough to bully."

She marched me to a door, shoved my nose up against it, let go of my hair, and strolled away.

I opened the door to a big, luxuriously furnished bedroom. The master bedroom, that used to be Leo's. Now it was my bedroom. What a weird, weird thought. I'd slept on the couch last night rather than face it.

In this whole messy house, someone had cleaned and replaced the sheets, and the bed was mostly made. Lisa could be thoughtful. We just had, um, cultural differences. Right.

Okay, my first quick chore would be a brief nap, then out for groceries, then fix the soul forge. No more bioengineering got done in this house until that forge passed the safety checklist. The official safety checklist, which I would dig out and follow just to make sure. It chilled me again to think I'd performed two high-powered rituals today with a forge in that condition.

But there was nothing wrong with it that I couldn't fix by myself, and it would give me plenty of time to refill my magic. After that I had a little experiment to try the repaired forge out on.

ChapterFive

I stepped out onto the street, my goggles high on my forehead and beheld my neighborhood. Goblita was... nice. Much greener than I would have expected. I'd heard things got pretty hot and dry down near the coast. And even here, out of sight of the sea, I could smell it faintly on the breeze.

"Let's head down to the beach. I'd like to stock up on meat. What is your preferred meat?" I asked my behorned cousin.

In an attempt to answer my own question, I looked down at the list she'd given me, and immediately rolled my eyes. "I admit I occasionally am insufficiently cynical, but no, I don't believe you actually want me to buy baby cutlets. You really are just putting on an act, aren't you?"

Lisa grinned at me, showing off her oversized canines and the pointy teeth on either side of them.

Another glance at the list, and I added, "I believe where you underlined chocolate twice, though."

The demoness's eyes bulged, suddenly unfocused. She curled her fingers up like claws, and gurgled in otherworldly hunger. "That stuff is *so* good. I never had it until I came here! I hope they have it in stock!"

We walked down the side of the road, which was lined with houses not quite as big as mine, but still very nice. Trees dotted their front lawns, and many more trees created a near-forest behind them. Again, we'd had a lot more up at the lake, I just hadn't been expecting this. I saw a little general store squatting amidst the residences, next to a plumber's shop. The former was tempting, but we had a lot more groceries to buy than a store for odds and ends could supply. Down a side street I saw a little building with colorful ornaments hanging from the two trees down front, which was probably a witch's shop, but again, food first.

Turning my thoughts back to chocolate, I chatted, "It was pretty expensive up at the lake, but we're right on the coast here and shipping might be better. We're going for the cheap basics today, remember. Familiars aren't cheap, but it was still just one job."

We passed the One-And-One, the ancient golden age road, rebuilt many times, that runs up the Pacific Coast. The maps my mom owned said it ran past Lady Angel to the South, and past Sin Fortress to the North, far past, North and North all the way to the Yukon. A much slower but a little safer path than the sea. For us, it was just a well-trodden road, paved as it passed through Goblita, which the street Lisa and I were following crossed at a diamond-shaped plaza not being used for anything. A sign post reared up noticeably at one corner, crowded with arrow-shaped signs. I gave it a glance. The signpost must have been a joke, although a joke raised and lovingly maintained by someone. Multiple arrows in different directions read "Goblita." There was an arrow for Lady Angel and one for Sin Fortress, one pointing out at the sea labeled "Tokyo," one pointing the opposite way labeled "Paree," one Northeast-ish with the bizarre label "Wall Dragon," and so on, and so on.

A little farther on, we passed a whole complex of big, boxy buildings with their own paths running around them in a web. They were too big and had too many windows to be houses, except the ones that had too few windows. Lots of people of various ages wandered those paths, mostly carrying small bundles.

What was up with this place? I stared, but I couldn't figure it out. They were just buildings, trumpeting no particular purpose. No carts carrying things to and fro, no signs.

Lisa noticed my stare, and supplied, "That's the College. They run this town."

Ah. "The Lady Angel College of Magic?"

She nodded. "Yeah." And that was it.

My curiosity also settled quickly. That explained everything. There must have been a lot of spellcasting in those buildings, enough even for my magic-desensitized nerves to stand on edge.

Then the beach came into view, and I stopped caring about the College anyway.

What was different about the grass near the edge? Something. It was tall, thin and sharp like blades, most of it, and grew in clumps. A few ponds here and there didn't seem to need filling or be attached by streams to anything. Big, skinny birds watched us from those ponds without looking alarmed.

That change felt like a barrier, or rather a gateway, entering another world. We passed it to the beach itself, where a small but sharp drop and a few rocks brought us down to sand. Like the lake, but more so, much more so. So much sand, wrinkly and shining pale blonde under the sun and blue sky. A long, smooth, wet, brown zone stretched the final distance into the sea itself, with waves sloshing up and down it lazily as if the ocean rolled around in its sleep.

The water was blue, darker than the lake, murky, but it seethed. It played with itself sleepily, rolling around caps of white and shadowy dents over the surface.

And it went on, and on, and on, and on, and on. A few ships' sails lurked here and there on that vast surface, but the endless emptiness of it filled my attention. Not a barren emptiness like the desert, or a nothing like the sky. This was a view of peace, alive like the land wasn't, but at rest.

The smell of it hit me, salt and old plants, fish and the smell after the rain. No. Those were all futile attempts to analyze it. This was its own smell, carried on a wind as soft and peaceful as the infinite water, along with a constantly changing hiss and the squeals of seagulls hunting for whales.

I'd expected a lake, but bigger. This was different. It was like coming home, when I never knew I'd been away.

I stumbled on the shifting sand, and Lisa hooked an arm into mine, maybe for safety, more likely impatience because I'd started lagging behind.

Right. I'd be living in walking distance of this for years. Right now, I had business, and two mouths to feed, one of those my own.

Not far down, I saw a pier thronged with fishing boats. Dull brown and wooden, they didn't look fancy, but they did look busy. People swarmed around like ants. There was a lot of action going on, and as my sandals crunching on sand took me closer, it mostly seemed to involve adjusting ropes and packing bottles into crates stuffed with straw. The bottles glowed light blue, the same color as the sky.

What I didn't see any of were fish.

The closest of the fishing boat people, doing the actual packing and padding of bottles into boxes, were two teenagers, a boy and girl. They looked up at the same time, the boy waved his arm, and they shouted, "Lisa!" So, we headed for them.

How old were they? I couldn't tell beyond "teenagers." They could be tall and my age, or short and seventeen. Physical work left them both muscular, in a merely visibly fit way rather than Joe's furry bulk. Both had dark skin, barely lighter than the wet sand, and coal-black hair. The boy kept his short and ragged, and the girl wore hers wrapped in a makeshift bun out of the way. For clothes, they both had a pair of tight and short shorts about the same color as their skin, with the girl adding a chest wrap tied up like a bandage. Those could not possibly be made of scratchy burlap, but sure looked like it.

The boy was wiry and sharp-featured. The girl would never be wiry no matter how fit she was. Whether she was my age or seventeen, she counted as an early bloomer. The chest wrap required several times as much fabric as her shorts, and neither were doing a great job. That was the impression she gave, at least. Still, she had to be young. She and the boy were too much alike in height and face and color. You might as well stamp "brother and sister" on their heads.

They also both had sharp, searching, dark eyes, which fixed my demonic cousin with interest. The girl asked, with a voice that had a touch of sardonic buzz built in, "Skipping school again?"

The boy jabbed the girl with his elbow, giving her a quick look of reproof. He had a smooth, kind voice, completely unlike hers, paired with an equally gentle smile as he told Lisa, "We heard. We're so sorry. Mr. Forge seemed like a good man."

Lisa barely shrugged, and even smirked faintly. "I was only going to school because he made me. Why are you two bookworms cutting class?"

The girl jerked a thumb back over her shoulder. "Mama and Papa called us out. The fleet caught a horseshoe crab."

Woah! Standing up on my tiptoes, I exclaimed, "Oooooh, one of the big ones?"

Tiptoes wouldn't even bring me up to a regular thirteen-year-old's altitude, so I scrambled up onto the pier, and then onto one of its stumpy supports.

There it was, a real giant horseshoe crab. A shield-shaped brown shell lurked at the surface of the water, just low enough that the biggest waves slid a coating of water over it. Fishing boats surrounded the enormous ocean bug, which was bigger than any one of them. Men and women in the boats held ropes tied and held taut to the horseshoe crab. Most of the ropes descended underwater, but many looped around the segmented mass sticking out of the back of the shield. As I watched the creature twitched, giving me hints of legs fluttering under the water. A tail lifted into the air, long and sharp-pointed, edged like a hacksaw and the same brown shell as the rest of the visible body. Then the tail slapped down into the ocean and disappeared, the creature going still again.

A man with a big syringe was at the very back of the shield shell, drawing out glowing blue blood and filling a bottle. Horseshoe crab blood. The stuff of dreams, for a mage. I wanted some. I didn't need it, but a bottle of what was essentially liquid soul fragment, oh, how nice that would be to have. Horseshoe crab blood wasn't nearly as concentrated as a soul fragment, but still, Dad said three of these creatures would be enough to distill down to make a gem that could run a soul forge.

Nobody knew, and bioengineers asked this question a lot, how any animal had developed blood that concentrated magic like this, especially a big underwater bug that ate mud. They did. Especially maddening, the little, common horseshoe crabs were useless. Oh, they had the same kind of blood, but because of their size you couldn't get it out in a pure state.

The big ones were also very, very rare. I hadn't expected to see one alive. What a hideous, beautiful, alien, magical wonder of nature. Also, I had to admire the strength and the bravery of the fisherpeople holding it still to be bled.

The man who had been drawing the blood hopped onto a fishing boat, then onto the pier. He added the bottle to a bag, and strolled up the wooden walkway to join us. He looked like a bigger, older version of the boy, with a huge grin and one gold tooth. As he approached, he called out to the teenagers, "Almost done. We can't risk killing it, or leaving it too weak to recover. I see the demon is cutting class again, but who is your new friend?"

Lisa, still holding my arm, lit up with acidly proud glee and announced, "Leonard's niece Artifact. She's a prodigy."

"I am," I admitted immodestly. Hey, was I going to deny it?

The girl snickered. The grown man, having arrived and handed her the bag, looked faintly amused.

I had Lisa to do my bragging for me. Whatever had cured her skepticism, she was into it now, and her sly glee curved her whole body into a bow as she asked, "I don't suppose any of you saw the dragon fly past this morning?"

The girl's cynicism disappeared in wide-eyed surprise. "Saw it? It ate a seagull right over our head half an hour ago. It was huge!"

"It was big," the boy conceded, in the cautious tone of someone who didn't want to exaggerate.

As satisfied as the cat who caught the mouse, Lisa bumped her shoulder to mine. "Artifact made it. I watched her."

Having her brag for me was great, but, um, the dragon had been here? On the shore? Half an hour ago? It had been supposed to fly straight to my parents' home, way north and inland, not hang around and eat wildlife! Normally messenger dragons never ate anything on the trip, not until they arrived and the spell wore off. Maybe the overcharge had made the difference. I'd been able to grow the dragon, but not fuel it, and it had to stick around and get a meal to sustain it on its journey.

My horror settling, trying not to look disturbed at all, I declared, "I'm Goblita's new bioengineer."

The adult still grinned, but the note of condescension had gone, or at least changed to that friendly condescension adults had for all teenagers. He put one hand each on the boy and girl's heads, and introduced, "I am Eduardo, and these are my prodigies, Emanuel and Elvira."

The teenage boy hunched up his dark shoulders until his darker hair met them, and protested, "PAPA."

His sister Elvira was busy shoveling straw on top of and around a bottle she'd just laid in the crate, and with none of her brother's embarrassment told me, "I won't say we're not good, but he greatly exaggerates."

Lisa crossed her arms, flicked her head away in disgust, and flicked her tail the other way. "They study magic constantly. They're so tediously good, I don't know why I put up with them."

Emanuel had just laid a bottle in place on its straw padding, but now he stood up like he'd been stung, pouting and giving me a pleading, soulful look. He waved his hands around emotionally as he asked, "Is it wrong to have a dream? There is so much magic can do for fishing, and nobody has even tried. Farmers, caravans, mages helping other mages find easier ways to make magic to sell. They all get spells designed and sold for them. No one is doing that for fishermen. I'm going to."

Packing up the last bottle, Elvira stood up more slowly. They were very close in height, so much that with all her hair I couldn't tell who was taller. A little like Lisa, she stood with crossed arms and a hip tilt, much more relaxed than her brother, and with heavy-lidded eyes, and a friendly, faintly sarcastic smile as her default expression. "I like fishing. I'm happy to be a fisher like my mother and father and their parents before them.

If magic can help, I want to do it in person."

Emanuel *bapped* her forearm with his, suddenly flashing a teasing smile. "Yes, by blowing up a fish's soul fragment to kill a whole school so they're easily caught."

I raised a hand and pointed a finger at Elvira. "That is definitely black magic."

If anything, Elvira arched her back more, and drawled with smug disdain, "Except no one cares about the sand grain of a tuna's soul fragment, and I know what I'm good at."

Emanuel's mouth tightened in discomfort at that admission. The teens' father fuzzled both their heads with his hands, and beamed with pride at his talented daughter and his morally upright son.

Affection filled me, until I had to laugh. "Okay, now I do wish I was going to school with you, but there's no way I'm holding down a job and—"

Emanuel interrupted me, holding up his hands. "Oh, we get it. You want this job." Yeah, I heard the faint hunger of ambition in his voice. He wished he was the one who could skip half a dozen years or so and get straight to his dream.

Everybody smiled, with a sense of mutual understanding. The strain of a first meeting disappeared, and Emanuel held out his hand. "Nice to meet you, Artifact."

"Likewise, Emanuel. Call me Art," I replied gaily, and gave his hand a shake.

He jerked, as if I'd poked him. Letting go, he gave his sister a significant look, and she reached out and shook my hand too.

She immediately jumped half an inch in the air, and let go. Looking straight up at him, she told her father, "Well, she's certainly not kidding about being a prodigy, Papa."

Ah, good. My strength must be coming back. Emanuel and Elvira were strong enough to be sensitive, but not so strong as to drown out their own senses.

Refusing to let the friendly tone die, Emanuel asked me and Lisa, "Where are you headed?"

"Shopping," I answered immediately. "I arrived to an empty kitchen, and we need to stock up. I was hoping to buy fish from you. Fish tacos sound—"

Lisa interrupted me by throwing her arms around my shoulder, and making the kind of drooly gurgles she'd made about chocolate. "Fish tacos sound like sin right now, and I mean the good kind. Which is most kinds."

Emanuel and Elvira giggled in unison. Well, at the same time. Elvira had a real giggle, high-pitched and wicked and awkward and wandering. Emanuel had a breathy chuckle that escaped in uncontrolled puffs.

Pointing up the road, Emanuel explained, "Mama already took all the regular fish up to the commercial district. How much were you planning to buy? I don't see any baskets."

Baskets? That hadn't occurred to me. After a couple of seconds of thought, I admitted, "Back home, we mostly get stuff delivered."

Elvira shook her head, not in the regular way, but tilting it towards one shoulder and then the other in a few rapid waggles. "I guess that's possible, but it's going to cost a lot extra."

Above us all, Eduardo boomed a sudden laugh. He waved his hand at his children. "I see where this is going. Go on, take those last boxes to Mama. We've bled this poor creature enough. I'll go talk to the other families about shares in the profit. Then you can carry the prodigy's groceries for her and make a valuable contact for the future."

Back rigid, muscles tense, arms stiff at his sides, and his face tight with mortification, Emanuel muttered, "Don't listen to him. I'm not that unscrupulous."

Merely scowling with her arms crossed under her chest again, Elvira added, "I am, but I'm not that mercenary."

Emanuel nudged her. They both stood straight in an officially alert, showily respectful way and singsonged together, "Thank you, Papa!" Then they crouched, grabbed their boxes, and scurried away before Eduardo could change his mind.

Lisa set out to catch them. Everyone seemed to know where to go, so I followed as they walked with brisk, long-legged paces towards the College, and then past it. I did not have long legs, but I knew how to scurry and kept up.

I didn't see what happened, but suddenly Emanuel barked, "Be careful!"

Elvira sneered back, "I'm always careful. You're the one with his head in the clouds. I know how dangerous this stuff is."

The proto-argument disappeared as fast as it had started, and instead Emanuel turned his head to me and asked, "So where are you from?"

"Lake Touhou," I answered.

Elvira giggled again. Wickedly. Absolutely everything she did looked and sounded wicked. Okay, she wasn't like Lisa, she put Lisa to shame, if Lisa was capable of feeling shame. In casual conversation, she almost barked her words, sounding as emphatic as she looked lazy. "No wonder you're a prodigy. They say there's a lot of wild magic up there. It's full of unexplored dungeons."

True, but still, I shrugged. "Nothing comes out of them. It's pretty, and it's quiet. I've met more people today than we had neighbors up there. My family are bioengineers, and it's a great place to research."

"Lots of places for the monsters you accidentally make to run off to," Elvira drawled.

Deliberately avoiding that topic, I described, "The water is lighter, clearer blue up there, and there are big shallow areas. I bet you don't get snow down here, either?"

Emanuel could drawl like his sister. "We'll take your word for it that snow is real."

With the sea behind me, images of home crept back into my thoughts. "If I climb the hill right behind our house, there's a huge tower out on the lake that I can see. It was cleared of monsters hundreds of years ago, but it's still standing. Sometimes I see dragons nesting in it. The regular, harmless kind, not the big ones."

Come to think of it, who even made the really huge dragons? Sure, the challenge was tempting, but a honking big destructive monster was not worth the effort no matter how proud you were. Then again, it only took one crazy and centuries of natural breeding.

Elvira's eyes unfocused at the pictures I'd created. "Mmmm, now that sounds enticing. I'd love to explore a dungeon someday. They say that earthmovers invent whole fake cultures, as if their dungeons are the ruins of real lost civilizations. It sounds beautiful. And sinister. But in a beautiful way."

"I got to watch it happen once," I said, distant as the memory unrolled.

Emanuel tripped over his own feet, and nearly dropped his crate. Elvira's dark eyes went wide like saucers. Even Lisa grabbed my hand with hers.

Emanuel spoke for them all, both hushed and aghast. "You saw an earthmover attack?"

Nodding, I mused, "Touhou wouldn't be surrounded by dungeons without them, would it? I..." The truth snapped into place, turning my tone more serious. "Okay, I was scared. Really, really scared. We felt the shaking, and I was upon the hill anyway, and Dad always said the first lesson of an earthmover attack was to get as far from the soul forge as possible, far from any active magic. He keeps his forge too well insulated to be the target, but when it happens, you have to wonder for a minute if you've made a mistake."

Emanuel shuddered. Elvira just kept staring. Lisa squeezed my hand harder. A couple of passersby must have heard something, because they watched me pass, but didn't follow.

I waved my free hand vaguely, groping for a description. "There's no way I can describe how big they are. It came out of the ground between our home and the Diggleton farm. It thrashed around like rats swarming food, and I got to see it make a temple spire. It just... puked the building up. Then it dove back into the ground and the shaking stopped, and it was gone. No monsters came out of the dungeon. It didn't have a soul forge."

Hushed by awe, Emanuel whispered, "Wow. We don't have any stories like that."

Extending my arm, I pointed back the way we came and accused, "You just caught a horseshoe crab. People write books about that!"

Emanuel hesitated a second, then tucked his head down and grinned, pride creeping up. "Okay, it was at least a little wild. The net was so heavy we thought it would sink our ship. We were about to cut the line when Papa sees the tip of the tail break the surface. We sound the horn and Elvira—"

"Stop," Elvira protested, turning her face away from me.

Emanuel did not stop. "Elvira casts a spell on it right there. The boat is pitching like a storm, and she's bolt upright as if it were a solid floor, hair streaming in the wind, rattling out code. The whole ocean turned black for a second."

Still not looking at me, Elvira protested, "That is a wild exaggeration. I stunned it with a basic neuro-shock. Vitality disruption wouldn't work on a horseshoe crab, and if it did, we couldn't harvest a weakened crab."

"So you know psychology *and* black magic," I accused.

Lisa leaned up against me, speaking past me at the siblings. "And I thought you were called out of school because of the horseshoe crab?"

"Family," Emanuel replied, terse and monotone.

Lisa snapped a nod. "Right. Topic abandoned."

Emanuel's passion came back as he resumed his story. "That gave time for the other families to get to us, and everyone throws nets, hauling the crab up to the surface. Papa actually climbs out onto the crab to catch people's ropes and tie them to it."

Elvira, rejuvenated by being teased, looked straight at me to give a serious nod. "That part is true. I thought he would be thrown off and drown every time it whip-snapped. I thought it would stab him with its tail. That's not how horseshoe crab tails work, but—"

I repeated, "When it's happening, you have to wonder."

Emanuel picked back up. "We got enough ropes on it from enough boats to hold it, and eventually it calmed down and we could take it back to shore."

Elvira, looking past him now, lifted her crate up in her arms and shouted, "Last delivery, Mama!"

I hadn't been paying attention to where we were. Now I did. Goblita kept its roads paved, and this one was wider than most, packed with people talking and doing shopping. Stores, some with stalls outside, some with open fronts and counters, some with doors leaning inside but big windows to show off the merchandise, sold everything, but mainly food. In front of a wooden stall sat straw-packed wooden boxes filled with big, lumpy green emu eggs that promised a future of good eating, and on the cart next to the stall one of several refrigerated metal cases stood open, with strips of emu meat inside.

Emus ran wild around Lake Touhou, which somehow made that funny.

Next to the stall was one of the closed stores, a butcher shop with beef cuts on display, and a cabinet of milk, both cow and goat. A bakery had out a tray of bread and multiple trays of corn tortillas and cornbread. Farmers must carry their produce to Goblita from many miles around, because there were fresh vegetables, tomatoes, hot peppers, citrus fruits and grapes in multiple shops. Down a ways, I spotted a dull grey, blobby, four-legged doll bigger than a bull, at the head of a chain of wagons. A caravan was in town, and they would have the rubber I needed, and fresh paper from the northern forests. Fantastic.

The diversity I hadn't seen until now was on display here, with a mix of furries of various species among the basic humans, and people who just had point ears or tails. No gobbos, to my surprise. Not even on the caravan.

I saw at least two restaurants serving the produce on display up cooked, and that included a plate of already prepared fish tacos that set my mouth watering.

A woman who distantly resembled Elvira, but older and with the softness spread more evenly around her body, bustled out of the store next to us. It was one of the open ones with a counter out front, a counter stocked with fish in buckets of ice. The woman beckoned her hand vigorously at her children and ordered, "Inside, inside. Stack them up on the others. I'm still deciding how to put up the display. The caravaneers want most of the stock to take to Lady Angel. They'll pay us a pittance and we'll make them rich, but what can you do?"

Elvira and Emanuel disappeared inside. I browsed the fish. Not that I knew much about fish, but they sat both whole and in filets white and orange, promising meal after meal of fish tacos until Lisa and I lost interest, which would take a long time.

I noticed something else a few doors down, and shouted into the shop, "I'll be back in a minute!"

With Lisa close behind me and peering curiously over my shoulder, I scurried down to the blacksmith's shop.

Chapter Six

Iliked what I saw immediately. Thick, stone walls. A safety focus. A round forge with a vent hood and chimney. The forge not only had the usual, professionally inscribed spells on it, it was covered with the sprawling diagrams of custom spells added by the owner, without the compact neatness of spells made for mass production. The metalwork on display was all well made and maintained, without a hint of rust and edges gleaming sharp. Swords, horseshoes, nails, hinges, hoes, this smith made everything, and I liked that.

Plus, the smith herself was shorter than me.

"An actual dwarf blacksmith!" I exclaimed out loud, and then felt like an idiot.

Fortunately, she gave me a merry, freckle-cheeked smile. "Oui! Funny, is it not? I am the only dwarf who took up smithing I have ever met, and out here in ze Wild West, I am the only one dwarf most Americans have met at all."

She looked the part. She so very looked the part. With her chubby cheeks, thick arms that didn't quite hide the muscle under a padding of pudge, black hair in a braid down her back, stocky and curvy figure not entirely hidden by a leather apron…

she seemed to have been born for this role. She certainly held up a hammer in her leather-gloved hands as if it were a feather and not at least twenty pounds of metal.

Stealing up between us, Lisa introduced, "This is Julianna. Julianna, this is Artifact. She's Leo's nephew." Enthusiasm broke through as she finished, "She inherited the soul forge, and she can use it too!"

Julianna took all this in with a quiet, somber frown, and let out a little sigh. Then she turned her blue eyes up to Lisa. "That poor man. How are you holding up, mon chere?"

Lisa answered with bored disdain, "Mortals gonna mortal."

All I had to say was, "I barely met him before. He was just my dad's favorite brother."

Still looking at Lisa, Julianna said, "You missed out on a very good man. I wish zere had been a body to bury, so we could have a funeral."

Okay, time to admit, "I haven't actually been told what happened."

I couldn't read the stare Julianna had been giving Lisa. Compassion, maybe? Softly, sadly, her strange accent lilting, the dwarf said, "It was sudden, but also not sudden. He told me long ago that he was sick with some magical sickness that would eventually kill him. The last time I saw him, a week ago, he acted as if he were fine, but he was…" She paused, face pinched, disturbed by the memory. "…transparent. Like a ghost."

Pursing my lips, I inhaled sharply, then winced. "Co-opted."

Oops. They didn't know what that meant. I explained, "It's an industrial accident for bioengineers. If your soul forge is out of tune, you can get linked to it, as if you were a monster it made. No wonder he left the soul forge in that condition. He didn't care about safety anymore. By the time you find out you've been linked, it's irreversible. Eventually you vanish, without even leaving a soul fragment."

Tears shone in Julianna's eyes. I winced again, and stammered, "Oh, I'm sorry. I didn't mean—" but wasn't sure what it was I didn't mean.

Lifting a leather-clad hand, Julianna took mine and gave it a grateful squeeze. "Non, non. Thank you. He would never explain. He wanted to pretend nothing was wrong, that our time together was always happy." She broke out in a wan smile, and with only a hint of roughness in her voice said, "I always thought he had romantic interests, but I told him he was too tall for me."

I had no idea what to say to someone grieving like this. Lisa wasn't leaping in, and didn't seem to even be paying attention. Would changing the subject help? Or was I about to say this because I wanted to know so badly? "Are you French?"

Eyes still shining, Julianna gasped and released my hand to press her fingers to her own chest. "Mon dieu. Did ze way I braid my hair give moi away?"

When I stood there with my mouth open like an idiot, she laughed. Still red-eyed, but now quietly merry, she explained with much less of an accent, "I am. There are many dwarves in France. It was a fashion for a while, so family history says."

My mind blank with awe, I asked, "*How* did you get here?"

She laid her hammer over her shoulder, and explained, "I had to leave France in a hurry. I—" She paused for a second, and her stare and tone turned serious. "The truth, Leo's niece, I killed a man. I thought at the time he needed to die, that it was the right thing to do, but hear me and remember, mon petite: Killing another human is a terrible experience. It shocks you to the core, changes you. I swore off all violence." Her smile crept back up. "And pacifism made fleeing the country much more complicated, let me tell you! Especially crossing America."

I lifted my hands and shook them in frustrated curiosity. "Okay, but how!? Did you go east or west? West, I guess, if you crossed America?"

Tears gone, Julianna was grinning hugely now, clearly enjoying my shock. She lectured with relish, "East was not an option. I have heard a dozen different tales for why, but what is sure is, Siberia is impassible. Those who try, never return. The Middle East is almost as bad. Americans know hardly anything of what happened on our continent after the Breach, but the earthmovers went mad in the Middle East. They built whole cities, rebuilt actual ancient ruins as well as making their own. People will live anywhere, and moved in, but the ruins took them over somehow. They live like they're in a dream, part of those ruins. They're not safe for outsiders to deal with, and you can get caught by the spell."

I continued to gape. "So you crossed the Atlantic, and then from the Atlantic shore to the Pacific. That's incredible."

The chunky dwarf tittered. "Ah, sea travel is easier than you think, little girl. There is good magic to keep ships from getting lost, or starved in a calm. If you don't have bad luck with a storm, you can travel from a major port in Europe to a major port on the American coast reliably enough, and with little pirate risk. Crossing from East Coast to West is much the same, although I admit it had its exciting moments."

Her smile disappeared, and her story stopped. She stared at nothing, at her own thoughts, and after a second of that looked up at Lisa again. "Merci for bringing her to me, mon chere demoness. A little closure that I needed."

Lisa waved her hands across each other and shook her horned head. "Nope. No kindness here. She came here on her own."

My memory kicked, I stammered, "Um. Yeah. On business, actually. Do you do goldsmithing, too?"

Julianna nodded graciously. "And silver, and even bronze. A bit of smelting as well, although I should not be your first choice for that."

"Can you make this?" I pulled out a diagram out of my pocket, unfolded it, and laid it on her counter. Then I scooped out the lump of gold Leo, like any bioengineer, kept for exactly this situation and set it next to the paper.

Lisa's eyes went wide. She stared at the gold with the surprise and interest of a demon who hadn't known something like that was lying around the house.

Julianna ignored her, smiling up at me now, both affectionate and businesswoman. "I can. For the forge, n'es pas? I will be great careful. You will not suffer the fate of your poor uncle if Julianna can help it."

She reached out and tapped my chest at my collarbone, then added, "More pleasant topic. Leo loved to hear this, and I am sure another bioengineer would as well. Ze big cities back East, especially Old York, they have a plan to rebuild ancient roads called railroads that stretch from East to West. The golden age men, they tunneled through mountains, leveled out passes, built huge bridges, all of which are still there to be repaired. The part you will like is that they plan to drag freight carts using dolls. Six legged dolls as big as houses, with bioengineers to keep them running."

"Ooooooh." She was right. I liked that part. What a project those would be. I'd never made a doll.

Well, I was a professional now. Maybe I'd get to.

Someone yelled, what sounded like curse words in Spanish. I looked. Everyone looked.

Elvira stood in front of the fish shop, whimpering. In front of her on the road, a big blue puddle spread slowly around a mess of broken glass.

More people swore. Elvira's mother yanked out her tablet and pointed it at the puddle. Sparks shot out of the tablet, and she dropped it with a yell. She'd tried a cleaning program, and no way she could handle the feedback from horseshoe crab blood.

Elvira and Emanuel got theirs out, swiped a spell, and pointed it at the puddle. They were more powerful than their mother, but nothing was happening.

Around them, people babbled in panic. A witch pawed at the potions she was carrying, desperately searching for something appropriate.

Confused, Lisa asked, "What's going on?"

In a hurry, I babbled, "Horseshoe crab blood contains—forget the details. Spill that much and you'll summon an earthmover!"

I shouldn't have said that out loud. A lot more people screamed, and started to run.

Me, I ran in the other direction, towards the mess. We had a chance, because of Goblita's paved roads. It would take a couple of minutes for the vitality in the hemomana to soak through concrete. If it had fallen directly in the dirt, we'd be doomed. An earthmover would detect that geodifferential spike dozens, hundreds of miles away.

This was the real danger never far from a bioengineer's

mind, because earthmovers and soul forges were inextricably linked.

I kept my tablet in my pocket, not on a wristband. Yanking it out, I swept the spell to put away clutter rather than the spell to clean dirt, and pointed it at the mess.

Behind me, a man barked orders to the people around him. "Get hammers and shovels. We'll pry up that section of the street and put it in a cart."

I focused on the blue puddle. My tablet got hot. Uncomfortably hot. Painfully hot.

The blue blood hissed. It bubbled. It and the glass shards poured up off the ground into the air, and reformed into the original bottle.

The shattered glass held together just long enough for Elvira's mother to scoop it up in a bucket.

I dropped my tablet onto the road. A great sigh of relief went up everywhere, including from me.

Except Elvira. She stood a few feet from me, using her long hair like a handkerchief to cover her face as she sobbed, "I'm sorry. I'm sorry, Mama. I should have been paying more attention. I was stupid and then I tried to catch it with—"

Her mother pulled Elvira to her chest, drowning out the sobs, and whispering, "No. Shush, niña. Our fault. We've been too casual with handling this stuff. It was going to happen."

A man stepped up in front of me. I vaguely noticed a badge and a big white mustache as his voice echoed. "So, I guess that makes you Leo's niece. I heard you've already opened up his forge, and now I believe it."

Lisa's angry voice came from somewhere, up close and distant at the same time. "Humans are all idiots. And *you're* the worst idiot."

A fingertip touched my forehead. It was attached to Lisa's hand. She pushed, and I fell backwards, but managed to keep my knees straight until I landed in what I already recognized by feel and smell as Lisa's arms.

As I let my eyes closed, I heard my cousin scold, "You would drown yourself in the ocean just to show off how long you can hold your breath."

A pause. A whisper in my ear, "I love you for it."

I finally noticed how tired I felt. Really, really tired. I let go, and it all slipped away.

The last thing I heard, in the distance, was, "Wait. Wait! You didn't tell me what groceries to buy!"

ChapterSeven

I woke up with something sucking on my face.

It had claws, little scratchy things that fluttered over my neck and jaw.

There was only one thing to do. I screeched, "AAAAAAA!" and sat bolt upright in bed. Also I may have flailed my arms around desperately, not so much swatting at it as just, you know, flailing.

A brown, hard-shelled, teardrop-shaped thing flew off my face, zoomed across the room, and landed on a lamp.

A second later Lisa sprinted into the room, wearing a bathrobe and brandishing a sword. It was an ornamental rather than practical sword. It had crimson inlay and a blade with jagged hooked bits sticking out the side, like if swords were trees. Practical or not, its edges and points sure looked deadly sharp to me.

"What in the bleached bone Hells is that!?" she shouted, pointing her sword at the buggy thing and shuffling sideways around the room to put herself between me and it.

Actually, with that long, pointy tail, the thing looked less like a bug and more like a... horseshoe crab. A horseshoe crab that could fly without wings and was completely ignoring us, rubbing itself over the lamp shade instead.

Extending my arms in caution, I exclaimed, "Wait, wait! It's not dangerous! It's... I think... it cleans up dust?"

My memories between the horseshoe crab blood incident and waking up just now were extremely murky, but I had that impression. This thing's purpose was to clean.

Lisa lowered the sword, turned, and gave me a stare of sour frustration, which, let me tell you, slit-pupiled glowing eyes are really effective at conveying. "You snuck out of bed in the middle of the night and made another monster, didn't you? You did. I put you to bed, and despite everything I told you, you snuck out and made... this." She waved a hand at the hard-shelled brown thing leaving visible dust-free trails over the lamp shade as it crawled around. "Why does it fly?"

Digging through the murk of... yesterday? I found what might be a memory and might be a guess. "Because the dust is everywhere? It's doing a good job. And it's not a monster. A monster doesn't have a soul fragment, it's supported by the soul forge directly. Um. Actually, I think it is a monster. I wanted to make sure it couldn't run away, and I could dismiss it any time I want."

A moment later, I added with helpless honesty, "I think."

Lisa stared at me some more. She lifted up the sword in both hands, in a "lugging around" rather than threatening position. Finally, she let out an exasperated growl and ordered, "Do... whatever it is you mortals think you have to do in the morning. Get dressed, probably." She rolled her eyes in disgust at our foolish modesty. "Don't you dare do anything productive before you meet me downstairs to eat."

With the stiff alertness of shock still driving me, a realization tumbled into my brain. I asked the question connected to it. "Why are you so determined to take care of me all of a sudden?"

She grinned. She grinned wide, so I could see the big canines and the odd, sharp teeth around them. Her eyes went wide, their glow making the rest of her face look subtly shadowed. It was an evil, deranged, demonic expression. Frustration gone, she answered with honeyed glee, "Because you're a weapon I can point at the world, if I keep you intact."

With that, she turned and stalked out of my bedroom, bathrobe flapping and still holding the sword.

Okay, um, this was the start of my morning, I guess. Time to take stock. I started by running my hands back through my hair. It was horribly tangled, but clean. Maybe the crab did that.

My teeth, on the other hand, felt and tasted like they'd been dipped in rotting applesauce. I leaned off the bed and fumbled around for my tablet and its cleaning spell.

A few minutes later, I bounced down the stairs, and took the turn straight into my workshop. I wanted to make sure I hadn't made that cleaning crab with an unsafe soul forge. I would be on edge until I knew.

Bending over the forge, I gave it a look over and did a bit of poking. The legs were properly insulated, thank goodness, and those loose wires fastened in place with lead. It still had that warped plate, but that wasn't immediately important. It would be fine as long as I replaced it before-

Lisa's fingers with their painfully pointy fingernails dug into my hair, grabbing a fistful right at my scalp. She yanked me to the side, and as I flailed my arms and squealed and tried not to fall down, she dragged me out of the workshop.

As she marched through the hall, making me stagger along sideways next to her, she snapped, "I am a demon. Do you understand? I am evil. I don't want to be nice to people. I can't torment you if you need me to take care of you all the time instead. How did you even survive this long!?"

Stumbling but staying mostly upright as she pulled me around sideways, I answered honestly, "I had parents to take care of me."

"And did you constantly try to kill yourself back home?" my cousin demanded.

"I did try to stick the soul fragment from Dad's soul forge in my mouth when I was..." I decided very quickly to lie about the number. "...four years old."

Lisa pulled me into the dining room, her hooves making angry little thumps on the carpet with every step. Whipping me around in a circle, she shoved me against one of the chairs until I climbed up into it. Only then did she let go, and march off into the kitchen. Mere seconds later she returned, with a plate in each hand, both held high.

She slid one of those plates onto the wooden tabletop in front of me.

It held one egg and a slice of toast. Technically. The egg was still in its shell, and browned in a way that I had never seen an eggshell colored before. It rolled at the sudden movement like a hard, solid object. I gave it a tap, and it felt like a rock.

I did not give the toast a tap. I didn't want to touch it. It was a big slice, but something unspeakable had happened to it. It was gooey in places and rough-edged crunchy in others, like it had been soaked in butter and then grilled relentlessly.

"Um...," I said, not wanting to insult someone who had gone to the effort of cooking me breakfast.

Lisa was not offended by my hesitation. Brisk and confident, she told me, "And now that you've learned what my cooking is like, here are some leftovers I reheated."

She pulled the plate of inedible pseudo-food out of the way, and slid a plate with a couple of fish tacos on it in front of me instead. The sharp, hot smell of tomatoes and peppers and fish hit me instantly. It looked delicious despite the mix of soft in some places and stiff in others you got heating up an old meal. Maybe it was a little over-cooked, but still mouth-watering to look at.

It tasted just as good as it looked. I wolfed it down, and drank a glass of goat's milk Lisa shoved into my hand. We hadn't had that milk, the egg, or the bread yesterday, so clearly some kind of groceries were purchased.

I opened my mouth to ask what all happened yesterday

that I forgot, only to realize that revealing how much I didn't know would give away just how badly I'd overworked myself. I'd managed to avoid killing myself. I didn't want Lisa to do it for me.

A stomach full of tacos felt so good. Mmmmm. Finally both awake and relaxed, I started to push my chair away from the table.

Lisa, standing next to me with her arms folded, declared, "*Now* you may go ahead and do your safety inspection."

She'd said that solely to make it appear like she was in charge. I glared at her. She grinned evilly back at me.

Neither of us were going to break, so I stopped wasting time and scurried eagerly for my workshop. Snapping my fingers turned the lights on to complement the sunlight filtering through curtains and the door into the house. Yes, the soul forge looked so much safer than yesterday. The whole place was nicer. The cleaning crab seemed kind of random, sucking the dust off of big patches, then leaving others still messy, but it had gotten a lot of the workshop done just since I'd made it last night. It had even made a start on the ground-in black grime on the floor.

I also noticed a metal jug on the supply shelf that hadn't been there yesterday. Flipping over the lid, I glanced inside and saw a little bottle of glowing blue horseshoe crab blood. Nice!

Cursory inspection done, I dug the actual official safety inspection checklist out of Uncle Leonard's papers, and started working through it.

I wasn't quite done with that when I heard a knock on the business door.

I straightened up from ticking off the list of sigils and their links. Raising my eyebrows, I lifted up my goggles and then raised my eyebrows again, because that was a lot more comfortable. "A customer? So early?"

Lisa slid off of the work table she'd been sitting on, from which she'd watched me like a sheep dog. With a smirk, she corrected, "It's not early. I fed you lunch, not breakfast. Somebody overworked herself so badly she slept until noon."

Which meant this could be anybody. I headed for the office to find out.

Started to head for the office. Lisa insinuated herself in front of me.

I started to push through her. She held up a palm of truce, and offered, "Compromise. No customers today, but I'll check and get their information. Okay?"

Mmmf. I wanted to argue. I felt fine. I was ready, eager, to start being a full time bioengineer! But... I did actually black out from overwork yesterday, using a damaged soul forge no less, so maybe a day of rest was acceptable. I might have mixed feelings about being pushed around, but Lisa was kind of right.

My acceptance must have been written in my expression. Lisa whisked away through the office to the door, and pulled it open.

Ruby stood there, the same as last time, with her burgundy hair perfectly made up and her expensive black dress pretending to be simple and her expertly applied makeup. The differences were that this time Sophie stood next to her, admittedly on four legs and way down at ground level, a wrinkly pink cat with a disapproving expression.

That, and Ruby was visibly swaying. Her eyes fixed on Lisa, and she squealed, "Eeee! My prodigy, my—you're not my prodigy savior."

Sophie sighed, and shook her head at her owner's bewildered babble.

Ruby's not entirely focused gaze wandered away from Lisa, and after a couple of seconds found me. She squealed again, face lighting up in joy. "Eeeeee! My prodigy savior!"

Launching herself forward, Ruby rushed across the room in a whipping flurry of skirts, and managed not to trip over her feet until she reached me. The bigger girl didn't actually fall over, but she wrapped her arms around my shoulders in a fierce hug and leaned most of her weight on me.

Me, I also didn't fall over, but my knees wobbled at the strain.

With her hair in my face, the teenage witch smelled weird. Sweet, but not pleasant sweet. Sickly, maybe a touch rancid. Not nasty, either, just odd, with a tang I didn't recognize. She also went back to babbling, her voice dizzy and erratic, passionately emphatic in some words and vaguely wandering with others.

"You're so smart an' you saved my cat an' you're so small. So adorably small. I'mma call you Lil Bits," she told me.

Twisting my head so I could look past Ruby and down at her cat, I asked, "Is she okay?"

The skinny pink animal strolled inside, not letting its hairlessness disturb a cat's usual grace and arrogance. A new collar around Sophie's neck held a clasp with a spell tablet fastened into it. Ruby's spell tablet, no doubt.

With a hint of sneer on her muzzle and more than a hint of resentment in her voice, Sophie answered, "Mistress Flora was displeased when she found out Rhubella got her familiar without permission, and assigned my—" The cat lifted one leg, and her altered, more dexterous paws flexed a couple of fingers in air quotes. "—'mistress' some difficult potions as punishment."

"I can do 'em," slurred Ruby into my ear. "Gotta gotta gotta show I'm as smart as my Lil Bits. My cute tiny big brain Lil Bits."

Sharp with strained dignity, Sophie continued, "And apparently this is what the fumes from stewing enchanted saguaro fruit does to you. I told her she wasn't in any fit state to go out."

Ruby pushed up off of me, and nearly achieved standing fully upright before she slumped back with her arms draped over my shoulders. Vehemently, she declared, "No! Made a promise. Said I was coming back today. My Lil Bits gotta know she can trust me. I say I'm gonna I'm gonna."

Suddenly she relaxed more, and OOF. I strained under the full weight of a girl at least six inches taller than me. Sleepily, right by my ear, she mumbled, "Tee hee. Lil Bits."

Yes, Ruby, I can tell you like that nickname. Sigh.

Groaning from the effort of holding her up, I suggested, "I think you need to lie down. Lisa, help me get her to the couch?"

Ruby's hands grabbed my chest, pushing, and she managed to struggle all the way into a standing position again. Offended, she argued with the ceiling, "Hey! I can walk! I can walk all the way to my Lil Bits house! Oh. I'm here."

She fell over on me again. I braced one foot behind me,

which was the only reason I didn't fall over, too.

Dour, Sophie observed, "I think she's actually getting worse. I suppose the chemicals take time to soak in."

Lisa, also scowling, watched me with arms folded and disdain at my request. "Keeping you alive is the limit—oh, never mind. If I don't help you'll fall over and break your leg, and we both know it."

So the demoness stumped over, and we each slid a shoulder under one of Ruby's, dragging her through the workshop into my still dusty living room. Her sandaled feet trailed across the floor, any attempt to hold herself up forgotten. She just kept giggling, "Lil Bits. Tee hee. Lil Bits. Oooooh, I like the flying ones."

That was her reaction to my new cleaning crab hovering past. She tried to poke it with a fingertip, and missed. It didn't even notice her.

Padding along after us, Sophie looked around curiously and commented, "I smell fish tacos. You will, of course, feed me."

Almost to the couch. Lisa was definitely doing the absolute minimum lifting to keep me from collapsing under Ruby's weight.

Fine. Be that way. I dragged Ruby to the couch, dropped her onto it, and rolled her over so she was lying on her back with her head propped up on a cushion. I'd slept on that couch the night before, so I knew it was comfortable and not particularly dusty.

As soon as Ruby was recumbent, Sophie leaped with liquid feline elegance up off the floor, and curled up in a mass of pink folds of skin on the young witch's stomach. She nudged her head against one of Ruby's limp hands and told her, "Just think, you could be at home petting me and telling *me* how great I am."

Blitzed out of her gourd on magic cactus fruit she might be, but Ruby immediately responded to the pressure, pressing back against Sophie's head and rolling her hand down the furless kitty's back, pushing up mounds of wrinkly skin. Sophie began to purr, loudly. Ruby smiled down at her familiar, and whispered, "You are. You're my kitty. Nobody else's kitty, all mine, forever. Did you know you're a kitty?"

Sophie rolled onto her back, batting at Ruby's hand with four long, scrawny pink legs while faux-exclaiming, "Gasp! Am I truly?"

Only one of Ruby's hands was busy playing with her cat. The other shot out, grabbed a strap of my overalls, and yanked my face close to hers. Hazel eyes watering, she looked up at me and whispered urgently, almost coherently, "You don't know how grateful I am, Lil Bits. Sophie has been my kitty my whole life. Her and me. It was always me she wanted."

Wriggling around Ruby's petting hand, Sophie commented, "I will let other people feed me, if they put the food down and stand far enough away." Going back to purring like an earthmover, she pushed her hand hard against Ruby for more pets.

Actually focused now, shaking her head with emotion, Ruby continued, "They let me take her to witch school, even. The other girls are dumb and they don't try and I don't know how they pass because some of this stuff is really hard, but I always had Sophie."

Tears welled up in the burgundy-haired girl's eyes, and immediately ran down her cheeks, leaving tracks in her makeup. Her voice turned rough. "And then she got sick, and she kept getting sick, and last week the potions stopped working, and she stopped eating, and I was going to lose her, and making her my familiar was all I could think of, and I didn't think a bioengineer would do it, but you did it and it worked and now I get to keep my kitty and you are my hero, Lil Bits. Mistress Hammerhead said if I think I deserve a familiar they'll make my work even harder but you inspire me and I have Sophie and I know I can do it."

Pulling me closer, Ruby shoved her face into my shirt and sobbed, and sobbed, and sobbed.

I patted her shoulder as tenderly as I could, and quietly asked, "Lisa, could you get some orange juice for our guest? And maybe there are some more fish tacos? I bet you bought a lot of them."

My demon cousin immediately turned and headed into the hall, replying mildly, "I bought so many fish tacos, but are you sure we should share them?"

Sophie stopped purring. She lifted up a paw that still wasn't quite a hand, and ordered, "Shhh. Wait."

We all waited. After a few more seconds Ruby's sobs stopped. She let go of my clothing, and sank back down on the couch, eyes closed. Her heavy, rough breathing slowed, and she went limp and quiet.

Sophie stretched her body up to Ruby's head, patting her owner's jaw, then peeling open an eyelid momentarily. Satisfied, Sophie murmured, "Well, thank goodness. I told her that she should sleep this off."

That said, Sophie clambered to her own four feet, walked up Ruby's body, and collapsed atop Ruby's face, draped over it and dangling on either side like a towel. Her eyes closed, and if she wasn't actually asleep seconds later, I couldn't tell the difference.

ChapterEight

Bok bok bok!

I nearly jumped out of my skin, then realized someone was knocking on my front door. The living room front door, the one behind me.

Neither Ruby nor Sophie budged. The witch girl could probably sleep through everything, as drunk as she was on potion ingredients. Hopefully. Anyway, ignoring the door would just lead to more knocking.

So I opened it, and told the man outside in a hushed voice, "Shhh. I have a guest asleep. I'm Artifact. How can I help you?"

He looked familiar. Tall, middle-aged, but hard rather than out of shape. A big man, but more because he was tall than broad. He wore a plain enough buttoned shirt and loose denim pants, with a copper ornament stuck to the shirt. A big, big hat sat on his grey-haired head, but it couldn't compete for attention with his big, big grey mustache.

He nodded, and answered in an equally gentle tone, "I know, little lady. I was there yesterday during all the fuss. I can't blame you for not remembering me. It was quite a hullabaloo."

With the door open, I caught the tiniest whiff of sea air. A haunting sensation that I didn't have time for.

Trying not to be too brusque while still conveying that I didn't have time to talk, I agreed, "I'm afraid that I don't. It was quite a hullabaloo, yes. Enough that the forge is closed today."

Something dropped into my hair. From the wiggling, it must have been the cleaning crab. I tried to ignore it.

Hooking his thumb into his big leather belt, the old man nodded. His face was so lined and grizzled, it was unreal, but in a leathery rather than fragile way. No, he looked like if you shot him with an arrow, or a lightning bolt for that matter, it would bounce off. He had a deep, gruff, but kind voice as he assured me, "I'll try not to keep you. I wish we were meeting under better circumstances, but it is what it is. This isn't about the forge. See, I'm the local sheriff, name of Westlake, and I've got some questions to ask about that girl Lisa that lives with you. The one old Leonard took a shine to."

My back immediately went stiff, a little with cold anxiety, but mostly with acid resentment. Was this going to be like that guy yesterday? Except... it was probably not a good idea to mouth off to the law, so I kept my tone studiously polite. "What about her?"

Okay, maybe that did sound slightly resentful, but only slightly.

He didn't seem upset. Crouching down to bring us a foot close to eye to eye, the dark little eyes within those wrinkles met mine. Not in challenge. Solemn acknowledgment. Respect, maybe. His voice stayed quiet, but sounded very, very serious. "Can you tell me where she was before noon yesterday? Sorry to leap straight to suspicion, young lady, but a very powerful tool called a breach detonator was stolen yesterday."

I tried to stare at him in convincing surprise, and probably pulled it off, considering how disturbed I felt by how this day was already going. "I know what a breach detonator is. What is one doing in Goblita in the first place?"

Sheriff Westlake's gravelly voice drawled, "The answer to that leads to why I'm here. See, one 'a the original Breach openings happened right here in Goblita. It got buried in a collapsed dungeon, but it's still there. There were incidents. The

College has an expert stationed here to bleed off pressure or something. I don't pretend to understand it."

I did, at least roughly, and it sounded majorly dangerous. It also answered another question, although I squinted at the old man and pressed for confirmation. "Would that expert be the guy who came to my house yesterday? He and Lisa don't seem to like each other."

Sheriff Westlake sighed. It was the most world-weary sound I'd ever heard. For a second I thought he would collapse into a pile of bones, but he got his grizzled fortitude back immediately, looked me in the eye again, and answered, "No, missy, I suppose they don't. Gregory's real dedicated to his job. He's mightily suspicious of anyone or anything not from our world. Like I said, the breach detonator got stolen yesterday morning, and he's convinced the demon girl did it."

"Yesterday morning? Lisa was with me all morning," I said truthfully.

"All morning?" he pressed, raising an eyebrow. When this guy raised an eyebrow, it was impressive. They weren't as bushy as his mustache, but they were at least three regular people's eyebrows.

I continued to tell the dishonest truth. "She was never out of my sight for more than five minutes. I don't want to go into details, but I just moved in, and there was a little tension about it while we sorted things out. I guess there's about an hour while I took my nap in the afternoon that she could have left the house. That might have started as early as one p.m., maybe?"

Sheriff Westlake sighed again, this time in clear relief. I actually felt bad about lying to such a nice guy. Clapping his hands on his knees, he pushed upright, and from way up there said, "No, little miss. It was definitely the morning. Thank you. Sorry to be a hassle. I'd have tracked down the thief and the detonator last night, but yesterday my forensic vulture got eaten by the biggest dragon you ever saw. Darnedest thing, let me tell you. Kind of a stressful day for everyone."

UM.

Um. Um. Um.

That was my dragon, which meant I had a big, big problem,

since it was *my* dragon that ate the local sheriff's bioengineered assistant. His expensive bioengineered assistant. His hopefully not intelligent expensive bioengineered assistant.

"Oh. Well. Um," I stammered, sounding like an idiot. Forcing myself back to coherence, I said, "I'd have to look it up, but I think I have the notes to make one of those, if you've got a regular vulture and a fragment to help upgrade."

Oh please, let the vulture part take a while. Nobody could just have a regular pet vulture waiting around ready to be upgraded, right? I would have time to clean up the feathery draconic evidence before he got back his ability to pin it on me, right? And track the breach detonator to Joe, and then my cousin? They might be guilty, but I badly wanted them both to be safe.

I still wasn't sure if they were morally right or wrong—no, no time for that now.

Whatever Sheriff Westlake saw my hesitation as, "suspicious" didn't seem to be it. He shook his head sadly. "Wish I could, but there's no city budget for it, even though I've got the replacement bird. Got a whole mews of 'em. Goblita's just about scraped together the money to come to you for some replacement slimes for the sewage plant."

Seriously? He had a pet vulture waiting around ready to be upgraded? The only thing he was missing was the money to pay me? Okay, that and the money to buy a soul fragment for the process. Right. Nobody could reasonably expect me to provide that myself.

Also, wait, the sewage plant was in trouble? Looking over my shoulder back at the kitchen, I asked, "Is there something wrong with the water?"

He grinned under that mustache. A tight grin with a bit of bleakness, but still a grin. The mustache if anything made the bends of the mouth it hid more noticeable. "Not yet. Figure it will be fine if we can get some more slimes soon. We lost most of them when some drunk adventurer fellow wandered into the plant and thought it was a dungeon. Killed all the slimes he could corner and stole their soul fragments. He's been dealt with, but Goblita will be rationing money out for a while to replace those slimes as fast as possible."

A touch of excitement at making water purification slimes mixed with the many other emotions storming within me, and I hazarded, "Well. Um. Civic responsibility and all, if you can get me the ingredients, I'll replace them two for one."

Down the hall and out of sight, Lisa shouted, "Don't you dare! You're going to suck yourself dry and shrivel up like a raisin overworking your magic, and then who will I mooch off of, huh?"

I rolled my eyes, leaning my head back to retort, "I can handle a few extra slimes, Lisa. Prodigy, remember?"

She stuck her head from around the corner, and grumped, "We'll discuss this after our guests are gone. Do you want ice cream?"

"Yes please," I answered, because yes, of course I wanted ice cream! We had ice cream? But I had a conversation to finish before that, so I gave Sheriff Westlake an apologetic smile. "Sorry. Like I said, we're still getting used to this."

He grunted, stretching out his back. Yes, keeping his head tilted down to look at me was probably bad for his spine. We were at the opposite ends of the unaltered human height scale. Unlike Lisa, he kept his voice low, thoughtfully trying not to disturb Ruby any more than we might have done already. "Don't worry about it. The main reason I came here was to check Lisa's alibi. Much as I'd like proper introductions to someone as important as Goblita's new bioengineer and the hero of yesterday's disaster, I'd better run off. I've got two emergencies to deal with. That breach detonator needs to be found fast, before we have some kinda outbreak or invasion, and I've got to track down that dragon even faster. It's so big, we think it might have come out of a dungeon."

Track down the dragon? I really did not want to have to admit I accidentally killed the sheriff's vulture. Hopefully my grimace looked like worry over the dungeon thing as I asked, "Close enough to Goblita that a monster can get in town?"

He nodded. "Figured you'd understand. Thanks for being so obliging, young missy. I hope you have a great day, and I'll talk to you more social like soon."

Giving him a pleasant smile, I closed the door carefully, bolted it, then turned around and grimaced with horror as I lay against the carved, lumpy wooden panel. My voice squeaky, I demanded, "Lisa. Lisa, where did you put it? We are in so much trouble." Pausing for a deep breath, forcing calm, I told myself, "No. I can take care of this. I'm a prodigy, right?"

Lisa wandered out of the kitchen. She never had changed out of the bathrobe, which made her look supernaturally lazy and relaxed combined with her holding a glass with a couple of scoops of ice cream in it. With the bland cheerfulness to match, she said, "A prodigy with a whole bucket of ice cream you got given for free! Plus, your witch girlfriend can help when she gets sober. I bet she'd do anything for you."

I didn't know where to begin to reply to all that, and while I tried to figure it out, the door thumped repeatedly, vibrating against my back. Someone was knocking. Again.

I looked up at the ceiling and let out a strangled gurgle. I had absolutely no time for this, but I couldn't ignore it. Unbolting the door, I peeked out through the crack and snapped out, "I'm sorry, we're kind of busy here—oh, it's you two. Hi!"

Because there were Elvira and Emanuel standing in front of my door, him in long brown pants instead of short brown shorts, and her in an ankle-length white gown that looked extremely comfortable and billowed and clung to her in the slightest breeze. Some people have the look where clothing does that. Elvira was one of them.

She nudged her brother with her shoulder, and told him with brusque satisfaction, "Told you she'd be home. Now you don't have to pretend you're here to see the demon girl."

Back in the hall, Lisa waved her ice-cream-smeared spoon with languid disdain. "He's too boring and nice for me."

Emmanuel was too busy glaring at his sister to notice. "You're the one who insisted on coming to see Artifact," he accused.

Lisa flounced up to the door, grabbed Elvira's hand and then Emmanuel's in one of hers, and pulled them inside. Gaily, the flame-haired demoness informed them, "Whatever your excuse, your timing is perfect. Come on in, and let me tell you a crazy story. Then you and Elvira can pay Artifact back for saving your family business and also your lives, by helping us commit a few crimes. Artifact has a plan!"

I did not have a plan.

Chapter Nine

I had a plan.

Leaning against the door frame leading into the workshop, I told my assembled friends, "First, the breach detonator can wait."

I paused long enough to shoot Lisa an accusing glance for dragging me into that.

That done, I resumed, "It'll be weeks before the detonator is needed. Months. It could be years. Returning it is important, but not an emergency."

A little prickle crawled across my shoulders, the guilty knowledge that I was waaaaaaay out of my area of expertise here. Dad always said that assuming that because you're a master of one type of magic that you know anything about others is the cause of most liches and dungeon masters. Come on, though. How often could inter-universe value differences need to be vented, or whatever they needed the detonator for? Goblita had survived for hundreds of years. It couldn't be that bad.

Reassured by my own logic, I got to the point. "Right now, the emergency is that if the sheriff finds out *my* dragon went rogue and ate his assistant, the best I can hope for is the forge taken away from me."

Elvira and Emanuel sat on the carpet, where they had attentively listened to Lisa's mostly accurate recounting of how we got in this mess. Ice cream had helped, and Elvira even now spooned up a mouthful of her third scoop. We sure had a lot of it, and ice cream was a whole lot more expensive than our mountain of fish tacos, so someone had been majorly grateful that I'd saved the city.

Or Lisa had stolen it. I was hoping for the "grateful" option.

Emanuel, mouth empty, gave me a sober nod. "I wish I saw a flaw in that logic, but yeah. I agree."

Elvira lifted her foot so that the horseshoe crab could suck clean the bit of carpet underneath, then settled down as it moved on in its quest to make the carpet they were sitting on less of a mess. Swallowing ice cream, she waved the spoon at me and said, "And we'll help however we can to fix this."

She didn't say it with passion. She said it like she was reminding me of a known fact.

Emanuel grimaced and asked with a little more emphasis, "I'm with you in sentiment, but can we at least find out what we're agreeing to before we commit?"

Elvira looked at him with a dismissive smirk. "No."

Emanuel didn't argue, and that complete lack of argument spoke volumes. It touched my heart. I needed this feeling that someone was on my side. Taking a deep breath, I explained, "Right. Priority one is to get the dragon back so that I can fix its transformation, or confirm that it has left on its mission. Odds are it did leave on its mission. Its problem is that it's overdesigned, too big and too smart and too everything for the soul fragment powering it. I mean, it's a transformed pigeon, for goodness sake! It must be running, what, at least a ninety percent vitality tension? I forced it into existence with a major power dump, but that left it with a hunger to achieve at least temporary vitality equilibrium—"

I paused, mid-rant and mid-arm wave. Nobody else in this room knew anything about bioengineering. They didn't understand a word of what I was saying. Emanuel and Elvira sat cross-legged, staring at me with dark, attentive, interested eyes, so at least they weren't annoyed, but I was also getting off track.

That track was kind of important right now.

I got back to it, dropping back to a more normal tone of voice. "Anyway, we need to recover the dragon, and quietly. Right now, only the people in this room know I made it."

Elvira sneered and rolled her eyes, a pinched expression of mild disgust and vast amusement. "And Papa, but he's not going to tell John Law about it."

She ended with a snigger, which at least got a smile from Emanuel.

"Yeah, you're safe there," he echoed.

Another little bit of much-needed comfort. Back to the plan. "I think we can do that with the help of a witch. A witch who can be relied on for discretion. I bet Ruby is grateful enough to mix…"

That was as far as I got. At the sound of Ruby's name, Sophie jerked her head up, gleaming green cat eyes wide. She patted Ruby's cheek with a paw.

Ruby's whole body twitched. She reached up to push Sophie up off her eyes to her forehead like a pair of goggles, and looked around, curious and confused.

She also winced, and grumbled, "Ugh. I am nauseous. Sophie, whose couch did I fall asleep—"

The young witch's roving eyes finally reached me, and locked on. She sat bolt upright, and the only reason Sophie didn't fly away like a catapult stone was that Ruby already had her hands on the cat, and tucked it into her lap.

"Oh, no," Ruby whispered. Her eyes darting again around the room, then back to me. Leaping to her feet, which did send Sophie tumbling to the floor with a thump, Ruby clasped her hands over her face and went running, stumbling, out of the living room and into the workshop, babbling, "I'm sorry. I'm so sorry, Miss Forge. I'll never bother you again. Please forget this ever happened."

She careened off the door frame from my workshop into the office, and I heard the click and clatter of her hands fumbling desperately at the door handle and latch to the door outside, until it squeaked open and her footsteps receded in the distance at a sprinting pace.

Sophie had landed on her feet with catlike grace. The skinny, wrinkled pink furless animal strutted up to me, looked around at all of us, and lifted one foot to hold palm up. "I warned her. You heard me say I warned her."

Um. I tried to recover from my disappointment, stammering, "Okay. I guess I was wrong about the grateful part. We'll figure out someone else."

Lisa convulsed, her upper body whipping forward as she slapped a hand over her face. Dragging that hand down and off, she lurched back up and snarled at me, "No, you lollipop! She admires you, and she acted like an idiot in front of you, and now she's scared of what you think of her!"

Emanuel leaned a few inches closer to his sister, his whisper fully audible to the room. "Lollipop?"

"She's sweet, innocent, and has a big head," Elvira answered back with the calm, smug assurance of someone who is making a good guess rather than already knowing the answer.

Sophie tilted her head to the side, joining the room in giving me a condescending stare. "Of course she's grateful. You saved my life. I know no one is supposed to admit this out loud, but that is *the* greatest act of heroism possible. Now if you'll excuse me, Rhubella needs me to love her and make her feel better, and I don't actually care about any of you."

Tail twitching and skinny pink cat butt waggling, Sophie slunk off towards the office.

I called after her, "Okay, but please, tell her that not only do I not think she's an idiot, I really need her help."

"If I remember," Sophie answered cheerfully.

She moved out of view past the doorway into the office. A few seconds later, I heard the outside door thump closed.

I turned back to face the dusty brown furniture packed living room, with Lisa and my two new friends who were probably sitting on the carpet because it was less messy than the chairs. As if responsive to my thoughts, which wasn't impossible, the horseshoe crab flew up onto a chair and started to feed on its coating of dust.

Trying to get my direction back, I said, "Okay, um, step one can wait at least briefly. Step two will give us time to see if the dragon flew off and delivered my letter."

Please, please let it have flown off and delivered my letter.

Right. My focus back, I launched into step two. "Even with the dragon dealt with, we need cover, because right now I'm the only person with a soul forge anywhere near here. The sheriff thinks the dragon is a monster, so we'll give him reason to think a minor dungeon opened up nearby, and the dragon came from there."

To my mild surprise, Emanuel nodded, dark eyebrows raised in surprised respect. "That works. There used to be a big city just south of Goblita. We could take a day trip if you want to see it sometime. Earthmovers wrecked it repeatedly. No one would be surprised if a new dungeon suddenly appeared, or one that had been hidden under rubble for a century opened up and spat out a few creatures."

Elvira put the ice cream bowl aside, sitting up with an enthusiastic smile. "I'd love to take you this weekend! There's not enough time to get there and back on a school day."

Tightening my lips, I met Elvira's gaze and went for it. "Well, that kind of sort of circles around to where I was going. You know some destructive magic. Could I talk you into actually fighting a monster?"

Elvira shrieked. Her already squeaky, sharp-edged voice echoed around the house like a saw biting metal. Leaping to her feet, she charged towards me, grabbed both of my shoulders, and demanded, "How did you know??? How did you know what I really want to be is an adventurer???"

My vision bobbled as she shook me, but I finally registered that Elvira was smiling. Elvira was smiling so big it looked like her head might split. Dizzy, I mumbled, "Oh. Well, that's convenient."

A knock resounded through the living room.

Someone was knocking at the business door.

Elvira let me go. I sighed in exasperation at the timing. "Again?"

To my surprise, Elvira and Emanuel immediately burst

out laughing. Emanuel, leaning heavily on one hand, choked down his laughs long enough to say, "You're an adult running a business now. Mama and Papa complain about it all the time. They say it's worse than school."

I thought about that, and glanced over my shoulder into the workshop. "Okay, but... I get my own soul forge."

Lisa stepped up next to me, one finger raised in warning. "Which you are not using today. Scheme today, act tomorrow. I'll go get the door and tell them you're unavailable."

I looked her in her glowing pink eyes, and corrected, "*We* will get the door and keep each other from getting out of line."

Unintimidated but also thoughtful, she met my gaze, and gave a small nod. "Acceptable, but I won't let you kill yourself. I've had enough of that from one Forge already."

We walked side by side to the door, matching each other's footsteps and watching to make sure the other didn't get even slightly ahead. When we reached the business door, Lisa reached out aggressively to take hold of the handle, but stepped back as she turned it, leaving me to greet the visitor.

Who was tall. And blue. Those were my first impressions. He wasn't actually crazy tall, but so thin that he looked like it. Most of his body stood ramrod straight, but at the shoulders he hunched forward to look down at us. Skinny, stick-like arms tapped the long fingers of spidery hands together in front of his contemplative grin. Decorate that scarecrow apparition with a nearly pressed, very straight blue suit with a number of faint but visible old stains, a wide and flat-brimmed blue hat, and pure white hair. Too pure white to be from age, and really, the man's face didn't look that old. "Over thirty" was all I could say for sure.

"Sorry to disappoint, but I'm actually closed for the day," I informed him. Lisa's proud smile approved of this approach.

The man's hunched head nodded, and in a jovial and surprisingly deep voice he said, "That's a pity, oh yes, but I am here to discuss future business, not make an immediate purchase, no."

He tapped his fingers together more as he talked.

"Then I guess I can give you a few minutes," I compromised. I was a professional. A professional needs customers.

Lisa spoke up, glaring at the tall, skinny man. "Miss Forge is being polite, but your timing really sucks. Hurry it up so she can tell you 'no' like Leo always did, Casper."

I shot her a warning glance, for whatever good that might do, but did switch to a wary tone as I told the man, "I can at least let you make your pitch."

His head bobbed. His fingers tapped together. His white-toothed grin never wavered. "Simple enough, oh yes. I have the honor to be the most successful butcher in Goblita, and most especially honored to be head of our trade union, yes. I make a special effort to recover the soul fragments from livestock wherever possible, and what better use than to recycle them into new stock? Efficient, yes, and I would be happy to offer you a half-and-half deal. For every fragment you restore to life, you get another to keep for your own professional purposes. Professional purposes are most important, we all agree."

That offer sounded straightforward, and certainly generous. It never occurred to me that butchers would be the main source of soul fragments, but even if they only recovered one percent, that would still be a pile, right?

So, why would Uncle Leonard object?

I realized why Uncle Leonard would object, and said, "I'm sorry, I'm not comfortable creating living things for the purpose of them immediately being killed again."

"Sorry, Casper!" barked Lisa, and made to slam the door.

I caught it with an outstretched arm, my eyes on the skinny butcher, and continued, "I can make you a counteroffer. I am willing to make exotic animals that would be allowed to grow up first. Ostriches, bison, and turkeys, for example. Better, I have recipes for truly exotic species. Even if you can't raise them yourself, I'm sure local ranchers would pay well for land catfish calves."

The butcher, whose name was presumably Casper, raised his pure white eyebrows for a fraction of a second. "Well, a very impressive offer to consider, yes, most impressive. More complicated, of course. I would have to consult with my associates."

I shrugged. "I'm not open for business today anyway."

Distant and thoughtful, but fingers still tapping, he said, "I have heard that land catfish grow quite large. Yes, that is what I hear."

Grinning because this was my subject, I filled him in, "The record is twenty tons. They never stop growing, but the owner couldn't afford to feed it anymore, and it couldn't move well enough to feed itself."

Personally and privately, I would not want my body made of delicious meat anywhere near a catfish that big. Nope, I would not. Heh.

Dragging myself back to business thoughts, I offered, "With three chicken fragments, I can make you a sucrow. As expensive as granulated sugar is, you'd make a fortune raising those. Ethics require me to warn you, sucrows don't breed. Nothing with more than one soul fragment breeds. Nature doesn't do more than one soul fragment, ever, but multiple fragment animals are highly magical and I can give you options. A few years of shed sucrow feathers are worth much more than three chickens, I'd say. Land catfish do breed, but it's not easy, and even a baby requires an adult cow's fragment. I have more recipes. I'll prepare a list for the next time we meet."

Finally pausing in his finger tapping, the skinny butcher reached up and tipped his hat to me, my first indication it wasn't welded to his head. He bobbed a short, quick bow, proving he also had hips. "Most generous, you are a most generous and professional young lady, yes. As I said, I must consult with my associates, but I believe they will find your offer favorable. Yes, favorable indeed."

"Which means our business is done," Lisa declared, and slammed the door in his face. I had just enough time to give him a helpless shut as it closed.

The gust of outside air from that sudden swing was nice, though.

I turned back to see Elvira standing in the doorway to the workshop, cracking her fingers with a sly, bright-eyed smile. It would have made her resemble the butcher, except there wasn't a straight up or down line anywhere on Elvira. "So, what's next? When do I get to blast stuff?"

Okay. A little more chaos than I'd expected, but basically a successful meeting. Holding up my hands, I answered, "What's next is that everyone goes home and I get my references and do a lot of design work, because I don't have recipes for the kind of monsters I need."

Lisa jabbed me in the shoulder with a sharp fingernail from behind. "And you're not making them today, anyway."

Accepting this truth, I told Elvira, "So you get to blast stuff tomorrow. After school."

ChapterTen

Tomorrow after school arrived.
    Except it didn't.
Because tonight had to happen first.

I closed my book, the unbound pages sticking out at odd angles because I'd been disturbing them. I looked at the office's window, out into indigo darkness, and then down at the off-white sheet of paper in front of me with the recipe I'd worked out. I couldn't see any flaws in my work. Ink blobs from an awkwardly wielded pen, yes, but I'd been very careful with the spacing and references and calculations. Everything balanced. There would be no overdesign issues like with the dragon.

I sat still on my stool in this grey room with its grey and brown shelves, the multi-colored block of the soul forge, and the clutter on the many shelves. Closing my eyes, I listened to the great, empty house.

Silence. Absolute silence. In the night, even the ice elemental had turned off. The house might be packed with furniture and books and knick-knacks, but it was still empty. It was the house of a man dead and gone.

Please, let Sophie have delivered my message. I badly

needed to recapture that dragon. I couldn't send my parents another message until I did. It might eat the messenger, and I would never know.

You know what my parents didn't know? If I'd arrived safely. They didn't know that Uncle Leonard was dead. I couldn't imagine what they were thinking, or what they would do. I hadn't specifically promised to send a message immediately when I arrived. Maybe they weren't freaking out yet. Maybe they were just worried.

My heart ached at the thought of Mom and Dad scared for me.

The ache spread like spilled vinegar, sour and repellant. It took two weeks to get from Lake Touhou to Goblita. I hadn't seen my parents in all that time. I had no idea if they were okay, either. Dad's job wasn't exactly safe. Lake Touhou was an isolated area, known for magical disasters.

The edges of my eyes stung. Heavy and tired, I listened to the silence some more. The silence of an empty house. Not like my parents' house, where at the very least I could hear them snoring, or the scraping and plinks of Dad's experimental bioengineering tools, and the hiss of the soul forge's special high-powered warding. This house didn't even creak. Goblita didn't seem to have weather to cause noises. No wild animals or harmless, tolerated monsters pawed at the woodpiles.

The stinging in my eyes sharpened. Tears went down my cheeks. I sobbed, hunched forward, arms wrapped around my own chest because my parents were far away.

With my eyes closed, I still noticed the change in lighting, and peeked enough to see Lisa in her bathrobe standing in the doorway to the living room. The only lights on in the house was the one in the workshop's ceiling, and Lisa's glowing tablet.

"I heard something—what's wrong?" the horned and flame-haired demoness asked, face pinched in puzzlement.

Pain surged up from my heart again. I clapped my hands tight over my eyes, which still didn't stop the tears from leaking around the edges as I whimpered, "I'm not ready for this. This house is too big. Running a business is too big. I miss my parents."

Seconds passed as I cried. Soft hands took hold of my wrists, pulling them away, so I could see Lisa standing in front of me, looking down. She looked baffled, lost, as if crying was something she'd only heard about in myths.

The tears rolling down my cheeks moved her to some decision. Putting an arm around my shoulders, she pulled me gently out of my chair, and towards the doorway to the house. "Come on," she murmured in monotone.

I tried. My feet stumbled over the cold, bare cement of the workshop, and then the soft, uneven, elderly carpet of the living room. I couldn't stop crying. The workshop felt too crushing and oppressive, every tool a relentless demand jabbing at me. The living room was vast and meaningless. I'd only turned on the lights in the workshop, and the living room's little tables and chairs and shelves all lurked in shadow, someone else's belongings, in every color but all faded and dull. Dead like their owner. Not mine. I'd never sat in them.

Lisa dragged me like a mannequin to the sofa, and we fell down onto it together. Her face still scowling and confused, she put her other arm around me. Not so much a hug as just holding me.

I didn't care about her expression. I grabbed fistfuls of her padded bathrobe, and buried my face in her shoulder. She smelled like strawberries and nothing human, but she was warm and alive and somebody, at least. Hoarse and shaking, I rasped, "It's so empty and I'm so alone."

Firm, not quite scolding but emphatic, Lisa corrected me, "No. I'm here. No building is empty if I'm in it. I've been toning it down for your sake. Plus, you've made friends already!"

I just squeezed and pulled myself against her tighter. "I've known them for one day. They don't really know me at all. They just know the thirteen-year-old prodigy who's as powerful as an adult bioengineer."

She shook her head a little. Her hair, with its mix of red and orange and hints of yellow, scattered over my face. Her arms around me gave a tentative squeeze, and she argued, "Then we'll spend more time with them. Your time can't all be taken up with work and fixing this dragon problem. Then when you get sick of me and tell me I have to go back to school or get kicked out, I can introduce you to some of those kids. They'll like you, I'm almost positive."

I just clung to her, my heart and head hurting, pouring tears onto her hot, inhumanly even-colored skin.

She shrugged in my grip, and with her hands busy holding me, her tail tip waved around helplessly instead. She complained, "Look, I was raised in Hell, okay? I'm not good at this comforting stuff. But I can promise I will be all the not-aloneness you can handle."

My voice barely more than a scratchy noise, I asked, "Don't you miss your home? Your mother?"

There was a pause. A long pause. The house was still utterly silent, but Lisa was next to me. I could feel the quilted softness of her bathrobe, the smoothness of her skin, smell that strawberry scent, and hear the steady thump of her heartbeat. I wasn't completely alone, and the house wasn't completely empty.

Also, as alien as Lisa was, we were cousins. Maybe physically she was pure demon, but she had inherited some familyness.

Finally, her tone non-committal, she answered, "My mother is fine. She's better than I knew, because she was right. Earth is better, and she had to get me out while I was young enough to appreciate it."

Curiosity surfaced above my misery. I croaked, "How so? People tell all kinds of stories, but they don't even agree whether it's hot or cold—"

Lisa let go of me with one arm, and put her hand over my mouth, holding it shut. Not quite angry, just stern, she informed me, "What you need to know is, nobody is having fun there. Demons are so busy fighting to make sure that they're the only one who gets to have fun that even the winners don't actually have any fun. The most miserable human is happier than the happiest demon. I need to stay here, which means I need you, and you need me even more than Leo did."

When her hand loosened, I asked, "Do you miss him? I didn't know him."

Stonily absolute, she snapped, "We're not going to talk about that. Ever."

I should feel stung by her harsh tone. Instead, a huge rush of sympathy flooded over my own pain. I let go of her bathrobe to slide my arms around her, and hugged her back tight.

She looked baffled again, slit-pupiled pink eyes staring at me, then looking around the room for escape or meaning, then they turned back to me. She also didn't resist.

Helpless and confused, she mumbled, "Look, the waterworks have stopped. Your work is done, right? It looked done. Let's go to bed. I'll harass you in the morning so you don't feel lonely, then I'll let you make those monsters, which I know you love done, and then we can go cause some chaos, which you know I'll love."

I loosened the hug enough to seek her hand with my own, and gave those warm, soft fingers a squeeze with my smaller but more calloused grip. She was right. I wasn't crying anymore. "Yeah, okay."

My head still hurt. I missed my parents like a hole in my chest. This big, strange house was weird and threatening. But I didn't feel alone.

ChapterEleven

A miserable night and a morning full of stress vanished as I crested the slight hill, and looked down at the pier and the sea beside it.

I stood there on that bump that marked the division between land and beach, and I took a deep breath. The air felt different, thicker, saltier, like it was scouring my lungs clean and pure. The sea breeze rolled over me, caressing the skin between my shirt and denim shorts, and cooling my body under the fabric. No, not a caress, just nature making me feel. I looked out over the water, which wasn't any less magical than before. It moved endlessly, a muddy dark blue, vast and peaceful, but not still. Still would be barren. The ocean was alive.

Thank goodness earthmovers didn't like water. I would sign up to be a mer-lich in an instant.

Even the weight of the eggs in my satchel was suddenly more comfortable and less scary. Also, I liked the satchel. I should carry one around everywhere. Maybe it could become my trademark.

The fishing fleet was all tied up at the dock, but people clambered all over them, working. That included banging, hammering sounds. Repairs? Renovations? I knew absolutely nothing about boats, but the horseshoe crab catch had to be rough for them, and they had to have made enough money off its blood for upgrades.

I pushed those questions aside. Leaning to the side and lifting my feet one by one, I slipped out of my shoes and socks. I walked up the uncomfortably hot sand until it turned into cool water. The water felt slick and sludgy at the edge, but then I was past the receding waves and it washed up around my ankles. I sloshed forward until the water was a little past my knees and stopped. I'd never expected how powerfully the current would pull at me, trying to push me backwards off my feet or drag me forward into the depths. Farther wouldn't be safe.

But the sound of the surf, that constant, sleepy roar, surged all around me. The current's pull felt like the ocean breathing. Seagulls squeaked overhead, and that endless, light breeze fluttered through my long, heavy hair, even flicking a few orange strands forward into my sight. Down at the pier, fishermen yelled, their words too distant and too muffled by the surf to mean anything to me.

The sea smelled. It smelled strange, like slimy dead plants and clean water, like salt and things I couldn't put a name to. It wasn't a good smell or a bad smell, but I loved it.

Reaching down, I ran my fingers through the water. It was murky with churned up sand, and I couldn't see even an inch under the surface.

Good.

Leaning forward like this, my satchel almost hung into the water itself. This was a perfect opportunity to slip out both eggs and drop them in. Which I did. They disappeared into the water with faint *blurp* sounds, sank until they bounced off my feet, and rolled away.

I probably shouldn't stay in this spot for too long, but I straightened up and closed my eyes, taking in the sounds and the feel, the experience, for a few more seconds.

Okay. Back to responsible mess fixing. I turned around and waded to shore, where Lisa waited with my shoes held up and a sneer on her lips.

Voice thick with disgust, she said, "Couldn't get me to set foot in that for all the chocolate in Anahuac. Are you ready to do this?"

I smiled. I felt quiet, calm, and devious. It was a fun sensation. "I've already started."

We wandered lazily down to the fishing boats. On the length of dock nearest to us, in a boat not too far out along it, Elvira and Emanuel were bent double laboring. Elvira saw me a mere second after I saw her, and she waved her arm and whistled.

Actually, scratch her seeing me after I saw her. She must have spotted me in the surf, because she cupped her hands around her mouth and shouted, "Someone's got the fisherwoman bug. Ditch that dusty old soul forge!"

I had no idea what it would be like to be out there totally surrounded by the sea, but…

"No, I like the job I have!" I shouted back, not just truthfully but honestly. If there was one thing better than the ocean, it was making life.

We got closer. Elvira stood up. She was wearing a shorter version of her sleeveless dress from the previous day, this one about knee-length, but in an ugly brown. Her brother was back to the barely fitting shorts. They both wore hats with wide brims. Both had rough sandals tied to their feet. The combination showed off how darkly tanned they were, and how crazy fit. Brother and sister might not be bulky, but they were lined with hard muscle.

Emanuel fished up tying a rope, then shuffled a couple of steps sideways. He picked up a paintbrush and a can of smelly, goopy black stuff, maybe tar. With those he painted a sentence on the inner surface of the boat in dots and dashes and little geometric symbols. Lisa and I had walked up the pier close enough to make those out by this point. When he finished, Elvira took his place, pressed her palm into the mess, and swiped her hand down the length. The symbols he'd written glowed gold through the now smeared gunk, which bubbled and dissolved with a hissing noise.

Something had changed in the planks. I was too inexpert to know what. They looked neater.

Seriously impressed, I turned wide eyes to Emanuel. "Did you design those spells yourself?"

He gave me an awkward, lopsided grin. When he didn't answer, Elvira playfully punched his muscle-padded shoulder and scolded him, "Stop pretending to be modest just because she's a bigger genius."

He punched her shoulder back, but launched into an eager, energetic explanation. "I'm learning spell compression and streamlining, but I've just started. The spell itself is mine. Don't be too impressed. The mana compression is nonexistent. It may be worse optimized than the spontaneous spell version. Fortunately, I have a powerhouse working next to me who doesn't care if the spell would shrivel regular people into a raisin. She would love a spell to shrivel regular people into raisins."

Elvira responded to his teasing grin by punching his shoulder again. Her own mouth pulled into a scowl, she hissed quietly, "Mama might hear you."

Anger washed over Emanuel's face, but not at Elvira. This was a distant, offended, resentful anger, and it felt freakishly out of place on his friendly face. It almost transformed him, drawing attention to the sharp nose and hard lined cheeks that were normally disguised by a smile.

Thankfully, that look of anger disappeared almost as fast as it had arisen.

My own voice just as low, I murmured, "I hope you can come up with one fast, because there are two monsters absorbing sea water and unfolding to full size right now. When you activate this they're going to home in on you." Out of the satchel I pulled a popsicle stick, and slipped it into Elvira's hand. I didn't know spell compression and was incompetent at spontaneous spell design period, but the paint on one side would give Elvira the same signature as my soul forge.

Elvira wasted no time, and immediately swiped her thumb over the flat stick. The spell glowed for a second as it activated, and when the glow faded she dropped the stick into the water.

I recoiled, then froze, locking my muscles and hoping no one watching had seen me jump. I hadn't expected her to do it instantly! The anxiety that had disappeared when I saw the ocean crept back up. The things I'd unleashed were now on their way, and I was right next to their target.

I wanted to run out to the safety of the sands right now, but that would be suspicious. The whole purpose of what I had done, what I was doing, was to turn suspicion away from me.

Emanuel and Elvira didn't seem the least bit bothered. As he painted the next section of planks, he asked me, "So, how is business?"

I tried desperately to push my jitteriness aside and focus on the conversation. "Beginning. I got a change request from someone who wants to go to witch school."

Emanuel turned his head to look at Elvira. "Peg?"

"Has to be Peg," she agreed.

Yes, the customer would be someone they knew from school, right? My ears straining to hear something that might interrupt the sound of the surf, I continued, "I told her to come back in a couple of weeks. I want to get used to this soul forge before I do human alterations, but I told her it would be free."

Em nodded, solemnly approving. "Your uncle did them for free."

"It's a family tradition," I explained. "Oh, and some rich lady wanted her daughter's pony turned pink. I felt a little weird about that, but it's not like the pony cares. Trivial. It was harder to get the pony to put its hoof on the altar than to cast the spell."

Next to me, but up on the dock where I'd stepped into the boat, Lisa grinned fangily. "But it's money, and money is honey." She licked her lips to make the point.

I jerked a thumb over my shoulder at my cousin. "Oh, yeah, and Lisa found a jar we missed in the kitchen because it was on the top shelf. So now she's had her first taste of honey."

Lisa tossed the coins we'd gotten from the pony job up in the air, and snatched them back out of it again. With vicious anticipation, she promised us, "But not my last."

I hadn't released the monsters far away. They must be fully revived by now. I shivered, and felt the sweat of nervousness on my brow, but managed to keep my voice steady at least as I asked, "How was school?"

Elvira had already activated the latest of Emanuel's spells that did whatever it did to the hull of the fishing boat. Now he bent lower, doing something even more mysterious with rope. It involved tying knots, and that was all I could identify. Strenuous knots, I guess, because he grunted a little as he said, "Elvira and Joe—you should meet Joe—"

Elvira gave him another punch to the bicep, and growled, "Mama will hear you. Knock it off."

The fishing boat lurched underneath us, tilting towards the ocean, then back towards the dock. I yelped, staggered, waving my arms, and almost fell backwards onto the dock.

"I didn't mean literally!" Elvira squealed.

The rocking settled into the boat leaning a little out towards the water, and the source of the weigh pulling on it became clear as a bone-white arm flailed up out of the surf, grabbing the edge of the fishing boat. A second arm lashed out beside it and grabbed. Then a third.

Those arms attached to the humanoid thing that pulled itself up to meet us. Its skin wasn't quite pure white, but had subtle, blue and yellow overtones that made it look diseased. Muscles bulged like beads along those arms, but strung out wrong, not like a human's. That third, extra arm sprouted from the middle of its back, and groped clumsily at us as it pulled itself up, and its mouth gnashed and bit.

Its mouth. Its face. Its lack of face. Wet black hair hung down from its scalp, but that was the only feature keeping the head from looking like a tube. It had neither eyes nor nose, just a huge, jawless, floppy mouth that took up the whole space where a face would be. Irregular teeth from the jaws of a hundred different species lined that maw, smacking together as its head waved blindly in our general direction and bit with squishy, sucking motions.

Ice spiked through every inch of my body, and I scrambled backwards with shaking limbs. I wanted away from that murderous nightmare.

And yet, as I retreated, I grinned like an idiot. The thing was terrifying. It was hideous. It was a work of deranged genius, and I was that genius. I had never been more proud in my life.

Also scared. I groped for Lisa's hand. Get me out of here!

Elvira didn't retreat, or waste an instant. She was up on her feet as soon as it rose over the rim of the boat. Grabbing a metal pail full of foul-smelling fish, she swung hard, slamming the thing in its soft head with that weighted metal.

Down several boats, people yelled, and another boat rocked. Something else pulled itself up onto the deck, or whatever fishing boats had. This thing didn't resemble the pallid humanoid monster at all. It looked like a giant worm, if worms were flat and made of ribbed, leathery rectangular segments. Bristles and groping claws protruded from the corner of every segment, and its head—yuck. A flattened bug head, eyeless, with huge serrated mandibles. Multiple sets of mandibles, and spear-like limbs that jutted out from between them.

This thing was doing a much better job of climbing up where it could get at actual people. It flung its coils up out of the water, and when they were in the boat lunged and snapped at the fisherpeople like a snake.

Elvira shot a quick glance over her shoulder the newcomer, and yelled, "Crap!"

But she didn't hesitate. She dumped the rotting fish from the bucket into the tubular mermonster's ugly mouth, an shoved the bucket onto and over the thing's head. With the biting mouth covered, she grabbed it by the shoulders, heaved, and shouted with acid satisfaction, "Bye, Felicia!"

At those words one of the innocent copper bracelets on her wrist lit up. She pulled the writhing creature right up out of the water, twisted her body, and flung it a dozen yards away, all the way up onto the beach.

Taking the thing out of the water revealed its lower body, a legless tubular mass like a whale's body, with black stripes mottling the grotesque off-white skin. Along that body, where a whale might have fins, it had more humanoid arms, these short and stubby. Two on each side, and one on top. The very end, instead of a flipper, ended in an oversized human foot.

It hit the sand, hard, not far from a stocky old woman in dark brown who didn't run, but did scoot nimbly out of the thing's reach.

With the help of Lisa's grabbing arms, I managed to climb back up onto the rough wooden boards of the dock. I couldn't have by myself. My heart pounded in my chest, and my own arms felt too weak.

The worm monster gave up biting at fisherpeople, and dove back into the water. A second later it burst back into the air in a different spot.

Right next to me.

Lisa and I scrambled away, and fear managed to spike even colder through me. The signature spell hadn't worked! No, it had, but this monster was still attracted to its creator more than to Elvira. Either it loved me and was going to betray that I'd made it, or it would try to kill me in the mindless hunger I'd built into it.

I didn't want to die, and screamed.

Elvira leaped between me and the worm. She'd found an oar, and slugged the worm in the head twice, babbling spell work.

I got my feet underneath me and ran back up the pier to the beach, and out onto the sand. The mermonster was up there, but it was built wrong to move around on land, and was too busy grabbing at the bucket and trying ineffectually to pull it off. It might have fingers, but I hadn't bothered to give them dexterity, or given it the knowledge to use them to do anything other than grab.

Like the worm, it didn't need eyes to know I was here. It turned towards me.

Now it was the old woman who stepped between me and the mermonster. She looked like a grandmother, with her grey hair and lined face and stocky body. Not so much fat as solid everywhere. The brown leather jacket and pants bulked like they were padded inside, which accentuated the solid appearance.

She wasn't all that tall, but she stood with the confidence of a colossus and the grimly protective zeal of a paladin, arms out to her sides and legs apart.

I looked back at the boats. Men and women were climbing around to join Elvira confronting the worm. She grabbed a harpoon out of someone's hands. Her long, straight, raven-black hair streamed out to the side as if the gentle sea breeze were a gale, and the short dress whipped around her slender, muscle-rounded legs. I had never seen spellcasting static before. It was just like Emanuel had described.

She stabbed the worm in the mouth with the harpoon. That didn't even slow it down as it surged up to try to bite her.

Stabbing light blinded me.

I blinked the blue flash away, listening to the sizzling and cracking noise coming from the action instead. Had I seen lightning hit the spear and flow down into the worm?

My vision, still rippling with blobby blue, crept back. The worm was gone. Elvira dropped the harpoon, turned, and sprinted up the dock and then up the beach towards me.

The mermonster had finally managed to clamp its hands over the pail and wriggle it nearly free. Elvira tackled it while its arms were free, slammed her fist into the bottom of the pail to force it back into place, and began to babble the clicks and beeps and abortive half-syllables of a spell. She squeezed the thing in a bear hug, with her fingers drumming on its pale stomach.

It thrashed violently, and the power of that elongated body threw her off onto the sand.

Elvira leaped immediately to her feet, but the old woman grabbed her shoulder and pulled her back out of the way. She had drawn a knife while I was distracted, a long knife with etched spell code covering the blade.

Eyes fixed on the flailing monster, the old woman lectured in a deep, imperious voice, "First, that spell won't work. Monsters don't have soul fragments."

A muffled boom thudded inside the mermonster. Its body spasmed once, harder than ever before, and collapsed limp. Over the next few seconds it dissolved into the air, leaving behind a pile of bloody gore on the sand. A much smaller pile of bloody gore than anyone would expect. About a bucket's worth.

Fisherfolk were rushing up off the pier, but the old woman held out a hand to them and shouted, "Stay BACK!"

She said it with such angry authority that they shuffled to a halt before they even reached the shore. Lisa stood at the front of that pack, right on the edge of the sand, but didn't approach further.

The stocky old woman turned her head to give me a searching, warning glare, but Elvira immediately blurted, "I trust her."

The old woman with the knife didn't argue. She stalked up to the chaotic depression in the sand where the monster had hit, lain, and thrashed. She bent over to stare down at the pile of gore with an angry scowl.

Timidly, Elvira tiptoed after her. I sat on the cold, wet sand where I'd fallen during my desperate escape.

Between the surf and the breeze, I barely heard the old woman's voice as she asked Elvira, "Do you know who I am, girl?"

Elvira shook her head, expression tight and scared like it hadn't been facing the monsters. "No."

In her deep, severe voice, the old woman explained, "I am a retired adventurer. The College asked me to look into monster rumors. You fed this thing dead fish so you could blow them up."

Elvira shook her head nervously, just little jerks side to side that made her black hair bob. "It just worked out that way. I was desperate."

A wave slid water up the beach far enough to just barely puddle around my butt, and then it slid away again.

The old woman answered Elvira irritably. No, more forcefully, authoritatively than that, but only a little angry. "No it didn't. Second, do not ever, ever cast that spell again where anyone can see you. I'm not the only person who might recognize it. You're smart enough to come up with a different plan. Third, that spell will get you killed. No matter how good you are, it almost never succeeds with living beings, and with dead ones you're more likely to blow your own hand off than hurt a monster." The anger solidified into stony harshness as she hissed, "Don't. Do it. Again. Do you understand me, girl?"

Elvira clasped her hands behind her back, wringing her fingers, and mumbled meekly, "Yes."

The lecturing old woman in the leather armor's face and

voice relaxed to mere elderly grouchiness, and her lecture softened the same way. "Last, you're as talented as you think you are, but you need training. Get your parents' permission, and I will find you a mentor."

Elvira scowled. More than a scowl, her whole face pinched up, and she answered bitterly, "That's not going to happen."

The old woman paused, studying Elvira's expression. Then she shrugged. "Not my place to get involved. The offer stands."

But she wasn't done. The elderly adventurer lowered her voice again, and I strained to make out the words that were spoken barely above a whisper. "Whatever, get yourself a combat spell stick. Learn to use that harpoon like it's a spear. People like us find monsters even when we're trying not to. Don't smile at me, girl, because that means family trouble is headed for you worse than any dragon."

Elvira, whose face had indeed lit up with hope, winced at that. Her smile still didn't entirely disappear. She stood quiet, respectful, waiting for if the old woman had anything else to say.

The adventuress pushed herself back up straight with a grunt of age, and growled, "Now, if you will excuse me, I need to talk to the sheriff about this. I don't like it. Those were not usual monsters. Did you notice how weird they are?"

Panic shot through me, and I exclaimed, "You think they were designed?"

Um. Okay, that sounded incredibly guilty, because I was incredibly guilty, so I added as a cover, "There's a dungeon master?"

That got me the old woman's attention. She took a few steps towards me, her heavy boots squelching in the wet sand. Elvira scurried after, explaining, "This is my friend Artifact. She's the town's new bioengineer."

The old adventuress stood over me with the scowl and searching eyes she seemed to reserve for anything, and answered us both. "I won't argue about her age. You just reminded me how fast kids can become mages. Maybe, Artifact. Maybe. They were sea dwelling, and there aren't a lot of underwater dungeons."

This was my topic. I picked up before she could continue,

"Plus, sea water will destroy a soul forge and erode its soul fragment."

The grey-haired, leather-covered woman nodded, and growled, "Old, wild soul forges do spit out oddities. Sometimes earthmovers leave a soul forge with strange patterns."

My mind was still racing. I continued for her again, "And the shock of sea water eroding a soul forge newly exposed to the ocean will badly warp any patterns."

She nodded again. Had I impressed her? Her scowl deepened. "That's the most likely explanation, and the one I'm most afraid of, because while the soul forge's fragment dissolves—"

That hadn't occurred to me. I grimaced. "Ooh. A leviathan."

One more nod, then she looked away from me, up at the seagull-strewn sky, and waved a hand. "On the other hand, there's that dragon. It was last seen over this beach yesterday, which is why I'm out here. I just don't know."

The conversation was over. She turned away from me and Elvira both, trudging up the sand. We stared. Behind Elvira, more and more seagulls landed next to the pile of exploded fish and squabbled over the bits.

As she stepped up onto the sea grass hump, the old woman added, "But I'm going to find out."

I did not want her to find out.

The adventuress stepped over that hump and out of sight. Elvira ran over to me, yanking me to my feet and hugging me to her tight. She squealed, "Did you hear that? A professional thinks I have what it takes! A professional accepted by the College!"

With the imposing old woman gone, the fishing families came stampeding up the beach. Elvira let me go, and stepped forward to be swallowed up by that cheering crowd. They clapped her on the back, and praised her in such a jabber I couldn't make out any words. Emanuel slipped into the press, and hugged Elvira like he was scared to let go.

Elvia and Emanuel's parents stood at the back of the crowd, watching with expressions I couldn't identify. Angry? Worried? Whatever it was, they weren't happy.

Lisa didn't care about any of that, and her little hooves

crunched on the sand as she stepped up to me and extended an arm to help me up. My own interest in the celebration was vanishing fast. I needed to figure out how to get Ruby to talk to me again. I needed to figure that out fast, because the old monster hunter did not strike me as a woman who took long to solve a mystery.

ChapterTwelve

"It's down this way!" Lisa urged me.

We had walked quite a way from the shore, inland along one of Goblita's biggest stress, then turned to a smaller but still impressively sizable street, then turned into a little bitty street with little houses amid a grove of tall, spiky-leaved palm trees. My expectations were steadily shrinking from this trip.

I also wished I could have brought Elvira and Emanuel, but they were getting way too much attention, and I wasn't sure the attention from their parents was happy.

Lisa turned down yet another side street that was more like a path between two houses. It descended quickly, becoming a man-sized ditch, which led to a tube. Seriously, a tube. A cement tube so big that a fully grown man could have walked through it. It ran right under the ground, the interior quickly turning dark as pitch, but with sunlight visible at the far end.

A puddle of water drizzled out of the bottom to run along the very bottom of the ditch, which was also lined with cement. It barely qualified as a puddle. More than a stain, but still only drops deep.

I trusted Lisa enough to follow her into this ominous tunnel without arguing, but not enough to do it in the dark. Flipping my tablet out of my pocket, I slid my thumb over the light spell, and hoped I wasn't giving it too much power.

The shine that came out of the little metal rectangle was bright enough to glare weirdly off the curved walls, shining brighter spots here and there, but it wasn't blinding. There wasn't anything to see. As far as we walked, the only litter in this tube was the pathetically minimal puddle running down the length.

We neared the other end, and the blank yellow sunlight of the exit resolved into something more complicated, an obstruction that still let in most of the light. Then we got closer still, and that obstruction proved to be a gate, with vines hanging over it on the outside.

The gate wasn't even locked. Lisa opened it, brushed the vines aside, and stepped out. I joined her, and we climbed up another brief, shallow ditch.

I tried to take everything in.

Like the College, this was a campus, if much smaller. Half a dozen buildings with their winding paths stood strewn over a big, big lot. Unlike the College which was open on all sides, a fence choked with vines ran all the way around this place, closing it off from the rest of Goblita. Also unlike the College, the buildings were distinctive. The College just went for big boxes. These were fancy, fanciful, bulging around rounded on the sides, with lots and lots of round towers sticking erratically up out of the pointed roofs. Not all of the towers were even straight. Plants crawled up the red brick, grey stone block, and even brown wooden plank walls. More plants filled the empty spaces, garden after garden, and a lot of trees, no two of them the same.

The Goblita School of Witchcraft.

The cement tube had come out inside the fence. Lisa jerked her thumb back at it, and then waved a finger around the fence. Dryly, she commented, "I don't know why they think all this would even slow down a school full of girls who want to go out and get into trouble."

That wasn't really an interesting detail to me. I looked at

the school itself, strange and official. I had to go deal with who knew what bureaucracy to try and convince someone I'd barely met to help me avoid "being arrested" type trouble. How was I supposed to do this without my parents. I wish I'd at least been able to bring Elvira and Emanuel.

Maybe I shivered. Maybe I looked worried. Lisa slipped her warm hand into mind and squeezed, leaning over to whisper, "You've got this. Do you know why?"

Fear and loneliness slid away, replaced by hot pride. I straightened up and declared, "I'm a prodigy."

Why say that? Because I'd earned it. I'd made two monsters this morning! Not just regular monsters, I'd made them amphibious and bound them into compressed eggs. Hardly any adult bioengineers could manage that. So if an adult could solve this, I could solve it.

It was still nice to have Lisa with me, to not be alone.

Which building to go to? A big, fancy gate marked a gap in the leaf-swathed fence down that way. The biggest paths, including a nice fountain in a stone nymph statue theme, ran up to the widest of the buildings. So, we would start there.

Nobody stopped us as Lisa and I ambled over the lawn, skirting around the gardens. I didn't even see anyone. This place wasn't crowded like the College.

We eventually reached the path. Not far from the main gate now, I saw it hung slightly ajar and unguarded. Good sign! Nobody would be freaked out that I was inside the fence.

I walked up to the big, arched wooden doors at the front of what I supposed was the main building, and knocked.

The door opened, held with a little effort by a girl in her mid-teens wearing a black dress. Her black hair had been partly tied up, but with lots of decorative stray curls. The glamorous effect was slightly dulled by big, circular-lensed glasses. She looked over at Lisa, then down at me, her face pinched in puzzlement.

Clasping my hands behind my back and trying to look as polite as respectable as possible, I asked, "Could I speak to Rhubella, please?"

The black-haired girl pushed the door open wider, her eyebrows pressing together and mouth opening in even more puzzlement. "Rhubella? You're looking for the Ice Princess?"

Behind her, I could now see three more girls. They all wore at least similar dresses, all black and with a rope belt, but the girl at the door, for example, wore her dress with the skirt hemmed above the knee, striped green and purple knee socks, and a lot of ruffles and folds in the skirt compared to the simple fit of the top. Behind the girls, I got peeks of a big, wood-paneled room that reminded me of Uncle Leonard's... of my living room, but with more potted plants.

The other girls crowded closer, regarding me and Lisa with similar astonishment. One said, "I didn't know the Ice Princess *had* friends."

A third girl, blonde with one icy white stripe in her hair, smirked and drawled, "Well, we finally know the Ice Princess's type. She likes little orange-haired gobbos."

The black-haired girl who had answered the door tensed, a scowl flashing over her face, swiveled and swatted the back of the blonde girl's head. Hard.

Stumbling forward a half-step, the blonde girl took a deep breath, and bowed her head to me sheepishly. "I apologize. I shouldn't take this out on you."

Still a touch puzzled, the black-haired girl gave me a friendly, even welcoming smile, and pointed out the door and off to the side. "If you must see Rhubella, she's probably in her room in the front corner tower. Good luck. I hope we see you again, sometime."

I bowed, replied, "Thank you!" and headed off.

The door stayed open for a while, and until they strayed out of my peripheral vision I saw the girls all watching me walk away. Never mind, they were watching Lisa walk away. I'd shown up at their front door with a demoness and pretended that was normal. That we got stares was no surprise. It took quite a while before I heard the big door thump shut.

The indicated building was the smallest on the lot, and a pincushion of seven towers sticking up at angles. The idea of living in any of those shocked me, but supposedly Rhubella did, and it at least "front corner" was easy to identify in the irregular mass.

Lisa and I walked across a lot of thick, ankle-high grass. Still we saw no one outside.

Up close, this building was surfaced in grey stone brick, with an unevenly colored brown tile roof. The whole building looked tilted, like it might fall over at any minute. Windows abundantly studded the surface, but all of them above my head height, and anyway, there was a door. The arched type resembled the one on the main building, but much smaller, fit for ordinary people.

Not sure what to do, I knocked.

"Pretty sure you just walk in," commented Lisa in a distracted tone. She was looking back the way we came rather than focusing on this building. Whatever was on her mind, she didn't volunteer.

My cousin might be supportive, but her respect for rules was just about zero, so I knocked again.

Absolutely nothing.

I pulled experimentally on the big brass handle. The door opened with only the slightest effort.

It was kind of a mess in here. Not the mess of filth or bad housekeeping. The big front room of this building was being used for storage. Barrels, pots, wardrobes, trunks, a few open so that I could see jars of leaves or piles of clothing lying inside to know the rest weren't empty. Back behind a pallet of crates I saw a door leading into another big room with a table and chairs that might be a dining room, but we wouldn't need to investigate that. The front room was also littered with stairs, spiral wooden cases winding around metal poles and winding up to a second story landing and then into the ceiling in odd places.

"Hello?" I shouted cautiously.

Lisa cupped her hands around her mouth and shouted, "HEY, ICE—"

I grabbed her mouth in both hands and pushed it shut. Lisa smirked at me. When I slowly, cautiously let go, she switched to grinning at me.

Which stairway went up to Rhubella's tower wasn't hard to figure out, so I dragged Lisa away from the box she was reaching into, and marched up the spiral that, sure enough, went through the ceiling into a big, slanted stone brick tube.

The funny unevenness of the staircase on the ground floor had just been cute. This was disorienting. It turned out, the tower wasn't even that tilted, and the steps were properly level, but the slight angle around me tugged at my eyes, made my stomach swim, and nagged me with a sense that I might pitch off the steps at any moment.

At least there would be something to grab. The tower continued the storage theme. Shelves, mostly with big drawers, lined the outer wall, a lot of them in arm's reach of the stairs. A lot of the ones that weren't could be reached by wooden boards that stuck off the staircase and looked terrifyingly dangerous. Many I couldn't see how they could be reached at all. Regardless, they looked stuffed.

The shelving left room for natural sunlight to illuminate the tower through several little windows.

"Rhubella?" I shouted when we were about halfway up.

Stupid mistake.

"RHUBELLA   RHUBELLA RHELLBELLRHULABELLBELLBELL," the echo pounded dizzyingly back around me. Literally dizzying, and I clung gratefully to the stair's railing, while Lisa took hold of one of my shoulders to keep me that much more safe until the sound faded.

Rubbing my ears, and then my burning thigh muscles, I finished this long, long climb, wondering if Rhubella could possibly be home and not have heard that, and whether her own legs must be made of steel to climb this stair at least once a day.

It all ended in a trapdoor in a wooden floor supported by a spiderweb of buttresses, or vaulting, or rafters, or whatever ceiling supports were called.

I tried one last knock, and listened.

Was that a squeak? It wasn't footsteps.

The trapdoor had a handle like a regular door. I tried it. Unlocked. Cautiously, I pushed the trapdoor open enough to peek in. It creaked loudly, but that was fine. I didn't want to be secret!

Sophie, sitting on Rhubella's slumped head, turned her own face to look at me and sighed, "Oh, thank goodness, it's the savior. I've rubbed my butt over every inch of her, and nothing is working!"

Pushing the trapdoor up farther, I stumbled into the room and tried to get a grasp on the situation as fast as possible.

First, despite all expectations, this room wasn't tilted at all. The final, and quite large top floor of the tower went straight up and down.

Second, it was a bedroom on one side and a workroom on the other side, with the workroom part much bigger than the bedroom.

Third, Rhubella sat in a chair just inside the workroom territory, slumped face-down over a long work table. Sophie, pink, furless, wrinkly, and kind of gross looking, sat on top of her head as stable as if it was a chair, peering down at her owner and poking Rhubella's head with a paw.

Chapter Thirteen

Tripping over my feet out of haste rather than any obstacle, I scrambled over to Rhubella, leaned forward and put my ear to her face while my fingers groped for her neck.

I felt a nice, even pulse under my fingers, and heard her slow, steady breathing. She was alive. Asleep, but alive.

My prodding didn't stir her even slightly. With my face so close to hers, I noticed the tear tracks staining her cheeks, subtle because she'd left off her makeup.

"Okay. She's alive," I reported to Lisa, while gasping to get my panicked breath back.

While I did, I tried to take in the rest of the room, at least a little better. The problem was, I didn't know what I was looking at, for most of it.

The table was impressive, and one of many. Rhubella had a crazy amount of potion-making equipment, way more than me. Bowls, pots, funny-shaped glass things, funny-shaped glass things connected by rubber tubes, plates, lenses, crystals, even the ones where I could identify what they were made of or some basic tool like a signature absorber, I still couldn't guess why they were there.

And boy, did Rhubella make use of it all. The work side of the room was littered with... stuff. Mostly plants, but in a variety of stages of disassembly and enchanting. Bowls of leaves next to wax-sealed jars of gooey stuff the same color as those leaves, next to what might be equipment to grind the former into the latter. Strips of colorful fabric laid out in size order on a bench. Tools sorted in racks. Glass bottles with goop in them bubbling gently over heating glyphs. A display of yellow stalks positioned in front of a window with a fancy lens pointed down at them. Tons and tons and tons of hourglasses in a variety of sizes, many of them in use next to something bubbling or crushed under a stone or sealed in a spell-inscribed box. The labels on the hourglasses glowed faintly, linked in serieseof descending size to each other, counting out some total deadline.

The walls were just as bad. Where there weren't shelves with pots of ingredients or books, she'd hung more components on the walls, in little racks or bundled around crystals or arranged in complex designs around each other. The only reason I couldn't say they took up all the space was because they were all kept carefully separated. Very carefully. Little pencil marks dotted the wall, and rulers the pencils themselves lay scattered across the desks, the only things left irregularly placed.

It all reminded me of the altar of a bioengineer working on a very dangerous transformation, all exact measurements and calculations, so that nothing whatsoever could go wrong.

The little living area, by contrast, was... okay, it was messy only in comparison to the workshop, but a couple of books did lie open on the perfunctorily made bed, and dresses on hooks lined the walls, and the makeup bottles and jars on the sink mostly stood open. If there was an actual bathroom I didn't see it and didn't want to know.

Back to Rhubella. Lisa was also bending over her now, and picked up a glass vial with a few drops of grey slime in it. The slime matched a pot sitting on an unlit warming sigil in front of her, at what looked like the end of an array of processing... stuff. I didn't know squat diddly about witchcraft.

What I did know was that when Lisa gave Ruby's shoulder a shake, Ruby didn't stir an inch.

"Rhubella? RHUBELLA! RUBY!" I shouted into her ear, giving her a shake of my own. Absolutely nothing.

Sophie, remaining perched atop Ruby's head, scowled at us both.

Yes. The familiar. We had a witness. "What happened?"

The cat crouched down and sniffed Ruby's burgundy hair, which had spilled almost completely out of its bindings and around the witch girl's shoulders. Poking Ruby's head again, Sophie answered, "She finished the advanced potion she's been working on, and drank a full dose. She'd been crying. She's been unhappy for a while now. She wouldn't talk to me. I even tried the beans, and that always works, but she didn't pay any attention this time."

Unhappy for a while now? But I'd just—oh, of course, Ruby might have had only a cat's intelligence before, but she kept all her memories from before being made a familiar.

I poked around a little more. Under Ruby's hand lay a pencil-written paper, line after line. The question-response style looked like a test, but I didn't understand any of it. The many, many red marks someone had made over the top of the writing with a colored pencil screamed bad news even to home schooled me.

My skin had felt prickly with nerves from before we'd even reached this room. Now cold jabbed out of my heart in spikes spreading to the rest of me, the cold of fear. I whispered to Lisa, "She overdosed. Maybe deliberately. I don't know anything about medicine. We have to find someone who does!"

"In a witch school, that won't be hard," Lisa reminded me, sniffing at the almost empty vial.

Right. Right. "Look after her, please," I told Sophie, and ran for the trapdoor.

"I'm trying! Don't you think I'm trying!?" complained the cat, her voice meow-y with no longer hidden anger and fear.

I didn't get to the trapdoor. The handle turned, the door pushed up, and a hat emerged.

I had never been so grateful to see a hat. This was the tall, pointy, wide-brimmed hat of a fully qualified witch. A second later, it turned out to be perched on the head of a grey-haired woman with a heavily lined face and a petulant, purse-lipped scowl. She wore little bitty round glasses, and a dress like the other witches, but instead of fine black and flattering cuts like the teenagers, she wore hers in frumpy straight lines and thick fabric so battered that both hat and dress had turned mere charcoal-grey. She had charms on her belt like Ruby had worn, which I hadn't seen on the other girls, but also a whole set of little leather potion cases.

Sourly, she looked me up and down and snapped, "Rhubella! What are you doing bringing unannounced visitors to your room at this hour!?"

Desperately, I babbled, "She didn't! I brought myself! I didn't know how to ask permission, and Ruby couldn't tell me because please, help us, I think she overdosed and she may die!"

Argument stopped. The old woman stormed up the last few steps and headed for Ruby, demanding, "What happened?"

"I found her asleep like this. She drank something and I can't wake her up!" I wailed, my cold worry meeting a pain of hope I was scared to let spread. Help was here, but what if it was too late?

"No vomiting," the old woman muttered irritably. "Was she shaking? Did you see any blood? Did you move her? Anything other than sleep?"

Sophie, who'd seen more than me, answered, "None of that. She drank a vial of that awful potion you ordered her to make, put her head down, and fell asleep."

"Off!" the old woman ordered the cat. When Sophie didn't immediately move, she held out both hands and pushed the cat off Ruby's head.

Sophie yowled and hissed in annoyance, but leaped off to the edge of the table before being physically shoved off instead. Back arched, tail raised, she lifted her chin and declared coldly, "Save Rhubella, Mistress Flora, and I will forgive—I will pretend that didn't happen."

Mistress Flora did some of the stuff I did. She checked pulse and listened to breathing. She opened one of Ruby's eyes and peered into it. She sniffed the pot, then snatched the vial out of Lisa's hand and sniffed that.

Finally, eyes closed tight, the old woman let out a sigh of

relief. Her lined face turned gentle and motherly as she crouched over Ruby's unconscious body, explaining, "Rhubella is in no danger. If she made this potion wrong, this might have been an overdose, but if it is prepared exactly right, no matter how much you take, you just sleep. You won't wake up until it wears off or is neutralized, but still, it's only sleep."

Fishing around in her belt, Mistress Flora the teaching witch pulled out a little tablet, broke it in half, and set it on the table in front of Ruby's nose.

The smell.

Even several feet away, I wheezed and took a step back. It was acrid, foul, like burning rubber. Mistress Flora's face grimaced in disgust, and she must have smelled this a hundred times. Sophie spasmed, made a number of hoarse horking noises, and leaped over to a windowsill to lean out and puke over the side of the tower.

Lisa just watched us all with a curious smile and her hands folded behind her horned head.

Face pinched, Flora hesitated a moment, pulled out a red pencil and a piece of paper, wrote "A" on the paper, and stuck it under the potion-filled pot. Then she took a big step back and let out her breath so she could inhale again.

Her expression changed several times. She grimaced, a disgusted old crone. She pinched up her eyebrows and frowned in soft concern. Her face relaxed into a different frown that made her look so very old and tired.

Putting her fingers to her forehead and rubbing from side to side, the old witch sighed, "If only she wasn't as bad at theory as she is at making the actual potions."

Silence happened. Sophie had stopped vomiting. Lisa just looked at me, letting me handle this. The witch teacher was lost in her own grim ponderings.

I wish I deserved Lisa's look of faithful expectation. What could I do about this tragedy? But I had to try something. If that test sheet had been any indication, I couldn't make things worse.

Lifting a hand, my voice a bit hoarse from hesitance and the really vile smell of the thing on the table, I said, "Mistress Flora,

I only know bioengineering, but… all those ingredients on the wall. Are those as well prepared as the potion?"

She gave me a new frown, not motherly, not angry. Enigmatic. It turned to the petulance of someone forcing herself to be polite as she turned to examine all the stuff on the wall.

That went on for a while. A couple of times she reached out to touch something with feathery delicacy, feeling its surface or turning it over, then setting it back exactly as she found it. Leaning forward, she sniffed what looked like a rack of drying leather, and measured the distance between a little metal badge and the bundle of flowers hanging beneath it. First she measured with her fingers, and then she used one of the rulers from the desk.

I didn't need an actual answer in words. Her thoughtful, analytical look was enough. I'd seen it plenty of times on Dad when he looked at my transformation designs. I continued, just as meekly, "In my field, you can't be that precise without an excellent understanding of the theory, not even if you have a great talent and manage to put all the symbols right by feel during transformations."

She looked at me as if she were seeing me for the first time, my obvious youth, my scruffy clothing, my satchel, my goggles, my lack of height and abundance of hair. The old witch looked more than a little disgusted as she tallied up the total, but her voice was merely guarded. "You're correct, but her tests say otherwise. When her answers aren't perfunctory, they ramble about trivialities."

"Then maybe the problem isn't what she knows, it's that she's bad at explaining it. Maybe she needs lessons about that," I suggested.

Lisa clopped her hoof on the wooden floor, and held up her own hand, palm out in warning. "Which we are not providing. She has a business to run, and that's enough responsibility at her age."

Frowning now in conventional puzzlement, Mistress Flora glanced at Lisa, again as if only now really looking at her, then back to me. "Who are you two, anyway?"

Nodding in a slight bow, because witches seemed to like

those, I answered cheerfully, "I'm Artifact Forge, Goblita's new bioengineer. I've taken over Uncle Leonard's soul forge. This is my cousin Lisa."

Behind the witch, Lisa reeled like I'd punched her in the face, and gave me a wide-eyed stare for about half a second before settling her features back in impatient disdain, complete with crossed arms.

Predictably, the witch teacher's grey eyebrows shot up and she asked, "At your age?"

My cheerful smile turned into a huge grin. "I'm a prodigy," I replied smugly, because hey—it was true!

Mistress Flora didn't argue. She studied me with the inscrutable frown for a few seconds. Then she turned it to Ruby for a few more seconds.

Who finally stirred, her hand fumbling, then sitting up and blinking owl-eyed. "Awake again," she muttered in bitter, groggy resignation. Then she noticed the little broken tablet, picking it up and turning it around curiously.

Sophie spun around on the windowsill and leaped over onto the table. The grotesque smell had faded a lot, but the cat still slapped the tablet out of Ruby's hand so hard it went flying out the window. Then she jumped into Ruby's lap and padded around in a circle, rumbling a loud purr and rubbing against her owner.

Mistress Flora stepped up to the table, and announced, "Miss Rhubella."

Ruby squeaked. She started to leap to her feet, then after rising a mere inch grabbed hold of Sophie and settled back into the chair. "Mistress—uh, Mistress—Mistress Flora, the potion works, please—what—" Surprised once, her head spun around, searching the room, and the sight of me and Lisa only seemed to increase her panic and confusion. The last thing she saw was the "A" under the pot, and she stared at it like an alien species.

For the first time, the old woman smiled. Like every change of expression, it transformed her, this time into the sweet grandmother you wished was yours. She gave Ruby's hair a tender stroke, and murmured, "Your assignment result was excellent. Dare I say it, perfect. Your friends have given me a chance to look around, and I've come to the conclusion that there is something wrong with your tests, not with your knowledge. We'll talk about how to fix that later. For now, you've overcome the challenge I gave you, and I'll leave you to your guests."

Scooping her arms under Sophie, Ruby stood up now hugging the cat to her chest, and gave a little bow. "Thank—thank you, Mistress Flora."

With the slightest of nods to me and Lisa, the old woman stomped down the stairs like they'd personally insulted her, and slammed the trap door shut behind her.

I turned an eager, happy, congratulatory smile to Ruby.

She stared back at me with the rigid frown of a glacier.

It was the last thing I expected. A purring Sophie still clasped in her arms, Ruby stood otherwise ramrod straight, so proud that her disheveled burgundy hair looked like the elegant disarray of an empress. This was the disapproving statue of a teenage girl who had first showed up at my office door. Bending forward with exact courtesy, she said, "Miss Forge. Once again, you have performed a great service for me."

I suddenly felt very, very awkward and unsure. It felt like the whole situation had reset into a new one. I took in the smell of the room, of old wood and the mingled hints of a thousand drying herbs and, even here fifty feet up and way inland, a hint of sea breeze through the open windows. The circular top floor of the tower surrounded me, with its grey stone walls, little bedroom area and its vast array of materials in different states of preparation. Faintly, the beams holding up the pointed roof over us creaked.

Trying to catch up, I bowed back and stammered, "Yes. Well. I was hoping to get your help for a very discreet job, Ruby—Rhubella. I can pay."

She nodded, in hard, practical approval. "Of course. You're a professional. As one professional to another, I cannot take your money—this time. I owe you heavy debts, and will repay them with my services. As for discretion, I have had to trust you with my secrets, so I will prove to you that you can trust me with yours. Whatever your project, I will make it a success."

"Oh," I said, feeling like the conversation had twisted

again. This result was good, right? Even if it was arriving from an entirely different direction than I expected. Ruby was so professional, and I was a professional too, so I settled into that mode, pretending I was an adult. "There is a dragon transformed from a pigeon loose in Goblita. It has been eating animals indiscriminately, but I believe is still somewhere between one hundred and one hundred fifty pounds. If it hasn't left yet, I need to catch it and transform it back into its original form, and do so secretly. I was hoping you could give me a lure and a tranquilizer. It looks like you have the latter on hand already."

Stiffly, only her mouth and the fingers scratching Sophie's chin moving, Rhubella corrected, "Not quite, but the alterations necessary to sedate a transformed bird can be made quickly. As for the lure, do you have an aspect chart or a signature sample?"

"Not on me. I didn't know what you would need. I can go home and get them," I answered, arms at my sides, hoping I didn't look as stupid as I felt.

"Send them to me. When I am finished, I will message you back, and you can tell me where and when you want to use them. I should be the one to do so," she instructed. Everyone was taller than me, but Ruby loomed when she stood like this, as hard and unbending as she was limp and affectionate when she fell on me yesterday.

"Sure. I can do that," I answered, not sure what else to say.

"Then I will see you then. Goodbye," Rhubella told me, pointedly.

Well. That was that. I walked back to the trapdoor, pulled it up, and descended back into the tower, with Lisa so close behind me that our shoulders touched.

The instant the trapdoor shut, Lisa hissed, "Shhh!" She put her finger to my lips, and tilted her head to listen. I did the same, because, well, what else could I do?

Very, very muffled, I heard Ruby babble, "Sophiesophiesophiesophie!" in a voice thick with emotion. What kind, I couldn't tell.

"Shut up and rub my belly," the just barely audible cat instructed her.

Smirking in satisfaction, Lisa slipped an arm around my

waist and nudged me back into descending the spiral staircase. My legs still twinged from climbing them, but at least going down would be easier than up.

My cousin added an encouraging squeeze to her grip, and flashed an even wider grin at me. "You did it, prodigy. Congratulations. Now let's go home and celebrate with the rest of the fish tacos."

I did it?

Well, I'd certainly convinced the authorities that there was a dungeon around. I'd obtained Rhubella's help, so that plan was progressing nicely. I'd gotten some paying, professional work done this morning, too!

Lisa was right! Today was a big success!

Wasn't it?

ChapterFourteen

I was new to Goblita, but I was pretty sure we weren't heading home. Lisa and I lived much closer to the sea.

My craning my head around figuring that out got Lisa's attention, and she explained, "When I realized where we were, I thought you'd like a quick detour."

We'd headed inland quite a ways to visit the witch school. Now we walked east along a road that almost defined the edge of the town. There were clumps of houses on both sides of it sometimes, but also long stretches where I could see flat land all the way out to the low hills in the north.

Lisa seemed to like sudden detours. I wasn't going to have much control over my life any time soon, was I?

No. I could handle this. I would handle this! I wasn't some regular kid!

A new building came into view ahead, and it had to be our destination because of all the people gathered in front of it. The building itself was big. Really big. Well, sort of. Instead of being solidly square, it rambled in a U shape away from the road, looping around a courtyard so big that it contained multiple trees whose branches sprawled like a spread-fingered hand, while still leaving more green sunny grass space than shade.

Well, green-brown. There were a few fully green spots in Goblita, especially near the shore. The witch's college had been downright lush. In others, the grass was clearly alive, but it sure looked dead or dying. That or grass gave way entirely to scrubby little bushes with the only bright green being the little kudzu beasts munching on those bushes. It was nice to not have to worry about stumbling into one of those by accident. They couldn't envelop any bush long, not with the massive, hump-backed bison wandering lazily about.

The wildlife was all in the distance, on that plain outside the town. Soon, the building would block that view, and the shouts pulled my attention away before that.

Because those people in front of the building were kids. They ranged in age from eight to eighteen, but no matter how you played with those numbers, this was more people my age than I'd ever seen before.

So the horseshoe shaped building must be the school the other teens kept mentioning. Wow. And this was at least two hours after classes ended!

Even in a city with its own soul forge, not a lot of teenagers had back-curved black horns, pink skin, and hair in multiple colors of fire. Even from a distance they recognized Lisa, and I heard her name called from a group of mostly girls perched on a big rock by the road. Angular and much more wide than tall, it reminded me of a table. They were certainly using it as one.

The girls waved at her with furious enthusiasm, and made beckoning motions. Lisa led me straight towards them. My heart thumped in my chest. In its way, this was as nervous and exciting as being attacked by monsters.

As soon as we got into range, a girl in an ankle-length dress and with golden hair tied back in dozens of braids leaned forward on the rock to call out, "Does this mean you're coming back to school? We were worried you might be leaving town."

"Or Earth," added a boy with a worried voice and worried eyes. Big, black, gleaming eyes, behind absolutely gigantic round glasses whose size, thickness, and heavy frames put the ones that witch girl had been wearing to shame.

Ginger fuzz surrounded those dark eyes. He was a cat. I saw a few more furries among the scattered children, but still no goblins. There was a girl with blue skin, huge animal ears, and a fuzzy-tipped tail across the street, but that was it.

A plump girl in a sweater and knee-length shorts propped her hands on the rock to give Lisa searching, sad, sympathetic stare. She wore glasses too, with dark lenses that hid her eyes entirely, and had astonishingly pale skin. Skin so pale that only her long, limp black hair assured me she wasn't albino. Her sad murmur resonated, like three identical voices speaking not quite at once. "I know you really liked Mr. Forge."

Still nervous and in awe at being around so many other kids my age, I looked back across the street again, to where the blue-skinned girl was playing with a ball at least a third her height. Not at her specifically, but the other kids, because there were still more in a playground, with swings, some metal frames that looked like gymnastics equipment, and a big stamped-flat dirt sports court. A circle of the youngest kids played jump-rope while the older ones played with that ball. On the far side of the court, a couple of children were riding around on a brown leather surfaced doll in the shape of a horse.

A playground doll? Any doll would have my professional interest, but such an unusual way to use one had my curiosity as well.

My attention snapped back to this side of the street as the blonde gave me an energetic, interested smile as she asked Lisa, "Who's your friend?"

Lisa shot me a questioning glance. I decided to announce myself. Touching my fingertips to my chest, I introduced grandly, "I'm her cousin Artifact. Call me Art," and was almost positive I didn't sound nervous.

My other hand felt Lisa's slip into it and give me a squeeze. A very tight squeeze. The rest of her expression looked completely relaxed and playful as she tilted her head to the side and prodded me coyly, "And...?"

A grin broke out on my face as the hot rush of pride replaced my anxiety. "And I might have inherited Uncle Leo's soul forge and I'm Goblita's new bioengineer."

Oh, the looks of astonishment. If I had a tail like Lisa's, it would be twitching right now.

The tip of the boy cat's tail wiggled like a flag in high wind as he asked breathlessly, "You can operate a soul forge?"

Another boy in a loose shirt had just drifted up to the group, raised his hand, and exclaimed in a squeaky voice, "Oh, yeah! My big sister Rita is a student witch. Some girl she calls Ice Princess got a familiar from a girl about our age. The whole witch school is in hysterics about it for some reason. It's all they've talked about for the last couple of days."

The pale girl with the sunglasses turned her face to me curiously. Louder than before, but still in a hush that echoed unnaturally, she asked, "Are you joining us at school, too?" The effect was extra jarring, because her tense, leaning posture, everything except those hidden eyes and quiet voice, radiated perky eagerness.

The blonde girl clapped her hands and grinned with the whitest teeth I'd ever seen. "That would be super cool! The genius and the demoness! Leaf will have a heart attack putting lessons together."

Realization hit me like a joyous hammer. Now I understood why my parents actually sent me to Goblita. My heart leaped in my chest at the idea of having so many friends.

The pale girl reached out and poked the blonde's knee, whispering, "We should introduce ourselves first."

The blonde in the long dress's eyebrows shot up in surprise. Her already pressed-together hands folded over each other and squeezed in a display of embarrassment. "Oh, right, our names! I'm Parsley."

"Yuki," whispered the pale girl. If her voice had a weird echoey effect normally, her name actually trailed out several seconds after she'd said it, repeated over and over by phantom voices. Neat!

"Everyone calls me Lucky," volunteered the cat boy.

Lisa, who presumably knew all these names already, was leaning this way and that, craning her head around to scan our surroundings. Finally she piped up. "I thought Joe would be here."

"He was," replied Yuki airily, which seemed to be her only option.

"Bonabelle walked past," Parsley explained, leaning on one hand on the rock she sat on.

Yuki and Bonabelle both sniggered.

The pale, rounded, black-haired, dark-glasses-wearing Yuki pointed at a small stack of papers and pencils and books next to the rock. "His homework is right there, so he'll be back. Eventually."

Lucky had been nibbling on a claw, frowning in thought, and suddenly stood up high on his tiptoes, asking me, "Hey, if you're good enough to run a soul forge already, you must have a lot of power, right?"

"Ooooooh," said Parsley, her smile and eyes alight with downright Lisa-ly levels of evil hope.

Yuki raised a warning finger. "Skill and power aren't the same thing."

"Okay, but come on, just try something for me, please?" begged Lucky, running around the rock to grab my hand in both of his. He dragged me with it across the street, and I dragged Lisa behind, since she was still holding my other hand.

We ended up on the sports rectangle, in front of a tall, older boy in shorts and a short-sleeves shirt that hung loose but barely reached his stomach at all. He had a lot of muscle, in the same lean way as Emanuel and Elvira. He gave Lisa a familiar and friendly smile, and then looked down at me with both curiosity and warm approval.

Of course, it was late afternoon, and everything was warm. Yuki had to be dying back there in her sweater.

The little (still taller than me) feline Lucky urged the bigger boy, "Hey, give Artifact the ball!"

"Sure," he agreed immediately. He radiated good cheer and easygoing casualness. The blue-skinned girl threw him her ball, he caught it, and he poured it into my arms.

It reminded me of a beach ball. Maybe not quite that big, and covered in brown leather. It was shockingly light for its size, bouncy, and obviously air-filled. I held it in both arms, my cheeks tightening and surely turning pink, and giggled awkwardly, "I have no idea what you want me to do."

The older boy was nice. His face didn't so much as hint at surprise or disdain. Stepping behind me, he reached around and laid his hands over mine. The sport area smelled like dust, but up close he covered that with the smell of clean sweat. Moving our hands up to hold the ball in my those instead of my arms, he raised it into a gentle lobbing position, and explained, "There's a spell-inscribed rubber interior. Just throw it at the board and put magic behind it."

So, I did that. The board in question was shaped kind of like a chevron pointing up, made of who knew what, and was fixed to the top of a metal pole well out of anyone's reach. Someone had painted a bullseye on it, and in front of that bullseye attached a vertical hoop big enough for the ball to fit in. I threw the ball up and forward towards that hoop, gently because my muscles themselves would never get it that far, and instead activated the spells inside the ball.

It launched out of my hands like a cannonball, and in that moment of panic it occurred to me that these might be the same spells that are used on cannonballs. Hurtling across the playing rectangle, the ball smashed into board off to one side. The hoop broke off, pinwheeling away, and the board spun twice around the pole before snapping off and spiraling into the grass outside the packed-dirt sport area.

"Sorry! Sorry!" I squealed. I should have known this would happen! I overpowered spells so easily!

Lucky stared at the devastation, his dark eyes behind his glasses somehow getting even bigger. "Ffffffff..." he hissed, and trailed off in wordless shock.

Parsley had wandered over to join us, which I found out when she declared in breathy awe, "She's stronger than Elvira. Nobody's stronger than Elvira!"

That didn't sound upset. I looked around. All of the nearby faces and most of the distant faces were turned either to me or the devastated sports target. Nobody looked unhappy, just impressed.

The tall, helpful jock, who I would guess was nearly

eighteen, snapped out of it first. He gave Parsley a look of desperate longing, and begged, "Please tell me she's going to our school." Looking down at me, he grabbed my hands again, this time from the front and to lift them cupped in his own as he continued, "You're a transfer student? Please?"

Still a little stunned, Parsley answered hesitantly, "She's with Lisa. She just moved to Goblita."

The older boy released my hands, clenching his into fists that trembled with eagerness. He raised his eyes to the heavens in rapturous anticipation. "We are going to wipe the floor with Depths Junior High. With Elvira and this girl? We'll stomp the College team. We'll be able to go down to Lady Angel to play in their championships."

His attention snapped suddenly back to me, and he reached up to clasp his hands in his short, brown hair. "How are you this strong?"

My whole body trembled. Not with fear. I'd never felt so popular, and it was amazing. I tried to shrug modestly, and knew I just looked and sounded smug. "I'm a prodigy."

Reality sliced the high painfully into ribbons, and I slumped and sighed. "But… I have a job. I don't have time to go to school."

Urgent and now a touch panicky, the tall boy argued, "Even Elvira and Emanuel's parents let them go to school."

Lucky bounced on his paw pads. "Yeah, but Artifact is the new bioengineer."

Oof. The new bioengineer, and I loved it. But this feeling of having so many friends was amazing. Why did I have to choose? I groped for the truth, speaking it aloud as I figured it out. "Right now there's a lot going on setting up." Like keeping me from being exiled from town for my ravenous dragon mistake. "Maybe I can figure out some kind of partial schedule when things smooth out."

Lisa took hold of my hand again, pink eyes looking into mine as she said, "I'll go back if you do."

There was emotion in that statement, and lots of it. I just didn't know what kind. This meant… something… to her.

Then her eyes flickered away, she let go, and raised her hand high instead to shout, "There's Joe. Hey, Joe!"

That was my out. Being popular was becoming too much, making me feel crushed. I lifted my hands, palms out, to the small crowd of admirers and declared, "As Goblita's new bioengineer, I am going to go do a bioengineering thing."

I left them, giving in to my curiosity instead and marching, no, scurrying over to the doll horse I'd seen earlier.

The two little kids who had been riding the horse were now brushing dust off its surface. The horse was more of a pony, sized so that if a tall adult rode it, their toes might touch the ground. Its body and the upper leg segments were still covered in old, old leather, which also lined the inside of the joints. Lower legs and the head itself had lost their cover, leaving just pale-grey ceramic and big black beads for eyes.

I crouched down to check the leg joints. Yes, the balls guiding movement were all covered in leather to prevent scraping, even where the leather outside had been lost. My fingers felt over the surface, both the hard brick and the soft as velvet ancient brown leather. The power flows down the legs would have to follow these lines. Aspects... it moved smoothly. More earth than strength aspects. Rows of smaller aspects rather than concentrations, I suspected.

What a beautiful creation. Not fancy, but flawlessly practical. And old. Shockingly old. Dolls were hardly ever old. This one might be... decades old? It had to be older than me. Amazing. A treasure.

Lisa showed up. Absorbed in my professional examination, I'd missed her hoofs approaching, but I saw her out of the corner of my eye standing near and watching me work with a proud smile.

The first of the two kids, young enough and baggy-dressed enough that I could not possibly identify their gender, bunched their fists and exclaimed eagerly, "His name is Herman!"

Folding my forearms over my knees, shorter than them crouched down like this, I asked, "Whose is he?"

"He belongs to the school," said the second kid, a bright red fox. They were both the same height, wore the same oversized shirts, had about the same barking, earnest voices, the only difference between the two was species. Well, apparent species.

Having a fuzzy animal face doesn't make you any less human inside, of course.

I tried again for the answer I actually wanted. "I mean, who powers him?"

The kids looked at each other. They both shrugged in unison. Kid One answered with obvious confusion, "Nobody? Herman is just Herman."

Joe had also arrived, standing right behind and looming over Lisa, and asked, "Does someone have to power him? Don't dolls just operate? They're fake animals."

I stood up, holding a silencing hand out to the others, and took Herman's bridle with the other. In a measured pace, I walked the pony doll around in a circle, watching how his legs moved. The age and fine craftsmanship of the original bioengineer were obvious in those smooth, natural steps. Herman had both time to learn and the ability to learn. Most dolls were physically more impressive, but their spellwork much more basic.

He also still showed no sign of a power source. He wasn't hooked to my soul forge. He'd have been deactivated when I did the safety check. There was no one visible who could be operating him.

I murmured my thoughts to him as I walked. "You can't be hooked up to a dungeon, can you? There can't be a secret soul forge just... hidden in a basement or something. There'd have been a degradation reaction by now, right? Surely... Uncle Leonard wouldn't have put a soul fragment in you."

No, even as slack about safety as he'd been while terminally ill... no. Giving a doll a soul fragment made it alive, and afflicted it with some of the fragment's donor's mind. The result was pure chaos. Herman was too passive for that.

I'd ruled out everything else. "That only leaves..."

Leaning down, I looked into Herman's black glass eye.

FORGET.

What had I been thinking about? Oh, right. I had to find an excuse to make a doll! No, just randomly making one would be irresponsible. Maybe I could start making up a plan, to be ready when I needed one. Multiple plans, for eventualities. Should I hook it to my soul forge? No, again, it would be irresponsible to do anything but power the doll personally. I didn't want to risk—

Leaning down, I looked into Herman's black glass eye.

THERE IS NOTHING TO SEE.

Well, so much for that. Someone had to have rigged Herman here with a soul fragment and he inherited a very gentle personality, maybe. The world was full of rarities like that, as unlikely as each one seemed by itself.

The only other explanation…

I beckoned Lisa over. Joe started to walk with her, but I held a hand out to him, then pointed at Lisa. Just her.

She wandered up to lay her hands on Herman's back and give he a curious but confused smile. "What? It's just Herman. He's the school's mascot. He pulls carts and lets little kids ride around on him and spends a lot of time standing in a closet because, you know, he's a doll."

"How does demonic possession work?" I asked her very quietly, so none of the other kids could hear.

Lisa reared back in shock, giving me a perplexed and mildly offended scowl. "How should I know?"

I did not dignify that with an answer, just stared.

My cousin relaxed slowly, laying her hands on Herman's back again, and gave her head a little shake. Softly, she answered, "No, seriously. Do you know how witchcraft works? I've only ever heard about possession." Looking down at the pony doll under her hands, her eyes widened. She was getting the picture, and her voice dropped further to a whisper. "You're not saying—"

I interrupted her to say quietly but firmly, "I'm saying that Herman has long since proven he's where he should be making people happy, and nothing else matters."

My cousin was a demon, and had proven to me that if they were all evil, it wasn't necessarily an evil anyone should ever worry about. If a demon was happy on Earth and everyone was happy around them, I wasn't going to interfere. Lifting Lisa's hands off the doll's back, I slapped Herman's butt and pushed him back towards Kid One and Kid Two.

Then, with Lisa's hands still held in one of mine, I gave her a grateful smile. "You were right. I liked this detour. But I'm getting really hungry."

"Joe can cook," Lisa assured me immediately, then nudged her head in the waiting wolf boy's direction. "We need to tell him what's up anyway."

Yeah, he'd stolen the key for Lisa. He was involved enough already that he deserved to know the rest.

I looked around at the scruffy playground, at the courtyard with its huge, spreading trees, at the horseshoe shaped school, and most of all at the children and teenagers. The children and teenagers who'd liked me. Some had even admired me. All had been friendly. The school area had a sandy smell, and its mix of desert dryness with grass and trees and civilization felt comfortable.

Wistful, I said, "When we get the dragon dealt with..."

I trailed off. I didn't want to finish that sentence. I didn't want to set myself up for disappointment when I couldn't have everything.

Lisa slipped her arm around my waist, and jerked me shoulder to shoulder against me. Grinning her just a little fangy grin, she said, "Hey. Demon wisdom for you, cousin. Worry about that later. When choosing time comes, it will be between happy and happiest. The big question we have to answer right now is—"

I felt an intense, tugging sensation of kinship with Lisa as I finished her sentence, "What we want Joe to cook for us."

ChapterFifteen

"Artifact! Food is ready!"

I did a few more scribbles. Oh, wait, I should answer. I shouted back, "One second, almost done!"

I was! Just a connection line here and here. Upgrade the junction symbol to reflect that. Now all I needed...

Lisa showed up in the office doorway, a pink silhouette against the currently dark workroom and living room behind her. Her glowing pink eyes glared down at me with imperious reproval. When I kept drawing, she stalked up like a jaguaress, tail lashing where it emerged under her dress, and she grabbed my left arm in both hands.

"Wait wait wait, just one more!" I squealed.

As my cousin began pulling me away, I stretched out my write arm to finish up the glyph that had to touch all four links and, "Okay, I'm done!"

Tossing the pen down, I snatched up the aspect chart. As Lisa hauled me by the arm to the kitchen, I rolled the chart up one-handed against my leg.

The lights might be off on the way, but the house I'd inherited's magical lamps bathed the kitchen in a glow as cheerful as noonday sun, but not as hot. Joe, with a too-small apron over his outfit of "a pair of shorts," was cutting a beef roast into slices using a jagged knife that was probably specialized for exactly this. The kitchen had come replete with tableware and pots and pans, just no food. A fact that Lisa and I had corrected, and now were reaping the rewards of.

The wooden chair with its thin, red-and-white striped cushion was strangely more comfortable than the huge, plush monster behind Uncle Leonard's desk, probably because I was going to need something to prop the office hair higher. Leonard has been a tall man, and his desk was awkwardly high. Not unusable, just awkward. Still, it was the most convenient flat space for writing on in the house.

The food smelled good. It smelled mind-meltingly good. The beef was covered in a purple-tinged sauce that must have come from the pot on the stove, and it smelled so rich and savory I could die. Underneath that exquisite aroma I could still make out the darker, earthier smell of brown-edged roast vegetables heaped around the beef, with their oniony tang.

I had no idea I'd gotten so hungry. Joe leaned forward and pushed a plate heaped with food across the table to me, and I had to repress an urge to giggle. He was too big for the apron, and all that fur and muscle looked like it was going to snap the fabric right off.

Stabbing a bit of beef that pulled apart at the slightest pressure into a perfect bite-sized chunk, I quickly speared a broccoli poof to go with it, stuffed them in my mouth, and oh, it tasted even better than it smelled!

After a ravenous swallow, I asked, my voice a bit hushed from awe, "Where did you learn to cook?"

Joe took his own place neatly right across the table from me. To my right, Lisa gobbled down food with the enthusiasm of a hungry opossum. More patiently, Joe answered me, "Practice. Cooking for myself," as he cut a forkful of meat that would never have fit in my mouth at all, then eating it only when he'd finished speaking.

He'd given me time for another bite, this time focusing on a chunk of onion-spiced potato, and now I was free to say, "Well, thank you for cooking for us."

Joe flashed me a friendly grin, which was a lot of grin thanks to that elongated canine muzzle. His teeth were sharper, not the same shape as mine, but I couldn't call them fangs. What they definitely were was bright white. He took care of them. "Thank you for the free food!"

"You sure made a lot of it." Really, he had. We were eating a few slices of a whole roast, and the vegetables absolutely heaped around it. Giving Lisa a suspicious look, I asked my demon cousin, "Leftovers?"

She licked gravy off her lips, and flashed her own almost-fangs, gleefully unembarrassed. "Do you want to eat our cooking?"

Joe burst out in a laugh, and I at least giggled a little, because Lisa had a point. The big furry boy diverted the mood from teasing by nodding at the rolled up paper beside me and asking, "What's that?"

I put down my fork and licked my lips, which would have driven my dad crazy but right now this was my house and I could be as uncivilized as I wanted. Giving the paper a wistful look, I explained, "A message I need to get to Ruby at the witches' academy. I'm not sure how. If I sent a pigeon the dragon might eat it. The dragon *was* my pigeon. It's still got my letter to my parents!"

Which, come to think of it, I really really really really really needed to reclaim before anybody else took down the dragon and saw it!

With less personal investment, Joe stuck to the topic, giving me a little nod. "That's right. You're from…"

I filled in the gap. "Lake Touhou."

"That's beautiful country," he said with the unfocused look in his pale blue eyes of someone looking at pleasant memories rather than what's in front of him.

Me, my eyebrows shot up in surprise. "You've been there?"

Returning to the present, he leaned back in his chair, which he slightly overfilled the way I slightly underfilled mine. Folding his thick grey arms behind his animal-ish head, he said lightly, "I've traveled on the caravans a lot. I stay in a town and try to get as much education as I can, then get moving to the next one before… legal problems happen."

Suddenly frozen with awkwardness, I said, "Oh."

Joe, on the other hand, was completely relaxed about the whole "thief" thing, although he grew steadily more passionate, more eager as he explained, "The whole idea is to leave that behind me. Learn enough math, polish my writing skills, and go somewhere where I'm just a poor, hardworking, down-on-my-luck boy who can do the bookkeeping for a business so the owner can focus on business. One of the caravan company headquarters would be perfect. They have a lot to keep track of, and a lot of calculations to make. At that point I just have to work hard, be reliable and smart and helpful, and I can have a steady, reliable, legal career. Once I have it... maybe I'll see a new goal to aim for."

I was boggled. Absolutely boggled. The big furry boy leaning forward in his chair, hands on the table and eyes alight as he regaled me with his dream was a side of the oversized, easygoing teenage thief my demon sister had gotten me mixed up in. It had been easy to forget the criminal part knowing him casually, and now as I started to get to know him better that seemed like an even less important part of his identity.

My eyes bugging out and mouth open did not escape my cousin, who chirped smugly, "Joe is a lot more than meets the eye, isn't he? Of course, what meets the eye is muscle."

Grinning slyly, Joe lifted his brawny arms and flexed. I smacked my hands over my eyes, because I just... I could not face it. My guts squirmed with mortification that was made even worse by Lisa's gleefully mischievous laughter.

Joe, thankfully, was a lot more sensitive and as I stared into my palms he said, "Change of topic. If you're from Touhou, what route did you take to Goblita? Did you pass through the redwood forest?"

Cautiously lowering my hands, I found Joe sitting up straight with all the dignity possible in that ill-fitting apron. Able to handle that, I answered, "Oh! Just barely. They're huge, aren't they?"

Huge was the only word I had, but it was pathetically inadequate to describe those... the trees were huge, okay?

Joe clearly needed no clarification on that, and leaned a little forward again, asking excitedly, "Did you see any of the forest people? Or the forest god?"

I shook my head thoughtfully. "No, we were only under those trees for a few hours, but while we were…"

I struggled for words, a way to describe the experience that would mean something. Joe and Lisa both watched me with breathless anticipation, waiting for the prodigy's word. I settled for, "I'm not very magically sensitive at all, but… if you asked me where the forest god was, I could have turned and pointed." Seizing on something more concrete to say, I added, "Have you seen him?"

Joe leaned back, arms behind his head again, eyes going distant, and nodded. "Yeah. Once."

Ooooh. Now this was going to be way better than my confusing non-story. It was my turn to lean forward eagerly. "What was it like?"

Still distant, quiet, and thoughtful, he said, "He just looked like a big deer, with big, complicated antlers that had vines growing on them. Not that impressive in my memory, but when he appeared between the trees, all we could do was stop and stare. Except one person. One of the caravan drivers got down off the wagon and followed him into the forest. They went around a tree and were… gone. We all snapped out of it, and when we checked, they'd left no footprints."

I let out a low, awed whistle. "Can you imagine the soul fragment a being like that must carry?"

Lisa burst into laughter so convulsive she immediately fell out of her chair. Shaky and with an unnecessary amount of drama she crawled back into it, still wheezing.

When she got back high enough, Joe reached over and nudged my cousin's shoulder with a scolding finger. His eyes still on me, he told me firmly, "I for one admire how professional you are. You know what you like, and you think about it all the time. As a reward, and as a thank you for dinner, I'll take your letter to the academy when I leave."

Her smile still crooked and spasmodic, her voice a touch husky, and eyebrows raised in sardonic surprise, Lisa asked, "They don't throw you out when they see you?"

The big wolf boy shrugged, back to his casual good cheer. "I'm not popular there, but they're not suspicious of me, either. They know I'm not going to steal any expensive potion components. It would be suicide. Witches are people a thief sells to, not steals from."

Ignoring that part of the conversation, I laid my hand on my so-important aspect chart and said sincerely, "Thank you, Joe. I really do appreciate it."

Warm and pleased, he responded, "And I appreciate how you talk to me like a regular person. To stop you from feeling too awkward about me saying that, I'll change the topic again. How was the trip itself?"

"Boring," I answered immediately and with disgust.

That got a merry chuckle. "You do seem like someone who needs to be constantly mentally active."

With a sharp nod and a roll of my eyes, I confirmed, "I spent most of it looking at the caravan drivers' maps, rereading my bioengineering notes, and drawing out elaborate plans for monsters and battle dolls and refined versions of regular transformations."

Joe stared at me for a few seconds, a touch of curiosity, surprise, and amusement infecting his smile. Finally, he asked, "Okay, but what are your hobbies?"

I had been using the break to shovel down more of the now much cooler but still delicious, tender beef in sauce, and had to finish chewing and swallowing a potato before I could respond. I did so even more baffled than him. "My hobbies?"

He pressed further. "What did you do for fun back at Lake Touhou? That didn't have to do with bioengineering?"

I considered that, as an excuse to dip a chunk of crisp broccoli in sharp-smelling sauce and crunch it down. Starting to feel properly fed, I said, "Oh. I guess I went for walks a lot? I know I just implied that I don't care about scenery, but it's different around Touhou. Lots of magically touched animals, and our neighbors' farms, and little bitty dungeons everywhere."

I had Lisa's attention again. Eyes wide, she watched me, even more rapt than Joe.

And Joe sounded pretty interested, if surprised. "That sounds dangerous."

I shrugged. "Not really. They're all small, like a temple and a couple of basement floors. All the traps and loot were cleared out long ago, but they're covered in strange decorations. It's always fun to try to figure out what they mean, if they're from the golden age, or some foreign culture, or a completely made up kingdom and the history I'm trying to analyze exists only in the imagination of the earthmover that built it. There's only one soul forge around the lake no one has located, and the monsters it spits out are harmless. Like, cute little lizard guys that steal firewood to eat and play with our neighbors' dogs."

Joe sat up sharper in his chair. He was so grey, and Lisa was so pink and red, they stood out like the only objects in the relentless brown of the wood-walled kitchen. The frilly baby blue apron just made him fill the foreground more. Delighted, he enthused, "Well, if you like poking at ruins, you're in luck. Yuki, Elvira and Emanuel have a school-sanctioned club that goes out into the abandoned city and pokes around the dungeons. There are dozens, maybe hundreds. Mostly emptied out, but every once in a while someone finds a new one."

Lisa slumped back in her chair, folding her arms across her front and sneering. "Elvira and Emanuel's parents told them to stop, but they still do it anyway."

I nodded, my turn to be distracted by memory. "That was part of why I liked it. I didn't go alone. Ramona would watch out for me."

Joe started to relax, his slight, white-toothed grin turning approving. If he ever stopped grinning, the world would probably end. "I wondered. I hope you don't mind my saying, but you're pretty young still, and you'd have been younger. It would be brave parents that let you explore even empty dungeons alone!"

Pfft. Me, young? Look, Joe was big and I didn't actually know how old he was, but no way was he even eighteen. But I stuck to the topic. "No, I was safe with Ramona. She had a major talent for destructive magic, and spontaneous spells, too. She could cast a shockwave to knock a bear on its butt in half a second. She could fry it or blow it up if she wanted, but I never thought she would, until…"

As the weight of grief fell over me like a blanket, Lisa and Joe noticed. They couldn't help but notice. Suddenly they were both serious, Lisa's face uncharacteristically focused in concern. Joe asked softly for both of them, "Is something wrong?"

We were deep in a topic I had successfully been trying not to remember. Seeing the colored flashes through the window, and then the final boom. Ramona's smile like nothing was wrong in the world the day before. She'd only been the older girl who looked after me sometimes, but still… "It was a month ago, almost exactly. Ramona and Fiona from the opposite side of the lake got in a fight. A magic fight. They both… they both died. Left a smoking crater behind, even. I thought they were best friends."

"So Lake Touhou's reputation is real," Joe said grimly. Reaching his long arm across the table, he caught one of my hands and gave it a comforting squeeze.

I clawed my way out of those memories. I had a new life to lead, and this was a conversation about me. Grabbing Joe's tangent, I assured him, "If my talent had been for spontaneous magic, anything other than bioengineering, I'm sure my parents would have moved away from Touhou long ago. They announced I was coming here to meet Uncle Leonard the day after. I know they wanted to distract me from what happened." I tried a smile, and weak as it was, I managed it. "It worked pretty well."

This still wasn't nearly as far a change of subject as I wanted, so I asked, "What is your hobby, Joe?"

Squeezing my hand just a little tighter, Joe put that big grin back on, looked me straight in the eyes, and said, "I'm doing it right now."

SMACK. Lisa slapped her hand over her face, not fully concealing a scowl of disgust.

Joe, of course, responded with casual good cheer and kept answering. "I like making new friends. Meeting people. There's nothing more fascinating than people. There's nothing better in life than being around happy people. I spend all the time I can spare from studying and trying to survive enjoying other people."

Letting go of my hand, Joe leaned back in his chair and took another huge bite of his own meal.

Lisa was having none of it. Behind her hand, sounding to me more embarrassed than actually disgusted, she growled, "You mortals are so smarmy it's insufferable."

Folding my own arms and smirking, I demanded, "Fine, what's your hobby?"

Lisa stopped covering her face. Snatching up her fork she pointed it first at me, then whipped it around to point at Joe. Back and forth, like a knife held to ward out danger, she aimed it at us as she barked, "I don't need hobbies. I don't need ambitions. That's the point. That stuff is for short-lived humans who die if they don't eat. My plan for my life? Find a mortal to mooch off of. String that out as long as possible, then find another. When I finally get banished back to Hell, trick my way out of that pit of whiny misery as fast as possible, then start the process over."

My folded arms and smirk did not stir.

The fork pointed solidly at me, Lisa snapped, "Don't give me that look. You know what I'm going to do if the college decides to take me away from artifact?"

She dropped the fork. Her hands flew to her head, fingers dipping into her multicolored hair, flailing around to turn it into a disheveled mass. Then she grabbed her purple dress at the neckline, digging in her sharp fingernails and yanking. The seams split all the way down over one shoulder.

Looking like a beaten mess now, she shrank back in her chair, shoulders hunched, face-down and to the side but eyes up. Lisa's hands trembled as she raised them with her palms out, like she was begging. Her expression twisted with fear, her voice squeaky and desperate, she pleaded, "Please, Sir. Wait. You don't have to send me back yet. If I'm living with you, if you're watching me all the time, I can't do any harm, can I?"

Again, I boggled. All I could do was stare.

Lisa rose back up like a snake to her defiant, back arched, sneering demon poise. "Freaks like him are obsessed with being in control. He'll fall for it, and my mom taught me all the tricks. Two weeks, tops, he'll be putty in my hands, I'll be the one actually in charge, and he won't even know, but…"

Her arm had been sneaking out towards me under the table as she spoke. She grabbed hold of my hand, and squeezed so tight it hurt. Her slitted eyes glared at Joe like he was the one who wanted to banish her, and she told him loudly and defiantly, "I'm staying with Artifact as long as possible. Artifact gives me respect. I don't get a lot of that."

Joe's canine face grinned bigger than ever before. Lisa pointed a sharp-nailed finger at him and snarled, "Don't. Don't even start. Ugh, this is the most obnoxiously human conversation. I'm going to take a bath, and then nap. You two do your stupid human things."

Standing up with so much force she shoved back her chair until it fell over, releasing my hand before it could ever be visible to Joe that she'd been holding on, my pink and red and black-horned cousin stomped across the kitchen to the hallway and its stairs. Her little black hooves rapped loudly on the wooden floor.

Joe gave her a little wave. "Have fun. I'll deliver Artifact's message, and see if I can negotiate cleaning up into a couch to sleep on until school tomorrow."

Lisa just growled, stomped her way down to the stairs, then stomped her way up them.

I watched all of this wide-eyed until she rose out of sight, and then… burst out laughing. I met Joe's grin with my own. Lisa had the strangest way of making me feel better, and if making friends was Joe's hobby, he was good at it.

Chapter Sixteen

Joe was gone, as promised, before I got up the next morning. I determined this for sure by stumbling downstairs and looking in the kitchen and living room before I went back up to get clean for the day.

Lisa snored. She snored like a stampede of dinosaurs. I could hear her from downstairs as I made myself breakfast, cooking cheese between a couple of slices of bread using my tablet's heat spell. Who needed stoves? Not this prodigy! I hardly burned it at all, even.

It felt surprisingly alive and in good spirits. Yesterday had been absolute chaos, but the lesson it had left me with was that friendship was great. Surprising. It came out of nowhere and kept coming out of nowhere. But great. I kind of envied Joe going to school where all the other kids were waiting, even if he had to get up early to do it.

My philosophical mood lasted past my gooey cheese sandwich, right up until someone knocked on the business door.

A burning eagerness replaced it. Time to create life again!

I hurried through my workshop and office to open the

door. Above me, blocking out the morning sunlight, stood the lanky and slightly bowlegged silhouette of the sheriff, with his thumbs in his belt.

Not exactly the person I'd been hoping would knock. I was covering up an awful lot right now. Anxiety started gnawing away at my joy.

Nodding his head and touching the brim of his hat, the supremely grizzled old man greeted, "Morning, little miss. Hope you're having a good one."

Okay, he sounded friendly, if a touch worried. That was good for me? Maybe I shouldn't be scared? Clinging to my cheer, I greeted, "So far. How can I help you, Sheriff?"

He nodded again. "Official town business. I told you about the slimes, I believe?"

My glee lit up in my chest again. Eager for this topic, I echoed, "Oh, yes! Killed by an adventurer?"

The sheriff scowled. At least, I think he scowled. His huge mustache drowned his frowning mouth, and the dark, leathery wrinkles around his eyes made it hard to be sure when his gaze hardened. He definitely sounded sour, and gave one foot a quick stomp. "Drat idiot. Dumbest thing I ever heard, killing them for their fragments. Lost two-thirds of the fragments at that, and it's not like a real dungeon slime would have them anyhow."

That tickled a thought for me, and I gave in to my love of showing off my expertise. Chest puffed out, I corrected, "Not... necessarily true, Sheriff."

The pause was to not seem too egotistical, you know.

"Call me Greenlake," he husked. His voice was so gravelly.

"Call me Art," I returned automatically, then focused on the important topic. "The thing is, as monsters age, and especially as they eat, their vitality tension drops and they become less dependent on their soul forge. It never gets anywhere near zero, but if they become close enough to real, and their model is good enough, they can breed. Their children will have soul fragments and not be tied to the dungeon any more. So I guess I'm asking..."

I paused for a second, to let him catch up, and finished, "... are the slimes you got from Uncle Leonard able to reproduce?"

Grey eyebrows that would have been impressively bushy if they didn't have that mustache to compete with raised. Sheriff Westlake's thumbs shifted in his belt. "Why, no, missy. They're not. Are you saying you can make ones that can? The town scraped together the funds to buy two from you to take at least a bit of pressure off in the plant, but we're going to need at least eight more we can't afford yet. It would be a mighty big help if they could make themselves."

Pondering the reproductive rate of the standard orange detritivore slime, I speculated, "Well, if I make adults, they'll be able to start as soon as they reach engorgement. A lot will depend on population pressure. Slimes only reproduce when they detect there is more food than slimes to eat it."

Sheriff Westlake let out a dry chuckle. "They'll be feeling the romance for a while then, miss. Can't believe old Leonard Forge didn't offer us this option."

Stung by the need to defend my uncle, I assured the sheriff, "He probably didn't know how. I'm sure Uncle Leonard was a fine mage, but no two bioengineers have the same list of recipes and techniques to work from. I have his files, plus a lot of recent research with me, and this, um... it's not exactly a basic technique."

Holding up my hands quickly, I added, "I'll only charge you as if they were basic slimes. Civic duty and all."

Doubt niggled me. I couldn't believe I was offering to do something that might make the sheriff get his forensic tools back faster, tools that he would use to find out I was guilty, but... well, who wanted to make the cheap version when I could make the cool, advanced version?

Hands still up, I reminded myself and informed the sheriff, "But, um, professional responsibility time. There are two problems with this plan, Mr. Greenlake."

He nodded, very solemn. Probably very solemn. His expressions were naturally hard to make out, and he was standing with his face in deep shadow. That did let the golden sunlight into the room around him, along with the fresh outside air.

Resolute, he said, "Life doesn't hand away freebees, even if people sometimes do."

I switched to holding up one finger. "The first one is my problem. I'm going to have to see the treatment plant and take a lot of measurements, including some inside. Slimes have to adapt to their magical environment to be fully adult, so if we want them reproducing any time soon, I have to work out exactly the conditions at the site."

He shrugged naturally slumped shoulders. "Your nose's funeral, Artifact. I'll be there suffering with you while we do. We can go immediately if you want."

I nodded slowly. "Better to get it over with. The other problem is that the new generation of slimes will all be wild. That's not a big deal with a slime, but they won't automatically see humans as friends and you'll need to start taking safety measures."

The old man rubbed his stubbly chin, making a noise like sandpaper. "Wild, eh? So that there dragon that's been troubling us—it could be wild as well?"

I blinked at that question. There was no way the one I'd made could reproduce, but I absolutely and definitely preferred the direction the sheriff was thinking. I answered as contemplatively as I could fake, "Possible. There's a colony of wild dragons that size of at Lake Touhou. They stick close to their nesting site, but there's no reason you couldn't get wanderers looking for new territory."

The sheriff was still looking thoughtful, still scratching that chin could be used to light matches. Oh please, let me have diverted all his suspicions about that dragon!

Aloud, I said, "Let me get my tools, and we can get going."

Chapter Seventeen

Sheriff Westlake had a horse, which was almost as brown as my house on top, and almost as grey as the sheriff's mustache underneath. We rode it out to the plant, which was near the coast out west at the edge of the city.

I knew when we were getting close. An earthy, compost smell crept in, despite the sea breeze and the weird, hot smell of a horse.

The sea breeze still dominated. We had ridden up the ancient One-And-One road, and off to our left stretched the exquisite blue flatness of the ocean. Looking at it filled me with peace, blotting away my troubles, and even when I looked away I felt buoyed, like I could do this. Keep the law's attention turned away until I removed the dragon myself, and there was nothing for anyone to find out. Just one of those weird wandering monster episodes.

Big, round, very low buildings reared up as we passed a low hill. They didn't rear up much. They looked like the tops of downright enormous buildings mostly buried underground. At the end of the pair of lurking cement circles reared a bulbous-topped water tower.

The tower looked old, for no reason I could put my finger on. The blue paint was fine. Nothing was visibly broken or insecure. I couldn't make out any hint of rust. Just, the tower and its pipes gave me the feeling they'd been there for a long, long, long time.

The horse trotted to a halt next to one of the round buildings. I slid down to my feet, and wobbled. My hips ached. I definitely preferred a cart. The sun was nice, though, covering me in bands of warmth from my legs to the bare stretch of my stomach and then above my shirt. It was moving a bit past "nice" towards "intrusive," and maybe I should have worn a hat like the sheriff, but we weren't there yet.

But, no time for that. To business! I pulled out of my satchel what I should probably have been carrying around since I got to town: the ID pendant from my soul forge. Sliding it into the round casing of the detector, I dug out a compass with my other hand, and spent a moment being amused at how similar they looked. The former could be mistaken for a much bigger version of the latter, just with prettier colors.

Walking around the circle, working the knots out of my muscles from horse riding, I took measurements at the north, south, east, and westmost points of the building. Each time I compared the glittering colors on the detector to the pendant's glow. I wrote the results down, finished my circling back to the sheriff, and planted my geoenchantment and geovitality stakes to let them calibrate.

The human rawhide old man pointed down the coast. "That tank over thereabouts is the incoming waste tank, and this here is the processing tank where the slimes live. We give them time to convert it all to fresh water before it moves on to the rinser."

"A cube jelly, I assume," I said as I calculated some aspects by distance and the color differences I'd written down. Trigonometry was not my strong suit, although I knew I'd get used to it eventually.

The sheriff smirked. Probably. Again, that mustache. "I take it this isn't your first sewage plant."

Still distracted, I said, "It is, I just know my monsters. You'll have to ask your engineers if it's the right idea, but you may want to put the first two breeding slimes in the incoming tank, where they'll have the most to eat and will reproduce fastest. That would take some of the pressure off the purifying process."

He slid his thumbs back into his belt, considering that. Those stiff, leathery lines on his face were good for hard, serious old man thinking. He gruffed, "The College built it, near three centuries ago, and does the maintenance. I'll ask them."

I was feeling so much better. I'd slept deeply last night, but the real reason for this sudden good mood was off to the left. I took one last look down the scratchy grass hill, past the slope of white and then brown sand, to the constantly rippling edge of the surf, and out along the ocean's perfect blue. In the distance, I could still make out subtly moving shadows. The sea was never still. I took a deep, deep breath of the cool breeze blowing off that infinite expanse of water.

Theeeeen I turned around, faced the pungent cement disk, and admitted what had to come next. "I'm going to need to take a look inside the processing tank."

Sheriff Westlake nodded. He rummaged around in his saddle bag, and pulled out two long, rough strips of fabric. Holding one out to me, he muttered, "Figured. Wrap this over your nose and mouth as many times as you can, and wash in the ocean as soon as the cover's back on, even if you don't touch anything."

Well, that warning confirmed all my fears. I shuddered in anticipation, but wrapped the scarf over my face tight, just like the sheriff showed me. Then I trudged away from the sea to the short iron ladder that led up maybe twice my height to the top of the rough grey cement circle.

When I pulled myself up that final step, the building looked even bigger than when I'd circled it down below. It was like a huge cement can, stuck into the ground so far only the top was barely visible. The top was flat and completely featureless, except for one dot exactly in the middle.

The sheriff climbed up to join me, and led me to that dot, which turned out to be a metal hatch more than a yard across set into the surface of the processing tank. It was the kind with a metal wheel on it, which the old man turned with obvious effort and obvious strength. I tensed.

He pulled the hatch up and open.

The stench was awful. Filthy. Foul. So nasty.

I didn't have a choice. I needed these last two readings, and I'd volunteered to take them rather than doing the sane thing of making a generic slime that would need to adapt before it could start reproducing. I'd set myself up for this.

Trying to the pendant to a cord I had looped up in my satchel, I leaned over the hatch and—

—nearly puked my guts out.

FOUL. SO FOUL.

Screwing up my face, I forced my spasming stomach still. I could see nothing but blackness in that hole, which thankfully gave me an excuse to take two long steps back and ask, "Are there lights in there?"

My voice was so muffled by the fabric I could barely understand me. The smell was this bad *with* all that wrapping.

Equally muffled, and with a naturally hoarse voice, the sheriff said what I was pretty sure was, "Yes, Miss. I'll get the activator panel."

I snapped my fingers. The lights went on inside the tank. Steeling myself for the stink, I leaned back over again and looked inside.

This time I could see the ladder, which no slime could hope to climb, going all the way down. The tank was deep, but not nearly as deep as I thought. The blue walls looked shockingly clean, and at the bottom four orange blobs bounced around in brown mud.

Best to think of it as mud.

The smell was so, so, so bad.

I could do this. I had to. Keep under control, stomach. Try not to breathe, nose.

"Looks like we're lucky. They're most of the way through eating this load," grumbled the sheriff over my shoulder.

Focusing on breathing as little as possible and only through my mouth, I lowered the ID pendant down over the edge, reeling it down towards the bottom of the tank on its line. The sheriff, slightly farther away and with enough self-control to spare to think about safety, grabbed me by the back of my belt to hold me secure.

I just needed to get the pendant all the way to the bottom. That was all.

It was taking a grotesquely long time to do. Bathed in that stench, I could have counted every heartbeat.

As the pendant approached, the slimes clustered towards the center of the tank, hopping higher, trying to reach it. Yes, they were made by Uncle Leonard, all right. They remembered the signature of his soul forge.

I let one of them grab the pendant as the cleanest way to get to the bottom, and nearly got yanked off my feet as it fell back to the floor of the tank. I didn't know if I'd have been able to keep my feet without his help, but for a flash-frozen instant I was very, very grateful the sheriff had thought to brace me.

Reeling out the last few feet of the line, I felt it finally go slack. Yanking a pen out of my bag, I marked the line and started pulling it back. The measurement wouldn't be exact. Fine. If it took an extra day for my new slimes to get used to their home, nobody would care. What was important was that I backed up as fast as I could, tugging at the weight of the fat, mature slime holding onto the pendant.

That weight let go and I staggered back into the sheriff's arms exactly at exactly the same time as I heard the dragon shriek.

Oh. Right. Carrying the pendant, I must stand out like a beacon to the dragon, the same way the slimes felt it, and the same way the monsters at the beach had been drawn to me.

Feeling like an idiot warred with the strangling grip of panic. I wasn't ready!

But… the sheriff didn't know what this meant, right? He wouldn't understand the connotations of anything I did.

Running back towards the edge of the tank's cement surface, I pulled up the cord holding the pendant as fast as I could, until the pendant itself dragged back into my grip. Thanks to the slime, it was perfectly clean. It just smelled awful. Everything smelled awful.

The dragon circled the hatch, craning its neck to peer down into the hole. Was it still wearing the collar with the message? I couldn't see it. The dragon looked bigger. Maybe the collar had snapped off, or been clawed off. If I could catch the dragon now, this would be over, right?

Behind me, one arm loosely around me, the sheriff gruffed, "I think it wants to eat the slimes. Figure we can seal it in?"

Not a bad idea. When the dragon choked to death on the smell, the slimes would eats its corpse and leave no evidence to get back to me. I hated to kill what had once been a harmless, idiot pigeon, but these were extreme circumstances.

Getting some rationality back, thoughts whirring, I whispered to Sheriff Westlake, "Dragons are too smart. It won't take the bait without help."

Without bothering to unhook the cord still scattered across the cement, I took hold of the pendant in both hands. Gem side out. Fingers touching the jewel on either side, but with my hands and arms not touching each other anywhere. The current had to run through me. As far as the dragon was concerned, right now I was the soul forge that had made it.

"Sit!" I yelled.

The dragon screeched, head snapping back.

"Land! Sit!" I ordered at the top of my lungs, louder because all the movement caused the scarf to fall away from my face.

The dragon let out its distorted, warbly, predatory bird scream again. Its head and wings flailed, fighting for control of its own body. Flapping furiously, it reared up, and instead of landing it shot up into the air and leveled off to look at me.

Then it opened its mouth and breathed fire at me.

No, not quite. Steam. That approaching mass of white was fresh, concentrated steam. It would still boil me alive.

The sheriff, less a mage and more a man of action who actually had some common sense, yanked me off my feet and out of the way. My view spun for a second and I wasn't sure which way I was pointing or what was going on, but I wasn't dead, and that knowledge hit like a spike of relief.

I squealed in shock, "It shouldn't be able to do that!"

The old man, as strong and tough as his leathery appearance

suggested, set me down on my feet and grabbed for a pouch on his belt, growling, "Way I hear it, breathing fire is a dragon thing."

Shaking my head furiously, I squeaked, "Made by a skilled dungeon master, or after generations in a magically charged location! Not just some random dragon!"

The dragon flew around in a wide circle, like a vulture, watching us. The sheriff turned to face it at every moment, always between me and it.

It did that thing where it reared back, inhaling so it could breathe steam again. Sheriff Westlake yanked a pistol out of his belt and fired.

Pop! The gun going off sounded exactly like a cork pulled out of a bottle, but much louder. I couldn't even see the bullet, only a couple of feathers get knocked off the dragon's hip.

It screeched, puffing out its neck muscles as it swerved to the side, then dodged the other way, and turned in the air to speed off in the direction of the sea.

I stared at the pistol, impressed. Very impressed. Bullets were incredibly expensive. It was hard engraving the same spells that powered the ball from the school playground on a tiny metal ball. You also needed serious raw magical power to activate those spells. The sheriff was no slouch.

Pistols themselves weren't exactly easy to make, although I didn't know the details. Weren't they mostly found in dungeons?

A sound I'd been hearing suddenly made sense. Galloping hooves. I looked, and saw the old woman adventuress galloping up the road towards us on a big, solid donkey, grey as the sheriff's mustache on top, brown as my house underneath.

She leaped off it before it finished slowing, skidding to a halt with her feet spread. Her hand moved in a jerking motion.

A fist-sized rock from beside the road catapulted into the air, sailing after the dragon. She launched another, and another. They flew shockingly far, shockingly fast, but the dragon was now over the ocean and out of reach. It rapidly became a speck, lost among the agitated seagulls.

I was impressed all over again. The old woman hadn't needed a staff, hadn't even needed an incantation. She knew that spell so well she could cast it with a literal wave of her hand, and cast it hard.

She didn't just stand around staring at the now-disappeared dragon. She stalked over to the ladder, and climbed up as nimbly as a child to join me and the sheriff on the roof of the cement processing tank. If she even noticed the smell still emanating from the open hatch, she didn't show it. She just growled to the sheriff, "Missed. Didn't have a chance at this range, but I had to try."

Was the sheriff shaking? He stood straight, eerily still in every other way, as he formally tugged his leather hat forward. "Sorry, Ma'am. I should have held my fire and let you deal with it. You wouldn't have missed the shot."

Her wooly white hair bounced under her even bigger leather hat as she gave her head a single, savage shake. "You dd the right thing and you know it, Greenlake. It's not your fault I couldn't get here in time. The College won't let me ride Sabertooth in town. I didn't come an inch from getting my throat ripped out taking him away from a lich to ride around town on a donkey, but they act like he's going to eat little kids on the street. Speaking of which, we need to get that one out of here."

The old adventuress and the old sheriff stared at each other, like they were communicating something I couldn't hear, or just waiting for the other to attack. Without looking at me, the sheriff ordered in a low, gruff voice, "Artifact, go wash up. I'll close the hatch and join you."

No. Not yet. Resisting the urge to grab the old woman's armor with hands that were probably unclean, I stepped up to her and blurted, "Did you see it use its breath weapon?"

"Yes," she answered.

Just one word, but with a flicker of her expression, confusion and worry. She understood just as well as I did, so there was nothing more to say. I obeyed the sheriff, heading for the ladder and down to the shore for a much-needed rinse and prayer that salt water would remove the stink.

But my thoughts were whirling the whole time. I did *not* give the dragon a breath weapon! No matter how overdesigned,

I hadn't done that! Yes, it had fire aspects, but they would need to grow enormously, and where did it get the water aspects? There was no room in the design for that kind of power!

Stepping into the surf, I bent forward to dip my hands and the pendant into the cold water, then splash my face, as the first step in decontamination.

And, um. Actually, I had given the dragon that elaborate containment, hadn't I? The really fancy one I'd learned from my father, which was designed to stretch, unlike normal containments? Okay, yes, but this was still nuts!

I absolutely had to get rid of that dragon soon!

ChapterEighteen

Sophie was standing by my door when the sheriff and his uncomfortable horse brought me home, and she was just about the most welcome sight there could ever be, especially with the folded paper in her mouth. Folded into an elaborate, spiky shape, but still obviously a letter.

The furless pink cat spat the paper onto the ground, revealing the letter had been folded into a vaguely birdlike shape. Soft of swan-ish. Hoisting her head high, the familiar complained, "Apparently I'm a messenger now. No one else can be trusted with letters to you, because you're *important*." Her contemptuous disbelief dripped from that word, then returned to mere indignation. "Just put a little cap on me and give me a bicycle to ride, I suppose. I keep telling myself that I'm going to refuse one of these demeaning demands and that will be it, but Ruby gives me that look, and who can resist that adorable face?"

The cat sighed. I bent down and picked up the paper, unfolding it several times until I could read it. That felt incredibly awkward with the sheriff only a few feet away, but he made no move at all to get an angle where he could read too.

Yes, this was a letter. The top line had three words scratched out so thoroughly I couldn't even guess what they had been before the actual contents started.

XXX XXX XXX To Artifact Forge

I did it. The potions are done already. You gave me the aspects and they were perfect like I knew they would be and I had most of the ingredients already prepared although I don't have time to prepare the neutralizer so the invigorated apocynum will make me a bit wired. Please think nothing of it as I know you are a professional and understand the hazards a professional faces and also that sometimes we have to accept mild side effects when time is short. The potions are ready did I write that already I should read back to the start but it feels so good to finally be writing to you lil bits lil bits lil bits lil bits lil bits lil bits lil bits lil bits sorry i just love that name it suits you so well i know it must seem undignified but you are as cute as you are a wonderful heroic super genius oops wait gotta

Please Please Please Please Please Call me Ruby Lil Bits

Staring up at me sourly, which might be the only expression her wrinkly cat face could manage, Sophie said, "She measures five times to make sure everything is exactly right when she gets like this. I suppose that's admirable."

The much appreciated point being that Ruby herself might have been high as a kite, but her work would be flawless.

I unlocked my business door and strolled inside, crumpling up the letter to stick in the pocket of my shorts. The sheriff followed me in, politely several steps back and not intruding as I held a conversation with a talking furless cat.

So, I conversed with the talking furless cat. "Well, um, if you'll wait in the kitchen, you can have some fish while I get this customer sorted out, and then I'll write you a letter to take back." Raising my voice, I called out, "Um, Lisa! Are you up?"

She shouted back from the direction of the kitchen, "Yes, but I'm not dressed!"

Of course not. At least she'd warned me this time.

I shouted, "I'm sure the cat doesn't care. Feed her anything she wants!"

Licking a paw, Sophie conceded, "I do smell some intriguing possibilities. Don't think this means you can pet me, but I'm willing to take your message back."

Bustling into the workshop, I set down my satchel, pulled out the ID pendant, and returned it to its slot under the soul forge to absorb. I found two large metal pails to put the new slimes in, got the notes I'd taken out of my satchel, and from the pile on the workbench pulled out my dad's notes about adding a wild framework to monster-based life, allowing them to reproduce.

Suspicion about my involvement might be going down, but yeah, that dragon had to go. Now. What if it attacked me at home?

No, I wouldn't think about that. I would let Ruby's professionalism be my guide. I would triple check everything on these slime designs, and focus on nothing else. They would be exact and perfect, because I couldn't afford to fail.

Worse, I couldn't afford to do too good a job again!

ChapterNineteen

The hardest part was waiting after the sheriff left for him to get safely out of sight.

He walked out the door in a stilted, bow legged march, because he held a rust-speckled bucket out on each side. Big buckets, theoretically filled with water, but actually filled with orange, pulsating slimes big enough to bulge over the top.

Sophie scurried out through the open doorway barely a step behind him.

Shocked, I called out to her, "Wait! Could you carry a message back to Ruby, please?"

The hairless cat stopped mid-trot, looked back over her pink shoulder, and answered, "No."

"It's urgent! Please!" I begged

"Did you change your name to Rhubella in the last ten minutes?" the cat replied sarcastically.

Out of the corner of my eye, I saw the pink shape of Lisa step into the doorway between the workshop and office, her arm raised as she shouted, "I did!"

"Still don't care," announced the familiar airily, and resumed trotting away with that deceptively fast kitty gait. She was around a corner and out of sight in seconds.

Giving up on that, I tried corralling the other troublemaker. "Lisa, put some clothes on. The door is open!"

Laying her hand on the door frame, tossing her hair to bring her curvy black horns into relief, the demoness grinned defiance. "You're the one holding it open."

I pushed the door shut as fast as I could, spun around to lean my back against the lacquered brown wood, and pointed back at the house. Giving my modesty-free cousin a ferocious glare, I told her, "Get dressed. I'm going to go get the potions from Ruby. We're catching the dragon today. As close to Now as possible."

That at least dragged Lisa out of the hip-tilted, taunting pose. Straightening up and all business, she lifted a black-clawed finger. "I'll go to Ruby. I'm faster. You go get Elvira and Emanuel. School is over, so I bet they're heading for the docks right now."

Why would I go get—I didn't finish the question, even in my head. It was obvious. I needed all the help I could get, and they were already in on the lie. Elvira would probably be offended if I left her out.

I nodded. My heart thumped in my chest, excitement and nervousness suddenly back and thrilling through me, but it wasn't time to act yet. Grave and measured, I told Lisa, "First we have to wait to make sure the sheriff doesn't see us."

Tense and uncomfortable enough that I wanted to scream, I returned to the workshop and used the time to get prepared. First, I turned off the soul forge, pulling the discreet lever at the front end that closed up the inner shell around the forge's huge soul fragment, and sent the rest of the cage rattling part by part into a more compact cube. I wiped down the altar, lined up my tools on the closest work bench, and copied the outer set of symbols for the procedure onto the altar. That was the set that needed careful measurement with my tape ruler. The now-shiny grey stone surface, with its built in channel grooves and the copper dots where the wires poked up through the underside, looked elegant and waiting with its web of fresh black ink symbols.

That was enough time. I shouted, "Lisa?"

"I'm gone!" she shouted back, flying down the stairs three at a time. She'd put on one of her short dresses, and the skirt flapped around her legs. The deep neckline in back billowed too, showing off more and less of the elaborate circular tattoo on her right shoulder.

In less time than it took to notice that, she reached the front door, yanked it open, and charged out. Through the workshop window I saw her running up the street. The hooves. It had to be those little black hooves. Lisa could run. She zoomed up the pavement in a series of sharp clicks, as fast as a horse but much better at dodging around carts and pedestrians. In a couple of seconds she also turned a corner and disappeared, but she'd been nearly out of sight anyway.

Still, it was a much longer trip to the witches' academy than the docks. Pulling my sweat-curled hair back behind my shoulders and grabbing my bright red satchel, I stepped out into the sunshine myself and headed for the beach.

I had time to merely walk briskly, and let the sun and blue sky try to soothe my nervousness. When I reached the College I started to smell a hint of the sea, which calmed me a bit more. When I passed the campus and could hear the susurration of the waves, I spotted a familiar and unexpected figure standing between the ponds on this side of that hump that separated grass from beach sand.

Even with the sun behind him, those shoulders and all that muscle were unmistakable. Surprised, I called out, "Joe? What are you doing here?"

He turned and gave me that friendly grin I already had memorized. At least he'd added a loose shirt to the shorts this time, and looked less like a fuzzy grey wall. As I closed the distance, he didn't need to shout and answered me normally, "Lingering after escorting Elvira and Emanuel back from school. They've been scheming about combat spells, and it's fun to listen. Are you here to see them?"

Joe already knew, so I didn't bother making up a lie. I jerked a thumb behind me and explained, "I'm getting rid of the dragon, and I thought they might like to help. I just have to ask them without their parents finding out, right?"

I'd heard some pretty strong hints that Elvira and Emanuel's parents were not enthused about their daughter's adventure lust.

He nodded, putting his huge hands on his hips. "Leave that to me. I'm a master at misdirection and finding ways to insert myself into other people's plans."

For the first time in what felt like hours, I grinned. Like my demon cousin Joe had no shame, and he was very welcome. "You're a prince, Joe."

"Yes, but there's no money in it," he answered with a grimace so wry that I half wondered if he really was some kind of dispossessed prince.

Grateful for another task off my shoulders, I said, "I'll wait for you at my house. I need to do more getting ready."

In fact, I had just unlocked my door and was opening it when Joe, Elvira, and Emanuel scurried up. The siblings had both changed into those tight brown outfits they wore to help their parents with fishing. Perfect clothing for unexpected chaos. I wasn't expecting chaos. The plan was smooth and comprehensive. Except I hadn't expected my dragon to have a breath weapon, either.

I stepped inside and let them in, noticing as I did that Elvira and Emanuel took quick, worried glances over their shoulders and back towards the sea before stepping inside. Guilt poked through the curtain of stress around my heart, and I said, "I hope I'm not getting you into trouble."

Elvira planted her feet apart, drawing up to her full height, towering over me with a proudly raised chin. "You're not. I'm getting us in trouble."

Laying a hand to the center of his chest and with a wounded, open-mouthed stare, Joe protested, "Excuse me, I'm getting you into trouble."

Emanuel, hands in pockets his shorts barely had room for, noted, "At least with me along our parents won't think it's a date."

The three all burst out laughing, so I gave up and decided not to worry about it.

The seriousness of my plans came crashing down on my thoughts instead. I told them quickly, "I'm waiting on Lisa to bring back some potions. I'll do the rest of my prep work. Maybe Joe can check if we have any ice cream left." I hesitated half a second. "Um, that's a big 'if' in a house with Lisa in it, but you're welcome if there is any."

Leaning forward with a bright-eyed and admiring smile, Emanuel said, "I'd be fascinated to watch you work."

Elvira nodded rapidly, echoing her brother with her rapid, buzzy voice. "Yeah, they don't teach us anything about biotech in school except some monster definitions, the importance of soul fragments, the most absolute basic stuff."

Joe didn't say anything. He didn't have to, he was pointing that stare of approving fascination at me again.

My cheeks tightened with embarrassment at all this attention, but... I also loved showing off!

Hurrying back into the workshop, I pushed the power lever for the soul forge back on. The inner shell around the soul fragment cracked open, and the machine shuddered as it began its boot sequence.

"I'm starting it fresh so there will be no contamination from previous rituals," I explained to my rapt audience.

Scouring the workshop's shelves, I grabbed the rest of the tools I might need and set them out. Then I finished writing the transformation pattern on the altar, then went back and engraved the areas that needed deeper channels with my stylus. I set out all my necessary element samples in their slots, including the elemental ice and elemental fire I never imagined I'd need until the dragon breathed steam at me.

I had just finished that when a firm, polite knock sounded on the business door. It was immediately followed by a sharp banging and my cousin yelling, "I forgot my key!"

I went and opened the business door. Sophie scooted in when the gap was mere inches wide, before I had the chance to open it up and see Ruby and Lisa standing outside.

I blinked in surprise, reflexively pulling my hair back where it had fallen over my shoulders again. "Ruby! I wasn't expecting you. You didn't have to come. You're welcome to, but, I mean, um… are you in any condition?"

Because she looked awful. Her clothing was just as shiny as perfect as ever, and she'd added a crude wooden broom thicker than my arm that she leaned on like a staff, its bristles pointed up in the air. One of those tall, pointy witch hats perched on her head, covering most of her burgundy hair, and the hat was shinier than most with a stiffer brim.

It was Ruby herself who looked bad. Her eyes were sunken, bloodshot and surrounded by dark and hollow lids. She looked like she'd lost ten pounds in twenty-four hours, her cheeks less full, her nose pointier, and her whole face and stance rigid like someone forcing themselves to be awake. Those red-tinged eyes sparkled with manic, furious determination to not give in, not collapse.

Her tone just as stiff and severe, she informed me, "I promised you my best, and you are getting my best. Would you ship someone a dangerous creature without a discussion of handling, first?"

I confessed, "I'd be uncomfortable with anything except handing it over in person."

The young witch gave me an imperious nod. "Well, here I am. My best work includes my personally applying the potion."

Looking in from the workshop, Joe pointed out, "Artifact, I don't think Miss Rhubella is allowed to have either that hat or that broomstick, so maybe she shouldn't be standing in the street."

Giving a little jump, I backed up quickly to welcome Ruby and Lisa inside, then closed the door again as soon as they stepped into the office. "Oh, I'm sorry! In! In! You're always welcome, Ruby, I was just surprised and worried about you."

Closing the door made the environment a little greyer, a little more shadowy brown. All the lights were on, but they couldn't compete with Goblita's sunshine. Ruby twirled the broomstick like a baton until the bristle end was down, hung the pointy hat over the top, and leaned them against the wall. Her face might be haggard, but her immaculate black dress stood out like an obsidian statue among the dusty, dark wood of the house I'd inherited. The cleaning crab still hadn't quite gotten the office freshened up.

A new thought clicked into place, and I raised my fuzzy orange eyebrows. "Wait, you rode the broomstick here?"

Lisa bunched up her fists and squealed, "It was cool! It uses a ton of power. I helped provide a lot of it."

"Your demoness said that this was urgent," Ruby declared, extra stiff at the implication she might have made the wrong decision.

"It is, I just..." I trailed off, unable to say out loud that I felt bad accusing Ruby of stealing something. Especially to help me.

"I did what it took to make the delivery on time. I strongly appreciate what a compassionate person you are, Artifact, but I would rather you let me handle my own professional risks," intoned the grave young witch. Her expression did soften maybe a touch around the word "compassionate," but I might have been imagining it.

And yeesh, she looked *really* tired, while clearly being in complete control of herself.

There was nothing I could do but let her make her own decisions.

Elvira peeked around the door jamb, more than a head below the still-curious Joe. "Is this everyone?" she asked.

"I hope so," I answered. I was glad for every single person here, but I hadn't dared even hope for more than me and Lisa when I'd started this.

Elvira gave a few bouncy nods. "Then what's the plan? I'm with you, I just don't know what I'm with you about." She added a miniature head twirl at the end to emphasize the irony.

From by Ruby's feet, Sophie announced, "Well, first, the slobbering hairy dog boy is going to get me some fish."

Lisa shot an offended scowl down at the cat. "I just fed you."

"And now it's his turn," Sophie answered airily.

Joe, never daunted, flashed one of his merriest grins and stepped across the doorway towards the hall. "I'll be listening from the kitchen."

Sophie, head and tail lifted with all the gloating smugness a cat could summon, trotted after him.

Making the best of it, I said, "We're going to need the rest of the beef on a platter anyway, Joe. Thank you."

I'd taken a couple of steps after Joe, which let Emanuel take a couple of steps himself into view in the workshop without doing the leaning thing like his sister. Hands clasped behind his back politely, the lean, dark boy said, "Not to be pushy, but we're all ears."

Walking slowly back into the workshop, I ran my fingers through my mane of orange hair and let out a long, whistling breath. "Okay. So here's the deal. Something has gone wrong with that dragon I made. I not only need to get its collar off before someone kills it, I need to reverse its transformation before it kills someone. It attacked me with a steam breath weapon, and it wasn't capable of that when I made it. It's growing, not just physically, but adding to its formula."

The grins were gone. Ruby, Elvira, Emanuel, even Lisa watched me with completely serious expressions.

I moved on to the practical part. "So we're going to set out a food bait in that window, lace it with a tranquilizer Ruby made, cover it in a lure she also made, and drag it onto the altar so I can activate this ritual and turn it back into pigeon."

Elvira jerked her head and her thumb both at the window in question. "That window is right out on the street. Wouldn't your back yard be more secret?"

I raised one eyebrow. "I was worried that if it's altering its aspect ratios, the tranquilizer might not work as well. Do you really want to carry it all the way in here from the back yard if it's not completely asleep?"

Looking up at Ruby, I asked, "Am I right? How much do I need to be worried about this?"

The hollow-eyed witch pursed her lips in thought. She was so tired it looked like thinking hurt, but she did it anyway. "That depends. How different are we talking? Is everything there that was before?"

I nodded. "It should be. The containment won't have changed, only expanded and added more aspects."

After a few seconds more thought, Ruby declared, "It would be irresponsible to pretend that I know for sure, but if that's the case the lure and sleep potions should be less effective, but still sufficient for the purpose."

Joe emerged from the kitchen holding a big platter with the cold remains of last night's beef.

Ruby popped three fist-sized—well, my-fist-sized—clay pots off of strings on her belt. Holding them up between her fingers, she listed, "The lure. The tranquilizer. A stable meld of both, since I suspected you might use them together. I'll apply the dosage myself."

I took a deep, deep breath, gathering my bravery. Everyone watched, curious: Ruby standing in front of me, Joe back at the entrance to the hallway, Elvira sitting on the edge of a work bench with her hands gripping the wood and one foot kicking, her brother cross-legged on the floor next to her, and my pink cousin Lisa leaning languidly against the other wall with her tail tip twitching. Indulging one final flinch and grimace, I followed by letting the breath out in a rush and said, "Then I'll send the invitation."

Bending down to reach under the soul forge, I pulled the ID pendant out of its slot. Being plugged in during the slime creation ritual had its crystal shining nice and fresh. Holding the pendant up in my left hand, arm extended, I used my right hand to snap my fingers.

A rush of dizziness, tiredness, hit me, but rapidly ebbed towards normal.

Elvira, Emanuel, and Ruby all stared at the pendant with identical expressions of wide-eyed surprise.

Soft and cautious, Emanuel spoke for the three. "I'd say if its signature matches and it's anywhere near the city it heard that, yes."

Elvira chirped, "I've got the window." Leaping over to the far wall, she unfastened the latch and pushed it wide open.

Next step, I put on my safety gear, all of it. Lab coat. Goggles. Heavy leather gloves. Rubber soled boots. Pulling my hair back into a ponytail, I bound it with the rubber band I kept in the desk.

Ruby poured the entire contents of the potion, a rainbow-glistening brown slime, over the beef, then set the plate on the window sill. I had wondered how much would be the right dose. "All of it," apparently.

And that was it. That was all there was to do.

We waited.

ChapterTwenty

A nd nothing happened.

And then nothing happened some more. Everyone was too tense to say anything, to break the silent, stretching eventlessness.

I almost jumped out of my skin when Sophie complained from the kitchen, "Don't you dare pet me."

Someone giggled. I thought it was Ruby, but by the time I looked at her face, she was as stone-faced and exhausted as ever.

Joe wandered out of the kitchen, padding on his big dog feet, shrugging amicably. Then he stopped, ears raised. "I hear something."

Elvira's hands jerked up, fingers curled like she was about to cast a spell.

I waved my arms at everyone and hissed, "Get out of sight!"

They all ducked into different rooms. All except me. I stood against the wall opposite the door, holding up the ID pendant.

Heavy wings *whumph*ed. Resplendent, iridescent, multicolored, the dragon landed on the windowsill, claws reaching out to grab the wooden sill like a perch, and wings still half-spread after it grabbed hold.

This pushed the plate into the room. It fell to the floor, dumping the beef onto the concrete and sending the plate itself clattering away.

The dragon hissed at the noise. Its feathery, lizard-like head slipped into the room on its extensible neck. It looked down at the sauce-covered lump of meat. It looked up at me, suspiciously, accusingly. Then it looked down at the meat again.

The lure worked. The dragon stopped paying attention to me, leaned way down with its tail sticking up and out the window, and started eating the beef. It snapped up and swallowed one bite, then another, and paused. After a few long breaths, it gave its head a little shake and ate the rest in two more bites. It had seemed like a lot of beef, meals and meals worth, until the dragon got to it.

With the final bite down the dragon paused again. Its wings fluttered restlessly.

Then it slid forward into the room, down the wall, its talons finally let go of the windowsill, and it landed on the floor in an unconscious heap.

My heart leaped in my chest. "Joe, get it on the altar," I ordered in a hush. I definitely wanted Joe to do it. The dragon was way bigger than when I'd made it. It looked intimidatingly heavy.

For Joe, it was no big deal. He hefted the thing off the floor and set it on the surface of the altar. Elvira ducked behind him, snapping the window closed to give us privacy. Emanuel turned the dragon around so it was oriented correctly, tail towards me, head away, wings lined up with the air symbols on the side. Pretty good for someone with no bioengineering training. Head, tail, and wings all slumped over the edge. I probably should have set up the elongated slab for humans and farm animals, but this was fine. The body fit the diagrams I'd drawn.

"Stand back," I warned my friends and co-conspirators. "Here we go."

The designs were all laid out. I reached into the forge and took hold of its soul fragment with my gloved left hand, and touched the fragment to the appropriate leads as I tapped symbols with my stylus. Everything glowed in the correct order.

The dragon's neck twitched. Then one of its claws. It rustled its wings, but still lay limp. It wasn't completely asleep, just heavily drugged.

Everyone was standing around us, barely breathing, watching. Waiting for me to finish.

The problem was, I *had* finished. The transformation spell was active, power was flowing, just... "Nothing is happening!"

They all looked stunned. All except Ruby, whose tired, diamond-hard eyes regarded me emotionlessly. She asked in an equally cool voice, "What is plan B?"

I winced, flashing my gritted teeth, and muttered, "I hate to do this to you, pigeon, but transformation reversal is a failure. I'm going to remove all the dragon elements from... whatever it has become instead."

There was already a lot of power flowing, and I shoved the crystal hard into a socket as I took my stylus to the fire aspect, breaking lines of transformation and redrawing them as pure negation.

The feathery beast on the altar did not like this, and I didn't blame it. I was chopping bits off of its magic rather than its meat, but it must feel about the same. Even drugged, it started to thrash, weakly flapping its wings, lifting its head and groggily biting the air.

I couldn't let that get started, and barked, "Joe, grab its mouth! Don't let it breathe on us!"

He did. That upset the dragon even more, but his hands held its muzzle shut, and his brawny arms kept its head in place despite its neck lashing from side to side. When the body on the table started to buck, Elvira grabbed a wing, and I had to scold her, "Not on the sides, you're in my way!"

She didn't argue. Grabbing the tail instead, the fisherman's daughter dropped to the floor, pulling the dragon's body taut between her and Joe. I couldn't tell her not to. I needed the dragon held in place. I stammered, "Yes, like that, just... try not to touch the altar."

My stylus flew from point to point on the slab, changing diagrams, setting more and more aspects to draining. The dragon struggled weakly. The symbols were all lit up.

The fire aspect was still glowing. It should have burned out by now. Putting my stylus hand to my forehead, I babbled, "I'm missing something. Lisa, grab the injector probe and the tracer."

"I have the tracer," Ruby answered immediately.

She did. She grabbed not just the pot, but the big brush meant for exactly this purpose. Dipping the bristles in the tracer, she painted a line of sticky glitter around the dragon's head, right up to the edge of Joe's tightly gripping hands without getting any on him, then drew a line down its back to where the tail hung over the edge. That took only seconds, and then she moved on to the wings, drawing a line out over the struts, then down the legs, and only after that started filling in the rest of the upper body, starting around the shoulders. She moved fast, she moved precisely, and she had the order and priorities of what to mark exactly right.

Setting the stylus down in a slot on the forge, I held a hand out. "Lisa, get my polarized glasses." I didn't see them on the surface of the desk, so I pointed. "Right-hand drawer."

She pulled open the drawer. Glowing pink eyes pinched in worry, she said, "They're not here." Faster and faster, she started pulling out the rest of the drawers.

Not there? I spun through my memories. Did I skip over the glasses while laying out my equipment because they weren't where I first looked, then forget to go back and find them?

Ruby cut through the confusion, saying, "Use mine." She pulled a pair of dark lenses out of another clay pot on her belt, this one oblong. Without pausing painting the tracer, she tossed the glasses to me, and thankfully I grabbed them out of the air on the first try. I slid them over my eyes, and while they fit badly, I didn't need precision.

Husky and emphatic, I told the student witch, "I'm so glad you're here. You were right, we needed you."

I wasn't sure if she was happy or sad to hear that. Her face took on that same look Lisa gave me sometimes when I said something that should have been innocuously positive, like she was so grimly determined she might be about to commit murder.

I grabbed the probe from Lisa's outstretched hand, and

realized Ruby even understood safety rules. She had tossed me the glasses so we wouldn't both be touching them at the same time.

No time for side speculation. The dragon was stirring more, getting angrier. I smacked the probe into the transformed bird's spine between its shoulder blades. The tip didn't actually penetrate its skin, but the creature whined uncomfortably.

Lines of light spread from that point through the already glittery tracer, and I traced them with the probe, making them brighter, spreading more lines faster into a pattern. Ruby painted around me as smoothly as a dancer.

A brilliant light lit up on its lower neck, maybe six inches up from where I'd first stuck the probe. Okay, that should be the soul fragment.

Except two more lights immediately lit up at the base of its wings, where they had no business being. As for the rest…

"What are those?" Ruby gasped. The three brilliant lights could even be seen without special lenses.

I shook my head, little rapid motions, and babbled in shock, "I have no idea. I didn't make any of this! This isn't my dragon!"

"Yes, it is," corrected Emanuel calmly. He'd been on the floor out of sight, but now he stood up next to Joe, holding the purple collar with the message tube and the shears he'd used to cut the collar off the dragon's neck.

No way. No wonder nothing was working. All I vaguely recognized in the patterns of color revealed by the tracer was the fancy, adaptable containment I'd put in. It was doing exactly what I hadn't realized I was designing it to do—shifting and blocking my attempts to drain the dragon's magic.

The feathery lizard bucked hard. Its tail flipped up, knocking Elvira on her back. She rolled right to her feet, hands out, and started to trill spell code.

I shouted over her, "No magic! You'll feed back into the forge!"

The teenage sorceress stopped, and without delay dropped back to the floor, grabbing the dragon's tail again. Her brother scrambled around and put his arms around her, with the two bracing their feet against the base of the altar to hold the creature steady. I wasn't thrilled about that, but it was the least dangerous thing going on right now.

"And if it dies while Artifact is working on it, that might kill her," added Emanuel as a warning to everyone. He wasn't a bioengineer, but that was too close to true for my comfort.

Close, but not quite true. I stared down at the struggling beast whose magic had defeated mine. Confused, sick at heart, I saw only two options left. One was to let the dragon go, which was just too dangerous.

Offering the probe back to Lisa, I told her, "The chisel on the end. Hurry."

She hurried, taking the pointy stick and handing me instead what looked and felt a lot like a knife with a flat rather than pointy end—because that's what it was. My heart clenched. I felt, somehow, that I owed the dragon an explanation. Bending over it, I said aloud, "I'm so sorry, little pigeon. I'm ejecting your soul fragment."

With two quick motions, I pulled off my work gloves. My left hand dove back into the soul forge, grabbing the huge, warm, glowing crystal at the center with the bare skin of my palm and fingers. With my right hand I stabbed the chisel into the dragon at the base of its neck, carving the eject sequence into its flesh. The cuts weren't deep, but blood welled up in them that glowed green like the forge.

Behind me, my ponytail lifted away from my body, and the few loose hairs I could see stuck out straight from my head.

The dragon shrieked, and I couldn't blame it. It wrestled with Joe, Elvira, and Emanuel, flapped its wings, but they held it in place as I carved more lines.

The containment was trying to get away. The patterns under the tracer were changing. That was crazy! But it wasn't better than its creator. I carved new designs to block those paths and force others, then dragged one final sweep up the spine from the shining light marking the soul fragment to the ejection sigil, and stabbed the chisel in hard.

My upper body shivered and tingled with the power transferring through me from the giant crystal in my left hand. The last thing any body, natural or magic, ever wanted to do was reject its own soul fragment. I was using the forge to force it to do exactly that.

My shoulders shook, hard enough it must have been visible. Ruby let out a tiny whine, lifted her hand, and took a half-step towards me.

"Don't!" Emanuel warned her.

She stopped, her face locking down again, voice bleakly emotionless. "I know, but..."

The dragon's neck bulged and bubbled, feathers fluttering and sucking into scaly pink skin. The whole neck popped off near the base, its length shrinking and rolling into a ball. The smaller head slipped out of Joe's grasp, but he ducked and caught it before it hit the floor. Standing up, he held in his palms a twitching, apparently alive pigeon.

The rest of the dragon's body contorted. Extra wings burst out of its back, shoving my arm away. Two new necks burst out of its shoulders, which now supported forelegs.

Above the meaty noises and the hiss of two newly formed dragon heads rang a metallic snap. My head turned down fast enough to see the warped golden sigil in the soul forge break into three pieces and fall to the floor.

All at the same time I threw away the chisel, let go of the forge's soul fragment, yanked my left hand out, and grabbed the power lever with my right, yanking it back. At the top of my lungs I yelled, "Emergency shutdown! Everyone back!"

They dove aside, with Elvira and Emanuel immediately releasing the dragon's tail. The two-headed beast, now slightly smaller than before but still impressively big, reared up on the altar and screeched out of both fangy mouths.

Actually, Elvira didn't dive aside. She dove forward, and now grabbed the window latch, yanking it back open. The two-headed dragon, angry as it was, decided that freedom was better than revenge and leaped to the window, crawling out into the sunshine.

Elvira leaped to her feet, starting to high-speed babble spell code, but not nearly fast enough. The dragon flapped its four wings and took off, out of sight. The sorceress had to let the spell trail off into dots so it wouldn't blow up.

That left me holding up my left hand, the inside surface of which glowed as brightly and with the same green as the now hidden soul forge gem, and even with the same purple highlights around seams and edges.

Lisa walked up to me, pink eyes wide. I grabbed my left wrist with my right hand to put my arm in the way as I pulled the hand back and ordered, "Don't touch!"

Lisa's arm swung. *WHAP!* I heard the sound of her slapping me, felt the pain and the shocking force jolt through my head before I realized that's what she was doing. Stumbling backwards, I hit the wall and slid down to the floor, blinking until the room stopped spinning.

Ruby rushed forward, but Emanuel grabbed her with his arms around her waist, hissing, "Nobody but the demon can touch her!"

"I know!" Ruby yelped back, grimacing miserably.

Shaking with anger, Lisa grabbed my shirt in both fists, leaning down over me to snarl, "You stupid licorice! You... you... I am NOT losing a second Forge to that contraption! Do you hear me!? Is that it!? Do you get sucked into it too now?"

My head was clearing. I stammered, "No. No, I'll be okay. I shut down the forge in time. Look at the formulae painted on the floor around the walls. If I'd grounded, they'd be glowing. I just need to—"

"Decontaminate," filled in Ruby.

With something she could do again, a stone-faced Ruby spun into action. She grabbed the correct jar off the storage shelves, along with a leather left glove Uncle Leonard had left behind, one way too big for my tiny hands. She lugged the heavy jar over, and set it and the glove on the table nearest me. Pulling another little pot off her belt and grabbing the brush she'd used for the tracer, she ordered, "This first."

Lisa pulled me to my feet, then with a ferocious scowl stomped hoofily out of the way. I still had my glowing hand held up and the wrist held in my right hand, to make absolutely sure I didn't touch anything by accident. Ruby scooped some clear goop out of the pot with the brush, and painted it delicately onto my palm and fingers. It felt cool and wet, soothing the stiff, scratchy heat of my glowing skin. When she had every inch of that covered, she held out the glove, hanging open with the fingers down, and poured a little powder in. Without touching my skin, she helped me pull the glove on, pouring in more and more of the grey mix of lead and sand that made up the decontaminating powder.

I had to admit, this was a way better plan than letting my hand soak in a pan under this stuff like I'd intended. Trust a witch to know cures for magical injuries.

Everyone else stood around silently until we finished, and I wiggled my fingers inside the heavy, awkward mitt of a lead-filled glove. Someone had closed the window, but I hadn't seen it, and now they all stood staring at me with anxious blank expressions.

Emanuel asked the question for the others. "What happened?"

I answered, tired and grumbly, still putting together the pieces myself. "Those other two lights were soul fragments. It had three fragments instead of one. It absorbed them after I made it. I have no idea how it could do that. I couldn't make an animal capable of that if I tried."

Lisa, arms folded, asked, "You didn't happen to use any of those brand new experimental runes you got from your dad when you made the dragon, did you?"

She'd sounded more concerned than sarcastic, but I still flinched because, yes, I had. They'd worked better than me, Dad, or even the Dollmaker could have dreamed.

Loud knocking echoed from the business door. Not just knocking, fist banging. Muffled by the wood, the old adventuress's voice shouted, "Is anyone alive in there?"

The banging didn't stop, and it was the kind that hinted she would break the door down if she didn't get an answer. I took a step towards the office, and gave my cousin a nod. "Lisa, get the door."

Shuffling onto the office carpet, I cradled my gloved hand in my other arm and left a trail of lead dust that the cleaning crab was already sucking up. Lisa opened the door and stepped out of the way.

The adventuress in her leather armor and Sheriff Westlake in his faded denims stood on the other side of that doorway, and neither of them looked happy. The old woman had her knife out, and the sheriff his hand on the pouch I now knew held a pistol.

Taking one step inside, the adventuress's eyes swept the room, taking in Lisa behind the door and Ruby standing in the doorway to the workshop, with Elvira and Emanuel peeking around the corner behind her. Brisk, wary, and ready for action, the old woman demanded, "Is everyone alright? What happened here?"

"We saw the dragon escape from your window," rumbled the sheriff, still lingering outside.

"A dragon," the grey-haired adventuress corrected him.

"The dragon," I corrected her.

Taking a deep breath, knowing exactly what I was going to tell them, I looked the poised, grey-haired old woman straight in the eyes and reported, "It's an exotic magical animal. As the town's bioengineer, it's my responsibility to try to neutralize it, figure out where it came from and what's wrong with it, and control it if I can or deconstruct it if I can't. It responds to my soul forge. Summoning it was worth a try. My friends helped me."

The woman's slightly hunched, big cat stalking pose relaxed a little. Her face softened into a weird mix of pity and admiration as she looked us over. Softly, she said, "Children...," but didn't seem to know how to finish.

The sheriff's fluffy mustache twisted first left, then right, and he squinted even more than his wrinkle-crowded eyes usually did. Like someone without the heart to be angry, he scolded, "That is not your job, Miss Forge. I admire your gumption, but it's not."

Still cradling my arm, I stood up more straight, and let my pride show through. "I'm the only person who could have found out what I found out. Miss..."

"Franklin," filled in the adventuress when I looked up at her.

I nodded. "Miss Franklin, that is not a normal monster, by

any definition. It is able to absorb soul fragments from animals it eats. I managed to remove one, but it has two left."

That changed her stare again. This time it turned dark, thoughtful, and distant. Grimly, she muttered, "A chimera. A real chimera."

"Those—" I started to argue, but caught myself. "Five minutes ago I would have said they don't exist."

"I ran into another, thirty years ago," she informed me. Her distant stare focused again. She drew herself up, and slid her knife back into a pocket sheath. Stepping back to the doorway and the sheriff, she looked back at me over her shoulder and asked solemnly, "Do you need any help?"

"We'll take care of her," declared Ruby firmly.

"We already have a witch here to provide medical aid," Emanuel pointed out.

The sheriff smiled. Probably. The corners of his mustache turned up, and his gravely voice lightened. "So I see. Alright. We'll leave you to it."

Miss Franklin took hold of the door handle, and nodded her head to me in respect. "Thank you for the information, Miss Forge. I have to go talk to the College. Now."

Sheriff Westlake added his own nod. "You did good, but this is it, you hear me, Missy? You've done your responsibility and then some. From now on, you leave it to us."

"Yes, Sir," I agreed with more than a little passion.

He hesitated, obviously hating to leave, but pulled the door shut and did it anyway.

I slumped into Lisa's arms, the strength I'd summoned to deal with the adults leaking away, leaving my body heavy and thick and my left hand still uncomfortably hot. I grinned weakly up at my fangy, horned, slit-pupiled cousin and chuckled, "You have no idea how happy I am to obey, Sheriff."

I hated having unleashed a beast like this on the town, but we had the collar, I had a fantastic cover story, and there was now officially absolutely no way anyone could trace the dragon back to me. I was about to pass out just from relief.

Ruby beat me to it. Her dark-rimmed eyes slipped closed and she dropped. Her body plummeted towards the floor only to be caught by Joe, who dove out of the workshop where he'd been lurking discreetly out of view. He scooped her up in his right arm, and held her unconscious body tenderly to his chest.

Sophie stalked into the office, looked at her collapsed mistress in Joe's right arm, looked at the cooing pigeon held up in Joe's left hand, and asked, "Are you going to eat that?"

Chapter
Twenty-One

Joe leaned over the sleeping witch, his hands on his hips. "I'd be happy to carry her back to the academy. She doesn't weigh much. I don't think she eats enough."

Ruby lay draped over my couch the same as last time, with her hands folded over her stomach because we couldn't just let one hang limp over the edge. She slept quietly, breaths slow, with no sign of stirring. Sophie lay draped over her eyes again like a wrinkly pink washrag.

The wrinkly pink washrag extended her forelegs, waggled her toes, and announced airily, "She would rather die than find out you did that, and I would rather die than put up with the dog hair you'd leave all over her clothing. As it is, I'll have to lie to her and tell her the short one caught her, or she'll spend the next week crying under the waterfall where she thinks nobody can see."

Joe, Lisa, and I stood around avoiding each other's faces as an uncomfortable silence descended on the living room. When the awkward, pained sympathy eased a touch I decided Sophie must be exaggerating. She wasn't exactly the most literally honest and unbiased witness in the world. The basic point would still be true. Ruby would not want Joe to save her.

The big wolf boy came out of the cloud of guilt as well, and shrugged. He turned a much milder smile than usual at me. "Then I suppose I leave this to you. Thank you for a wonderful time. You really know how to throw a party."

Pffft. He didn't pause for me to think of a witty rejoinder, just opened up the living room front door and left.

I looked around, taking in how empty the place felt with our only remaining visitor asleep on the couch. After the chaos of fighting a dragon, a disastrous transformation ritual that ended in the emergency shutdown of a broken soul forge, confronting the law, and seriously contaminating my left hand, the living room's peaceful nature pressed on me. It held no ticking clocks. The crowded furniture was all heavily padded. The carpet was battered and soft under my feet, and the brown wooden walls a soothingly shadowy color. Hints of the chaos still lingered in the form of smells, the acrid animal scent of the dragon's feathers, the sharp tang of the sauce Joe had made for the beef, the always present smells of dust and wood, Ruby's smell mixing mushrooms and grass, Lisa's strawberry scent even more intense when she sweated, and the oil and metal scent from the decontamination mix in my oversized left glove.

The horseshoe crab floated by, its dozen legs scraping at its mouth parts and shell to eat up the last traces of the dragon lure's beef mess. The vitality tension of that monster had to be getting low, which would help keep it alive until I fixed the soul forge. I still needed to make sure I was keeping it powered and bind it to me.

Sophie lifted a paw and batted at it as it hovered past.

I clapped my hands together. Speaking of the soul forge... "Lisa, would you mind running down to Julianna and picking up—I take it that's a no. I mean yes. I mean you're not going to do it."

My demon cousin didn't actually say anything, but she was looking up at the ceiling with a sharp-toothed scowl and pulling on her own horns in agonized frustration. The message was clear. I was overworking again.

With a heavy sigh, I accepted that she was right. The heavy glove on my left hand was an irrefutable argument in her favor. I defeatedly slunk across the room and dropped down into one of the living room's padded chairs.

Oh. Ooooooh. I let out a groan of exquisite pleasure. My voice weak because my body suddenly refused to do anything, I wheezed, "This is the most comfortable chair I have ever sat in in my life."

It was so comfy. I wanted a chair like this for my own.

Wait, this one was mine. I closed my eyes and let go of everything but enjoying the utter, plush softness. This was just so nice.

Hooves clumped on carpet rapid-fire. I heard them stop as L leaped into the air. She hit the chair butt-first right next to me, and wriggled into place. I scooted a little to give her room. It was a big chair and could handle us both.

I felt her body go limp. Forcing my eyes half-open, I looked over and saw Lisa's slit-pupiled eyes wide and staring upwards.

Soft, with a touch of wheeze, she asked, "Why is this the one chair I never tried until now?"

"It was buried in dust," I wheezed back.

Her head moved, the faintest of nods I wouldn't have spotted if we weren't side by side on the same cushion. "Oh, yeah, that's true."

Immediately, a knock sounded on the door. Very stiff, regular, and formal.

Okay, it might not have been immediate, but I had no sense of time lying in that plush upholstery embrace and it sure felt like I got to enjoy it for about one peaceful second.

Again, I forced my eyes open and looked at my cousin, who gave me the same blank, sessile stare. Neither of us wanted to get up, but there was nothing for it. I summoned all of my power and threw myself forward, leaping to my feet and escaping paradise.

As soon as I was upright energy returned to my body. Was that chair magic? I would have to be careful with it.

A little lead dust sprinkled out of the glove on my left wrist, and I pulled it up snug. I needed to be more careful with it. My hand needed to soak until bedtime.

Lisa took the opportunity to slide into the middle of the chair, splaying her arms and legs and hogging the whole space.

Despite the taunting, I could not resent her joy. My energy returned, I trotted over to the office and opened the door.

Two witches filled the doorway, tall and shadowy silhouettes in the late afternoon sun, rigid and crowned by huge pointy hats. A second later my eyes adjusted and identified the one on my right as the grey-haired Mistress Flora, towering and studying me like a judge weighing execution.

The witch on my left was new, and much less stark than Miss Flora. She wasn't quite as tall, although she still loomed over me with the hat making it worse. Her hair was deep blue, and her face less lined, making me not quite sure of her age. I had an impression she was about the same age as Miss Flora and merely looked much younger. Where Miss Flora's witch dress was faded and frayed at the hems, this witch was as shiny and sleek as Ruby. Both wore collections of charms, little clay pots, and pouches tied to their rope belt. A lot of them. Her stare was a lot harder to pin down. Alert, searching, but not betraying any emotion.

Mistress Flora's head turned like it was dragged by a signature beacon to the broomstick leaning against a bookshelf, and the pointy hat the stick held up. Her tone icy and official, she declared, "I see Miss Rhubella is present."

I didn't see the signal, but there had to be one. Suddenly Mistress Flora looked questioningly at her companion, and then followed the blue-haired witch's gaze to my wrist and the oversized leather glove on it. I'd opened the door latch with that hand, and it wasn't quite hidden.

"Decontamination powder," Mistress Flora said. She'd spotted the contents of the glove.

Mistress Flora reached for her belt and the tubes and jars on it. Her companion reached for my arm. I took a step back, cradling the heavy glove in my other arm, and warned, "Don't take the glove off. It's been treated already."

Mistress Flora's demeanor changed. She looked older, her scowl tired and troubled. "By Rhubella, no doubt. Did she apply leeching gel?"

I nodded. "She didn't name it, but yes."

The blue-haired witch had a soft, even voice, as mysterious in its mood as her expression. Just someone pointing out facts. "Rhubella wouldn't use it if it wasn't perfect. Describe the injury."

They were witches, after all. I reported, "Second degree soul fragment burn. Severe for second degree, bright glow, but no mutation or transparency. I confirmed no grounding."

I would swear Mistress Flora shrank at least an inch as she listened, mouth pursed in sour contemplation. She stood that way another second after I finished before grumbling, "Well, I can see why Rhubella thought this was an emergency that needed all possible speed."

"Well, um... no, it wasn't this that she hurried over for. This happened after," I said.

The old witches both gave me identical blank, expectant stares, and I kicked myself mentally. I'd gotten Rhubella back in trouble, and now I had to scramble and do it again!

Desperately hoping the truth would work, because I certainly thought Rhubella was a hero, I cradled my injured hand and babbled, "I decided that it was my responsibility as town bioengineer to deal with the rogue dragon. I got specialized potions from Ruby to help, but when I sent a message that I was going to do it immediately, she insisted on being here. If she hadn't... I think someone might have died."

That was the truth. If any of my friends hadn't been there, someone might have died. It all went so spectacularly wrong, but as a team my friends and I made it through.

And of course Mistress Flora asked, "Did you succeed?"

I faced it. I stood straight and accepted my responsibility and looked her right back in the eyes. "No. It is not a normal monster." I hated using the inaccurate, vernacular meaning of "monster," but now was not the time to be pedantic. "We weakened it and gave the College information they will need, that they could not have gotten elsewhere and probably don't want shared around."

Both witches nodded at that, maybe an inch, just a reflexive acknowledgment. As witches, professional secrets would make perfect sense to them.

Actually, I just didn't want people freaking out about a soul fragment absorbing chimera.

Mistress Flora smiled, just faintly, her eyes still focused and searching as she looked down at me. This must be what she was like as a teacher. She sounded sweet and grandmotherly as she said, "I can see what you and Rhubella see in each other."

Again, there must have been some signal, because there was a slight pause and Mistress Flora looked at her friend, then sighed. Her head and shoulders sagged, and she looked older than ever, her dress greyer as if covered in dust. She sighed, and told the air above us, "Of course, because this wasn't complicated enough already." Looking back down at me, she asked, "Where is Rhubella now?"

Whatever was going on in Mistress Flora's head, all I could do was stick to being straightforward and responsible. With my arms busy, I ticked my head in the direction of the living room. "Asleep. She was in no physical condition to help out. She insisted on doing it anyway, until everyone was safe."

Again Mistress Flora looked up at the ceiling. Again she sighed. Again she looked at her blue-haired companion, and then back at me.

The quiet second witch finally took a half-step forward, and bowed deeply. Formally but with a touch of sweetness, she said, "I'm sorry for our bad manners. You've met Mistress Flora. I am Mistress Hammerhead."

I was suddenly glad cradling my injured hand kept both my arms tucked against my body. The hand kissing still weirded me out, and I wanted to avoid it whenever possible. I bowed back. Not being a witch myself I should probably curtsey, but I wasn't sure I knew how to do that right.

Mistress Flora walked past me into the office, far enough to see through the workshop and into the living room. Rhubella would be visible on the couch from that angle.

I heard Sophie say, "Oh look, the old biddies are here. She's out like a light, or she'd be having hysterics that I called you that."

Mistress Flora took it well, or maybe just didn't care what cats think, which struck me as wise. She turned an enigmatic face back to the enigmatic Mistress Hammerhead, and asked, "What are we going to do about this?"

Folding her hands together, Mistress Hammerhead answered almost casually, "Take her home. Other than that, no clue. I know a lot of things we're not going to do."

Mistress Flora's troubled frown returned. "Not what I wanted to hear."

Troubled or not, she strolled through the door into the workshop and presumably into the living room, because she returned seconds later with Ruby held in her arms like an overlarge baby. Ruby was still asleep, with her head supported on Mistress Flora's arm. Sophie was still draped across Ruby's face.

Mistress Hammerhead picked up the broom and hat. She gave me another little bow, and said, "Thank you for your honesty and hospitality, Miss Forge." With a slight smile and a quieter, confidential tone, she added, "Don't worry too much about your friend. You're the best defender she could ever hope for."

The witches stepped out the door side by side, and I closed it behind them.

Immediately, from the workshop, Lisa hissed. "Hsssst!"

I scurried hurriedly in, and found Lisa pressed to the wall by the window. She had it pulled just the tiniest crack open.

That was enough for me to hear Mistress Flora's faint voice, now matter-of-fact and maybe even argumentative. "If we could graduate her early we could give her a hat, push her out the door, and she'd stop being our problem, but…"

When the first witch trailed off, Mistress Hammerhead filled in, "She's not ready."

"No. She's good, but she's not that good," agreed Mistress Flora.

That was enough. I pulled the window firmly closed.

After that I stood still in the dim, grey, cement-floored workshop, and took a few deep breaths. My heartbeat slowed. I hadn't realized just how nervous that conversation made me.

Lisa just grinned at me, back against the wall, mischievously amused as usual.

The witches couldn't possibly hear me. Nobody but Lisa could possibly hear me. Still, I lowered my voice to barely over a whisper as I said, "I can't believe they believed me."

Lisa tilted her head forward sardonically, one glowing eye uncovered and the other peeking through red and yellow locks of hair. "Of course they believed you." The disdain in her tone was *thick.*

Uncowed, I argued back, "I know I was telling the truth, but that doesn't make it believable!"

Lisa stared for another second, her smile turning from sardonic to boggled. "You have no idea what you look like, do you?"

I blinked, my head giving a little jerk, and asked, "What does that have to do with anything?"

Now my demon cousin's mouth fell open. She gaped as she pushed off the wall and started walking slowly around me, looking me up and down like I'd turned into a bizarre alien from one of the really weird cross-breach universes. "You don't. You really don't. Artifact, you are the most trustworthy-looking person on Earth."

I turned to face her and asked intelligently, "Um?"

Lisa posed in front of me, hand on a jutting out hip, arrogant and authoritative. Her purple dress swished as she shifted her weight that way, and her tail emerged from it in back, curled up and then down right at the pointy arrow tip. Lifting her other hand, she extended a finger and its claw-like pointy black fingernail. "First, you're short."

I put my fists on my own hips and told her dryly, "Yes, I know, thank you."

She pushed her hand and its raised finger forward, for once sounding firm and serious, even if she didn't look it. "No, it matters. You're not threatening. You're adorable. You have round apple cheeks." She extended both arms, and pinched those cheeks. "You're just the slightest bit pudgy—" She prodded my belly with a fingertip between shirt and shorts. "—but no one could ever call you fat. You're just the slightest bit muscled—"

She pinched one of my biceps. "—but no one could ever call you buff. You have huge blue eyes and huge orange hair, and I don't know how you get that kind of volume. My mother would kill for it, and probably has. You're *adorable*, cousin. You look earnest and wholesome and you could be twelve or you could be twenty. If you told someone they had a second head, they'd start feeling around for it and ask you where when they didn't find it."

All I could do was stand there. I didn't know whether a description like that should make me self-conscious or not. She wasn't actually wrong about any of it, especially the "slightly" parts.

Not knowing what to say, I did what came naturally to me. I crouched down and looked over the soul forge. My gaze quickly came to rest on the gap where the broken glyph should have been. Hmmm. "Do you think you could go see if Julianna—"

Lisa cut me off. "No. You are actually physically injured from overwork already. We're staying in the rest of the day."

"Tomorrow—"

Palm out, she swept her arm out to the side and down. "Maybe after school. You were interested in school, right? I will actually go back to school myself if that's what it takes to slow you down killing yourself with that soul forge. Besides, it's starting to rain."

It was. The tapping of raindrops on the window picked up quickly to a steady drumming. The sound was nice and peaceful, and I had to admit to myself that a relaxing afternoon and evening sounded appealing.

Chapter
Twenty-Two

I hadn't been sure that Goblita had weather, but it rained all
night, just hard enough to be a constant pat-pat-pat on every
window. I slightly opened the one in my bedroom so the smell of
rain would drift into the room and replace the house's lingering
dusty smell. When I woke up the horseshoe crab was on the
floor in front of that window, licking up raindrops that got in.

I muzzily remembered the occasional distant thunder and
flash of lightning, but the boom of one must have just hit nearby
and woken me. The bedroom was quivering, and the whole
house rattled a second before it settled. Thunder followed, but
this time from much farther away.

It seemed like only moments later when the bedroom door
opened, revealing the pale outline of Lisa stumbling into room,
her body just a suggestion among shadows except for pink eyes
shining like searchlights in the dark. Even mostly closed, those
crescents of light glared in the gloom. She lurched up to the
bed, crawled up into it, and growled groggily, "Fine. If you're
going to keep screaming and waking me up like this, I'll come

stay with you. Being afraid of thunderstorms is stupid, do you know that?"

"Um...," I said, not the slightest bit bothered by the latest flash of light and quiet boom from outside.

As she pulled open the covers and crawled in, Lisa mumbled, "Look, I got dressed and everything so you don't have to freak out. You Forges are all the same."

She had done that. Next to me in the bed I could see she was wearing a shirt sized for someone so much bigger than her that it went down to her thighs. It was enough to not be embarrassing, but looked completely comfortable to sleep in.

Pulling the blanket completely over herself, she curled into a ball and snuggled right up against me like that.

It was the middle of the night. I hadn't been completely awake anyway. I draped an arm over Lisa and went back to sleep.

Chapter
Twenty-Three

The room was much brighter when Lisa shook me awake. She wasn't curled up next to me anymore. She was standing by the bed, fully dressed for the day, holding my shoulders in both hands and jostling me until I had to open my eyes.

"What time is it?" I asked blearily. A quiet ticking pulled my eyes to the clock on the wall, but early morning light wasn't enough to read it. It was only bright compared to the darkness when Lisa had crawled in with me.

She let go of me and answered with a hard scowl, "Seven a.m. I let you sleep in, but if you don't hurry we'll be late. Breakfast is waiting downstairs. Get dressed. Move it, Forge."

Lisa whisked out the door into the second floor hall. I stumbled out of bed. No time for a bath, from the sound of things. I waved the cleaning spell on my tablet over myself. Still waking up I was moving slowly. My skin felt raw when I finished, my hair hanging down around my shoulders was definitely a shade light, and I didn't dare touch my eyebrows in case I found out I'd disintegrated them. My left hand looked normal, but I kept the cleaning spell away from it anyway.

Grabbing my shorts and shirt from yesterday, I used my tablet to clean those too rather than dig something out of my trunk. Everybody dressed like this in Goblita anyway. It was usually so hot and bright you'd be crazy not to.

By the time I was dressed I was fully awake and had my energy back, so I bounced down the stairs two at a time, a little anxious about what I would find in the kitchen. I detected no aroma of burned food. What I actually found was that Lisa managed this miracle by not cooking at all. A burrito wrap waited for me on a plate on the kitchen table. As I slid into my chair, a peek inside the tortilla revealed Lisa had made it by heaping up beans, fish, cheese, and vegetables diced so fine that I had no clue what they were. That all looked great to me.

Lisa was already wolfing down the last of hers, which looked the same as mine but sprinkled with sugar. I took her example and stuffed my burrito down my throat as fast as possible, drowning it with orange juice.

It was a long walk to school and Lisa was a fast walker, but with a good meal in my stomach I had no trouble keeping up. I wore the soul forge pendant around my neck because I should wear it more often, and for the same reason had a few measuring tools in my satchel. It was mostly empty. The tools didn't weigh nearly as much as the only other contents, a pair of cloth-wrapped sandwiches Lisa had stuffed in. I was actually carrying the satchel because I wondered if I might need it to carry stuff back from school with me.

Lisa gave the glittery green crystal hanging around my neck an occasional dirty look.

Early-morning Goblita was pleasant and only slightly warm, with a few passersby, a lot of little white houses with the occasional clump of butcher/produce/dry goods shops. A couple of carts passed by loaded with mysterious boxes and barrels under wraps, and we passed a few kids with backpacks who I suspected were also heading to school. Palm trees, incredibly tall and impossibly skinny, stuck up out of the ground and gave the impression they would fall over in the slightest breeze. A sheep trotted past us once, its origin and destination unknown.

One of the carts did get my special attention because it was pulled by goats as big as horses, which could only have gotten that way thanks to bioengineering. If anything I'd heard about goats was true, they'd also have to be altered to be more obedient. Did I have a recipe for that somewhere? How would I do it if I was starting from scratch? Hmmm.

The school was too low and wide a building to loom, so we were close by the time I spotted it ahead. It looked the same as last time, a sandy building stretched out in a long, wide U and with lots and lots of big windows. A large overhang held up by thin metal pillars shaded the double doored entrance, and kids ranging from "might not be teenagers anymore" down to "shouldn't a child that small be with her parents" trickled inside.

"We made it," declared Lisa with relief. Taking hold of my elbow, she dragged me forward into the building, even though I'd have been happy to keep up with any pace or even take the lead.

Inside was a long, long, long, bland hallway. The building had a lot of stone brick painted a nondescript pale cream color, which did amplify sunlight filtering in from the huge windows on the outside rooms through smaller but still big windows on the rows of doors. It was a jarringly different experience from Uncle Leonard's brown, crowded house. The place felt sterile, even though it was far from empty. Between the regular doors, long stretches of wall were lined with rows of identical wooden lockers. A sign made of cut out letters in a multitude of colors stretched above one set of lockers, reading "Welcome Back Goblita Murder Hobos." Scruffy plants in big pots needed more light than they were getting, and from the way my pendant flashed when I passed one, they'd been altered to survive these conditions.

I didn't have much time to gawk. Lisa knew exactly where she was going, and pulled me into one of the seemingly endless identical doors. Nearly identical. This one did have "12" in black numerals painted over it.

The huge windows meant the room we entered was as brightly lit as the outside. A bunch of single person wooden desks with matching chairs filled most of the room in untidy rows, with a proper desk for an adult at the far end. A blackboard dominated the wall behind the big desk, and the walls were lined in shelves, mostly stomach high on me, with books and paper supplies and oddball objects crammed into them. Posters of educational-looking things like a chart of the solar system freckled any otherwise unused wall space.

Of course, there were other kids here, already at their desks, either sitting or standing next to the desk fiddling with books and stationary. I recognized several of them. Joe, Elvira, Emanuel, the little cat boy Lucky, and the sweater-enveloped Yuki were all here.

Elvira, standing by her desk, spotted me and Lisa immediately. Grinning in frenetic triumph, she pumped her fist and shouted, "Yes!"

The room contained one adult, standing by the big desk and reading or at least scanning a book. Fluffy red hair with golden highlights topped his head, and when he looked over at me even across the room I could make out his golden eyes with their more subtle red highlights. I couldn't place his age. Not all that old, just an adult. Still slim and fit, which with his full-length black suit made him look like a building column when he stood too still.

I couldn't tell if he was looking at me or Lisa, and he addressed her first, absolutely radiating delight as he did. "I was hoping we'd see you again. Is this the new girl in town I've been hearing about?"

I took a step towards him, and flashed a grin. I had butterflies in my stomach, but they were excited butterflies. "I'm Lisa's cousin Artifact. Call me Art."

Lisa, meanwhile, leaned away and crossed her arms, putting on a scowl. "I hope I'm not back. I agreed to bring in Artifact so she could see how boring school is. Even if she's dumb and dooms us to this misery, I knew she'd be in this class, so I just brought her straight in."

The teacher—he had to be the teacher—stepped quickly and lightly over to us, holding out his hand. As I shook it, he explained, "I'm Mr. Drake. What Lisa means is that this is the class for kids whose education is so irregular it's hard to sort you into normal classes."

Elvira had something in her mouth she chewed on idly as she jerked a thumb at the big wolf boy at the desk in front of her. "Joe is here because he's too smart. He keeps finishing everything."

"So are you," murmured Yuki from her chair on the other side of the square of desks. Her voice still echoed with itself, as if she was multiple people speaking not quite in sync.

Elvira rolled her eyes sardonically up at the ceiling, and wobbled her head a little. The constant, patient chewing only made her look more sardonic. "Only if it has to do with magic."

I tried to keep my attention on Mr. Drake, telling him, "That would be me. I was taught by my parents and this is my first time setting foot in a real school. I'm a bioengineering prodigy, but I don't know how I measure up on any other topics."

Goblita was a city of people with sly smiles. Mr. Drake's friendly teacher smile took on at least a touch of that slyness as he assured me, "That is what placement tests are for."

Lisa groaned and shuddered next to me.

I shook my head. "Don't listen to her. I like tests."

Mr. Drake tilted his head back for a brief laugh. "That's a relief. I hate beginning someone's school experience with a bad surprise."

"Yeah, they might think it's as tedious as I do," Lisa grumbled.

Lisa's complaints didn't budge Mr. Drake's smile at all. The teacher clearly wasn't bothered by her grumpy-bad-girl act.

No, the teacher just waved a hand at the desks and said, "Take a seat anywhere you like while I get the tests." Then true this word, he headed back to his own desk and started rooting through the shelves and filing cabinets behind it.

I took another look around. So many books in one room! And that curious globe on a stand that would let it rotate and spin. Those lines on the globe... were a map!

I drifted over to look at it, intrigued. A map of the whole Earth. Amazing. The surface was badly faded, more brown than anything else, but you could tell the oceans used to be blue, and nations were picked out in every other color imaginable. The arrangement of those nations made no sense. There was the West coast of our continent, which would put Goblita right... there, but it was only a part of a huge yellow block.

Emanuel stepped up behind and to one side of me, leaning over my shoulder to explain, "It's pre-Breach. Preserved by witchcraft. Those are all how the nations were divided up during the golden age of mankind."

Impressed, I murmured, "They're enormous. How can one country spread from the East Coast to the West Coast? This one north of us is even bigger! Is that the Yukon up there? I didn't realize just how far away it is."

I swiveled the globe around, getting my first good look at the shape of our planet's continents. So that was what Asia looked like. It was gigantic. What strange, squiggly contours of coastline, and so many islands! No wonder hardly anyone ever crossed the Pacific. It was also absurdly big. That trip would take months.

Flipping the globe around some more, I said, "It's neat to see an accurate map of Europa. None of my Dad's maps were pre-Breach. I know the shape of the land hasn't changed."

Emanuel smirked a bit, not sarcasm, just the love of trivia. "The names all have. Any labels you see are at best clues to let you find modern cities. You'll learn the ones we know in class. I'll help you catch up. Geography won't take long, if you like maps this much."

A clawed hand grabbed my elbow. Lisa's. She hauled me away from Emanuel and the globe, back to the wooden desk next to her own, and pulled me into the chair.

The reason became immediately clear, as Mr. Drake approached with a stack of papers and set them down on my desk's wooden surface. He set a couple of pencils next to them. The papers were all covered in neat writing, with a lot of free spaces.

Lisa recoiled in horror, leaning away from me like being tested might be contagious.

Mr. Drake just smiled encouragingly and sympathetically at me. "I know it's a lot. If you need a break, let me know."

"Won't know until I try!" I chirped. I was looking forward to this. What a neat opportunity to explore what I knew, and what other people knew.

The results of that question and my ability with the tests varied wildly. I would have felt worse about that, but I wasn't sure how good I was supposed to be at any of it anyway. There were half a dozen calculus questions I didn't know the answer to, and I sweated on the trigonometry, but thankfully the desk contained a slide rule. Other than that, I breezed through the math. I was pretty sure reading and writing went well. I knew most of the big words already from my dad's books.

Some of the questions were weird, but I got the hang of them. Like, "A sheep is to wool as a goat is to ___" I had to stare at that one for more than a minute trying to figure out what it was even asking. I didn't want to give up, or ask for help if I didn't have to. Then it hit me that "is to" was just testing jargon for "produces," so I wrote "milk" on the empty line.

The next question was "A boat is to water what a bicycle is to ___." Okay, "is to" clearly didn't mean "produces" after all. It was just generally about relationships. I wrote in "roads" and was pretty sure I had that right. More questions of this type only made me more confident.

On the other hand, most of the geography was a mystery, and I could barely answer any of the questions about the meaning of spell parts or their construction. And what even was sentence diagramming?

Admitting defeat on that one, I shook my head to clear it of the feeling of being stuffed with wool. Out loud, I declared, "Okay, now I need a break."

Looking around, I found Lisa hunched over a page of multiplication tables on her desk. She muttered, "I'm surrounded by brain freaks."

I'd gotten Emanuel's attention. He was looking up from whatever he'd been doing and at me instead. He suggested, "I saw you looking at the books. Mr. Drake, why don't I take her to the library?"

Joe nodded in approval, without lifting his fuzzy wolf head from the book he was taking notes on. Next to him, Elvira seemed oblivious to all of us, with her head leaned way forward and her long black hair almost hiding a page of what looked like spell code.

Emanuel leaped from his chair and rushed over to hold the door open for me. Happy for the break, amused at his eagerness, I grinned as I followed him out into the hall.

A loud bell rang somewhere in the building while we were in the hall, and kids stampeded out of rooms, rushed around in every direction talking to each other at the top of their lungs, and streamed into new rooms. Or were sucked back into their original rooms, I couldn't tell.

Emanuel ignored them, leading me through the river of teenagers and little kids to a stretch of wall where there was a lot more space between its one door and the nearest other than in the rest of the school. Grinning enormously, he opened that door and ushered me inside.

I looked around.

"Um. Wow," I said cogently.

In one sense it wasn't that impressive. The whole thing was the size of maybe three or four classrooms strung together. There were just so many books. They weren't piled up on floors or anything. They didn't have to be. Walls lined with bookshelves and two neat rows of shelves going down the center were enough to hold more books than... well, it was a lot of books. I'd thought Uncle Leonard's house had a lot of books, with like a dozen in each room. Every book in his house, including my bioengineering notes, would fit on a few feet of the shelves in here. There wasn't much free space on the walls, but what there was continued the educational posters theme, with places for odd decorations like stuffed dolls hanging by one hand, or cut out pictures of pumpkins.

My feet padded forward as if the bookshelves were tugging me to them. This shelf was lined with short but thick books with wrinkled backs that looked like they were made of thin cardboard or something like that. Despite the wrinkles of overreading and the faded colors, the spines were readable. They had names like Dying Sun and A Boy And His Cat.

My voice sounded hollow, like someone else was speaking.

"I didn't know there were this many books in one place anywhere."

Em stepped around me enough to watch my expression, which meant I could see his. He was grinning like a loon at my reaction. This was why he had volunteered to bring me!

"Most of these are pre-Breach, of course," he said, giving his head a little dip and with his hands clasped behind his back.

These books were hundreds of years old? "Did I say 'Um. Wow' yet?"

Slowly, gently, Emanuel took hold of my wrist in his rough, calloused fingers, lifting my hand to a random book. My own fingers closed instinctively, and I responded to his guidance by cautiously pulling it out of its place and flipping it open. Emanuel assured me, "You're allowed to touch them. You're allowed to take them home, if you sign them out. We're very lucky. A lot of books were left in this area after the Breach, and witches got to them before they rotted."

Despite its worn and faded appearance, the book pages felt firm and supple and sturdy under my fingers, and the spine didn't creak when I opened it. I let it fall open to wherever it wanted, and scanned the text in fascination.

Then I blinked, and frowned. "Wait. This doll has way too much angst. She wants to sneak off and see a human friend? Dolls don't work like this. They don't even work like this if you're crazy enough to give them a soul fragment. It's not how they worked pre-Breach either. Dad and the Dollmaker have shared some notes from back then, and it's bizarre stuff, but nothing like this."

Emanuel's grin somehow got a little brighter. As smugly as if he'd written everything in the library, he informed me, "Nope, this is the fiction section."

Fiction section? I looked down the row. "That is a lot of storybooks. It's going to take me a while. At least it's something to do when Lisa won't let me work."

Emanuel had not run out of smug grin. No, not smug, whimsical. He gave his head another slight dip, as if conceding a mistake. "Actually, I should say that's the section we know is fiction. This—"

He'd been partly behind me, and I didn't see him reaching until his hands took hold of my waist. He lifted me easily up off the tiled floor, which left him completely behind me and out of sight as he carried me down to the next row of shelves.

I folded my arms and put up with it. Some people enjoyed my being short way too much. Anyway, there was an extra element to this, something comforting. Emanuel was telling me that he and Elvira didn't just see me as a friend, but the kind of close friend you get silly and physical with.

My heart knotted with a sudden, unexpected pain and a vision of brown bangs. Ramona was dead, a part of my life left behind at Lake Touhou. But still, we hadn't been close. For this feeling of being loved now, I would deal with any amount of "small enough to be portable" humor.

Now Emanuel definitely sounded joking as he set me down in front of a lot more books and declared, "And these are the books that we're not sure if they're fiction."

I giggled, and confirmed for him that I got the joke. "There's a lot of them." A *lot* of them. The sections had numbered divider signs showing where they began and ended, and this one stretched all the way to the end of the library.

In the grand tone of someone sharing their favorite facts, Emanuel explained, "The ancients didn't leave guides to what they wrote that is or isn't true, and they loved stories that were sort of true. Like this one." He reached up and pulled a book out an inch to get my attention. It didn't have a cover picture, just the words "Valperga" and "Mary Shelley" on the back. "It's a fictional story, but it's a fictional story about something that there are enough other sources to be sure it happened. The ancients loved writing those. They loved writing stories set during big historical events. Last fall I snuck in here and listened to some historians from as far away as Sin Fortress get together and argue about whether there were vampires in the Golden Age."

Okay, I laughed, and pushed my hair back behind my shoulders with both hands, because it was starting to fall forward and get in the way again. "Thanks for helping me over the hump of feeling like an idiot because I was never taught much history. I'm not used to feeling stupid."

And thanks to Emanuel, I didn't feel stupid. Just like there was a lot to learn.

Emanuel squeezed my waist with the hand still there. His tone was still glowing with delight, but settled from playful down to friendly. "You're welcome, but honestly, Artifact? You seem like someone else who loves knowledge and words for their own sake, and I don't have enough people to talk to about this stuff. Even if you're starting from scratch. Joe is the smartest person in the school, but that intelligence is all driven. He doesn't enjoy learning, he's doing it because being smart is useful. Elvira is distracted a lot. Another friend who saw a library and wondered how much time she could free up to read for fun is exactly the kind of person I wanted to meet."

I twisted around and leaned my head back to smile up at him. "That makes me feel better for dragging you into trouble. Thank you."

He met my smile, but only for a moment before his eyes darted back up to the shelves. "Now, let me show you some of those vampire books."

Chapter
Twenty-Four

I was picking up a few spilled books off the floor when the loudest school bell yet drove the conversation Emanuel and I had been having out of my head. The books fell out of my stiff hands, and I had to scramble to get everything back in place.

"How long have we been here? I should get back to the tests!" I babbled frantically.

Helping me pick up and still calm, Emanuel reassured me, "That's the lunch bell, and the way you were cruising through them you'll get done before we go home. Come on!"

His hands lifted suspiciously, and I giggled and scooted a few steps out of reach, warning, "I can walk this time."

Lisa had been right. I wasn't just small, I was adorable. The things you don't find out until life dumps you into a crowd of strangers! I still wasn't at all sure how I felt about it.

We struggled through the crowds, which were now positively frenzied. I remembered where we were going this time. Classroom twelve!

We were late. We had to be late. Gasping for breath, I

squeezed out of the torrent of teenagers and into the class room. Emanuel emerged with more grace. Everyone grinned at us.

Everyone but Lisa, who scowled and pointed an accusing finger at me. "Thank goodness. You're carrying my lunch!"

I had brought my satchel with me, yes, and it did have our food in it. I pulled out the wrapped up burritos, peeked in to see which one had sugar on it, and passed that one to Lisa.

"We should have brought water," I *tsked*.

Emanuel had been just starting to sit down at his desk, but rose up again. "I see—"

Lisa reached out and put her hand over his mouth. "You've wasted enough of her time. Artifact, look out the door at the metal thing on the right."

I peeked out. The rush was over, with only a few kids sitting against the wall here and there eating. I could see clearly now the students had gone. I could see the one obstacle Lisa had directed me to. A curious thing. It was a metal box, nearly shoulder height. It had a few protrusions and a handle. One of those protrusions looked an awful lot like a faucet.

Experimentally, I pushed the handle, and water pumped out of the faucet, up into the air and arching back into a convenient drain in the center of the box. How nice! This town had a great plumbing system, and now I was even more motivated to help them preserve it. Plus, the water was refreshingly cold.

Artifact, try to remember to offer to help power the refrigeration system. Saving whoever ran this school that effort and money was the least I could do to show my gratitude.

I drank my fill, ducked back into the class room, and devoured my burrito. I ate surrounded by friends all eating their own meals of varying levels of fanciness. Even Mr. Drake had some food at his desk. It felt great.

When I finished I waved my tablet's cleaning spell over my face to make sure there weren't any embarrassing bean stains or some such, and pulled up my tests.

As I picked up my pencil, Lisa swatted it down again and scolded, "Not until the bell rings. What is wrong with you?"

"I don't think it's wrong at all," declared Lucky, bouncing in his seat.

"I like her spirit," agreed Emanuel.

Mr. Drake raised his hands and put on a responsible adult face. "No, no. Lisa is right. If you keep coming to school there will be plenty of nose-to-the-grindstone days, Artifact, but this isn't one of them."

I shook my head and told him, "No, really, it's not about responsibility or anything. I'm just a bit overloaded and getting back to words on a page would be a relief. We didn't have nearly this many kids around up at Lake Touhou."

Yuki's head shot up from where she was packing away her lunch box. She rose to her feet like she'd been pulled by a string, and she hurried over to me with a strange grace. If I didn't see her legs moving, I'd have thought she was floating. I had a lot of hair. Elvira had long hair. Yuki's hung down to her knees. She put her hands on the surface of my desk and leaned over me. This sweater was light blue, different from yesterday's, and the collar went all the way up her neck. Between her hair, the big dark glasses, and the sweater, I couldn't see much skin. What I could see was as white as chalk, without even the blue or pink of veins underneath.

Lucky crowded up on the other side of me. I patted his feline head without paying him much attention.

I couldn't gauge Yuki's expression, but her murmury, echoing voice sounded fascinated, even hopeful. "Touhou. Are the rumors true?"

Again I felt a little pinprick of grief, but with so many friends around, it faded immediately. I was much closer to the people around me than to a girl who hadn't been much more than a babysitter.

Lying to myself didn't help, but the friends part did and I moved on.

Plus, my friends were nice. Joe shook his head in warning at the sweater-wrapped girl with the long, long hair. "Dark topic, Yuki."

"I mean the ruins. The background magic," she pressed, her dark glasses still fixed on me.

"Oh, that." Cheering up immediately, I pushed myself back and straight in my chair and answered, "It's a pretty magical place, but not as much as you'd think. We do have a lot of empty ruins."

Her voices even more echoey and out of sync, Yuki whispered, "I would like to see them. Do any of the ruins have this symbol on them?"

Picking up my pencil, she drew on the back of one of my test papers. It was an odd symbol. Not complex. It reminded me of a forced nerve channel aspect in a containment formula. It was shaped like a box, but with no bottom line and an extra-long second line right under the top.

"Not that I remember," I hedged, trying to rack my brain and come up with a more certain answer.

Instead of letting me think, Yuki asked immediately, "Any gods?" Her near-whisper might drain it, but that magic-induced resonance in her voice made the question sound passionately interested.

Out in the hall, somewhere in the building, the bell rang.

Mr. Drake clapped his desk with his hand. "Alright, now you can stop talking and get to work."

"Later," Yuki promised, and drifted back to her chair.

As Yuki passed, Lisa told her, "She loves dungeon diving."

The extra-long-haired girl pressed her palms together. "Wonderful."

I finally got back to the tests, and was greeted with a pleasant surprise. The first topic on the remaining papers was aspects. The questions were all laughably easy.

I finished the last answer on the last page of the last test seconds before a bell rang, and this one must have been important, because Elvira leaped out of her chair and shouted, "Woo!"

All the kids started shuffling around, tidying up papers and putting books back on shelves.

Mr. Drake strolled up and took the pile of tests off of my desk, clumping them a couple of times on the wooden surface to make them a neat stack again. He told me with a warm smile, "Thank you, Artifact. I'll know where you need to pick up by Monday, and I hope we'll see you then."

"Monday?" I asked, surprised. They didn't want me back tomorrow?

Lisa arched her back, extending her arms and then clasping her hands behind her back with as much lazy, evil satisfaction as even Sophie could muster. "No school on Saturday and Sunday. Best mortal tradition ever."

The other kids took some books and papers with them when they bustled out of the classroom. It made sense that I didn't have any, since I hadn't been sorted yet.

Leaving Mr. Drake flipping through my tests, I followed Lisa out into the hall, and then out onto the lawn. Like the last time we'd visited, kids were scattered all over under the shady trees, and out in the playground across the road. A clump had already taken up position on the big rock. The blonde braided girl, Parsley, lounged on it like a queen on her throne.

The tall, sports leader boy from my last visit loomed suddenly over me, making me squeak. I hadn't seen him approach!

He looked happier to see me than Emanuel had, if that was possible. "You're back!"

Lucky popped up next to us and crowed, "She is!"

The tall boy leaned forward, and I froze up, for a split second afraid that he intended to pick me up and carry me over his shoulder. No, no. He just took my hand in one of his and placed the other behind my shoulder blades. It was more very, very eager guiding than pushing, so I went along with it and let myself be hurried across the street to the dirt ball court.

Elvira was already there, her hair tied in a bun. She crouched, holding the big leather-covered ball in both hands, aiming it at the backboard on the pole at the far end of the court.

I felt a touch of relief at seeing that board. It was back up already! Maybe it got knocked off often and I hadn't hit it as hard as I thought.

Her eyes fixed on the board, Elvira surged upwards, pushed her hands forward, and fired the hidden spells inside the ball. It shot through the air across the court, flew precisely through the hoops, hit the board itself in the center of its bullseye, and bounced back out. Elvira took off, sprinting over the packed dirt, leaped up, and grabbed the ball out of the air. She landed with her tightly sandaled feet skidding and kicking up dust as she swiveled to face us.

Kids around the yard applauded.

Elvira trotted back to us, and tossed the ball to the older boy. He held it out to me. Like he was talking to an easily spooked kitten, he urged me gently, "Give it a try. Just go a little easier than yesterday."

He left me alone to do it. Other kids backed up to give me room. I stood on the hard, dusty, flat earth, among the distant shouts of younger kids having fun, looking down the gold-brown barren rectangle surrounded by dark green grass. I aimed the ball at the board on the pole, and at the painted bullseye behind the layered wooden hoops.

I activated the spell.

My breath puffed out from the rush of effort. The ball went *whoomp!* It rocketed away like a blur, got nowhere near the goal, and instead flew right off the end of the court and kept going. And going. And going.

Elvira grinned and gave me a wink as if we'd planned this.

The head sports boy took it well. He told two of the nearby kids, "You go get the ball. You go get the spares. We'll need them."

Then he turned back to me, his arms wide and his grin completely encouraging. "Nothing that practice can't fix. Nobody but Elvira was born with good aim."

Elvira stomped on foot, standing up straight and with her chin up, perhaps honestly offended. Her cream colored dress whirled around her legs. Glaring, she told the older boy, "I worked hard and I work hard for this."

Wherever that argument was going, it didn't have a chance. Yuki arrived. Her hand closed on my bicep, and on this warm, sunny day her skin against mine was shockingly cold. She told the sports boy, "I saw her first," and then Elvira, "Artifact is into dungeon diving."

Elvira leaped two feet in the air, swinging her fist above her, and landed giving Yuki a high five. "I knew it! I didn't want to speak for Artifact, but I knew it!"

Elvira gave me another of those conspiratorial winks where

I didn't know what I was conspiring with. Then she lunged forward and actually did scoop me up in her arms. I saw Yuki stick her tongue out at the sports boy before Elvira carried me past her, whisking me away back to the big rock. She laughed the whole time, as merrily as if we were sharing a joke.

Trotting up the last few steps, Elvira sat me on the flat top of the rock as regally as if I were a treasure on display. Taking a step back, she spread her hands and said, "Everyone, welcome the newest member of the East Goblita Wastes Exploration Society. Assuming you are interested, Artifact?"

Chapter
Twenty-Five

On the other side of the boulder, Emanuel added, "Despite the show she puts on, you do get to say no."

Elvira clapped her hands together and nodded. "You do. Rico needs to be reminded that people have interests other than sports occasionally, that's all."

"I'm interested!" I promised the top-heavy dark-skinned girl, her brother, and everyone else gathered around.

Lisa stepped up to the rock, arms folded and tail raised like a scorpion's. "And I'm not letting my cousin with no sense of self-preservation do anything dangerous without me."

A few feet away, Parsley, the other person sitting on the rock itself, clapped her hands in triumph. Lucky crowded up in front of me, glasses magnifying his dark eyes until they looked huge and soulful. "You won't regret this!" he gushed.

I scratched him under his chin. His eyes slunk closed in bliss.

Parsley clapped her hands again. "First order of business. Everyone noticed the earthmover attack last night, right?"

"Yes!" shouted Elvira gleefully. She unfastened her hair bun with savage glee, shaking the long black locks out again.

Emanuel, leaning his elbows on the speckled grey and white surface of the irregularly faceted boulder, remarked dryly, "She's been waiting to talk about it all day."

Lucky raised his hand and bounced on the balls of his feet, while his tail curled sharply left and right behind him. "I did!"

Yuki leaned her hip up against the rock. She was a vaguely feminine, vaguely pudgy shape masked by her enormous sweater, enormous hair, and enormous glasses. Her hands still gripped the rock surface with more excitement than anyone. "My detectors said it came from the Wastes. I got a soul forge jingle, but just one. Inconclusive."

Joe was sitting on the grass, his back leaning against the rock, scribbling on papers and not part of the conversation. I still saw one of his triangular ears cock backwards to listen.

Smiling, but still crisp and all business, Parsley pulled her knees up under her long, charcoal-grey skirt and said, "Then confirming monster presence is our top priority."

Me, I felt like an idiot. I had successfully avoided that sensation all morning, but now it hit hard, because I of all people should have recognized that vibration last night. "I thought it was thunder."

Lisa sneered, and told us all, "*I* actually value my sleep."

Nobody laughed at me or frowned at Lisa. Parsley's attention was all on Yuki. "Any kind of fix on location?"

"No. Just east," murmured the echoey girl.

Parsley looked around at the rest of us, face stiff and official. "All in favor of mounting an expedition tomorrow?"

Every hand went up except mine, Lisa's, and Joe's. Even a few kids I didn't realize were doing more than just standing around raised their hands.

Maybe I looked confused. Parsley relaxed a bit, giving me a cheerful smile as she explained, "What our club does is go on expeditions into the ruins of the city that used to be next to Goblita. We make maps and take notes of what civilizations are represented, since the adventurers who clean the place out aren't big on learning, just treasure."

Emanuel raised a black eyebrow on a brown face and flashed white teeth at me. His words drawled with amusement. "We bring back a lot of books. They don't take the books for some reason."

Parsley rolled her eyes so hard that her head lolled to one side. Scowling in deep disgust, she said, "We need a better next generation of adventurers, which is why we're here."

The blonde turned her proud smile back to me. "Normally that's easygoing and we only have to worry about rubble, that sort of thing. When there's a new dungeon, though, we try to find it and report its location to the authorities, so they can make sure it's cleaned out by a competent and responsible team."

"And if it has monsters, we report that, and type of monsters," added Elvira with unholy relish.

I leaned back on one hand on the pleasantly cool rock surface, looking around at the excited faces. Mine probably matched their expression. "Does this happen a lot?"

Elvira's head bobbed from side to side in energetic non-committal emotion. "About once a year, but we got lucky last year. Four dungeons, one with a soul forge."

Parsley scowled, her mouth pursed like she'd bitten the mother of all lemons. "Which was destroyed by an incompetent recovery team. One of them tried to go lich. Franklin is in town. She's a legend. Even the College approves of her. She'll make sure whoever clears this dungeon is professional about it."

Rubbing her right arm with her left hand, Elvira grumbled, "Wish it could be us."

"Not yet. Your day will come, sis," promised Emanuel, sidling around the rock and putting an arm around her waist to give her a hug.

Parsley's gaze swiveled back to me. "So the question is, do you want in on the expedition?"

I was still reeling from the suddenness of all this, but, "I'd love to."

Lisa's shoulders slumped, and she let out a gurgly groan. "Of course."

Parsley's approving smile lingered on me for only a second before she turned regally solemn, looking out over all the assembled kids. Her tone just as sober, she said, "There may be monsters, so only the core, necessary group who can defend themselves go on this one. I wish that included me, but it doesn't. Elvira, Emanuel, you two of course. Yuki, and Artifact and Lisa."

I jolted up an inch in surprise. "Wait. Me? I'd love to, but I can't defend myself! My soul forge is shut down for the weekend. I can't even make a monster or doll to protect me."

No one looked convinced, and Parsley didn't look even slightly surprised. She did give me a probing look, and asked, "You know a lot about monsters, don't you?"

I admitted, "Everything. I'm a prodigy. That doesn't mean I can fight or control them without resources I don't have available." The pendant hanging around my neck was nothing but a piece of cheap quartz to monsters not connected to my soul forge.

Parsley nodded in satisfaction. "You can gather information others can't, and I've seen Lisa fight."

She had? I shot a curious glance at my cousin, whose resentful frown betrayed nothing.

Lucky jumped up and down, pleading, "I can gather information. Please let me come!"

"You know you can't, Lucky," Parsley told him with the wistful gentleness of someone who wished she wasn't in charge so she could beg, too.

Me, I stared at my hand, at the end of my outstretched arm. The hand that had been scratching Lucky's chin until he bounced away from my touch. I'd forgotten I was doing it. Where... "What's going on? Why was I petting you? I didn't intend to!"

And every girl around the rock burst out laughing.

Even businesslike and authoritative Parsley let out a quick, wry chuckle. "The Lucky Curse claims another victim."

Lucky pulled his hands behind him, his ginger-striped cat face pulled into a sad, big-eyed, apologetic frown. "I'm sorry. I can't control it."

Parsley wagged a finger at him. "Liar. You love it and indulge it to the limit." To me she explained, "Lucky has an inherited magical power that makes people want to pet him. You get used to it."

That shocked me. I wanted to say that for a bioengineer to give someone powers like that was wildly unethical. Forget the moral considerations of psychology magic. You didn't mess with what humans were inside, especially not to just give them extra abilities. You risked making them not human anymore in serious, not-just-a-technicality ways.

There was no point in saying it. Everyone must know already, and whoever did it was probably generations dead. It still bothered me much more than finding out I'd been petting the cat boy without realizing it.

The awkward topic was broken by Elvira declaring, "And you can so defend yourself, Artifact. Better than I can, I bet. Here."

Where she kept it in her loose gown I hadn't a clue, but Elvira was now holding a thick wooden rod a little longer than my forearm. She tossed it to me, and I caught it in both hands without making a complete fool of myself.

There was nothing complicated about the stick. It was made of the same kind of rough but cut straight wood you'd use for a broomstick. As thick around as three of my fingers, maybe. Its only special feature was all the dots and dashes and squiggles and little geometric shapes of spell script covering one side of it from top to bottom.

My knowledge of spell script and spontaneous spellcasting in general was feeble, but this sure looked like some kind of directed destruction spell. Which I'd have guessed even if I couldn't read any of those symbols at all, since Elvira had given it to me.

Bouncing from side to side, Elvira bragged, "Emanuel made it. It's one of the oldest adventuring spells. It's called Magic Missile. Nobody knows why."

Her brother shook his head, his much shorter black hair flying from side to side. With almost acid emphasis, he denied, "It's not. It's a crude, amateur attempt to reproduce the spell. The real thing has been refined for generations and is way better, but the only way I know to get a copy of the formula is the library at the Goblita branch of the College, and they'd never let a fisherman's son wander in to look at destruction spells. The stick won't last long, either."

It was Elvira's turn to put her arms around Emanuel's shoulders and give him a fierce, loving squeeze. "It'll last long enough, and it's plenty for defense against a wandering monster. I think it's brilliant. How many kids your age could do that? You do miracles for me. If anybody's doing a bad job, it's me. If I could quick cast the spell, I wouldn't need your help."

Pushing her arms off, Emanuel folded his and leaned back to give her the weird scolding look when you're mad at someone for not being nice to themselves. "You just learned it. Of course you can't quick cast it."

She took a step away, giving her enough room to raise a forearm and flap a hand around in a circle. Exasperated, she answered, "I can't quick cast anything. I'll be fine, I can get hard copies like this, but it's the thing I just... can't do."

Emanuel wasn't having any. He put his fists on his hips and argued, "Yes, you can. You quick cast Bye, Felicia all the time."

His sister held up her wrist, the sleeve of her dress falling back to her elbow to show off her shiny metal bracelet, a thin chain holding a not much wider plate cramped with engraved script. She told Emanuel sharply, "I activate the spell you made."

Emanuel's face pinched in shock, squeezed more on one side than the other. He even tilted his head an inch to the side, asking, "Have you believed that all this time? I can't fit a kinetic spell like that on a bracelet now. I sure couldn't when I was twelve."

Fired up and determined, head bobbing from side to side, Elvira snarked, "Yes, I've—" Her deeply tanned face went blank as her thoughts hit a wall of logic. Suddenly confused, she asked, "Wait, if it doesn't cast the spell, what does it do?"

Emanuel spread his hands, explaining slowly with carefully held back frustration, "It's a trigger. That's it. I made it when I saw you were only having to cast half the spell to throw things. I knew you could cast the whole spell by reflex if you had a script to get you started, and I was right."

Elvira stared at him. And stared some more. Her mouth

dropped open. She stuck one hand on her hip and flapped the other as she said, "You mean it. I mean you're right, duh, it's obvious, but I never put it together."

Leaning towards Elvira rather than away again, Emanuel lowered his voice to firmly affectionate and encouraging, while looking straight into her eyes. "You just need access to real combat spells and a chance to practice. You're going to be a force of nature, a one woman army someday, sister mine."

They grabbed each other, the startlingly similar siblings squeezing with loving appreciation of each other. They were so physical with each other. Maybe they had begun manhandling me because they thought of me as such a close friend I was almost family. It was a nice thought.

Then the hug let go, and Elvira whirled around to face me, ready to pass on the support. "As for you, just activate that. But don't point it at anyone."

Yeah, I definitely was not going to do that. I pointed the stick up at the pretty blue Goblita sky and ran my other thumb up the spell to activate it.

BOOM!

Wind hit me like a wall, knocking me back off my feet to land in Lisa's arms. That same wind mashed the grass flat and shoving all the nearby kids backwards.

The sound had been like thunder. Every kid on both sides of the road was staring at us now, as were adults at the windows of the school and two looking out the front door.

And we'd been behind the blast, not its target.

Elvira was holding onto Emanuel, who had fallen over backwards like me. Their hair was a disheveled mess, with Elvira's hanging all over her brother. Her shocked gawk rallied quickly into a big, proud grin. "Now imagine what that would do to a monster, Miss Defenseless."

Chapter
Twenty-Six

I stepped out the work door the next morning into fog.

Way too early the next morning. Maybe Lisa was trying to send me a message about what going to school every day would be like.

If so, it wasn't working. The Goblita streets hazed with gentle white, everything clear up close but turning into a cloudy murk several blocks away, it was a beautiful sight worth getting up to see. The slightly chilly air refreshed me, giving me more energy by the second.

Glancing back at both the front doors of my house, I didn't see a sign hung on either of them. That surprised me a little. Absolutely no one had interrupted us the whole rest of the day after getting home yesterday, and I had thought for sure Lisa must have done something to ensure it.

The main part of the house bulked up in three stories of an irregular box with lots of curtained windows. It made me think of a wooden castle all scrunched down so that none of the towers and parapets and stuff could get out, only make the walls bulge in curves and rectangles.

Lisa, looking grumbly and resentful this morning, extended her arm and pointed a clawed finger towards the ocean. "That way."

I shifted my satchel up more securely onto my shoulder. It contained a little analyzing gear I doubted I'd need, and more wrapped up meals. We were likely to be making a full day trip, after all.

She might have been putting on a grumpy face at home, but now that we were out on the street Lisa strutted like she owned it, head high, horns sweeping backwards, smirking and placing her hooves in front of each other with sultry demonic grace. It was a show for nobody. Between the early hour and the fog, I couldn't see any other people around.

Oh, wait. There was someone to see. Ahead of us, a dark shape quickly became the big furry shape of Joe, leaning against the weird signpost at the intersection with the One-And-One. He watched us approach with his welcoming, interested smile.

The mist wasn't really that thick, but it created an intimate feeling, and walking up to Joe reminded me vividly of just how big he was. So big, and so friendly. It felt weird and awkward to have that intense smile directed at me. The wolf boy face didn't help. Sure, he was as human as me, but I hadn't grown up around a lot of furries. That smile on that face coming from up above me made me feel like a mouse walking into a trap. It also didn't help that I knew the smile, the interest, was all completely honest.

I stopped walking because it was that or run into him, and stood there with no idea what to say.

Fortunately, I had an immediate opportunity to completely stop thinking about that when a cart pulled by Herman, with Yuki driving, pulled up to a stop on the road. Emanuel and Elvira must have been waiting just out of sight, because they drifted out of the fog to meet it.

Joe hadn't spoken yet either, but now he leaned down a bit, put his big not-actually-at-all-pawlike hand in my hair, and gave it an affectionate ruffle. "Good morning, little prodigy."

Lisa struck a pose with her fists on her hips, slightly turned away from Joe, one hoof tucked back, and stuck her tongue out at him insolently. Her petulance was utterly unconvincing. They both radiated amusement.

Elvira hopped up into the driver's seat of the cart. Em vaulted lightly into the back, then took Yuki's hands, or at least the ends of her sweater arms, and helped her climb back with him. Once solidly on the cart bed, she knelt down and opened up a box I couldn't see much of.

Instead of picking up Herman's reins, Elvira twisted around in the seat, leaning against the corner of the cart to flash a huge grin in our direction. No, a leer, accompanied by an equally sly call-out. "What an amazing coincidence meeting you here, Joe."

Joe rose to the challenge, and rose to it with joy. The smile he'd been giving me turned like a lighthouse's glare to Elvira. It couldn't get more eager, but now it added a touch of wickedness as he told her, "I'm always up at this hour, Elvira. You know that."

Boy, Elvira could smirk. She even propped her elbows on the rim of the cart and cupped her chin in her hands. "And you hang out at this intersection of the One-And-One? Is there something to buy or sell here that I didn't notice?"

Joe put a hand to his chest, where the mist left dew all over his fur. "Our school's finest talents were all going to be here before going off on an adventure. How could I resist seeing you off?"

What was going on in this conversation? Did I want to know? Emanuel was sure grinning a lot. Yuki was focused on her box. Next to me Lisa was watching the two with a sneer, but that could mean she was amused as easily as upset.

Elvira leaned forward a little more, her smile turning so demonically lazy my eyes kept expecting to see a twitching tail. "If you really wanted to see our talents on display, you could come with us. I won't tell Parsley."

"And I won't tell our parents," added Emanuel dryly.

In a rustle of loose skirts, Elvira slipped her leg over the edge of the cart and kicked Emanuel in the shoulder.

Joe rubbed his chin, which thanks to that elongated snout took a lot of rubbing, but he had a lot of hand to do it with. "Are we going to be looting any treasures?"

Yuki answered this one. "No." She sounded disappointed.

Elvira jerked her leg back into place to resume the leaning far forward and smiling slyly at Joe. "Afraid not, tall, grey, and cupiditous."

Joe watched her with his smile turned more sly and lazy to match Elvira's, and his tail waggled slowly behind him, ending each sweep in a sharp jerk. Drawling and honeyed, he declared, "Then I'll wait until you get back to see your talents."

This was now definitely flirting, so I rooted around between the cloth-wrapped food packages in my bag, checking which pieces of equipment I'd brought. Yes, that was a much less awkward thing to pay attention to.

Elvira's loud, wicked peal of laughter broke through my attempt to not listen. She held out her arm towards me, and, well, there wasn't anything else to do but walk over and place my hand in hers. She grabbed and pulled, hauling me up onto the driver's seat next to her. Keeping one arm hooked around my waist, she patted Herman's leather-covered clay butt with her other hand. When he plodded obediently forward, she waved back at Joe and called, "Have fun eating our soggy dust, and think about everything you could have had instead!"

Emanuel started laughing. Yuki, head bent forward, grinned behind her broken veil of black hair. Lisa hopped up into cart, and her sneer still didn't tell me what she actually felt, but she sprawled out on the boards like it was a couch.

Joe was immediately swallowed by the mist. I didn't know if he was close enough to hear us, but Yuki made no attempt to keep her voice down as she said, "We would never have gotten any work done if Joe came along anyway."

Everyone but Yuki and I snorted laughter, even Lisa. Yuki didn't laugh, but she did grin as wickedly as Lisa or Elvira ever could.

Me, I tried to avoid the whole embarrassing conversation by staring at the doll horse in front of me. Was I really the only person here who knew that dolls don't do this? Yes, dolls were expert level bioengineering, but "everything needs a power source" was such a basic, obvious rule.

Emanuel hopped over the barrier between the cart and the driver's seat, scrunching up close and squeezing me between him and Elvira, hip to hip to hip.

Looking past me, he said, "And you watch the road, sis. We don't want to go off the edge in this mist."

"Especially when we get to the seaside cliffs," echoed Yuki behind us.

Elvira, holding limp reins in one hand, flapped the other at her detractors and waggled her head from side to side. "It will have cleared before then. It's only this bad now because you're here."

I took a deep breath, inhaling through my nose the damp sea air, with its hints of seaweed and fish and yet smelling so clean. Letting that out again, I sighed, "I like it."

Elvira and Emanuel leaned in closer, squeezing their shoulders to mine in an armless hug.

Straightening back up, Elvira said, "It's nice to get you out of that gloomy workshop."

I couldn't see Yuki behind me now, but I heard her say, "It is. Everyone else is into dungeons for the action or the treasure. Now I finally have someone interested in soul forges, in creation and transformation and the cultures earthmovers invent."

Emanuel pouted back at her, stung. "I'm interested. There's nothing available to learn about bioengineering!"

Still grinning lopsidedly, Elvira waved a pointed finger between us. "And while you two drag information out of her, we can drag a real life into her."

"Just keep Rico's hands off of her," hissed Yuki.

Elvira shrugged. Cocking her head to look at me sideways, she said, "That's not up to me. How do you feel about sports, Artifact?"

"Um...," was the only answer I had.

Brother and sister squeezed up against me in one of those almost-hugs again, and Elvira declared, "Exactly. You'll figure out what you want, and we'll make sure you get it."

Emanuel leaned his head closer over mine, and added, "Then if you change your mind later, we'll make sure you get that."

From back in the cart, Lisa groused, "Good. Someone to take some of the work off my shoulders."

Lisa might be playing extra grumpy today, but I read the real message there. She would help, too.

I didn't know what to say to all this, so I didn't say anything.

The mist cleared, and I didn't need to say anything, because I could see the sea.

We were high up now, at the top of a cliff that ran down to the beach, and stretching on and on to our right was the perfect blue of the ocean. I didn't know why, but just looking at it filled me with relief so intense I could almost cry.

My meditation was eventually broken by a particularly nasty pothole bouncing me a foot in the air out of my wooden seat.

Elvira hooked an arm around me, holding me steady as she said, "Sorry. The caravans try to maintain the One-And-One, but around the Waste they don't do a very good job."

Em hopped back into the bed of the cart, and pulled out a bag I hadn't noticed when he arrived. There were actually half a dozen bags back there, and even a couple of shovels and a pickaxe. It made sense. To begin with, Lisa and I weren't the only people who would need to eat.

Now that I had the room to look around behind me, I could see that Yuki was still messing with her box, and I was even close enough to get a peek inside. It was filled with racks of detecting equipment mixed with rolled-up paper, some of it blank. Most of the devices were unfamiliar to me, but some I could figure out at a glance. The little water filled box with the multi-colored, many-sided block floating in it would detect major aspect imbalances. That was an odd thing to detect, since it wasn't the kind of thing I associated with dungeons. On the other hand, if you got a dungeon with a lava moat or shadow fountain or something easily crazy, you would want to know *before* your leg got burned off.

The glass tube with soul fragments embedded in metal caps at either end… hmmm. Subtle purple sparks flickered in the gas inside it. That would be a monster detector, I bet. Imprecise and short range. Reaching back, I ran the tip of my right index finger over the glass. Was there a slight increase in glitter? Shifting position, I ran my left index finger over the glass, and this time there was definitely a brighter trail of following sparkles inside the tube.

Joy.

Yuki looked up from her box at the pendant hanging from my neck, then up some more at Elvira. Breathily, the only way she could, she asked, "Are we getting you in a lot of trouble?"

Elvira rolled her eyes, and smirked with a particularly whimsical twist of her lips. "Probably, and I'm grateful you all give me reasons to."

"And you too, Emanuel," Yuki added, peeking up at him past her hair. Probably peeking. She tilted her face up a little, but I couldn't see anything past those big, dark glasses.

Emanuel had a stylus he'd gotten out of the bag, and was busy scratching spell code into the wooden bed of the cart. Without taking his eyes off it, he answered cheerfully, "Same as Elvira. Besides, it's not like I can bring you out fishing. Speaking of which, how's your health? How's Lizzie?"

"Fine. Lizzie's in a bad mood from the damp." Yuki's smile grew, soft and sweet and affectionate, talking about whoever Lizzie was.

We hit another bad pothole, and the wooden boards bounced painfully under our butts, cutting off conversation.

It resumed by Emanuel saying, "Okay, time to give this a go."

He swept his hand over the spell he'd written out. Golden light trailed after, lighting up the spell symbols.

Suddenly, this was the smoothest cart ride I'd ever been on. It was like sitting in a chair.

"Oh, Emanuel, this is heaven," Elvira hissed. It was almost a moan.

I sighed in relief, which might also have sounded like a moan.

"Oh, yeah. This one is genius, Emanuel," whispered Yuki.

Emanuel warned, "Don't get excited. If I'm right—"

The cart started to jostle again, cutting him off.

Sliding back into a sitting position on the cart bed, Emanuel said, "That's what I thought. It needs frequent reactivating. It uses up a lot of power. It's not ready for regular use. Anyway, it's also not new. The caravans have something like it. I just thought coming up with one myself would be a good learning exercise, and helpful."

Twisting around to face backwards, Elvira ruffled Emanuel's short, glossy black hair. "My hard-working brother. You and he are a lot alike, Artifact."

At the back of the cart, Lisa stuck out her tongue and mimed gagging.

"Don't miss the turn," murmured Yuki.

There was indeed a turn. The hills on the left side of the road opened up for ramps to curve off of the One-And-One, twisting around like an elaborate and silly calligraphy version of an intersection. The new road led through that gap in the hills, into the remains of a devastated town.

Elvira turned the cart into it, and as the wheels skipped over the particularly jagged spot of broken concrete where one road became another, Emanuel gave another hand sweep over his spell, making the ride smooth just for those thirty seconds when it would have been at its worst.

This process didn't require any expert driving, so Elvira was free to point down the road the way we'd been going and tell me cheerfully, "The crypts are down there," and then everyone, "I want to take Artifact there sometime."

"That would be fun," agreed Emanuel with an eager nod.

"Time to get serious. Stop here," murmured Yuki.

Elvira gave a little tug on the reins, and Herman stopped. Unlike all the banter, this had felt like an order casually given and instantly obeyed. Yuki was in charge of this adventuring party, I guess.

I slid off the drivers' seat onto a clump of grass, and took a good look around.

Chapter
Twenty-Seven

The first thing that was clear was that the hills had mostly been an illusion. There had been a whole city right here, with maybe ten, twenty feet of rock that sloped gently and blended into the ground on this side hiding the view.

Now the patchwork of the East Goblita Wastes was mostly visible in front of me. It had streets. We were on a street, which stretched North towards the next set of real hills, and side streets I could see. It had buildings. Barely. To my left looking in was an irregular warren of long-collapsed, dome-shaped clay buildings. To my right, there weren't so much walls as square shaped lines of heaped stone blocks marking where buildings used to be.

Yuki saw me staring, and pointed at them, murmuring, "Original golden age buildings. Long since mined out for steel."

I looked past the place where the golden age buildings were. Way, way down the street towards the hills I made out the spires of a half-collapsed cathedral that must have been huge. Much nearer, a boxy, turreted stone building sat with a big chunk bitten out of the side, in which stood a tower like the one I'd seen out on an island at Lake Touhou, but smaller. Past it reared a triangular, black rock hill that was obviously unnatural with a mine shaft set into the base and leading down.

"This... this is crazy," I said, stunned.

Even Lake Touhou wasn't this riddled with dungeons. Not anywhere near.

They'd said once a year, most years, but sometimes more. That would mean hundreds of dungeons in an area the size of a small city.

I pulled my signal detector out of my satchel, unhooked my ID pendant from its necklace chain and slapped it into the wheel. Nothing stood out obviously on the circle of colorful crystal shards set into the rim. I hadn't been expecting it to.

Pulling out my stakes, I yanked a couple of glass clumps out of the dirt and planted the carved wooden posts instead. The only thing universal about the chaos of earthmover-provided architecture in the Wastes was the grass and little trees growing around and through it.

The gauge on the first stake lay limp. On the other, colors slowly coalesced in spots on the regularly marked strip of metal running up the side. I pulled out a fistful of tags and stuck them to the spots.

At first glance, none of this looked weird enough to explain anything, but powerful magic wasn't always simple.

As I leaned over the stake applying more stickers, I asked Yuki next to me, "Can I have a pencil and some of your papers?"

When she didn't instantly answer, I looked up at her. I looked around at all my friends, because they were all standing around watching me with smiles on their faces. I hadn't bothered to give them a good look in the fog. Not that any of them looked much different than usual, but there were little signs they'd prepared for this to be physical. Yuki had on long pants instead of a skirt, and a double layer of oversized knit sweaters, with collars climbing up her neck to her chin and sleeves that engulfed her hands. Emanuel wore a very loose short shirt and tight knee-length breeches, pretty normal for him, the same as Elvira's loose-skirted, knee-length dress, but both of them and Yuki wore boots that went way up their shins instead of regular shoes or sandals. Even Lisa was wearing pants and a shirt, although her shirt wasn't much more than a tight tube with a couple of strings pretending to be shoulder straps, and the striped grey-and-darker-grey pants gleamed and fit like silk stitched onto her. Both pieces were so shiny I wondered if she'd ever worn them before. She liked those short skirts. She didn't need any kind of shoes, but multiple bracelets dangled around her wrists today, except the one she'd allowed to slip low enough that she held one side palmed in her fist and the other metal edge stretched over her fingers.

Lisa's smile turned into a sneer when she saw me look up. Everybody else kept watching me like I was their favorite kitten doing a trick.

Whatever her expression, Yuki showed she took me seriously by holding out a big piece of paper. "Will this help?"

It was a map. The coastline had been drawn out, and the One-And-One. Goblita's boundaries were shown on the west side. It ran right up to the edge of the Wastes. We'd taken the road to go right to the center. Otherwise, the map was a litter of little symbols making different types of dungeons.

I stared at it for a few more seconds, tempted, but... "Not at the moment. Can I get a copy to keep? Maybe I can work out a plan after I analyze these results at home."

"What are you trying to do?" asked Elvira, and she also sounded serious and sincerely interested. Maybe this happened to everyone, and the real problem was that I wasn't used to having so many friends.

"She is trying to find out why the Waste draws so many earthmovers," Yuki answered for me. Yes, she really had been paying attention!

I tapped the first stick with the flat gauge. "I'm not seeing a geodifferential. Not even ripples. Earthmovers don't just attack anywhere. They have to be drawn to something. Lake Touhou is a strong natural magic area. These readings look totally normal."

Lake Touhou's magical background was one of the big reasons I was magically deaf, or at least deaf compared to what you'd expect from someone as powerful as me. Even that field didn't draw earthmovers one tenth as much as this place. Of course, it was changes in magical level that were the big draw, not the static level. I wasn't detecting anything here that could spike and cause a differential.

Elvira sidled over to her brother and nudged him with her elbow. "Why don't we find something to climb up to get a good look around, and leave the magic geeks to bond?"

Emanuel gave her a wounded glare. "We are the magic geeks!" It dissolved instantly into a huge grin, and he jerked his head down the street. "I'll go see if the stairs in the tower are still up."

Lisa leaned against the cart, arms folded, and gave Elvira a grumpy nod. "I'm not leaving Artifact's side. She makes you look timid and safety-focused."

Now, that was just unfair. I performed bioengineering following all the recommended and even suggested safety procedures. The only thing I'd even touched my soul forge to do since its sigil broke was moving the ID pendant in and out of its charging slot!

Before I had marshaled my objections into words, Emanuel told Lisa over my head, "I have juicy gossip if you come with me."

"… how juicy?" Lisa asked cautiously.

I didn't look at either of their expressions. Yuki had passed me the paper and pencils I wanted, and I was busy copying down geolevel notes. The amount of soul fragment dust in this soil was only barely over nonexistent, for example, as I would expect from earth left behind by an earthmover.

Emanuel coughed, the signal of significant secrets kind of cough.

Sullenly, Lisa said, "Alright, but I'm watching her from the windows."

They left. I kept writing.

Yuki crouched next to me, reading my notes as I made them, although they probably didn't make sense to her. I was already trying to figure out what I could do with this information. The obvious would be to draw it out on a Rozen Diagram and compare that to diagrams of other magically significant locations. I was pretty sure I'd seen a copy of that book on Uncle Leonard's shelves, and there had to be one in the College library if not.

When we couldn't hear any footsteps at all, Yuki said, "I think it's a god."

I opened my mouth to say that we would know if it was a god, but... would we? I thought out loud, "A god in hiding or imprisoned that peeks out occasionally might create an earthmover-drawing geodifferential. I don't know enough about them. I don't think anyone does."

I kept scribbling. I wanted this chart to be complete. The difference between .1 and .4 might be huge when I got to comparing ratios.

Still, I wasn't totally focused on the post or on my writing now. I kept watch on Yuki's face sidelong. She wore her glasses so close to her face that I couldn't peek around the edges and see even her eyebrows, but the rest of her frowning expression looked troubled. I was getting concerned.

Her head moved enough that I could guess she was staring at the pendant I'd hooked back around my neck. She asked, "Is that what I think it is?"

I put the paper and pencil down. The pendant was still slotted into the detector, so I unhooked them both and held them in front of us. "My soul forge's ID pendant. This is a signal detector. The pendant's strong signal reacts to the strongest signature in any direction, which lights up the reactive prisms around it."

Yuki leaned in a little closer to peer at the colorful ring of tiny crystals. She whispered, "You can use that to find other soul forges?"

Finally, someone who knew something about bioengineering, even if only a little! I leaped eagerly into explaining, "That's the idea. It doesn't work all that well. If my soul forge wasn't sealed it would show up as a bright dot the same color as the pendant about here." I tapped the ring in the direction of Goblita, and specifically my house. "We're only... five miles away, I think? It would be easy to read. There is no other clear signal, so if there's a wild forge it's a weak one. I mean, by forge standards. The smallest soul forge is as much power as a thousand human soul fragments."

Yuki pouted. "Awwwwwwww." The perkiness of her disappointment clashed with her ghostly appearance and quiet, echoey voice.

I assured her, "We're not out of luck—woah." I'd cut my own encouragement off because for about half a second the colors on the detector wheel all spun around in a circle. Then they were back to normal, like nothing had happened.

"Ooooooooh." Yuki leaned even closer, so close I could feel cold radiating out of her cheeks. It was like standing next to the box containing our house's ice elemental.

Me, I just stared. "I've never seen that before. I have no idea what it means." My mind tried to race, and got nowhere fast. "I don't even have a guess."

Yuki did. She jumped an inch like she'd been stuck, whispered, "Wait, let me check!" and scrambled over to her own box of detection equipment. Pulling out what looked like a thumb-sized glass tube filled with ice, she gave it a shake, peered close, and declared, "It's a breach!"

The word "breach" echoed over and over, lingering well after she'd actually said it.

My mouth flapped until I found my voice and squeaked, "It's a what!?"

Yuki held her hands out, palms forward under the camouflaging lumps of orange knitted wool, signaling me to relax. "Calm down. We get pinprick breaches around here all the time. It's why I think there's a god hidden in the Waste. It's why…"

She trailed off, paused, took a deep breath, and let it out in a sigh. The sigh echoed around us like the rustle of blown leaves.

Shoulders slumping, Yuki murmured, "They left us alone so I could say this in private. Emanuel and Elvira want us to be close friends. If we're dungeon hunting together I suppose I have to tell you anyway."

I raised my eyebrows curiously. What was left of them after yesterday's magical over-cleansing, anyway. "This has something to do with your bioengineering transformation, doesn't it? Who did that?" I hadn't wanted to say anything, but the more I saw the more I wasn't sure I even could alter someone like this, even if I was willing to do something so wildly, insanely unethical. Although the idea was intriguing, like making a giant monster using a soul forge's full power or finding a way to turn myself into a self-controlled lich. One of those things that needed to stay crazy thought experiments.

Yuki upended that train of thought by correcting me. "It's not a transformation."

"You're extra-dimensional!?" I squealed. Oops. Had that been loud enough to carry? It was crazy, but it made so much sense at the same time. It would explain her interest in breaches. Was Yuki a demon? From somewhere else? It's not like Hell was the only dimension that human-ish people escaped from to Earth…

Maybe Yuki's powers included reading my mind, because her smile turned so, so very amused. "No, not that. My great grandmother was adapted."

"I don't know that term," I said, and it was a really, really weird thing to say.

Yuki lowered her face again, her smile tightening into something wry, maybe a touch bitter. I couldn't identify emotions good or bad in her quiet, resonant voice. "She was on a mountain in Nihon in the winter. She got caught in a blizzard, followed some wooden gates shaped like this—" She drew that same three-sided box symbol, which could be a kind of gateway arch, sure. "—to a little shrine. It was a very high-magic area. She fell asleep, and instead of dying, woke up not human anymore. A creature of cold. She was still able to get married and have children, as was my grandmother and my mother, but only one girl who was exactly the same."

"Um. I never knew that could happen. It makes sense," I stammered, trying to file this new information away. This wasn't technically bioengineering, which is why I hadn't known about it, and no one ever knew everything about magic anyway. It really did make sense. Humans were magical, magic-reactive animals after all.

Yuki shrugged a little, her shoulders blobs rolling against other blobs under the heavy sweaters. "That's all I know. My mother hated it. She crossed the ocean to get away from this legacy. I think she was wrong. I want to know who I am, what I am. There must be more of us somewhere, even if it's in another world. I'm sure a god was involved. The shrine might have been a dungeon. Even if it wasn't, earthmovers repeat landmarks like that. I know there are clues out there, if I can just find them. There will be a way to find my people."

Despite her inability to speak above a hush, passion grew in Yuki's story with every word. I reached out and lay my hand on the cool knit covering one of hers, and promised, "I'll help you if I can."

She took hold of my hand and squeezed. Even through two thick layers of knitted wool, I felt the cold of the fingers underneath.

Then she giggled, her small, full-lipped mouth on her plump-cheeked face turning in a grin. She whispered, "For someone obsessed with this, it's weird how I hate telling people I'm not human. Emanuel and Elvira are good judges of character and it's obvious how they feel about you."

At that appropriate moment, Emanuel yelled something from the top of the tower a couple of broken blocks down. I couldn't make out any words, but it sounded like a call for attention.

Elvira apparently understood, because from the other direction and not quite as far I heard her shout, "Here?"

Emanuel yelled again.

Yuki and I stood up and put our papers and equipment away, and a few seconds later Lisa came bounding out of the tower's ground floor doorway. She not only ran with incredible demon speed, she bounced off of and balanced on the uneven rocks making up the road as easily as a goat. It might as well have been flat ground.

She got to us fast, hooked both her arms around one of mine at the elbow, and pulled me back next to the cart. "You are going to do something stupid, I know it, and I am *not* going to lose you." From Lisa, the babbling and worried sincerity was shocking.

Yuki on the other hand clasped her hands together in eager excitement, and as Emanuel and Elvira came running up asked, "You saw something new?"

Emanuel, only breathing the slightest bit heavy, pointed. "Brown earth, that way. It's nearly hidden by buildings. Not far, either. The view isn't great from the tower."

Yuki nodded. "I know."

Elvira pointed back the way she'd come from. "Don't go that way. There's a chasm. It's new, but I checked it out and I don't see any sign of intersecting tunnels. Just ground stress from the attack."

"We'll have to leave the cart here," murmured Yuki.

"I'll get out supplies," Emanuel told her.

Elvira just pulled her spell rod out from wherever she'd been hiding it, holding it ready in her right hand.

Emanuel ran back to the cart. The dark fisher boy pulled a heavily loaded backpack out of the bed, and was still fitting it over his arms as he ran back to his sister.

Momentarily separated from our three friends, just me and Lisa, I remembered the worrying breach signal. I whispered to my cousin, "Now that the dragon is taken care of, we should start planning the next step. What did you do with the breach detonator?"

"I threw it in the ocean," she whispered back.

Oh.

Um.

Well.

Chapter
Twenty-Eight

Elvira yelled back at us, "Get a move on, shorties!" and flaunted her big, long, tall people legs by climbing up a chunk of rock next to the road in one step.

Lisa and I wandered over the badly broken road that led subtly upwards to meet our friends, who were already hiking in the direction Emanuel had pointed, past the mined-out remains of golden age buildings and through a grove crisscrossed with lines of heaped up white rocks, as if a maze had been built and flattened there centuries ago. Which it probably had.

We caught up to Yuki holding her map out in both hands and scowling down at it. Elvira, half a dozen paces ahead, grinned hugely and spent more time marching backwards than forwards, spinning her spell rod like a baton.

Emanuel told us all, "We should be able to see it past those trees."

I trailed behind. Lisa put on a show of scowling and dragging her feet, but she stayed right by my left side and slightly behind me.

So. Lisa had thrown the breach detonator in the ocean. It was, what, ten pounds? Twenty? Not huge, but big and solid metal? There was no way that would get washed up on the beach anywhere, right? Could that be recovered at all?

Also, it might have looked like an oversized key, but it was a sophisticated magical tool used for major spellcraft. Was dumping it in sea water and letting fishes prod it around safe? That hadn't even occurred to me until now. Just because it was only part of a spell needed to open or close doorways between worlds in a controlled way didn't mean it was powerless by itself.

That it couldn't be recovered was why Lisa had dumped it in the ocean in the first place.

But Lisa didn't know any more about oceans or breach detonators than I did, right? I needed a private moment to ask Emanuel and Elvira for more information. I had a soul forge at my disposal, and I was no ordinary bioengineer. I would figure out something.

I just might have less time to do that than I'd thought.

No, the breach had been a blip, and Yuki said those were common. I still wasn't in a hurry, it was just time to start working on this issue. Right.

I bumped into Yuki's back and had to stop walking and actually look around.

Elvira, Yuki, and Emanuel stood close together. Elvira had her arm draped around Yuki's shoulders. The pale ice girl's head slumped forward over her map, shaking and trembling in despair. Her hair hung from her head and spilled over and around the page like a shroud.

Past them, we had just arrived at the edge of a circle of churned brown dirt and rocks and bits of debris, a circle so big I couldn't see the other side. It had lots of irregular hills and pits in it from how the debris was randomly scattered, so I actually couldn't see that far ahead anyway, but it stretched way, way out to the sides as well.

The brown dirt didn't actually cross the hill to the road, so maybe it wasn't a circle, just round where we were. Anyway, it was big. Maybe miles across, unless the little hills were hiding a sudden cut-off.

I'd retreated automatically after bumping into Lisa. Now I stepped close again, just barely touching. As a friend I should be there for her in case it was comforting.

Yuki pushed her hair off the map page, and drew an imaginary circle on it with her finger. Her voice rasped as much as it echoed. "Look at this. Right in the middle. Everything gone."

There were a lot of symbols for dungeons in the area she'd indicated. Yes, this earthmover had done what they so often did, what made them so scary and dangerous—it had destroyed everything in the zone it attacked. It ate the buildings or plowed them back into the ground, stirred the dirt and rock, and left nothing living or intact in the spot that got its attention. Only the dungeon it had built would be left at the site of an earthmover attack. That spot cold be as small as the ball court back at school, or as big as a city.

Elvira gave Yuki a tender squeeze. The energetic, top-heavy, adventurous fishergirl was not good at sounding gentle, but she at least tried. "Look at it this way. If the cleared-off area is this big, there's probably a huge underground labyrinth we can explore when the adventurers are done with it. If there's no soul forge, maybe we can lure Joe in to do a little light clearing before the adventurers arrive. You know how good he is with traps and locks, and how good Emanuel is with puzzles. We might get away with some treasure, even intact magical artifacts. We'd see the best inscriptions before looters got to ripping the inlay out or breaking the walls to look for secret rooms."

A step away on the other side, Emanuel offered, "If nothing else, it's an excuse for multiple major expeditions for the whole club. We have to scout what's gone and what's still here, especially underground."

I offered my two cents of encouragement. Pointing out in the middle of the devastation, I said, "At least we know the dungeon's that way."

Elvira rolled her eyes and her head, scrunching up her nose in disgust. "I wish. It could be a shack built right on the edge, or a door in the ground leading to a complex that we're already standing on and goes down a dozen floors." By the end there, she sounded a little enthusiastic.

Emanuel raised his hand. "But this does make it much easier to search, yes. Come on, Yuki. We've almost found a whole new dungeon, before adventurers, before the College, even before the sheriff."

Yuki started walking, and we left the trees and grass behind for empty piles of dirt. We climbed the nearest hill, its soil squishy underneath. We were the first people to ever walk on it.

At the top, Emanuel pointed, hope in his voice as he declared, "That flat line way over there. I think that's a roof."

Elvira rose up to her full height, then pulled her head back a few inches in surprise. "If that's a roof, the new dungeon is huge."

I couldn't even see it, just more lumpy brown terrain, but I assumed the tall people had a better angle.

Excited now, Elvira squealed, "Come on! Let's go find out!"

She skipped down the hill from rock to rock, at a speed I would have been guaranteed to slip and break my ankle. Emanuel and Yuki hurried after her, but she left them far behind, skirting around the next hill before I'd even reached the bottom of this one.

Emanuel shouted after his sister, "Elvira, don't you dare get out of sight of the rest of the party! You know better!"

From the other side of the big dirt mound she called back, "Okay, fine, take—YAIEEE!?"

Chapter
Twenty-Nine

Skirt flapping, Elvira came running back around the side of the hill, waving at us to back up with a horrified look on her face. When we started to edge back around the hill we'd just crossed, she spun around and stopped with her feet planted apart and the spell rod pointed at whatever she'd been fleeing from.

A big animal stepped into the gap between dirt mounts in front of her. It was squat and burly, but still taller at the shoulder than Elvira. Hooves splayed out of the ends of its thick legs, and huge golden wings spread from its blocky quadruped body's back. An oversized human head, a man's head with a big, braided, squared off beard emerged from its shoulders in more or less the right place for a head, or at least a neck. On that head perched a golden crown.

The monster yelled words in a deep, rough, but human voice.

Yuki husked, "He says we are trespassing on sacred ground."

I gawked at her. "You speak Sumerian!?"

Emanuel was back by me now, and whispered, "Yuki speaks all the tongues of men. So does Lucky. It's a whole Thing, we'll tell you later."

The question of whether I should ask more became moot as Lisa's hands took fierce hold of my arm, and pulled me back a couple of steps. I had to plant my feet and resist to stop her from dragging me away.

Yuki yelled Sumerian back at the beast, or at least spoke with more carrying resonance than usual. Everyone, not just me and Lisa, started to back away.

The monster shouted again, exactly the same words as before, I was pretty sure.

I knew I was right, because Yuki flinched, then muttered, "The warning is a fake. It can talk, but it's brainless."

I agreed, "Most monsters are. They're spells wearing a fake body, following the spell instructions."

Lisa growled by my ear, "Which means it can't be reasoned with. We're getting out of here, Forge."

She locked her arms around my elbow and dragged me backwards again, hard, forcing me to stumble after her.

Whether the monster would have attacked otherwise, the sudden movement was enough to set it off. It charged forward like a stampeding ram, but much, much bigger.

Elvira whisked her fingers over the spell rod. Its code lit up, and while the spell itself might be invisible, we could see the beast stagger as if it had been punched, trip over its own feet, and fall sprawling in the dirt.

It immediately started rolling right back to its feet. Elvira hit it with the spell again, and again. It twitched like it had been shoved each time, but still managed to get its hooves underneath it and claw back upright.

Yelling its repetitive battle cry from its now bruised face, the monster charged Elvira. Straight on, the spell blast barely shook it. The next blast hit it in the leg, causing it to drop and roll, but again it got right back up.

Every blast, every movement of the monster was reflected in glitters and shifts of color in the detector I still held in my hands. That it showed up at all proved this was a dungeon monster, not my chimeric dragon mutated again.

Elvira yelped. The monster was now close enough to swing its head at her. Thankfully, it was big and strong, but not agile. Elvira was the definition of agility. She grabbed its wing and actually hopped up onto its back, then leaped away as it bucked. She landed in a roll, fired her spell rod as she did, and knocked its legs out from under it.

As she hopped back to her feet, she yelled, "Run, you fools! It's too tough! The spell barely hurts it!"

We had all stopped, frozen by the scene playing out in front of us. Now we started backing up again, with Lisa pulling at me fiercely.

Moving reluctantly, Emanuel shouted, "You can get away?"

"If I can't, nobody can!" his sister called back.

As stupid as it was, the monster stopped being stunned, or confused, or whatever had made it lie still for a few seconds. Its legs clawed at the ground, spraying dirt as it pushed back up, and started a new charge.

At us. At me, Yuki, Lisa, and Emanuel.

With its back to her, Elvira shot its legs out from under it again. She ran forward, and its head recoiled as she hit it in the face with that spell again. The black-haired adventuress-to-be growled something I bet was profanity and added loud and clear, "Prodigy, it's your time to shine!"

She threw the spell rod to me. It arced through the air with perfect aim. I shoved my pendant and detector into Lisa's hands and grabbed the weapon.

Lisa put her arms around my waist. I couldn't see her face behind me, but her voice rasped like someone trying not to cry. "No way. You're not dying on me, Artifact! Not again!"

Elvira and the monster had been fighting while my eyes were on the flying weapon. I looked back up at them to see the girl's arms around its neck, hear her yell, "Bye, Felicia!" and watch her pull the beast up off the ground and fling it into the air.

While it flew, Elvira barked out spell code.

It hit the ground hard, on its back, a few yards from me. It started to twist around, but Elvira's spell finished and its legs spasmed, twitching randomly instead.

I didn't wait to find out how long that would last. Straining against Lisa's grip, I pointed the rod, swiped my other hand over the still glowing spell, and made no attempt to hold back.

Thunder *BOOM*ed. I went over backwards onto Lisa, who landed on her butt in the dirt.

The monster disappeared, blown into splinter-sized fragments that instantly and bloodlessly vanished.

Its crown sailed way, way up in the air, fell back down, and landed with a *clang* and a *snap*.

At the end of my extended arm, I was still holding out the handle of the rod. The wood continued about an inch past my thumb, the rest gone, exploded by the force of the spell.

Elvira stood alone in the chewed up dirt field, hunched over and panting. Her dress was so badly ripped that she was lucky that the only audience was other girls and her brother. The red marks showing on her exposed dusky skin didn't seem to be bleeding, at least.

Little by little, she staggered more upright, and asked in the ringing post-explosion silence, "Why was that thing so tough? Those monsters—at the seashore weren't that hard to kill."

I climbed back to my own feet, like everyone else was having to do. I also noticed with gratitude Elvira remembering to be discreet with Yuki around.

I answered her question from hundreds of afternoons of reading books about the patterns used by dungeon soul forges. "Shedu. It was a Shedu. A Sumerian temple guardian. Soul forges tuned to Sumerian patterns turn out a small number of very tough monsters. The authorities will want to know."

Picking his wobbly way over to her, Emanuel told his sister, "You could have taken it with better spells, sis."

She let him put an arm around her to help with her first few steps, and grunted, "Maybe, but if we don't warn them, a few of those will stomp a regular adventuring party into a bloody pulp."

Which was my time to add, "Also, that was a really weak Shedu. There are probably stronger ones at the temple. Much stronger."

"We're getting out of here now," Lisa snarled.

"Seconded," declared a weary and grateful Elvira.

"Yes," agreed a stained and disheveled Yuki.

"Wait!" I yelled.

"I'm giving you thirty seconds, Forge," Lisa growled.

I took two steps and scooped up the dropped pendant, and pointed at the director ring fitted around it. "There. The soul forge is that way. That was the color of the Shedu's signature."

Yuki looked in that direction, looked back at the buildings in the not-complete-leveled ruins, laid her map out on her box, and drew a quick, straight line.

Something in her box went *ding*! A little sparkle flashed on the spot marking the soul forge on my detector.

"I think it just made a replacement Shedu," I said.

"Yes," the ice girl agreed.

"Time is up," Lisa declared. This time she picked me bodily up off the ground, carrying me like a baby back towards the maze rubble-strewn grove. Everyone else crowded close, but we hadn't gone very far in, and almost immediately we were off the loose brown dirt and back on the broken pavement road. I could even see the cart.

Walking on her own, but with a lot of wincing, Elvira asked, "How much tougher than that do Shedu get?"

As I hooked my ID pendant back onto my necklace, I dredged my memory to report, "Bigger, up to 20 feet tall. Stronger. Bronze armored skin, even spellcasting ability. Usually breath weapons. The worse problem is that there might be a Lammasu in there."

"Do we want to know?" asked Emanuel with a grimace.

"Yes," chorused Yuki and Elvira.

We'd gotten back to the cart. Emanuel slipped his arms around his sister, and despite her still being able to move lifted her up and set her into the bed of the cart, among the limited cushioning of the bags. The rest of us climbed in on our own as Emanuel turned Herman and the cart around, climbed up in the seat, and droves us back down the horribly bumpy little ramp to the One-And-One.

Scared to try to activate Emanuel's shock absorber spell

in case I catapulted us into the sea, I put up with the banging and focused on explaining instead. "A Lammasu is a goddess. Supposedly. Sumerian soul forges sometimes try to make a copy. You'll get maybe three Shedu, and a Lammasu that is a more powerful spell caster than any human can be, and looks like a winged woman in a fur dress. She won't be stupid, either. Weird, but able to think and think well. Even a tiny soul forge, if it devotes all its power, can make a scary Lammasu. Until it detonates, anyway."

Pulling her knees up against her chest, Yuki asked, "Is there a real goddess? Would there be information in the temple?"

"You tell us. Read this," said, Elvira. She pulled the Shedu's crown out of the ripped up fabric of her dress, and tossed it into Yuki's hands. The crown was dented badly, and snapped in places to show that it was actually a gold coating over wood. The crown design itself was simple, just a thick circlet with a rectangular plate in front. On that plate was stamped writing made out of a lot of little pointy triangles.

Yuki squinted at the plate, and turned it around a few times. Finally, she said, "These letters look a little like the gate symbol, but not enough. The message is about respecting the Queen of the Earth. The ground, not the world. She is a connection between humans and gods. I don't think this is what I'm looking for, but when it's cleaned out, I need to go back there. Especially if it's a big temple."

"We'll take you," declared Elvira immediately.

"That includes me," I promised.

"After it's safe," Lisa corrected me. She scowled, fists clenched, brow furrowed, sitting in the corner of the cart so tense that she looked nauseous. Her voice came out scratchy with anger as she said, "I swear, I will tie you down if I have to, Artifact. You scared me. You're my meal ticket and I am not, *not* losing this easy life, okay?"

I scooted down the cart bed to my cousin, slipped my arms around her, and gave her a hug. She sat there tense and sour looking in my grip, but she didn't push me away, either. The cart crossed through the hills and out onto the sunny One-And-One, with the sea breeze rolling over us. Maybe that would help.

Finished reading, Yuki held the crown back out to Elvira.

Elvira didn't take it. She tilted her head in my direction. "Artifact's loot. She killed it and saved our lives."

Oh, no. I kept my arms around Lisa, but protested, "You did almost all the fighting. I might as well have just been a cliff you threw it over."

"We can't keep it," said Emanuel from the driver's seat, his voice touched with bitterness.

An idea occurred to me. I offered, "I'll give it to Joe. He needs the money more than any of us."

Everyone but Lisa smiled. She didn't look disapproving, just still worried. Her arms slipped stealthily around my waist and held me, too.

Taking a deep breath of wonderful sea air, I shook out my hair and added, "And I am joining the East Goblita Wastes Exploration Society. This is way better than throwing a ball."

Elvira cackled in glee.

Chapter Thirty

Herman's patient clip-clop eventually brought us back to the weird signpost where the road I lived on met the One-and-One. The mist had cleared without a trace. People bustled about on important adult business. Warm sun gently soothed us from our adventure, while the sea breeze gently soothed us from the warm sun. Houses and shops in every faded stretched off in three directions, and in the fourth dark green tufted grass, a few ponds and the sprawl of the College created a horizon blocking the view of the distant sea.

Lisa and I hopped out of the cart, and I shouldered my satchel. Time to home and plan out the rest of my day, and start thinking about what I could possibly do about a breach detonator dropped in the sea!

I was a bioengineering prodigy. There had to be something. There would be something.

Elvira and Emanuel stood to climb out of the cart themselves, but didn't get that far. Elvira moved slowly, wincing a lot and wheezing. She didn't even fully unbend. Her arms didn't clutch her wounds, but that was because they were too busy holding her damaged dress shut.

This was worse than when we'd left the Waste. Emanuel immediately leaned in concern over his sister, hand on her shoulder, looking her over from every side. "How badly are you hurt. Elvira, you're still bleeding from some of these hits?"

Elvira's voice at least was strong, sly, and accompanied by rolled eyes and that little head shake she often did. "Well, I'm sore, but nothing serious." Her growing smile disappeared, and she closed her eyes to groan. "That is, until Mama and Papa see me."

"If they see you walking around in public wearing that, they won't notice the wounds," Emanuel said, and it didn't sound like a joke.

Elvira's smile returned, even if grim, and she looked up into his eyes. "Calling you on that one, Emanuel. Their priorities are straight, even if their standards aren't."

Emanuel hunched over her even closer, too concerned to argue. "You need medical treatment that won't report to our parents."

Matter of fact, Elvira answered, "We have plenty of sympathetic neighbors. Hide me in Gwenda's shop and get that witch student, Ruby. I guarantee she'll come running. Can you think of any student witch who wouldn't?"

"I'll drop you off there," echoed Yuki.

It looked to me like Elvira was in way more pain than she wanted to admit. Desperate to help, I asked Lisa, "Would you go run and take the message? Make sure she knows she doesn't have to steal a broom and hurry this time."

My pink and red cousin twisted her body away in a display of reluctance, her already small mouth petulantly pursed.

I was imposing, I knew, but this was important. Lisa was way faster than anyone else. I argued, "We have to buy groceries anyway, and I need to pick up my replacement forge seal, and yes, we are doing that today. You want me feeling grateful when we pass the candy counter."

That did it. She took off at a run, speeding up the street with her gazelle-like speed and grace.

Yuki tapped Herman with her foot. The cart pulled away from me, heading up the street next to the One-and-One. As slow as it was, it kicked up a dusty smell in its wake. Emanuel crowded to the back of the wooden vehicle and told me, "Gwenda sells pottery, right on this end of the street row our shop is on. It's the perfect place to get cleaned up without our folks finding out."

I wandered back home. Me hurrying wouldn't help anything right now, no matter how many things I had to feel urgent about. In the shadowy grey interior of the workshop I'd inherited I offloaded my notes and most of my detecting equipment. I got the money from the slime creation out of the drawer in my desk I kept it in. Then an idea hit me, and I wandered into the better lit, lighter brown kitchen and rummaged around.

There! In the pantry I found what I hoped would be there: Some big, sturdy cloth bags with shoulder straps for carrying groceries. Uncle Leonard had only two hands, same as me.

On the way back out I checked the pigeon in its pigeon-hole nest in my workshop. It had kicked out all the nesting material I'd given it except one crumpled piece of paper, which it sat in as it stared at me with the standard horrified, orange-eyed pigeon expression.

The little wooden compartment was remarkably clean. I was very glad my horseshoe crab—reminder, repair and reboot the forge immediately on getting home to recharge it—had decided on its own to clean up the pigeon droppings. I was kind of glad it had taken a liking to my pigeon and coughed up little blue balls of organic detritus for the pigeon to eat. Still, they couldn't be healthy, and I made another mental note. Buy seed.

Why was the cleaning crab acting like that? It was an effectively mindless true monster. It couldn't take a liking to anything except in the crudest sense of what it did and didn't want to eat. The strangest things could sneak into a spell formula. Especially bioengineering, where a few simple designs had to build on themselves to create a complete animal.

That was a fun question to roll around on my simple walk to the market. Now that the mist had cleared, it was such a beautiful day. A hint of salt in the air. Blue skies. Goblita residents in the varied styles and colors of clothing favored by a dozen cultures inhabiting the West Coast, and a few immigrants from who knew where. Some of the residents themselves had fur, scales, big ears, horns, tails, or brightly colored skin to add even more variety to the view. Much more than up at Lake Touhou. The town sure had plenty of furries.

Still no gobbos. I was starting to wonder how the town had gotten its name.

The market was packed with shoppers. Were there other market streets? Presumably. Goblita was a whole town. This one right by the One-and-One would be convenient for deliveries and a lot of residents, so I bet it was the biggest and busiest.

People watching over, back to being productive. My first step: Figure out which shop Emanuel had directed me to.

The little shop on the nearest street corner sold jars. A small table out front held some misshapen red clay pots with no price tags. Charity freebies, I supposed. A counter inside but at the front crowded with sleek, professional work. Brightly colored ceramic pots, glass jars and bottles, even a few boxes made of expensive resin that looked much too fresh to be golden age salvage. Sophisticated stuff.

The building didn't have windows, just wooden panels currently slid up that would lock over the front at night. In the shallow, shady room behind the counter bustled a woman wearing an apron—no, a loose yellow shirt and skirt. She just looked like someone who always wore an apron.

She was a furry. A rabbit, to be precise. Chocolate brown fur in back, sandy pale in front. I had no ability to tell age on furries, but I wildly guessed not quite middle age, just barely too young for any grey hair. She bulged. Not fat, exactly. Or rather, her body as a whole wasn't round, but every individual part of her was "plump"? She bustled, too, moving in quick steps with her arms and hands always moving but her elbows tucked in.

The rabbit woman was also not much taller than me, but still tall enough to lean over and pinch both my cheeks, wiggling them as she gushed in a rich, adult voice, "Well, I know who you must be! I heard a rumor the Dollmaker was in town. I'm Gwenda."

Gently leaning back to dislodge the plump, pinching fingers, I corrected, "I'm not the Dollmaker." I paused, then smirked. "...

yet." My name is Artifact Forge. Call me Art."

"You don't look anything like your uncle Leonard, Artifact, but all the kids say you're even more darling. They're in the back, if that's what you're here for. If it's business, well, I know bioengineers need plenty of safe storage. When you want shielded or lead-lined glass, be a dear and order ahead, please?" She, well, bustled about as she talked, picking up pots and jars and showing to me, whether or not they had any relevance to anything, and walked back and forth within the limited confines of her shop.

I slid around Gwenda to peer through the doorway in the back of her sales area. The back room was much larger than the front, but still not as big as my living room. It just wasn't a big building. The only light in this dim storage area filtered in from outside. Shelves lined the walls, packed with everything, mostly strange shapes under draped cloth, but cleaning supplies, more jars, tools, all sorts of stuff remained uncovered and on display.

Elvira sat on a stool in the middle of the floor, drinking water out of a jar. She still hunched over, and was now wearing a pair of the ragged brown shorts she and her brother favored so often, hardly darker than her skin. She hadn't taken off the grey dress, but it bunched up around her waist in front and trailed down to the floor in back. It hung loosely off her upper body, and red scrapes, some oozing enough they might be cuts, peeked through the big slashes. The skin around those scrapes bloomed a much darker charcoal color than the deep tan of her healthy skin.

Emanuel hovered next to her, holding in both hands a rolled-up cloth that looked a lot like a bandage, but I recognized as one of the chest ties Elvira wore when fishing.

Elvira waved, but didn't straighten up from her hunch and there was a definite amount of grunt in her normally cheerful, chattering tone. "Ruby's going to need access to a lot of me, so I decided to keep this until she's done."

Her left leg bore its own wound, but it didn't seem to stretch up under the shorts. I asked anxiously, "Are you sure you're okay?"

Despite the husk, Elvira nodded her head emphatically and

was definitely still cheerful. "Oh, yeah. I just can't afford to go home looking like this." She waved a hand at herself.

"Or with cracked ribs," Emanuel added, solemn and looking his sister over with a worried frown.

Elvira tossed her head, rustling her long black hair. "Like you know. They're my ribs! Anyway, if they are, we have a witch on the way."

I hesitated, but... well, a witch was on the way, and I couldn't heal Elvira without strapping her to a slab and radically altering her species. Reluctantly, I told the siblings, "Alright. I guess I'll get shopping. Tell Lisa that's what I'm doing when she gets back. Give Ruby my thanks. She does too much for me already, just because I helped her with her cat. She's too kind and responsible and hardworking for her own good."

On my way back out, as I held up the flipping counter section that would let me leave the shop, Gwenda grabbed my shoulders. She lifted up one of the sacks slung over my back and chided me, "You're going to carry all your groceries in those? Sweet cakes, cherub dumpling, Leo's place is a few blocks away. Get a wheelbarrow or cart and I'll let you store it in the back between shopping trips. As I live and breathe, you children think you can solve every problem by trying harder! Now shoo! Shoo. Gwenda has mason jars to sell."

The jerk as she grabbed me, then let me go, pulled my eyes to my ID pendant. That faint glitter—either the sun was catching the crystal just right, or this shop radiated magic.

I extricated myself and dove into the crowd, but considered Gwenda's suggestion. Forget a cart. I should make a simple quadrupedal doll I could walk around. The power requirements would be low, the behaviors simple, and the distance to the market trivial, so I could hook it to my soul forge without any worries.

Bouncing from shop to stall to cart, I bought food. First, before I could forget, a little bag of sunflower seeds and another of dried corn for the pigeon. Chicken from a chilled butcher shop—I tapped the ice elemental's box and refilled its power as a courtesy—and tomato sauce from a woman with a cart full of everything pickled, crushed, or juiced. Still more beans. The number of stalls selling beans and the variety for sale absolutely bewildered me, so I grabbed what looked the most like the tasty black beans Joe had cooked for me and my cousin. Oh, bread from the baker, and cheese from a dairy shop.

We still had plenty of tortillas at home.

What did I still need? I would have to start keeping a grocery list, especially for not-food items. Did we need any of those besides the seed? Nothing leaped to mind.

I stood at the edge of the flow of shoppers pondering all that and resting my shoulder from lugging the increasingly heavy shopping bag when Lisa caught up. Before she said a word she leaned over and around me, examining me like I might be damaged, then she stuck her face into the bag. "Any candy in there?" asked the mass of hair in various colors of fire and the black sweeping horns over top.

"I was leaving sugar until last. I knew you'd want to be along," I answered.

Lisa pulled her head out, and stood back up straight with a troubled expression I wasn't expecting. Her face turned away, but I still couldn't miss how her expression twisted round. I caught "pain" and "lost" and "hopeful" and "about to cry" and couldn't honestly say if any of them meant anything or were just my interpretation. Finally it all settled into bland good cheer, with a tight frown offset by raised eyebrows that provided the good humor. Bumping my shoulder with her fist, she said, "Good plan. Thank you."

We wandered way down to the far end of the market to one of the most temporary looking stalls, a few crates and planks covered in tablecloth and strewn with products from the caravans. Not much honey or granular sugar were grown right around Goblita, apparently.

Back at Lake Touhou we'd had to get pretty much everything delivered in cartloads, so we could stock up. My dad could afford it. He was the guy you came to on the West Coast when you needed really exotic, high level bioengineering, like salamanders who could precisely control high temperature smelters or prism birds to transform aspects for arch-mages.

Give me a few months to get used to doing instead of just

learning, and I bet I could do transformations like that!

Anyway, the candy stand gnome. That's what he looked like as we approached, a wizened old gnome. Only when I actually stood in front of his stand did I realize that was just the impression he gave. He was thin, with long, pointy ears, so bioengineering definitely lurked in his family tree. I wasn't entirely sure he was old. His mixed grey and blond hair was both thin and poofy, yes, but while his skin might be the color of leather his face bore hardly any lines, mostly around the eyes and brow. He had an almost pretty face, in fact. He wasn't short, either, just sat on a tall stool with his stick legs tucked up on the bar just below the seat. His equally scrawny arms hovered in front of him, tapping his fingers together. That pose made him look short.

Lisa picked up a big, big glass jar of dark golden honey with flecks of wax, and stared at it with wide and longing pink eyes. The air around us bathed in sweetness, with a different rich overtone however you turned your head.

I looked at the price on the jar, and winced. Digging my remaining coins out of my pocket after shopping, I counted them.

A new, alien discomfort stung me. It felt weird and heavy and mortifying. I couldn't afford that honey.

Awkwardly, I pushed the jar back down to the pink tablecloth and told Lisa, "Something smaller, and I *have* to go back to work, okay? Feeding... just running a house costs more than I expected. I'll make plenty, but I have to bioengineer to do that."

Lisa pouted, hunching up her shoulders. "Well, it gets me out of school. I still won't let you kill yourself."

The woman at the next table, a wizened crone who needed no fooling to look like one, cackled in malicious, triumphant glee. She wore a lumpy dress and head scarf in blue and white, made of the kind of thick weave fabric I usually associated with place mats, or baskets.

Waving at her display of grains, flour, and hard little cakes, she crowed, "Sorghum! That's what you need, children. Little Hell child has an expensive sweet tooth? Sorghum is the answer.

Sorghum is always the answer. Here, have a taste."

She picked up a small, sandy white pot in one shriveled hand, opened it, and offered it to Lisa. It contained a golden brown liquid thinner than honey, more syrupy than goopy. Lisa accepted the treasure gingerly in both hands.

Then she drank it all.

She just threw her head back and guzzled the whole jar of syrup before I even registered that's what she was doing, gulping it down. Before I knew how to react Lisa finished, and set the jar down on the table, empty except for dregs.

I just hoped it didn't cost a lot. My eyes darted to a price tag on a much bigger jar. Okay, this sorghum juice stuff wasn't cheap, but it was a fifth as pricey as honey, and granulated sugar was worse.

My cousin licked her bright pink lips and sighed. "Not bad!" She sounded much more enthusiastic and satisfied than those weak words suggested.

I pointed at the big clay sorghum juice jar. "Okay, this time we'll take that one, and you can use it as a sweetener. If you let me work I'm sure next time we'll have enough money to pick up some actual candy. Sound good?"

Lisa hoisted the jar up in both hands with an eager, greedy smile.

I warned, "Don't you dare drink it raw, either. It's for sweetening your food."

She pouted, but only for form. "Yeah, yeah, okay. Here."

Pulling the empty bag from my shoulder, she redistributed the food between bags, then hoisted one on her back herself. From the looks and what was in each, I knew she'd taken the heavier bag. Plus, she held the sorghum pot in both arms like a treasure chest she had to protect from thieves.

As we walked away, I heard the gnome-looking guy grouse, "Got me again," and the crone's gleeful cackle.

The market was fun, but that was the last item, so I said, "We'd better go home and get the meat tucked away before it goes bad. I want to refrigerate the bread and cheese too, so they don't go stale."

Lisa's ears perked up. "Oh, yeah, good idea!"

As we started walking shoulder to shoulder, or at least shoulder to bicep, through the crowd, I related, "It's something my parents did, since my mom hated baking bread and my dad was almost as bad a cook as you. I'm sure not making my own bread."

Lisa snorted, a giggle totally lacking in her usual demonic poise.

My mind shifted to a darker topic, and I warned her quietly, trusting the noise of the crowd to prevent anyone from hearing anything, "Listen. We have to get that thing you dumped in the ocean back. I know you don't want to, but I detected a breach this morning."

That news didn't trouble Lisa at all. She raised a scarlet eyebrow and asked lightly, "Big or little?"

A bit stunned by her unconcern, I answered, "Tiny, I think."

The teenage demoness's small mouth bloomed into a huge, wicked, fangy grin. Her voice turned lilting with evil pleasure. "I'm surprised it took this long. That, my dear cousin, was the goofball who summoned me, summoning my mother."

Chapter
Thirty-One

Off-balance, I stammered, "Oh. I... never thought to wonder why you're on Earth. How, I mean. I thought your mother sent you."

Cinching her grocery bag up with her left hand, running the right back through her hair and between her horns, Lisa crowed, "Alone? Without all that fancy breach equipment? Naah, you can send someone from Hell to Earth with only a regular amount of magic if there's someone on both sides trying to make it work. Right? Stick-in-the-muds like that College guy hate that fact. There's a man in town who wants *so* much to summon a succubus. He got ahold of Mom's summoning name, but when he cast the spell she shoved me through instead. The dummy actually thought I was her shapeshifted into a kid! I played along until I could jump out of a window and run for Leo's place like Mom told me to. I guess it took him two months to get his nerve back up to try again. Probably thought I was going to expose him. Why would I punish anyone for wanting to summon hot demon women?"

I blushed, but also sputtered laughter at that embarrassing story.

Funny as that story had been, boy did I want to change the topic. I was about to suggest we peek in on Emanuel and Elvira when I heard the yelling. The angry yelling.

I couldn't make out the words, but I recognized Emanuel's voice in the mix.

Slipping and burrowing through the crowds like a meadow eel, I ran for the potter's shop at the end of the row. Emanuel and Elvira's parents stood in the doorway to the back room, exchanging loud, angry words with Emanuel.

Had I ever heard Emanuel and Elvira's parents' names? I couldn't remember them now. I was certainly struck again by how they looked like older, bulkier versions of their children.

Gwenda seemed to appear out of nowhere. I'd missed her standing out front until she threw out an arm and caught me, blocking me from stampeding in to join the confrontation. Turning me to look down into my eyes, she shook her head very, very seriously.

The message was plain. Stay out of this. I didn't want to, but when she turned serious the plump bunny woman looked like she knew what she was doing. So much so, I… would trust her. I just had to hope she was as wise as she looked.

But this close, I could hear everything clearly.

Inside the shop's storeroom, Emanuel shouted, "What if I have? What business is it of yours who she dates?"

His mother put her fists on her hips, where she wore a skirt that was as much tied-up sash as anything over a pair of long shorts. Parents and kids dressed much alike, but I'd never heard an arch tone like this from Elvira. "I'm more concerned with how many than who."

Emanuel wasn't having any of that. He shot back immediately, "And if it was me, you'd be congratulating me and encouraging me to spend more time out, maybe catch a bride."

Hard edged, but more approving, his mother argued, "You're spending your spare time studying, not practicing to become a looter."

I'd never imagined Emanuel sounding this angry. He was

such a positive, friendly boy. But now his voice seethed with offended fury. "She's good at it. She's incredible at it. Elvira is a genius, and she knows what she wants, and you don't like that it's, what, dangerous? She can't pick her own risks?"

His mother's tone spiked, and she tilted her head sharply to one side. Mother didn't do it as much as daughter, but this was where Elvira got her body language. "No, she can't. She's still a teenager. Picking her risks is our job as her parents."

Emanuel still didn't need a moment's pause before snarling, "All you pick for her is no risks at all. We never got near the dungeon. Elvira chased off a monster so we could escape. She's gotten hurt worse fishing. You were proud of her for winning that spellcasting duel with the octopus."

His father spoke for the first time, gruff, his anger simmering but leashed—barely. "She had backup."

I couldn't really see Emanuel past his parents, but I made out his arm waving. "She had backup in the Waste. She always has backup! She's not stupid. Stop treating her like she is!"

"Then why aren't you letting her speak for herself?" his mother demanded.

Craning my head around, I got a peek of Elvira, who was indeed lurking behind Emanuel, not quite cowering. With her chest tied up again, she showed no sign of wounds. Ruby had done her usual perfect job.

I thought Emanuel had been mad before. Now it got colder. He stood up very straight, arms at his sides, fists clenched, and didn't so much yell as tell his parents at top volume, "Because it's not her you're mad at. I'm the real problem, but you're scared that if you yell at me, I'll run away, so you're taking it out on her."

His father's crossed arms tightened visibly, and he snapped, "The only thing wrong with you is that you think you have to take your sister's side on everything."

Emanuel's volume dropped. Not that he was anywhere near quiet, but his anger and tone compressed into something bleak and hard, behind a stony face. "And that I'm going to leave. Leave Goblita, leave you, and most importantly leave fishing."

That scored a hit. Their heavily tanned faces turned a little more pale. His parents rocked back a few inches, and were silent for several seconds. After the loud back and forth, that brief silence blared.

But his parents didn't actually look surprised. His father twitched his chin, and gruffly denied, "You're young. You'll change your mind."

Emanuel shook his head emphatically. "You know I won't, and if you push me, you'll just guarantee it. So you're taking it out on Elvira, who wants to stay. Elvira loves our family traditions. She only wants to adventure sometimes. Her powers are great for the ocean, for making our family rich and famous because we catch sea monsters instead of running from them. You would brag about how wild she is, but you're so scared of me leaving that you crush her instead."

Behind him, Elvira moved, grabbing his hand. She spoke up for the first time since I'd arrived. "If you run away, I'm going with you."

Their father's anger now mixed with worry as he scolded, "You'd be destroying your lives. You're too young for any good job."

Emanuel tossed his head in contempt at that. "With our skills? The caravans would hire us in a snap. They know we're already good enough at magic to be useful, and we're only going to get better and better. Then our whole family legacy is ashes, because you want to keep your kids on a leash and Elvira is the one who cares enough to let you."

Elvira corrected, "Cared." Was she squeezing Emanuel's hand?

Emanuel's dad, blocky and hard muscled, swelled up like he was going to explode. A second later, he deflated again. As he shrank, their mother took hold of his bicep.

Angry, sad, but most of all calm, their father rumbled, "We're all overcome by emotion right now. Let's take a break. No matter who is right, this incident is not worth breaking our family over."

I wasn't sure Emanuel agreed. He still stood like a tower of pride and righteous anger, until Elvira slipped her hand up to his wrist and squeezed again.

That did it. Emanuel hung his head forward, torso relaxing, and in a gruelingly tired voice agreed, "Yes."

Gwenda pulled me farther back out of the way as the fishing teens' parents stalked out without another word, making for the docks.

I rushed in, ducking under the counter's flip up door, scurrying up to the doorway into the dark back room.

My rush stopped there. The room wasn't quite as dim as before. Ruby had left a little glass tube on a shelf with some murky liquid in it that shone as bright and clear as any script magic lamp. It still smelled like dust. Emanuel stood by the wooden stool in the middle, both arms around Elvira's shoulders as she pressed her face to his chest.

Except one of his arms left her to shoot out, holding his palm up. Still tired, his voice scratchy, he said, "Not now, Artifact. Elvira and I need to talk alone. You're not part of this, and you didn't cause this."

Lisa's gentle, clawed hands took hold of me by the waist, and she pulled me back from the doorway. I staggered through the now raised counter door. The rejection. I just... I couldn't process it. I wasn't at all sure I hadn't caused this, either. I'd been feeding Elvira opportunities to flex and show off her combat spell casting since we met. I was trying to help, but had been blind to what a violent ant nest I'd kicked.

Inside the shop, Gwenda pulled down the wooden shutters to close he shop, even though it was still the middle of the afternoon. She pulled the cords one by one, because she kept her face sunk in the other hand. Long, brown rabbit ears drooped forward to cover her face further.

I heard the other yelling.

Chapter
Thirty-Two

Not yelling exactly, which is why Emanuel and his family's fight had drowned them out, but raised, harsh voices.

I stepped around the corner of Gwenda's shop onto the regular, non-market street. At the far corner of the shop stood Ruby, Mistress Flora, and Mistress Hammerhead, a trio of slim figures in black dresses. Two of those figures wore tall, pointed, wide-brimmed hats, which made them even more towering figures of authority as they glowered down at Ruby.

Ruby didn't cower. The burgundy-haired young woman stood ramrod straight, her face and figure more elegant and cold than ever. An ice statue would betray more repentance and fear as she said, "I didn't break any rules this time."

Mistress Flora looked older than ever, her face a mountain range of wrinkles, but not soft. Oh, no. This was the stare of ancient, primeval judgment. Her eyes bored into Ruby as she declared, "No. Not quite. There's no rule against uncertified witches dispensing self-made potions, if they work. Or against treating your friends. Or against leaving school at this hour without telling anyone. Or bypassing the city's official medical witches."

Mistress Hammerhead didn't look as threatening, but that wasn't saying much. The shorter, fancier, blue-haired head witch had her nebulous, always thoughtful and searching gaze on Ruby, and her hands clasped in front of her. Quieter than the other two, which again was easy, she said, "But altogether, it's… inappropriate. Unwise."

I hadn't been able to help Emanuel and Elvira, but at least I could do this. Taking a couple of steps forward, raising my hands, I declared, "I sent that message."

Ruby twisted around, saw me, and barked savagely, "I don't want your help!" Then she snapped right back into position, meeting Mistress Flora's gaze, except now tense where she had been solid moments before.

I recoiled. I had actually somehow made things worse, and now Ruby was mad at me, too.

The silence went on, all three black-gowned figures as still as stone. Ruby's face was now a mask of horror. Mistress Flora loomed grim and merciless. Mistress Hammerhead… still just thoughtful.

The frozen moment broke when the blue-haired witch turned and told me, a little more frankly than gently, "I believe what Rhubella means is that she needs to learn to fight for herself. She needs to feel like an equal in your relationship."

I was totally, utterly out of my depth. I didn't even understand what Mistress Hammerhead just said. An equal? In what way were Ruby and I not equals? Why would this be a big deal? Did it mean Ruby was angry with me or not? At least I understood that I didn't understand, and could keep myself from sticking my foot farther into my own mouth.

Further helplessness settled on me like lead. If Ruby, if Elvira and Emanuel, if any of my friends were kicked out of their homes, I couldn't help them. I had a nice, big house, but I couldn't afford to feed anyone but myself and Lisa. Maybe later, but not yet. I couldn't springboard into an adult's life and responsibilities instantly. I was still stumbling over the little potholes of becoming a professional.

Apparently the other three felt my interruption was over. Ruby told the old women flatly, "I'm a witch. My services were needed."

"You're not a witch yet," Mistress Flora replied. I wasn't sure what was worse, if she'd sounded angry, or this matter of fact correction.

Mistress Hammerhead shook her head and echoed sadly, "No. You're not."

"Ice Princess" didn't begin to describe Ruby. Her moment of horror and weakness had passed. As hard as frozen steel, she asked, "I've taken enough classes about how a witch is supposed to act. Didn't you mean them?"

I would expect that to infuriate the old women. Instead, Mistress Flora seemed to shrink—slightly. She looked shabbier. Not weak, but old, like a woman carved out of wood. Her voice held no anger and maybe slight traces of sympathy under its grim, bleak seriousness. "That's why you're not expelled yet. This can't go on, Rhubella, and you can't change without losing what you're good at."

Miss Hammerhead's normally detached thoughtfulness now bored into Ruby like an awl as she said, "You're not talented, you're determined, which is better."

I agreed. I still barely knew Ruby, but that's what I had seen. Not that Ruby was stupid, but she was no natural genius like me or Elvira. What she was, was driven even harder than us. She achieved perfection by insisting on it. She prepared her ingredients ahead of time. She measured exactly and repeatedly. She took every precaution, using no ingredients and dispensing no potions she wasn't sure were perfect. She worked herself to collapse for perfection, and it worked.

Now I'd found out this meant fulfilling the responsibilities of a witch past the point where it became self-destructive.

Mistress Flora knew, and I was sure cared, nothing about my reactions. She continued after her partner, "But it has made you unsuitable to be a student. You are out of chances, Rhubella."

A weird, low-pitched ringing noise sounded behind me, around me. People yelled, in alarm rather than anger this time, and a lot of people.

I darted back onto the market street, and gawked. Something soared up into the air, from the direction of the ocean and heading over the city. Two somethings. It was hard to make out what they were. One looked like a ball, the other like a box, both shiny and with so many flailing limbs it looked like a slap fight.

That wasn't the even path of a thrown object. These things were flying. How? I didn't see wings.

Buzzes and bell tones, muffled by distance, filtered down to us on the ground.

Something happened in the fight. The round one dropped, catapulted down from the sky, and hit the market road not far from me. The violence of the impact cracked the pavement and scattered drops of sea water. One of those hit me in the face.

What was it? Was it even a creature? It wasn't just shiny like metal, but like a mirror. No, it had to be a creature because it had one big, perfectly round, glassy blue eye. It also had arms, four of them, mostly human, if simplified and flexible.

It looked like an appliance, not an animal. More than that, it looked like one of the bizarre machines from humanity's golden age.

Elvira yanked up one of the screens of Gwenda's shop, bursting out onto the street, already chanting spell code.

Code I'd heard her use before. I tackled Elvira, which was useless in terms of knocking the bigger girl down, but it let me reach my arm up and wrap my hand around her mouth. Trying to pull her ear down to my level, I hissed, "Don't cast illegal psychology spells in the middle of the street! Besides, that's not a monster!"

The round thing leaped back up into the air, only to meet the cube already diving for it. They met with a clang, dropped onto the road, and rolled around clawing at each other. If the rectangular thing had eyes, I didn't see them, but it had plenty of arms, and instead of the reflective shine of the sphere its metallic-looking surface shown with a rainbow that reminded me of spilled kerosene.

I found out Emanuel was standing behind me and Elvira when he asked, "It's not? What is it?"

"I don't know! I've never seen anything like them, which is why I'm sure they're not monsters! The only thing I can think of is extradimensionals," I whispered to the siblings.

POW-CRACK. Something hit the struggling beings invisibly fast. They shattered into jagged chunks that immediately began to slump and melt. Melt, but not vanish like monster flesh.

I followed the source of the pow sound back to Sheriff Greenlake, standing in the middle of the street with his revolver held up in both hands. Beside him stood the leather-clad old adventuress, Franklin. Except she didn't stay beside him long, stalking up to the corpses like a wary tiger, her heavy knife drawn and glowing, while her other hand held forward a fist-sized device I couldn't identify at this distance. It surely was meant to identify the beings.

Emanuel, Elvira, and I retreated into the doorway of Gwenda's shop to huddle together.

Into the enclosed space between us, one arm over his sister's back and the other over my shoulders, Emanuel murmured, "She's right, sis. Nobody will care in a dungeon, but you almost cast an illegal spell in front of them." He ticked his head subtly towards the sheriff and adventuress.

Me, I rubbed my face, suddenly understanding why Gwenda would do it. Plaintively, I asked, "Black magic, psychology. Aren't fire and lightning and force enough? What's left, necromancy?"

Elvira rolled her red-rimmed eyes in disdain. "Oh, like you've never tried to use your soul forge to bring a dead pet back to life."

Emanuel burst out laughing at whatever expression I now wore. He managed to choke it down to not escape the huddle, but his face twisted up convulsively and he couldn't stop the wheezy little barks.

Elvira shot him a disgusted expression next, and argued, "Come on. If it weren't for stalker zombies, every sheep on the West Coast would have been eaten by wild dogs. Necromancy isn't that bad."

Emanuel laughed harder. I was a little worried he would choke. I'd started to grin now, too.

Trying to be serious, I warned his sister, "If you keep this up you're going to get some nickname like Mistress of the Dark. Do you really want that?"

Elvira's eyes shone and her face lit up in rapture as if she had never been miserable. She whispered, "That would be the best. People would be seeking me out from the far side of the continent to raid dungeons!"

I was simultaneously helpless, horrified, amused, and awash in affection for Elvira. Giving up, I squeaked desperately, "Just don't get thrown in jail before that happens, okay?"

Elvira and Emanuel's arms tightened around my back, sweeping me into a hug with both simultaneously. My heart stung from relief, one of the fears that had been stacking up today taken away: Whatever else they were suffering, we were still friends.

I squeezed them back as hard as I could, which was pretty pathetic compared to their labor-hardened muscles. I also felt a subtle pressure around my ankle, a touch with an edge to it, like maybe Lisa had hooked her tail tip around my leg and squeezed.

By the time I struggled free from the hug, Lisa's tail swayed innocently behind her, but she was standing next to me with her arms impatiently folded and one of our food bags hooked over her shoulder.

We needed to go home soon, but I was bound to one more thing. I explained to the other three, "While the authorities are here, I ought to tell them about what we found in the Waste. Large temple in a widely cleared space in the middle. Weak soul forge, but it's producing Sumerian patterns so it's going to be dangerous and unstable."

Emanuel pointed his thumb back at the main street. "And Elvira and I will get farther out of sight. We need to talk about our future."

Oof. The worry came flooding back. "I wish…"

Elvira ruffled my fluffy hair, sounding different from usual only in not being as bubbly. "Our parents will be calmed down when we get home, and Emanuel is right. I don't want to, but if we have to, we can get jobs with the caravans. You go talk to the authorities. They'll listen to you."

I smirked. "I hope so. I'm a prodigy."

Chapter Thirty-Three

Saturday afternoon was quiet, which weighed on me Sunday morning.

I finished going over the safety checklist for the forge one more time, and rebooted it. The new golden seal worked perfectly. It slid in and out of place with the others smoothly. The inner box opened, the glowing green crystal floated motionless in the center, and the cage layers drifted out into their places.

Goblita's soul forge was ready for business.

If there would be any business.

Finally tearing my eyes away from all the properly fitted parts of the forge, I asked my cousin, "Is there a sign to show when we're open?" I mean, maybe I'd missed something.

Lisa was in the middle of eating something in a large tortilla wrap. She leaned against a bench in the back of the workshop, in a royal blue dress that clashed violently with the red, black, pink, and white themes of her body itself. It had a shorter skirt than most, but its main feature was a very low neckline in back to show off the summoning circle tattoo on her back even better than her other outfits.

She had just torn off a section with her fangs, and after a few chews swallowed the whole thing, causing a bulge to roll down her throat. She chattered, "Leo would turn on the light in the office and workshop. That's what stores seem to do here. I'm not sure how much it works. People knock whenever."

I tried it. The light from the windows had seemed like plenty, but I snapped my fingers and turned on the lights in the workshop and office—and also in the living room and probably a few more rooms and I definitely heard the ice elemental start whispering through the vents.

But lo and behold, seconds later, the doorknob to the business entrance rattled, followed by a knock!

I dashed to the door, and checked myself. Goggles, lab coat, overalls, protective gloves. Not wanting to take any chances with a newly repaired forge meant I was dressed like a real bioengineer.

Which I was.

I opened the door to a woman with short brown hair, a blouse and skirt, and that was all I noticed before she grabbed the door frame, leaned in, and demanded—or maybe begged, "You are open! You're the new bioengineer, right? Do you do species changes? Please tell me you do species changes."

Um. She obviously meant human changes. Working on a human was dangerous, or rather, if I did mess up, the consequences would be awful. Tiny mistakes you wouldn't notice in an animal could be devastating for a transformed human. I had been hoping to warm up to this. I was still new to being a professional.

On the other hand, I'd jumped into the ocean and found out I could swim. Metaphorically. The actual ocean looked as intimidating as it was beautiful.

I would take inspiration from Ruby. I'd do the job, but I would measure everything repeatedly, recheck every calculation and line I drew. I wouldn't improvise, overdesign, or underdesign. I would make sure everything was perfect.

It's not like I wasn't good enough. My problems were always from doing things too well.

The woman took the brief silence as encouragement to launch another question. "Do you do goblins?"

FINALLY.

I mean, "Um…"

She lowered one hand, palm down, and tugged on her ear with the other. "You know, like you, but green skin, pointy ears? The cute kind."

Throwing my hands up in the air, I complained, "I'm just thirteen!"

That stopped her. Well, momentarily. She straightened back up, giving me a wide-eyed, searching look. "And you're running a soul forge?"

She hadn't sounded skeptical, so I puffed up and tried not to gloat too hard as I explained, "I'm a prodigy."

She gripped one fist into the other by her stomach, and leaned forward again, asking, "A prodigy that can turn me into a goblin? Pleeeeeease?"

It should have sounded like a child begging, but this held more tiredness, a touch of exasperation. Maybe desperation, like this was the tail end of a string of things going wrong.

"Sure."

"Woo!" She reared up so fast she jumped into the air, threw her fist up, and spun around in a circle. A touch of seriousness returned. She took a deep breath, pulling her hair back, although it was so short it didn't need that. She asked hopefully, "Can I bring you a picture? If I bring you a memory, you can make me look like that, right?"

Okay, take it for granted that if it was a memory recording, it would be detailed. "I can."

But my ethics took over, no matter how much I was already hungry to take this job. I warned, "But you need to be careful. The more your body changes, the more the person inside changes. Giving yourself fur or green skin or even an animal muzzle isn't a big deal as long as that's fur and a muzzle on," and I waved my hand at her from top to bottom. "Just making you shorter is going to leave your soul fragment overpowered for the body it's running. You'll be much more energetic, and that sounds like it's all good, but it can change you in ways you wouldn't expect."

She looked like she was paying attention to every word, but when I finished she squeezed her eyes shut and shook her fists emphatically next to her head. In a breathy rush, she explained to me, "Yes yes yes! This is perfect. I have it all planned. I've got a whole new wardrobe scoped out, a job lined up where being small is an advantage, my friends all say they think I'm super cool for wanting this, and my boyfriend is so supportive. He says he thinks I'm great the way I am, but I'll be cute to die for as a goblin. I've wanted this since I was ten and I've got the money now and it will be great!"

Again, um. Was this woman stable enough to make a decision like a species change?

She was at least twice my age. She obviously wanted this as way more than a whim. I was in no place to judge whether an adult was able to make her own decisions. I was having enough trouble myself.

So I took a deep breath, and decided to stop judging and be a bioengineer. "Alright. Yes, I can make you look like a picture, if you insist. It's expensive, and we can't do the transformation today. I have to take measurements today, and you'll have to come back another day after I've had time to make calculations. You'll pay then."

I would really like that money after watching it all disappear buying groceries. A species change seemed like even more money when I would be the one getting paid. That this woman had saved up enough for it was another sign that she was serious and I had to let her decide. But, taking the money before I was completely sure the transformation would happen would be unethical.

I took a step back from the door, and the woman walked in, playing with her hair and responding, "Can I have a copy of my numbers? You make up a whole diagram, right? I'd love a copy to show my friends."

Retreating to the door of the workshop, I beckoned. "Come on in."

Then I focused on getting out the tracer and extending the altar for a human subject.

Chapter
Thirty-Four

As weird as the woman wanting the species change had been, getting her readings went so smoothly that I was certain the soul forge was perfectly calibrated. That relief and confidence buoyed me when the next knock came.

I opened the door to that towering scarecrow of a man, the head butcher Casper.

My heart lit up to see him. Then it damped again, as he held out a handful of tiny, tiny soul fragments rather than money. Right, we'd agreed on trade. Sure, these were worth a lot of money, except I had no one to sell them to.

I still handled them very, very carefully as he poured them into my hands, and I took them immediately to the special bowl with its airtight lid for storing soul fragments.

As I walked, the butcher stalked behind me in long strides, purring, "Twelve fragments obtained whole from chickens, oh yes, obtained whole. Six for you, and six for a pair of most fine sucrows. The other two are from particularly fine bulls, and surely must have the power of three chickens."

With the fragments safely stored, I got out my notes for making sucrows, explaining automatically, "Doesn't work. It has to be three separate shards, and if you break the bigger ones, they'll be useless."

Breaking them precisely would be very difficult anyway, as small as they were. Chicken fragments were bigger than pinheads, but not by much. The bull fragments were about four times that, little green shiny things in the grey ceramic cup. "Dead" soul fragments were just bright enough that you couldn't be sure if they were glowing or not.

The former owner loomed over me with his stick figure in vertically striped pants and a vertically striped coat. His intrusive presence demanded an answer, and one popped into my head. Digging into my notes again, I offered, "How about a powerkeet? It's either saving you money on powering your appliances, or making you money powering other people's. You're the head butcher, right? Your guild's refrigerators must gulp magic."

"As always, a most excellent suggestion." He bowed his head forward, tapping his fingertips together. I had to wonder if he was related to the gnome-looking guy at the market.

So I spent the next hour making a pair of sucrows and a powerkeet, which was fun and distracting. Intricate, but no stretch for my skills. It wasn't like they were new, experimental designs, and while they required a lot of power to put flesh on, bare soul fragments are predictable.

Lisa spent most of the process lounging in the back of the workshop staring at Casper. Not exactly hostile, but suspicious, like she thought he would knife me in the back if she gave him a chance.

I sent him off with three of the four bird cages he'd brought inhabited, and as I held open the door I explained, "Remember they'll eat heavily for the first few days as they replace the forge's magic with real flesh and blood. And sugar, for the sucrows, of course. Let them gorge themselves, it's a good thing."

Closing the door, I turned around to Lisa holding out a sandwich. "Lunch," she told me, flat and expressionless.

When I accepted and bit in, that demeanor changed. She

slid up to sit on the edge of my office workshop, smiling and watching me eat. The sandwich was crude, with thick bread slices unevenly cut and materials stuffed in, but it wasn't cooked, so it wasn't a disaster. Apparently we'd had some cooked fish left. It hadn't been slathered in sorghum juice, thank goodness.

I was guzzling water out of a jar when another knock sounded on the door.

Holding out the jar to Lisa, I chuckled. "Turning on the lights worked."

She accepted with a detached, sardonic half-smile and a shrug. "Sunday was usually a big business day for Leo. Maybe it's the shopping day for everyone who doesn't run a shop themselves."

So there would probably have been good business if they had been open Saturday morning. Well, I wasn't going to miss out on that adventuring with my friends, even if it turned into a disaster for those friends.

I shuddered as guilt hit me again, followed by cold worry at how Ruby had yelled at me.

Another knock sounded at the door, and I could not have been more grateful.

I opened the door to another woman. This one older, with tied back hair, dark touched with grey. She had an expression not so much sour as dignified, a posture as straight as Ruby's, and wore a suit that was tight and dark, greyed out blue. She held a bird cage low in front of her, then lifted to show me the pigeon inside.

"Is this the soul forge reopened?" she asked crisply.

I nodded. "It is. I'm the new bioengineer, Artifact Forge. Call me Art."

She nodded back, sort of. It was a slight movement of her head forward and to the side. "I'm sure this will be simple enough, then. I'd like a messenger dragon."

Ouch. Way to hit me where I'm sensitive.

And ouch again, as I forced myself to say, "I'd have been happy to, Ma'am, but I have to recommend against it. There's a wild dragon breed hunting around the city limits right now, and if you send out a messenger dragon, it will probably get attacked."

It stung to say that, and not just because I was responsible. I liked making dragons, and again, having only a couple of coins rattling around in my desk drawer right now was making me uncomfortable.

Then I blinked. Of course!

In her stiff, official way, the woman's expression was turning disappointed. I interrupted that process by cheerfully declaring, "On the other hand, bioengineering may be able to help you after all. How far do you need to send messages?"

Solemnly, with maybe a hint of curiosity creeping into her voice, she said, "Mostly around Goblita. I live out on the northwest edge, and getting to the shops or contacting my nieces and nephews downtown is an uncomfortable walk."

I grinned enormously. "Then I can help you after all. How about a roadrunner dragon? They can't fly higher than a story, but they're fast and reliable on the ground. If you send it cross country it will get eaten by animals, but it could go up or down the One-and-One as far as Sin Fortress, if that's what you wanted."

She brightened up, eyebrows rising maybe a half inch and her mouth curling the same amount into a smile. "That sounds perfect."

I made sure it was perfect, and sent her away a little while later with a long-legged, long-tailed, bouncy and fangy little creature the size of her hand hopping around in its cage, eager to get to work.

The sensation of actual money in my hand filled me with relief, and I loved hearing the multiple clinks as I poured it all into the wooden drawer. Messenger dragons were cheap for bioengineering work, but shopping had made me realize that no bioengineering work was cheap. This and one more messenger dragon would cover the cost of feeding me and Lisa for a week, including sweets.

I wished I could write to tell my father how fun and heavy it was simultaneously to be a professional, and to tell my parents that I was actually succeeding.

Another knock didn't happen immediately, so I headed for the living room and sat down in the super comfortable chair.

Its softness didn't help my mood much. The joy of creating life was rapidly sinking into the pit of my worries.

What were my parents thinking? I had to send them a letter. The roads weren't great between here and Touhou. A roadrunner dragon wouldn't make it. Maybe I could make something more durable, or magical. Maybe stealthy. Or a burrower.

Except experimenting was how I caused all this trouble in the first place.

So far, I'd been able to fix my own troubles okay, but I'd gotten other people hurt, and my friends' troubles were my troubles. Emanuel and Elvira were being braved, but their life had cracked and was about to fall apart, and I'd given it the last big kick.

I might lose them. Like I'd lost Ramona.

I didn't want to remember Ramona.

What would happen to Ruby? I wasn't even sure if I was friends with Ruby. How would I feel, if Ruby, Emanuel, and Elvira all had to leave town?

Lisa dropped into the chair beside me, and twisted, forcing me aside until we shared the deep padding half and half.

I was about to ruin Lisa's mood, and felt even worse about it because I was partly doing it to distract from my own pain. Weakly, my head tilted back to look up at the dull brown ceiling currently being sucked clean by a horseshoe crab, I asked, "You know we have to get the breach key back, right?"

"If we do, you have to promise to not let them send me home," she answered.

She'd said it like a casual warning, as if it wasn't a big deal, but I put my arms around my demon cousin and squeezed her fierce and tight to me. "I promise," I whispered into her shoulder, and made it emphatic.

Lisa didn't hug me back, but she was warm and had that nice fruit smell and it was comforting to me, too, to have family here I could touch. She pouted vaguely, looking away from me, and her voice dropped into a sullen grumble. "Okay, then, fine, but I don't know how you're going to. It's in the ocean. It's gone."

I eased up on the hug, but didn't let go. Managing a bit of whimsical sarcasm myself, I said, "Yeah, I know it's in the ocean. It opened an underwater breach yesterday, remember? Next time it might open one enough for more than a couple of bucket sized weirdos to get out. We have to get it back."

She hunched up her shoulders a bit, her scowl deepening. "I get it, but that still doesn't mean I can help. You're the bioengineer. Make a… retrieval fish or something."

Hmmm. I let go of the hug, leaving only the arm wormed between the chair and Lisa's back. Scootching up even closer to her, I walked through that idea out loud. "Making an aquatic monster that wants to retrieve something won't be hard. I can give it whatever senses it needs. Self-defense that doesn't make it look like offense, so it doesn't scare anyone. Maybe something like a lobster. Everything is easy except finding the detonator itself. Any residue of your scent is long gone. Or your signature, for that matter. I'm sure a breach detonator has a strong signature, which would be great, except I don't know what it is."

I drummed my fingers on the arm rest of the chair. With padding that soft, they didn't make much noise.

"Except someone does," I mused.

Lisa's head jerked around to give me a glare. "Do not go talk to that freaky old guy who wants to exorcise me, Artifact."

I waved my not-pinned hand to reassure her. "No, no. I'll get the information from where he gets it. The college library. While I'm at it, I may be able to do a favor for Emanuel and Elvira."

Because if I was going to get them kicked out of their homes, I could at least send them on their new life well armed.

Chapter
Thirty-Five

A n hour passed with no more customers.

The comfy chair was nice. The comfy chair was so nice.
Still, there was only so much rest I could do, and with only a
little effort of will I sprang to my feet and declared, "Might as
well go now. Why waste time?"

Lisa spread out to contain the seat entirely, leaning her
elbow on one of the rests to look up to me with a skeptical pink
smirk. "You just want to make a weird new monster nobody
else has made before."

I pulled papers into a pile and added some pencils and pens,
a bottle of ink, and dug out my slide rule. Then I wandered
around the living room until I found where I'd put down my
satchel, then did the same for my shoes.

Somewhere during that process I noticed the comfy chair
was empty, and glanced over my shoulder. Lisa, with diabolic
stealth, was now following me around. She frowned a lot, and
when I finally had my shoes on and my satchel on my shoulder

she crossed her arms and shifted her weight to one side. "I can't come with you."

Slightly disappointed, I raised a bushy orange eyebrow at her while my hands scooped bushy orange head hair out from under the satchel strap that had trapped a lot of it. "Because that guy who hates demons works there?"

Lisa turned her head to one side so sharply that it flung her hair about. "A lot more than just him. You don't notice. They would never let me into the library."

Aw. With one hand remaining on the strap of my satchel, I stepped up to my red-haired, black-horned, glowing-eyed cousin and slipped my other arm around her shoulders. She rolled her eyes at the hug.

Then I admonished her gently, "It's a library, Lisa. I can take care of myself for a few hours in a library. I'll be safe. My burning hand really spooked you, didn't it?"

She gave me another of her weird looks. This wasn't the one where all sorts of contradictory expressions flashed over her face. This one was an intent, searching stare that didn't seem angry and didn't have anything to do with the situation that I could figure out.

Her answer, at least, made sense with its crisp, accusing tone. "If you'd seen someone fade away into nothing, you'd be spooked too. Go to the library." And she stomped off into the kitchen. A girl with hooves can really stomp, too. Once she got off the carpet she sounded like someone hammering a nail.

I was becoming sure that Uncle Leonard being Lisa's father was more than just an unconfirmed technicality for her, but if Lisa didn't want to talk about it there was nothing I could do.

I stepped outside. It was late afternoon now, but hopefully not so late that the College library was closed. People seemed to still be out shopping. They wandered up and down the street alone or in small groups holding packages. A woman in a flower print dress carried a big bag in her arms, followed by children in flower print clothing holding bags in descending sizes. That is, bags and children both got smaller towards the far end.

That was a good sign. Just because a school for kids and teenagers closed on Sundays didn't mean the school for adults would, right? Especially since the College was more than a school.

I mean, I actually only assumed they did classes at all because of the name. The only things I'd heard for sure the College did was magical research and the kind of big magics governments need. Building a sewer system and maintaining its pumping systems, say. Or blowing up pirates.

I bet the witch school wasn't closed. I hoped that Ruby was still in it. The harder I tried to be nice to Ruby, the more I seemed to blow up her life. Had Ruby started to hate me for it? How could I keep up with the feelings of someone who only showed them when she was drunk on magic? Maybe it would be better if Ruby did hate me, for Ruby's sake.

The College wasn't far. I only had to go down to the One-and-One to see it, and it only took that long because other buildings were in the way.

I was so busy brooding instead of paying attention to the world around me that I only noticed the hulking shadow slide up next to me at the last moment. A big, claw-tipped hand slipped into my hair, vigorously rubbing the top of my head.

Way up at the top of that shadow, Joe gave me an amicable wolf grin and asked, "How's the cutest goblin prodigy on the West Coast?"

The whole world suddenly smelled like sawdust, sandy street dust, and salt. Joe must have to bathe in the ocean a lot. At least he didn't naturally smell bad. In response to his question, I ticked off on my fingers, "First, you know I'm not a goblin. Second, do you always lurk at the crossroads?"

His grin only widened. He extricated his hand from my hair, which left some of it floating in the gentle sea breeze. Tucking his thumbs into the waistline of his shorts instead he said, "Not hardly. I was about to knock on your door when I saw you walking down the street."

"Which door?" I asked automatically.

Joe's grin got wider still, like that was the best question ever. "The personal door. It's not a big deal, I just wanted to thank you for the crown."

Oh, right. So much happened so far, I'd forgotten about it.

"You mean from the Shedu yesterday? We all wanted you to have it."

I would never say this where Joe might hear it, but after I'd gone grocery shopping the appeal of keeping that golden treasure really hit home for me.

"I've been thanking everyone," he assured me. "You're next to last. They all say you beat the monster anyway."

I shook my head at that, and had to push back some of the hair that Joe had dislodged. "I hope Elvira is last, because she did all the work."

Joe's eyes watched me like… well, not like a wolf watching a rabbit. He just seemed delighted to look at me, the same way he looked at everyone. Raising a finger, he corrected merrily, "No, Bonabelle will be last, because she's across town. Elvira was passionate about the whole thing. She said it taught her why adventurers work in teams, that she can't blast a monster and wrestle with it at the same time."

I guessed lessons like that were very much on Elvira's mind if she was planning on leaving home.

Instead of following that topic, I said, "You need the money the most anyway."

Which was true. I could earn enough for me and Lisa. It had just come as a shock that I had to.

His grin faded to a bittersweet smile. "I do. It's just the windfall I needed. I hate to say it, but it's time for me to move on."

Oof. Another heart clench moment. Another friend leaving. Even though Joe was only a friend at the level of he liked to see me smile. Did anyone know Joe better than that? He said himself that his defining feature was his interest in other people. As a result, he was even more opaque than Lisa and Ruby.

A fact I would never have noticed if I wasn't trying to deal with the mysteries of Lisa and Ruby already. Joe had been someone who could make any situation fun and easy, and I'd been happy to go along with the ride.

Did adults always have to think like this? Because it sucked. I wanted to think about bioengineering instead.

But this was an important topic, so I focused on it again and said, "I guess it's expensive to move around a lot."

He snorted and rolled his eyes, even his irritation cheerful. "I can do it for free, it's just miserable to do it that way. I was going to use the money from the opportunity Lisa pointed at me, but everything I picked up is too specialized to sell locally. Another reason to move on. I wish I could stay here, but," and he shook his head wistfully, "Goblita isn't cheap, and it doesn't have the opportunities I need for a real life. It's probably time I headed down to Adventure and looked for a real job."

I tried to sound as unbrooding as possible. "Congratulations. I'll miss you, but that sounds like a thing to congratulate you on."

Joe took a deep breath, and with that huge, muscular chest it was a lot of breath. "It is, but... I got to like Goblita. It seems like every week I meet someone new and fascinating." He ruffled my hair again, sending it spilling over my face. I probably looked like an orange haystack with legs. "If you're heading to the College, I'd better turn around. You'll see me before I go, I promise. More than once. You'll get plenty of warning."

I leaned my head back to smile back up at him. "Thanks. Good luck, Joe! In the future, I mean. And also right now." Throwing up my hands in exasperation, I declared, "I don't know! I'm only good at bioengineering!"

He walked off laughing, his head turned so he could watch my face as long as possible.

Wait, who was Bonabelle?

Too late to ask. Joe was gone.

I'd reached the College campus, too. A lot of rectangular, multistory buildings with small windows looked very generic, and I had no idea which one was which. Nice greenery around the paths, at least. Nothing looked particularly magical. It was absolutely nothing like the witchcraft academy.

I did the obvious. I waved my hand in front of an adult walking past holding a book, and asked, "Excuse me, where is the library?"

The man pointed a finger. "That building down there. Sorry, I'm in a hurry." He had been walking pretty fast, and now he swept past me, scurrying towards... somewhere. The paths looped around a lot.

I followed his direction. This building was thinner and taller than the others, but not by enough to stand out. It did have an arch around the door sculpted in wavy designs. The door opened easily enough, and I stepped inside.

Yes, this was a library. No mistaking it. The front room was pretty small, with a lot of tiling in swirly blue and white that just might be marble. The room did go up two floors in the middle, with a circular balcony looking down on us at ground level. I saw bookshelves up there. I saw bookshelves through two doorways off to either side at ground level. I saw tightly packed bookshelves and a skinny metal filigree spiral staircase through a doorway straight ahead. The floors and bookshelves were different colors in each of those rooms, and arranged differently besides.

A hand caught the back of my shirt. I looked up at the dimensional magic specialist, the one that I'd mistaken for a priest. He still looked like a priest, with that big but neatly squared off beard, his white collar and black coat, and overall fastidious tidiness. Also that sour-faced priest look. I'd heard there were fun gods and goddesses, but I'd never met any.

"What are you doing here, Artifact Forge? Where is the demon?" he demanded, all stiff and suspicious, but not actually visibly angry.

My mind started buzzing, searching for an excuse. That stopped abruptly, because… the truth would work just fine!

I told him honestly, "She's at home, and I'm here to look up the exact signature of a breach detonator."

His scowl had been suspicious and not quite angry. Now it turned suspicious and confused. But very suspicious indeed. "Why?"

"So I can make a monster to find it," I again answered honestly.

I had him. I could see it in the way his face froze up, unfocused. It was obviously the last thing he expected. Plus, if Lisa had stolen the device, why would I want or need to find it?

"Why is that your business?" he demanded, his grip on my shirt weakening, his tone less suspicious and more just not understanding.

I adjusted my bag, looked up into his beady little eyes, and said with still perfect honesty, "Because there was a breach event yesterday, and somebody said you need the key to prevent those? I saw some interdimensionals I've never heard of land in the street, and hundreds of them fighting a war in Goblita seems like a bad idea. They were covered in seawater, so I thought maybe the detonator is in the ocean. I'm going to make a monster to go find it."

All true! Not just technically, but in spirit. I'd left out why the detonator was in the ocean, but the point was I wanted it back before the Breach replayed in the town I lived in.

"That's not your job," he pointed out, probing at my unexpected answers.

I shrugged. "I'm the only one who can do it."

It's not like the priest-looking guy stopped scowling. I doubted he ever stopped scowling. But now he spent several silent seconds with the brow-furrowed, detached surliness of someone scowling at his own thoughts.

Finally, he said, gruff and glaring, "You need to understand some things, Miss Forge. You think I don't like your house guest, and you're right. You badly underestimate how harsh the Hell she comes from is, and how hostile most of its occupants are. Even if she is somehow an exception, her presence is a constant pressure in a vulnerable area. The other Hell proto-universes are even worse than hers and she scratches at their walls."

"Then we had better find that breach detonator so you can stabilize things, fast," I answered, calmer but just as determined as him.

Or maybe more determined. He let out a long sigh, and let go of me completely. Muttering, "The book you're looking for is *Annotations of the Golden Age Conferences of Quantum Theory.* Look in the appendix."

I put the books down on the low table in my living room, and opened up the shiny, soft, slick one to flip through its pages. As I turned to the appendix with all the statistics and measurements of a breach detonator, I told my cousin enthusiastically, "It was so easy! A librarian only asked me anything once, and I said I was the town bioengineer and she didn't even mention my age. All you need to take a book home is just sign and date a little card so they'll know what happened if someone else wants to check the book out."

Lisa tapped the book that had a cloth-covered wooden plate cover. Her pointed fingernail made a little clicking sound. "This one doesn't have a label."

I pulled that book up on top of the shiny one. The pages inside were much more ragged, yellowing, and written, not typed for a press. Every page seemed to have a hand-drawn picture on it. "It's some adventurer's journal. He recorded dungeon designs. But he *also* recorded..."

I turned a few more pages, and pulled out one of the many pages tucked rather than bound into the journal. It contained nothing but a compact, carefully calligraphed design of squiggles and dots. I crowed, "Magic Missile! And there are other spells, I just can't read magic code well enough to know what they are. Emanuel will know."

Pushing both books aside, I pulled up my own stack of blank papers, not fancy and pure white or old and yellow. I drew out the basic diagram to make a lobster, then expanded its containment. Not in an experimental way this time. No more chimeras! I knew how to draw in signature sensitivity by heart...

Standing over me, Lisa let out a groan. "You're going to try to make this tonight."

A lock of my hair fell forward, over my face and down to pool onto the papers. I blew it aside with a puff of air before chattering back, "Sure. This isn't anything strenuous. Once I get the design done, it will take half an hour. Five minutes to make the egg, ten minutes to walk down to the ocean and toss it in, ten minutes to walk back home, and another five minutes in there somewhere while we argue."

Arms crossed, Lisa watched me, briefly silent. Then she pouted. "Fine, but I'll be watching you. It had better only take thirty minutes."

It only took thirty minutes. Five minutes of creation, ten minutes of walking down to the ocean in the dim purple gloaming, ten minutes of walking back in a night lit only by lamps, bathed in quiet and sea breeze, and another five minutes in there somewhere while Lisa made me eat a sandwich.

Chapter Thirty-Six

L isa did not wake me up to go to school the next morning. I wasn't sure how I felt about that until I wandered into my workshop and saw the little bead I'd attached to my soul forge blinking red.

Questions of whether I should have gone to school today became moot. My monster had retrieved the detonator.

That fast? Well, it was heavy metal and highly magical. Maybe it hadn't gone far, and was easy to find.

I ran upstairs, feet thumping on the stairs, to grab the rest of my clothing. The sound of feet on wood got Lisa toddling groggily out of her bedroom. I yelled, "Get dressed. Hurry! We have to go retrieve my monster before someone notices something is pulsing satisfaction aspect and goes to find out why. I'm sure the College has detectors." It would be weird if they didn't.

Anxiety tickled me, but it was ridiculous and irrational. The geodifferential from a fluctuating signal like this would be much too tiny to get an earthmover's attention. The College produced more activity all day just from people casting spells, I'd bet.

Besides, earthmovers didn't like water and hardly ever

attacked oceans or lakes. You'd need a much bigger provocation than my little crustacean monster's beacon.

I pulled my freshly charged ID pendant out from under my soul forge and hung it around my neck, then I checked the pigeon's feed. It stared at me with creepy orange eyes, and as if those eyes were looking into my thoughts it pecked a sunflower seed, scooping it up and swallowing it down.

I had my satchel on my shoulder when Lisa came clip-clopping down the stairs. With mussed hair slightly shiny from not having been washed yet, she of course looked even more fabulous. Also, could I alter myself so that my sweat smelled like strawberries? That was a completely unfair advantage.

We hurried outside, into beautiful sunshine. It was too late in the morning for mist, but the sun was warm, the air was cool, and the sea breeze was drifting inland all the way to my house. Nobody paid the slightest bit of attention to me and Lisa as we walked down to the beach.

I leaned close to Lisa as we walked, opening my satchel to show her the wood-and-cloth–bound book inside. I explained cheerfully, "Once we've got the detonator, I want to see if Emanuel is down with the fishing fleet. If we can get him alone, I'll give him this."

Lisa rubbed her rounded little chin. She'd painted her fingernails black since last night. "Diabolical schemer working on it now."

I flashed her a grin. "Thanks."

As she stood back, I walked up to the edge of the water, just inside the wet line on the sand, so that the water splashed over my sandaled toes every few waves. It felt slightly sticky today, but I didn't care. The cold rush of water that then withdrew was still nice.

I waited, looking out over the water, drinking in the blue. I floated on the rhythmic rush of the waves moving in and out. I listened to the squeaks of the distant seagulls. Very distant. This beach was apparently a very boring place for seagulls right now. Maybe some huge, dead fish was floating around a mile out. Maybe traces of its blubber were why the water felt sticky. Ew.

After a few peaceful minutes, my monster came crawling out of the surf. It dragged itself forward, not great at moving on land, leaving a wide line in the wet sand. Of course the breach detonator would be weighing it down, hidden under that rounded brown shell.

At the last minute, I'd decided to switch the monster recipe to something I already know, so now a lumpy, chitinous horseshoe crab crawled up the beach in front of my feet. It seemed extra appropriate because I added a few drops of horseshoe crab blood from my supply, so it would have the extra vitality to operate keen magical senses.

Where *was* the detonator? Sure, its gripping claws were under the shell, but the big, metal key ought to stick out somewhere. I crouched down and pulled up the armored hood at the front of the monster, and it spat out a hexagonal metal plate the size of my spread-fingered hand.

This was not the detonator. I picked it up. It was heavy, and looked like iron, except it hadn't rusted. It was encrusted with brown gunk and striped, fruit-shaped barnacles, but the uncovered sections revealed engravings on one side. It felt a little odd, too, prickly at my fingertips, and my ID pendant hanging over it definitely sparkled a little more than normal.

Out loud, I asked, "What is this, and why does it have the exact same magical signature as a breach detonator?"

Shadows shifted as Lisa leaned over me. "I don't know any magic, but that doesn't look like any of your symbols, and it doesn't look like spells on a tablet."

I rubbed uselessly at a wet brown crust that looked like sand fused by years into cement, and guessed, "No, it's... I think this has to be an earthmover creation. This corner looks like that gate Yuki is looking for, but there's more underneath that's covered up. I don't think it's the same symbol."

Lisa jerked upright, clasping her hands behind her and grinning with shameless delight. "I guess you've got a neat extra treasure, and finding the key is off!"

Straightening up myself, I nudged her shoulder with my fist. "Sorry to disappoint you, but with this not distracting it anymore, I'll just send my little guy back to find the real—"

Multiple somethings screamed, all at the same time. Animal sounds, but in the sky.

I looked up, and identified the four-winged, three-headed silhouette descending towards us as the chimera, then was yanked away by Lisa's hands gripping my wrist. I stumbled as she dragged me away from the surf, and away from the landing chimera.

Although "landing" implied a certain grace it didn't bother with. It dropped out of the air onto my retrieval monster, flipped the marine bug thing onto its back, and began tearing into it with all three heads, each one darting on its sinuous, swan-like neck to bite down, rip up, and swallow.

The new head was more than a little out of place, and looked like a smaller wolf's head.

Not much smaller. The thing was bigger than before, bigger than an adult.

"It remembers you!" yelped Lisa, still dragging me away.

I corrected, "It remembers my soul forge, and it's desperately hungry for magic. I'll dismiss the monster, so at least—"

The air rippled, like a thin line of heat haze. Something invisible smacked into the chimera. Repeatedly. It was like watching the thing get hit by a rapid series of powerful punches. They knocked its head and wings about, sending it sprawling. Its joints no longer looked right, but I watched a wing bent in a disturbing angle twist back into place and start flapping. It rose ponderously up into the air.

A big, heavy, black-painted crossbow bolt hit it right in the center of its body, knocking it out of the air to flop into the surf. Red blood ran from the wound, and its erratically waving wings brushed over the tracks my monster had made, erasing them. The monster itself was gone, dissolved into the air and water when it died.

Another crossbow bolt hit the chimera farther up its rib cage, and I definitely saw the point jutting out the back of the body this time. More blood splattered into the waves and was washed away. The magical impacts had definitely hurt it. The wing may have straightened out, but one of the dragon heads twisted at a creepy angle at what looked like a broken neck.

The wolf head was underwater.

The last head screeched, only to be literally drowned out as an extra big wave washed over it. When the water pulled back, the chimera was gone.

The old woman in the leather armor rushed up, holding a crossbow covered in magic script engravings. Her armor whisked and clunked with every heavy step.

My heart leaped into my throat, then I remembered it was fine. We hadn't been caught doing anything. My sending out this monster was no secret.

Which was good, because I had a very, very important question to ask her. "Do you think you got it?"

Her tightly curled locks of grey hair bounced as she shook her head. She kept her voice low. "I don't know. If it were a regular animal, a monster, even something tough like a dragon, it would have died with the first hit, if it even survived the spell. Chimeras are tough."

Water splashed, more than it already does on a beach. Several yards out, something jumped up out of the waves, then fell back in. I made out four wings, but now they looked like oversized flippers. A white, scaleless, reptilian head held up a horseshoe crab, which it had just bitten in half. Glowing blue blood poured down into and around the creature's mouth, splattering its face.

Then it was underwater and gone again.

The old monster hunter, Franklin, grunted. "That's not a good sign."

"I saw the arrows, and it's still flailing," Lisa pointed out.

Looking at me, Franklin said, "It may still be dying. If it's not, and it goes fully aquatic, it won't have reason to bother us anymore. The ocean is a bad place for most magical animals. It's going to be a target for every predator for miles. Still… not a good sign. I'm going to go talk to the College, and see if I can contact the Adventurers' Guild in Lady Angel. What did your scavenger turn up?"

The answer was harmless, so I picked the dropped plate up off the sand and showed it to her. "Any clue what it is?"

She stared at it. "Dungeon loot. Highly magical. That's all I can tell you," she answered flatly.

Then she walked away.

Lisa patted my shoulder. I turned my head to see her waving at Emanuel and Elvira running up from the direction of the docks.

They were already almost on us, and it only took a few seconds before Elvira ran right past me after Franklin, but the old woman could move fast without seeming to run. She was a ways away already. Elvira trotted to a stop after a few steps, then whipped around, fists clenched and arms straight down, face aglow with excitement. She bubbled enthusiastically, "Did you see that Magic Missile? Nine hits! I bet the Shedu would have felt *that*."

Elvira's perky energy shouldn't surprise me by now, but it always seemed to. I recovered quickly, reaching into my satchel. "Speaking of which…"

I pulled out the untitled adventurer's journal out of my bag, and placed it in Emanuel's hands. He immediately let it fall open to a random page.

It chose to open to a page with one of the loose sheets tucked in, the ones with spell code written on them. His eyes and smile widened in delight, and his lips moved subtly as he translated.

Elvira saw the page too. She descended on me much like the chimera had dropped onto my monster, but with friendlier intentions. Much friendly, and at least slightly less deadly. The bigger girl cinched her arms around my middle, pulled me off the ground, and squeezed me in a ferocious hug.

I had never been hugged so tight. All the breath squeezed out of me, and my back and ribs ached.

I could still move my head, so I got to see tears shining at the corners of her eyes as Elvira pressed her face to my shoulder and squeaked, "You are so nice to me."

Someone yelled in the distance. Two someones, a man and a woman. They sounded angry, and they sounded like Emanuel and Elvira's parents, although too far away to make out any words. I was glad I couldn't make out the words.

Elvira dropped me onto my feet. I wheezed a little.

Emanuel looked at his sister, both of them tense and serious now. He said, "I have to hide this. I can get their attention in the process."

The sorceress in the long brown dress and long black hair replied, "That will be plan A."

Emanuel nodded at her. I might feel like I'd just heard half a conversation, but they clearly understood each other. Both took off back the way they came, but with Elvira angling towards the beach and Emanuel away.

Behind me and off to my side, Lisa grabbed tight hold of my shoulder. "Home," she ordered.

I looked back at her with surprise. "What? I guess, but—"

Lisa stared right in my eyes, although I personally found glowing, pink, slit-pupil eyes adorable rather than intimidating. She explained firmly, "Home now. In case that thing comes back. It's hungry for magic, and you are full of magic. It can track that—" she jabbed the ID pendant hanging against my chest. "Or maybe it was just after the thing you dug up out of the sea. I don't like any of those options, so let's put some more distance between it and you, okay? Besides, the professionals are on it. It's not your job anymore."

It was good advice, and I appreciated Lisa's concern no matter how pushy she was expressing it. "Okay."

Chapter
Thirty-Seven

I managed to not be my job all the way to Wednesday.

We left the damp, lovely mist behind us as we walked inland up our street in the early morning.

Lisa sparkled as if she knew some way to deliberately collect drops of mist all over her and then make them shine in the rising sunlight. It was a technique that did not merge well with her staring down at the road sulkily.

My turn to tease, I grinned lazily over at her. "Sorry, cousin, that goblin job got me enough money I can afford to go to school the rest of the week."

Lisa grunted. Then she peeked up and side at me slyly, with a smirk instead of a pout. "And you're still floating on it."

Pushing my fluffy hair back, I gushed, "Who wouldn't be? I got to turn a human into another species. When she sat up and stretched her arms and looked at how green they are and said, 'Everything is so big,' it was the biggest rush in the world. Did you see her expression? Did you?"

Lisa clasped her hands behind her, just above the base of

her waving tail. "You did make her look just like the picture. If she hadn't wanted to look so grown-up, she'd have been as cute as you."

I waved my hands wide, like I could form a rainbow in the air. "I did all kinds of readings. Mental alteration was practically zero. I've always been proud of being a prodigy, but I never felt it like I did seeing the results. Even the Dollmaker couldn't have done better."

Lisa's smirk widened. "And you're not the only goblin in town anymore."

I stuck my tongue out at her.

Back to being the teaser instead of the teasee, she flashed a shameless grin back, but it faded into something gentler immediately. Rapt, but not playful or malicious. It was the same smile Joe usually wore. Lisa was enjoying seeing me happy.

That just put the capstone on that happiness. It was hard to feel lonely and rejected with someone who loved me this much at my side.

And then I saw Ruby walking along the street, wearing a towering witch hat and holding a ratty old broom that dragged in the street next to her. She had her head tilted back just enough to look up at the cloud-dappled sky.

I... didn't know what to say.

A little pink arm stuck out from under the hat and patted the side of Ruby's head with its paw. It pointed at me at the same time Lisa shouted, "Hey, ice witch!"

Would kicking Lisa in the tail make this more awkward? I grimaced at Ruby, the most embarrassed person in the world, as she walked up to me with her calm, unreadably solemn face. She tried to clasp her hands in front of her, but she was holding the broom, so the stick ended up turned at an angle across her front.

Stepping up to just out of arm's reach, she stopped and said softly, formally, "Good morning, Miss Forge. May I ask where you are going at this time in the morning?"

Oh, oof. What a question. Uncomfortably aware this might be a painful answer, I pointed inland with just a finger and mumbled, "Um... school."

Her sober expression tilted just a bit towards sadness, and she nodded.

I was now stuck with the questions I desperately craved answers for, and was afraid to ask. Except... my work yesterday and the sense of security of having a desk full of money at home gave me strength. I burst out, "The hat. Does that mean you've graduated?"

"I am afraid not," she answered. "There is no law against non-witches wearing one, after all. Only student witches are forbidden."

Guilt squeezed my throat, flooding away the remains of yesterday's joy. My voice rasped as I asked, "You were expelled?"

The burgundy-haired girl's frown deepened, her face lowered an inch, and for a moment her eyes stopped focusing on mine. "I'm not... sure."

Suddenly she bowed, so deep that her tucked down head made it more than double. Her hat hissed, but stayed on. The calm voice became a stiff, formal voice. "I apologize, Miss Forge. I felt, I feel keenly that you should hear what happened, but it is difficult to make myself say it. I hope you can overlook my unprofessional awkwardness."

Lost and aghast, I waved my hands in front of me. "No, I would never force you to tell me anything."

Ruby remained bowed, but her hat wandered up to the back of her head, far enough for the brim to lift and Sophie's wrinkly furless cat face to peer out at me. The cat owner, still formal, echoed, "No, of course you wouldn't. You are a deeply considerate person. I am being kicked out of the school, but not out of witchcraft. The headmistresses have concluded that I am unsuited to a classroom environment, and would benefit more from practical education. I am being sent to an apprenticeship."

"Where?" I asked immediately, and then my shocked brain caught up with what must mean more to Ruby. "With who?"

Finally, she stood up straight. Her hat scrambled back up to its proper place on top. The calm had definitely been replaced with a hard, icy mask, although there wasn't much difference between sober detachment and formal reserve. A bit of tension in the same expression and tone, that's it. "That is not decided.

Mistress Flora said she had a friend she thought would be perfect, but that friend lives in Sin Fortress."

"Hundreds of miles away," I filled in, stunned. Ruby wasn't just leaving. She was going unreachably far away.

"Yes," Ruby confirmed.

Sophie's leg extended from under the hat again, whapping Ruby in the face several times. The cat hissed from under the hat, "Tell her!"

Ruby swept forward in that super deep bow again. She declared, if quietly, "I might be asked to leave any day now, and I wanted to say..." She hesitated, long enough for it to be very obvious, to even start to drag, before continuing, "It has been an honor to know and to work with you, Miss Forge."

Sophie meowed, and sounded angry.

Ruby swept back upright. The broom had turned horizontal whenever she bowed, and now up at an angle again. She told me, focused very much on me, as if I were the only person in the world, "Until then, I am officially a witch, and I am occupying the same room at the school as I prepare to move out."

Sophie stuck her paw out of the hat and whapped Ruby's face some more.

Ruby nodded curtly. "Yes, Sophie. Please, if this does trouble you, Miss Forge, know that without you I would have flunked out of school. Now I am on a path to accomplish all my goals." The formal mask slipped. A touch of pain cracked it, tilting her mouth and eyebrows at an angle, and adding a noticeable hoarseness to the next word before she recovered. "Almost. Thank you, Miss Forge, from the bottom of my heart."

She turned around so fast that her skirts whirled around her, and walked away as fast as anyone can without looking undignified.

I suddenly realized something. "We're going to be late!"

Lisa gave me that special grin that said she'd been letting me miss that fact.

I burst into a run, my satchel flapping uncomfortably at my side. Lisa trotted next to me, keeping up easily with long, light, skipping steps, keeping that grin trained on me as I labored.

Me, I wasn't in shape for this. I had to slow down to a jog.

Lisa responded by turning around and trotting backwards, still matching my pace with those almost lazy strides. Always a master at taunting, she kept her hands behind her back so she looked even more casual.

And of course, Lisa didn't get her comeuppance by tripping over anything. No, she hopped backwards all the way to the door of the school, including jumping up onto and then down off of the big rock in the front yard.

At least she turned around once we reached the front hall. It was clear of students. My cousin and I got into our classroom a little late, but I thought only a little late.

The first thing I noticed was... no Joe, no Emanuel, and no Elvira.

Mr. Drake was still there, with his mixed red and gold hair, and his mixed red and gold eyes gleaming with delight as he spotted me. Rising up from behind his desk, he greeted, "Miss Forge! I was hoping I'd see you again."

Being formal felt weird after talking to Ruby, but I managed to be both politely respectful and not actually as stiff as a stone wall as I explained, "I'm interested in school, Mr. Drake, but I have a job. I'm hoping I can figure out a schedule where I go to school some days, and work others. I'm still figuring out how much I need to work to support my cousin and I."

That seemed to work, because he merely watched me with an approving smile as I wandered among the desks to sit in the one next to Yuki. She and Lucky were the only kids left in the room that I knew.

As soon as I sat down, Yuki looked up sharply from her work, and leaned over the arm of her desk chair. Her dark glasses hid half her expression, but her whispered questions were anything but stiff. "Where is Elvira? And Emanuel and Joe?"

"I was going to ask you!" I whispered back.

She shook her head, rapidly but just a tiny bit from side to side. "I haven't seen them since this weekend." Up close, even her breath felt cold as it puffed over e.

Lucky was not a subtle cat. He leaned way over Yuki, out of his chair and leaning his hands on her desk, and at least wasn't loud as he said, "I haven't seen them since last week. They haven't been coming to class."

I patted the fuzzy feline boy on the head, but most of my attention remained on Yuki. "Emanuel and Elvira got in a lot of trouble with their parents. I think… I think all three are preparing to move out of town."

They took the news much like I had. That is, they sat back in their chairs, Lucky falling into his, and they stared into space with expressions of horror.

Drake slid up in front of me. At least he was still smiling, rather than scolding us for talking. Maybe he'd been hoping for answers. Whatever his motivation, now he placed a book on the desk in front of me and said, "Your placement test results were interesting, Miss Forge. You may know more about math than even Joe. Your knowledge of bioengineering is far beyond anything we teach here, and so is your knowledge of magical properties. It seems the price has been knowing anything about other magics, so why don't you start by getting familiar with this book?"

I looked at it. The book was old. The book was battered. It was a paperback with stiff covers and pages made of high-quality paper that I suspected had been rejuvenated by witchcraft many times. Its damage all looked like overuse. The spine wasn't creased anywhere, it was creased everywhere, like an accordion. Little nicks, barely visible stains, and dog ears plagued the pages. It was still completely readable, and showed no sign of falling apart in my hands.

The cover read "The Different Types of Magic." Well, that was an intriguing name, and might distract me from my anxieties about losing my friends.

It did. There were more kinds of magic than I'd dreamed. It shouldn't have been a surprise that music wasn't just magic, it could be controlled and directed. Materials Magic, Channeling, Rift Engineering, Witchcraft, Enhancements… Code magic, in script and incantation forms, Bioengineering of course.

The Bioengineering chapter began with a line that it was considered to be in the same "family" of techniques as Materials and Witchcraft. That was fair. I didn't understand any of the details, but when I looked at Ruby's room I had a good idea of the kinds of processes going on everywhere.

It was an interesting book, but sometimes my attention drifted away to the huge windows, letting in sunlight, looking back at the endless clutter of little buildings that made up Goblita filling the distance. The hard wooden seat and desk felt uncomfortable, different, and official in a way I wasn't used to. The white walls and ceiling made the big room feel empty without my friends, no matter how many kids or how much clutter it contained.

My attention never drifted for long. I liked books and I liked new knowledge, and I had a lot of book with a lot of new knowledge in front of me.

I read, fascinated, about the two branches of Channeling, drawing energy from a god and manipulating naturally available magic. In both cases the rawness of the process was as utterly unlike bioengineering as I could imagine. Channeling reduced everything to quick casting, and the practitioners trained to manipulate magic as if it were part of their body. Magically adapted humans often could do that automatically. For everyone else, the amount of practice and discipline involved awed me. Also precision. The charging and appliance activation spells I could do were technically channeling, but I couldn't aim those and they were the simplest channeling you could get.

Quick casting in general was a natural process of your body learning to repeat as channeling magic you use a lot from other disciplines. That made sense.

The part about adaptation kicked up a reminder in my brain. I looked over at Yuki's work instead of my own. She and Lucky seemed to be working on the same thing, sweating over a page of sentences in other languages. In a space between each, they were writing sentences in English. From their expressions, it was hard. Even with her eyebrows hidden, Yuki's face was pinched enough to look strained.

She noticed my staring and looked up.

I murmured, "Sorry. Everyone said we'd discuss it later, and it's… later, I guess. Is this something to do with you being able to speak Sumerian?"

She gave a little nod, voice low so as to not disturb the more productive students. "Yes. Lucky and I both have it."

Lucky had noticed. Lucky's self-control was limited to a hushed kind of shout. "We speak in all the tongues of men!" It really was barely louder than Yuki's voice, it just gave the impression of shouting.

Yuki's sweater bobbled as she laughed silently. When she got control of that, her echoey voice corrected whimsically, "Mostly we understand them." Settling down to more seriousness, she went on, "You know there are different languages, but Lucky and I—"

"Her more than me, but me too," interrupted Lucky, waving a pointed finger between Yuki and himself.

Rather than irritated, Lucky just seemed to make Yuki perkier. "We don't hear that. You have to learn words and put them together. We just... know what it means. The problem is—"

Again, Lucky interrupted, crestfallen, with his ears flat out to either side. "We can't tell languages apart."

Yuki gave a little nod. "Yes. Each of you uses just a tiny fraction of the words out there, and it's so hard to know which fraction. Speaking English is easy because I'm surrounded by it so much that I have a feel, but writing it is another matter. So Lucky and I have to take special classes."

Lucky enthused, "Plus there's all this detail and stuff. You know what, um, twinkling is. I hear how it's being used. The word itself, um..."

Yuki told him, "It's like when a piece of glass rolls around and shines in different directions."

Lucky, whose smile had faltered as he groped for understanding, came back bright as ever. "Yes, twinkling means when something twinkles."

Mr. Drake, at his desk, was looking right at us, and smiling. Well, we were learning.

That was when the weird noise started, like something howling but going up and down in a slow, even pattern, never pausing for breath. It sounded distant, faint here, but must have been impressively loud at its source.

Chapter
Thirty-Eight

Yuki sat up straighter, looking around, her incredibly long, straight black hair splashing around her sweater worse than mine ever did. She asked everyone and no one, "The emergency siren?" Her voice echoed more than usual, lasting well after she'd actually stopped talking.

Voices chattered and yelled out in the hall. Feet stamped. More than that, stampeded.

My anxieties about everything that had been happening spiked up through my heart, and I ran out into the hall to find out what was going on, with Lisa close behind me.

The kids were all pouring out onto the lawn, so I did that too. With the open air rather than the window in the way, the siren was easier to hear, but no more informative.

Everyone was talking. I overheard, "What is it?" "It's got to be an earthmover attack!" "My parents are downtown!"

Parsley climbed up on the big rock, and yelled over the crowd, "It's not an earthmover! We'd be able to feel it, remember?"

A witch on a broomstick soared up to the school from the

direction of downtown. She hovered too far up to be more than a figure, but I was still sure it wasn't any of the witches I'd met so far. I didn't recognize her magically amplified voice when she announced, "Teachers and students! Stay where you are! A giant sea monster is attacking the Goblita Magical College. Everyone is instructed to go inland to be safe until it leaves!"

"Leaves. Not is killed. Leaves," I noticed out loud.

Action came faster than thought. I snapped my fingers.

Lights flashed inside the building. A few kids yelped as the spells they were using on their tablets overcharged. I shouted, "Herman!"

That would get his attention, and hopefully the possessed doll would think of me as someone to obey.

Sure enough, a door out of sight *bang*ed as it was kicked open, and Herman the horse doll came loping or cantering or whatever horses do when they're moving fast but not full-out. He stopped next to me, looking brown and worn and docile and artificial, but still a horse.

I jumped on his back.

Lisa pointed at me and shouted, "Don't you dare!"

I ignored her, pointing at the street into town. "That way."

Herman took off, and I had to cling to the ropes around his neck, leaning forward until I could smell the old leather. My legs and butt got sore fast from being bounced around as he ran, but I would have to put up with it.

I didn't leave Lisa behind for long. She caught up in long, leaping strides, the clicking of her hooves higher pitched than the clomping of Herman's. Horrified, she demanded, "What are you doing!?"

"My job!" I yelled back over the siren and the wind. Herman's squat, ragged body didn't look like he could run, but boy, he could.

Lisa slashed her hands furiously in front of her. "I don't care if it's the chimera. There are adventurers for this!"

"You don't understand! I'll explain at home, while I'm working! We'll be there soon!" I yelled.

We would be. Buildings, two story houses and wider, single-story shops, flew past. Herman was faster than even I'd hoped, knowing how strong and tireless dolls could be. Lisa even had to stop arguing because she needed her breath to run and keep up.

I jumped off Herman's back as he clattered to a halt in front of my house. Fumbling for my keys in my pocket, I took too long to unlock the door, then I rushed inside to my workroom.

Ow. My hips and legs really hurt, but I had no choice but to ignore it.

I grabbed my goggles, coat, and gloves. If this went wrong, they were about as much protection as a sheet of paper would be from that old woman's Magic Missile spell, but I'd take all the safety I could get.

That done, I bolted from work bench to work bench, dragging bundles of papers off shelves, yanking off strings holding those bundles together, and scattering them around as I searched with desperate speed. I focused on my notes. If Leo had what I was looking for, I'd never seen it. I would trust my own design better anyway. My dad had certainly never showed me his. I was pretty sure he'd never had to use it. How many bioengineers ever did? I'd made it as a fun hypothetical!

"What is going on?" demanded Lisa, behind me.

I couldn't waste the attention to look at her. As I confirmed the page I was looking for wasn't in this pile and moved to the next, I rattled off, "The chimera is coming here. It hasn't figured out what it's doing yet, but it's hunting for my soul forge. When it eats the soul fragment, it will go off like a bomb that will turn Goblita into an ocean bay."

Her hands grabbed my bicep, and she started to tug. "Then I'm getting you out of here."

"No! Listen!" I demanded, vehement.

She paused, her delicate pink face pinched up in disapproval and worry, but waiting and giving me a chance.

I fumbled to explain, which was hard, because my thoughts were full of diagrams of what I had to do, and it was an awkward topic to begin with. "We don't talk about this. It's not a secret. Everyone is supposed to know. You just hope it will never come up. A soul forge is as powerful as thousands of adult mages. Even a little one is the most powerful weapon that exists, by a long way."

Lisa's mouth tightened, her frown tight but getting deeper, and her eyes wide as she stared at me. "I really don't like where this is going."

Pulling my arm gently free of her grip, I ran my fingers back through the air, and tried to think of what needed to be said next. "There are a bunch of reasons why it's not used that way. When it comes down to it..."

I stopped, found my rubber hair band, and tied my hair back. It could not get in the way today.

That calmed me down a little, and I started over. "The difference between a dungeon master and a bioengineer is training and safety equipment installed in the forge. The only thing you can safely do with a soul forge's incredible power is make monsters, and they have a limited range."

Understanding dawned in Lisa's eyes, and not a happy understanding. "You're not—" she started to say.

I put my hand over her mouth. I wasn't done, and this was important. Crucial. "A bioengineer is the last line of defense of the town she lives in. That's our job. That's our responsibility. We can't replace an army, but we can smash one if it gets close. If an earthmover attacks and it doesn't hit the forge first, or a big enough pack of magical creatures, we drive them away."

Lisa's eyebrows pressed together. Through my hand she growled, "I can't let you—"

Anger roared through me. Trying not to cry, because I desperately needed to stay calm, I shouted over her, "You can and you're going to! This is what I have to do." Weakly, desperately, I tried to calm things down with a joke. "Besides, if the chimera eats this forge, there goes your meal ticket."

Lisa screamed, "I don't care about the meal ticket! I care about you!"

She stood there rigid, quivering, fists at her sides. I opened my mouth, but this time it was her grabbing my face. She pulled me close, looking me in the eyes, with only the glass of my goggles in the way.

Voice shaking, she told me, "I don't understand why you're doing this. I don't understand this bioengineering stuff. But you don't understand me or my life or what it's like to be a demon.

Have you noticed something? I know you haven't. Everywhere we go, everyone we talk to, they talk to you, not me."

I said, "Um," because she was right, and I had no idea what to make of it.

Bleakness stained her anger and desperation, and Lisa's voice got a little higher as she went on, "No, obviously you don't know why, and that's why I care about you. People don't talk to me because I'm your dog. I'm your pet. Do you understand? I'm a demon. I'm beautiful and fun, but I'm only safe because I belong to you, so they talk to you. Demons are just a bunch of hungers, so we don't have anything to say anyway. They're pretty close to right about that."

That last sentence came out sour, and ended in a bitter pout.

Confused, a little outraged, I said, "But you're—"

She cut me off again, talked over me, gripping my head tighter in both her clawed hands and pressing her forehead to my goggles. "Yes, you talk to me. Better than that, you listen to me. You may not agree, but you respect whatever I have to say as if I was human." Tears welled up at the edges of her glowing pink eyes. I hadn't been sure she could cry until now. "You tell people that I'm your cousin, you stupid lollipop!"

I couldn't help what other people thought, but I grabbed at that. "You are my cousin. If we're mistaken about Uncle Leonard, then you're still my cousin, just not by blood. But this time you have to respect me, and let me do this."

She shivered. This close, held like this, I could both see and feel it. She had a lot more self-control than me, and asked merely quietly and solemnly, "Is it dangerous?"

Unwilling to lie, I nodded as much as her gripping hands would allow. "Yes, but I know most of the ways it usually fails, and I've covered for them. The biggest problem is that you have to be able to channel a huge amount of magic to survive. You have to be some kind of prodigy."

Lisa made a faint *pfft* noise, amused despite herself. She let go of me, and stepped over to the back wall of the workshop. The wall lined with cement, because a workshop is a dangerous place, too dangerous to be contained by wood. She leaned her back against that wall, arms crossed, and watched me with eyes that were already pink but had that tight look of someone who's been crying.

I went back to searching my notes, and found what I was looking for. There. My fantasy designs for if I ever made a giant fighting monster. They'd been just an idea I didn't think I would ever use, but right now I was grateful I'd put so much work into doing them right.

I pushed up the slab extensions for my altar, the ones I used when I was working on a human. Grabbing my stylus, I started carving symbols into the surface. After a few seconds of that, I yanked my gloves off. They were too clumsy, and I had to write small, and cut lots of little symbols into the stone surface as fast as I could without making a mistake. Every minute this took might be one I didn't have.

Lisa drifted over. Her face was still sour, but she peered over me and sounded curious, if dubiously so. "It's so cramped, and it repeats so much."

Having someone to talk to while I worked was a relief. It kept me from getting so absorbed that my mind skipped ahead of my hands. I chattered, "It's not much more complicated than a regular monster, but everything has to be thirty times as intense. The containment that messed up the chimera is going to be the chimera's downfall, because I'll be able to pour all the power my soul forge can project into my monster. This one doesn't get its own soul fragment."

That was one of the things that got other bioengineers trying this killed. Giving something this powerful its own mind at all was disaster. Trying to spontaneously spawn anything this big would blow up the forge or the monster. So much could go wrong, but I'd accounted for all of it.

Most of it.

Scratch scratch scratch went my stylus. Little aspect sigils. Lots of concentric hexagons. The room smelled of dust and the tang of my soul forge's metal cage and the sweet fruity scent of Lisa close by.

Outside, something boomed, but in a weird, buzzy, hissy way. The College mages had tried something. From the distant roaring, it hadn't stopped the chimera.

I added an extra touch I'd just thought of to the design, hoping it would fit in the way I thought it would.

Okay. Time for the next step.

Bending down, I reached into the cage that made up the forge, closing my fist around the limiter plate on one of the innermost rings. I twisted, pulled, twisted some more, and with a *THUNG* it snapped off.

"What are you doing?" asked Lisa, one hand raised to her lips, openly worried again.

"Soul forges are built to not let you make something like this," I answered honestly.

I pulled off the backup limiter plate. Then I jimmied out the filter from up front. Then I broke off the projection interface. That one took extra twisting, and I spilled back onto my butt on the hard cement floor. Ow.

"I'm right about how not safe that is, aren't I?" asked Lisa, calm but haunted.

"Yes. I'm sorry," I answered, trying not to look at her.

I wished I could say that I planned on surviving, but I had done my best and it would or wouldn't happen. Either way, this was my duty.

Lisa stiffened up again, raising her chin. Voice quivering, she declared, "No. I can't let you."

I answered with something painfully on my mind. "Emanuel and Elvira are out there. Elvira will try to fight it, if she hasn't already."

That shut Lisa up, which cheered me up a little even though I was walking up to the gates of death. I knew Lisa cared about more than just me and herself.

That's it. There was nothing left. Time to go.

I reached all the way inside the soul forge, which with several interior plates gone was much easier, and grabbed the oversized fragment in my bare fist. I touched it to the leads in the correct order. The whole cage hummed and vibrated from the power being used.

If I got this wrong enough, the chimera would die from being caught in the blast, so there was that.

No time for jokes, bitter or not. I needed to focus. I watched the green glow spread through the diagram I'd carved, switching leads at the right times.

When the diagram was almost fully lit, I called out, "The bottle of horseshoe crab blood! Pour it on the altar! In the middle!"

"How much?" Lisa called back, as loud as me, even though there was no read. The forge only made a faint hum.

"All of it!" I shouted.

My hand stung. The power wasn't going through me, but just the flickering around the edge here would burn most people's hand. I wasn't most people, and could handle it.

As instructed, Lisa pulled the glass bottle out of its metal jug, and poured the glowing blue stuff like syrup into the middle of all the hexagons I'd drawn. The blood smoked, crackled, fizzed, and bulged up into a round shape that eventually became an egg, as big as the milk bottle I'd kept the crab blood in.

Lisa said, "It looks like the ones you threw into the sea."

It did. Scaly and blue, but basically the same. It looked like it was made of stone, but polished silky smooth.

"That's part of the secret. One of my safeguards," I said.

I grabbed it. Forget my satchel. My goggles would only be a nuisance, so I tossed them away. I ran out the office front door, leaving it open.

The street was empty. Just the noises of an angry monster from the direction of the shore, and West a little.

I ran as fast as my sore legs could manage to the One-and-One, then past it. I didn't see anyone I knew. Goblita looked peaceful, and sounded like a war.

Lisa kept pace beside me, watching me, not our surroundings.

Past the One-and-One, I could see the College. One of the buildings had been smashed. People were gathering around the rubble.

They must have driven the chimera away. It approached this beach now, splashing through the water clumsily. It had been given a beating. Scorch marks mottled its pale chest. Fins on the back hung broken, or had chunks carved out. Its huge mouth was missing a few teeth.

None of that seemed to be even slowing it down.

What a mess of conflicting parts. The giant magical beast towered up and up and up, much taller than any building I could see. It stood upright, and had arms like a human, sort of, although they weren't quite straight enough, like tentacles bending in the middle to pretend they have elbows. At the end of each was a giant animal head, a wolf on one and a snake on the other. On its squat neck bulked a heavy, wide hammerhead shark head, with a shark's oversized mouth and triangular teeth. It had lots of smaller, bug-like, segmented arms sticking out of its belly and fins in weird places. Four huge fins projected from the back like wings, although they'd taken a lot of damage. Every part was a different color, but most of the front was a shiny, pale, bluish white, like a fish.

Lisa gaped up at it in awe. "How did it get this big this fast!?"

They weren't obvious with it facing us, but I saw the big, mud-brown armor plates on its shoulders and peeking around the sides. That answered the question for me. "It ate a giant horseshoe crab."

I might have sounded a little proud. This was a bad time for pride, but… drinking regular horseshoe crab blood would burn out the vital system of any normal animal, and overload any monster. The pure stuff from a giant horseshoe crab was ten times as dangerous. My adjusting containment formula had held all that power.

Hopefully not for much longer.

The chimera wasn't just heading in my direction. All three heads were looking exactly at me.

I grabbed the heavy necklace around my neck. It remembered my ID pendant.

It was practically onshore already. It was going to get to me before I could get to the water.

Lisa yanked the egg out of my hand, and sprinted with her incredible hoof-footed speed to the ridge that marked the edge of the beach, pulled her arm back, and hurled the egg forward. It sailed beautifully, with all the arm strength and aim I didn't have.

I heard it plop when it hit the water.

Chapter Thirty-Nine

I *felt* it hit the water.

The chimera was too close. The snake head reached out, mouth snapping eagerly, getting closer.

I couldn't run. I couldn't walk. Bent forward, with my arms around my stomach, muscles shaking and knees wobbling, it took all my effort to stand. The ID pendant blazed like a lighthouse. Enough power to turn a regular person into a cinder was pouring through me right now. Not into me. Through me.

Into the egg.

An iridescent shape speared out of the water, banging into the chimera. It wasn't much of a hit, but it rocked the enormous beast back, and that yanked the snake head away.

Lisa ran back to me, put her arms around my hunched body, and lifted me into the air.

I pointed, and croaked, "The beach. I have to be able to see what's happening."

One of the ways previous bioengineers had died was hooking up their giant monster's senses to their own. They hadn't been able to untangle their mind from it after. There was just too much power involved, and I would bet this was the biggest, most powerful monster anyone had ever made.

Except the Lady Angel, of course.

A thunderous sucking noise might have sucked out my words, but Lisa carried me at a demon run to the hump at the edge of the beach, but farther down, well out of the chimera's reach.

I wriggled gently out of her grip, landing on my feet in the stiff, tufted grass next to the odd, sharp up slope, maybe a foot high, that marked the exact edge.

I could stand again, and stand upright. The power was still pouring through me, a twitchy sensation not just in my muscles but everywhere, but I'd gotten used to it. Or maybe the flow was smoother. All that mattered was I was in control again.

Thank goodness the chimera wasn't smart. It stood there, rearing up out of the water, legs hidden, watching with stunned confusion as a whirlpool flowed into my own monster.

Huge. Scaly. A mane of spikes around its head. Taloned hands and feet, and a powerful, bulky body. The long tail came with a metallic arrowhead at the end, much like Lisa's. Unlike Lisa's horns, my monster's horns stuck forward as weapons.

I'd made a dragon. I liked dragons, and I designed this before one went rogue on me.

The chimera was dumb enough to watch until the flow of water out of the sea and the magic out of my soul forge slowed to a crawl, and my dragon reached its full size. In the water its wings wouldn't be of much use, but when I rolled my shoulders they extended and flapped. I twisted my head to loosen my neck, and the dragon leaned back and roared.

I swiveled my hips. The stinger-tipped tail jabbed towards the chimera's gut.

The thing wasn't so stupid that it didn't recognize an attack. The wolf head grabbed my dragon's tail, its fangs biting deep. I winced. Even without my senses hooked up to my creation, I still felt the ghostly, painful pressure of being bitten where I didn't have anything. Magical feedback.

I swung my hands forward, and the chimera and my dragon slammed into each other.

My dragon was too big. It wasn't fast. Neither was the chimera. I didn't know anything about fighting, either. We waged a clumsy, flailing battle.

Clawing at the wolf arm, I forced it to let go of my tail, but the monsters were belly to belly now, too close. I tried to sting, but I had no precision, and the stinger kept bouncing off the plates on the chimera's back.

The wolf head bit down on my dragon's bicep instead. It was hard to claw back at that, but I grabbed the serpent head arm, and darted my monster's head down to bite into the chimera's shoulder, just in front of the armor plates. I yanked my head back, and my dragon did the same, ripping out a chunk.

Blue blood oozed from the wound. Horseshoe crab blood.

Well, that wasn't good.

My monster didn't have blood, which was good, because the chimera liked my idea. It lunged its huge shark mouth forward to take a bite. I twisted, and managed to jam my dragon's useless right wing into the chimera's mouth. It bit, pulled, and the wing came off. The shark head gulped and swallowed, and the bleeding on its chest stopped.

It was absorbing my monster. The dragon was made of pure magic, after all. Vast amounts of it.

I leaned forward, snapping my teeth, and the dragon bit at the chimera's face. It abandoned what was left of the wing, and bit back. The two behemoths waged a brief struggle, but the chimera was controlling its own body directly, and had better control. It clamped its jaws down around the dragon's snout.

That hurt. That hurt like the worst stopped up sinuses from the worst cold. And this was only the feedback.

Both giants moved so slowly. They stood practically still there, under the bright blue sky and sun, water sloshing around my dragon's knees and the chimera's very low waist. Sunshine glittered off of both of them, and everything smelled of salt.

Also my face hurt. A lot.

The chimera's head wobbled, the tiniest bit, as if something had thumped it. Something too small to see, or too invisible to see.

A pair of human figures stood much, much farther down

the beach in the direction of the College. Only slightly past the chimera. Easily within its reach.

I slammed my hands together in front of me. The clawed hands of the dragon hit the shark head, tearing at it, spilling lines of blue blood.

Its shark jaws let go. The chimera's wolf and snake heads bit and tore at my dragon's sides, but that didn't matter. I held the chimera at arm's length long enough to take a deep breath, and I mimed a gag so hard it made me actually nauseous.

The gigantic dragon vomited grey and purple sludge all over the front of the chimera, because every dragon needs a breath weapon.

The chimera screamed. It could feel pain. All three heads screamed. I didn't know what that slime was. The papers my dad gave me labeled it a "necrotic" weapon. I suspected a lot of dead fish would be washing up on shore for the next week or so, but so be it.

I shoved he chimera away. My dragon staggered back, and the chimera slid backwards. The goo on its front bubbled, and pits and furrows opened in the patchwork monster's upper body. This still clearly wasn't enough to kill it. Barely enough to slow it down.

The chimera took my example, opened all three of its mouths wide, and a white ray, roaring orange fire, and twisted blue lightning hit my dragon. The feedback danced pain across my body, but this was perfect. All three of its heads were distracted.

I twisted my hips again, and stabbed it in the center of its chest with my dragon's tail tip. This time the stinger connected, penetrated. My whole body clenched, and the dragon tail rippled, injecting its poison deep into the chimera's body.

The breath weapons stopped. The chimera sagged to the side like a drunk.

Then it straightened back up, hissing. It had survived the poison.

But that hadn't been the point.

The point was eight bright lights springing into view in different spots on its body.

Ignoring the biting mouths pulling my dragon apart bit by

bit, I reached forward with both hands, dug my dragon's claws into the chimera a little below one armpit, and yanked out one of those lights.

A soul fragment.

The wolf head arm withered, falling useless to the chimera's side and continuing to shrivel like an ancient raisin.

I bit another fragment out of the chimera's upper chest. The beast was already starting to thrash instead of fight. One by one, I carved out the fragments my poison made light up, and spit them into the ocean.

Arms useless, head melting, the chimera slammed forward into my dragon, nearly knocking it over with the beast's incredible weight. The row of little clawed legs on the front scratched at my monster's already badly savaged torso.

Why wasn't it dead? If I didn't get every fragment out, it would still be able to absorb some new animal and start rebuilding.

I saw it. Another light behind the chimera. It didn't have legs at all. It had been standing on a thick tail that was hidden by the waves and its own bulk. Shoving the chimera's torso aside, I bent forward, and my dragon bit that last fragment out.

That did it. The chimera's body burst into a gory mass of blue blood, which rapidly washed out to sea.

I fell over into Lisa's slim, strong arms.

"I'm getting you—" she began.

"Not yet," I warned.

Her angry face twisted into a desperate, pleading grimace. Voice cracking, she begged, "Please tell me you're going to live."

"We're about to find out," was all I could say.

I grabbed my soul forge's ID pendant tight in both hands, and... squeezed the flow of magic inside me. Straining for delicacy and control I didn't normally have.

I didn't stop the flow. I strangled it, more and more, my body jerking from side to side as power the likes of which even I wasn't meant to channel flowed back and forth, into my monster and back into the soul forge.

Maybe the sheer, outrageous intensity of that magical flow kept my clumsiness from going too far. The dragon shrank, and shrank, water gushing out of it everywhere in a roar.

When the dragon reached, oh, fifteen feet tall, it vanished into mist and the waves slopped over the spot where it had stood.

The ID pendant died down to its normal faint glow.

I didn't feel anything but aching and Lisa's arms holding me up.

Holding a shaking hand up, I asked, "Any transparency?"

She got one of her hands free to take mine, turning it this way and that, scowling at it with furious focus. Only when she could say it with absolute conviction did she say, "None. It's not glowing, either. You're trembling, but you look and sound the same."

I gave my black-horned, flame-haired cousin a groggy grin. "Congratulate me. I survived."

Voice hoarse, she held me tightly to her, and squeaked, "Admit it. Nobody survives what you just did."

Trying to push myself back properly to my feet, I denied, "Some of them do." I didn't say, not a lot. "I told you, cousin. I'm a prodigy."

Lisa responded by my effort to support myself by hooking both arms under me and lifting me up like a baby to hold against her chest.

"Give me a minute, I'll be fine to walk," I protested.

"No," she answered, flat and simple.

I decided not to argue, and lay there in her grip, exhausted, achy, and twitchy, but alive and even intact.

Lisa didn't need to know that my odds of surviving if I ever did this a second time dropped to, um… no recorded instances. Anyway, the vast majority of bioengineers never had to do it once.

My head lolled to the side, and I saw Elvira running up, dull brown dress flapping around her legs. Lisa twisted, yanking me aside, and barked, "Don't touch her!"

"Is she okay?" Elvira asked in a hurry.

"Yes. Just tired," I croaked at her. If Lisa was going to hold me up, I wouldn't try to pretend I had any strength left.

Scared, excited, dark eyes so wide I saw whites all around

the edges, Elvira babbled, "I saw you fighting. That was the scariest thing I've seen in my life. It didn't even notice my spells. The sheriff and Franklin shot it and they might as well have been flicking sand grains."

The second figure down the beach had been that same Franklin, in her dark, bulky leather in contrast to her bushy white hair, who came strolling up behind Elvira. She had that deceptively fast walk, but still wasn't running.

Looking at the two of them, I said, "You two saved the day. Your Magic Missiles distracted it just when I needed."

With the quick, casual dismissal of a professional, the old woman said, "No they didn't. You did it all yourself. You were brave enough to take on the soul forge master's final responsibility, and you even survived."

Turning my head up to Lisa, I gave her a weak but smug grin. "Told you. It's part of the job."

Franklin's lip twisted with a hint of disgust, but her tone remained generically gruff. "One most bioengineers are too cowardly to perform when the time comes. In my unfortunately extensive experience, if you don't get a contract ahead of time you won't get a reward for saving a city from destruction, but you have my thanks. A little kid shouldn't have to do what you did. How sure are you it's dead?"

That was the hard question that had to be asked, and it felt intensely good to be able to honestly say, "Completely. The soul fragments all came out with no limbs, no mouths, just meat and blood. I didn't see any lights after I dropped them in the sea. They're dead, and so is the chimera. It's not coming back this time. The danger is over."

The old woman let out a deep, relieved sigh, and for the moment looked... old. Not quite looking at Lisa, she huffed, "Take her home and don't let her out of bed until the morning. Feed her until she bursts, too."

That felt a little unfair, since it was still about noon, but I didn't try to argue.

Elvira grabbed my hands in hers, and squeezed them together. Fiery and energetic, she said, "I have to go talk to my parents, but I want you to know you inspired me, Artifact.

Whatever they say, I can face it and my future head on, thanks to you."

She ran off, past Lisa where I couldn't see her. On grass, I only heard half a dozen footsteps before those got too quiet.

Franklin was already walking away, heading for the College.

Seconds passed. Lisa whispered, "Are they gone? Is anyone looking?"

I craned my head around. "You'd think there'd be a crowd. I guess everyone evacuated." The town, the beach, everything looked peaceful, except some remaining bits of blue sludge on the tide.

Lisa squeezed me, crushing me to her chest, head bent down over me. She hissed, "Every second of that was a nightmare. Now I know why demons don't love."

I wheezed a little at the pressure, but tucked my cheek up against hers as reassurance. "Sorry, you're still stuck with me. I'll buy you a jar of candy tomorrow to make up for it."

Lisa eased up her grip, raising her head. All a show of perkiness again, she said, "I like bribes, but I'm still putting you to bed."

Lisa put me to bed.

ChapterForty

In the middle of the night, my eyes snapped open. Something was there, out in the ocean. I knew it like I knew where my hand was. I could point at it.

It felt like a god.

Muzzily, surrounded by darkness and only the murkiest shadows revealed by starlight, I rolled over. A sea god, appearing suddenly near Goblita? Weird. But I was sure it was south, way south, which meant it was out in the water. It wasn't moving.

I went back to sleep.

Until the house started shaking.

ChapterForty-One

The house shook. It shook hard. The bed rattled underneath me. The walls and floors creaked. The window shutters remained closed, but banged and banged against the frame. I heard books fall off of shelves, and a distant clang must have been a pot falling out of a cupboard in the kitchen. Even more distant shouts meant that everyone's house was shaking.

The shaking didn't stop. I lay in my bed, where at least I was secure, and the house vibrated around me.

Lisa, struggling to fit her arms through her oversized bedshirt as she ran, stumbled and weaved into the room, every step having to stagger to stay up as the floor moved under her hooves. In the darkness, her pink eyes stood out like lamps until she dove into my bed. Those lights disappeared as she burrowed under the covers, and curled into a ball holding onto me with desperate tightness.

I put a loose arm over her, and my voice also vibrated a bit as I told her above the rattling, "It's okay. It's an earthmover attack. A big earthmover attack, but if it were going to eat us, it would have already."

"You said they eat soul forges!" she squeaked from under my blanket.

I remained calm, thankfully believing what I said. "Mine is insulated and the floor is shielded. The earthmover doesn't know my force exists."

Lisa just curled up tighter, a warm, tense ball next to me, and she demanded, "Then why is it here?"

The answer was unpleasantly obvious. "Earthmovers mostly attack geodifferentials—changes in how much magic is in the ground. Yesterday someone used an enormous amount of magic to make a giant dragon. Then they released an enormous amount of magic dismissing the giant dragon. They also spilled several tons of something a lot like horseshoe crab blood. Then magic levels went back to normal. I don't know how much of that got into the ground, but enough."

Lisa, whimpered, curled up even harder, and held onto me.

Eventually, the shaking stopped. It was much easier to hear people shouting now, but nobody sounded scared or in pain. They sounded like people with strong opinions and strong questions.

Lisa didn't move, but she did relax down to merely tense and clinging. Very quietly, she asked, "Should we go look?"

I murmured back, "No point. It's the middle of the night. We couldn't see it. Everyone running outside is wasting their time. Anyway, the earthmover is gone, and the dungeon will still be there tomorrow, wherever or whatever it is."

Lisa relaxed a bit more. She wasn't squeezing now, either herself or me, just a hot, curled up presence pressed against my side. Her voice calmed down too, dropping to merely haunted. "You said you saw an earthmover once. What do they look like?"

I patted her back under the covers. Our house was still here, the earthmover hadn't eaten us, and my shock was already wearing off. I said softly, "No one knows. No one has ever seen more than the piece they stick out of the ground. That might be all of it, or just a finger. What I saw looked like a snake that was square instead of round, made of steel but lined with rectangular glass scales that looked like windows. It churned the ground, eating trees and rocks, rose up and vomited out a building, then slid back underground. That's all anyone has seen. We only know what they do, and some diaries people wrote during the Breach saying that the golden age cities came alive and burrowed into the Earth."

It was a long explanation, and by the end of it I heard raindrops start to splatter against the window pane. That made the people shouting outside's actions extra pointless, and most of them went quiet.

Lisa didn't speak again.

Eventually, I fell asleep, my arm still draped over my demon cousin to comfort her.

Chapter
Forty-Two

I woke up. I kept the shutters on my bedroom windows closed, but they still let in some sun.

Lisa sat up next to me immediately, so immediately that I wasn't sure which of us woke up the other.

Instantly energetic, maybe not cheerful but urgent and without a trace of fear, she looked down at me and said, "We should go see."

Not quite as fast a riser, I yawned. "Alright, but let's get cleaned up first."

She hopped out of the bed, her hooves clicking loudly on the wooden floor. Grabbing my tablet which miraculously had not fallen off the bedside table, she thumbed its cleaning spell and waved it over herself a few times. Then she ran off to her room. The sound of her hooves told me where she'd gone.

I got the point. No lingering baths this morning. At least Lisa had dropped my tablet back on the table. That had been enough time for me to be wide awake, so I slid out of bed myself, and used the spell on me. Maybe it was because I'd drained myself yesterday, but I had a lot more control than usual and I thought I bleached or disintegrated a bare minimum of hair today. I grabbed shorts and a shirt and stuffed my feet into my work boots without socks, the fastest dressing I could manage.

Still not as fast as Lisa, who came running back in, dressed much fancier than my oldest, most worn clothes. It wasn't a dress this time. She actually was wearing shorts and a shirt herself, but hers had long sleeves but showed off a lot of stomach, and she had shiny bracelets on her wrist and even a band around her ankle above the little kink that started her hoof. The fabric was all shiny and stretchy, giving the impression it had been sequined.

Where did she get all this stuff? Uncle Leonard, presumably. He must have been making a lot of money to lavish it on clothes this fancy. Then again, a daughter he never knew he had showed up suddenly on his doorstep. I could imagine how much he would want to spoil her.

Her hair poured down in an elegant, fiery wave. Mine would just have to look like a haystack falling off a cliff.

Seeing me ready, she ran downstairs without another word. Interest nagged me too, but I merely hurried. In fact, as I passed through my workshop I stopped entirely.

The soul forge was still on! Big gaps showed in the already unevenly shaped gold middle layer. The layers still all floated in place with the hefty yellow-green soul fragment in the center. It hadn't so much as moved an inch from all the shaking. It had been and would be safe, but I still should have turned it off first thing when I got home yesterday. Being literally carried to bed at the time, that hadn't been an option.

No harm done, anyway. I did the responsible thing now, pulling the lever that closed the inner box around the crystal and settled the inner cages to the floor of the outer cage. I sure wasn't using that until I'd fixed it.

I'd leave the gold pieces I'd ripped out where they lay for now. They didn't look damaged.

I did put on my ID pendant and scooped my detection equipment into my satchel to take with me. You never knew, right?

Finally, I stepped outside, where Lisa waited, quivering with impatience. Her impatience hadn't been rewarded, because there was nothing to see. The same buildings, all intact despite the shaking. A few people standing in small groups in front of their houses talking. A standard morning in Goblita. The occasional person stepping out their front door or opening a window to look around didn't change much.

It was actually pretty quiet.

After a few seconds of looking around, I said, "If we can't see it, it didn't happen very close, which means it must have been a big attack."

Our timing turned out to be fantastic. Yuki came running up the street from deeper in town. She paused, sweater-enveloped hands on her knees, and panted for breath. She glanced up and saw us ahead, but too tired and distant to speak she just pointed towards the ocean and started running again.

I'd been about to head down that way anyway, because that constant presence of a god was that way, and maybe there would be something to see after all.

As Lisa and I walked at a merely fast pace down to the One-and-One, the direction of the god didn't change at all. That automatic awareness that *something* was due south remained the same.

When we crossed the road, the College came into view. A lot of scaffolding crowded around the collapsed building. Well, the mages must know a lot of magic useful for construction. If they'd been doing that much casting last night, they were lucky the earthmover hadn't hit them.

Yuki caught up, laboring now, almost staggering. She kept pointing.

The three of us reached the little ridge overlooking the beach, and looked over.

The old woman with the fluffy grey hair and the dark leather armor sat on the white sands of the beach, looking out over the ocean with a telescope.

Out there, where she was looking, where Yuki pointed, where that something always was, a spire jutted out of the water.

It was... an island? It was far enough that I couldn't see it clearly. An island with a very tall building on it. On the other hand, if I could see it at all it couldn't be that far out. A pointy shape rearing out of the water, grey with distance, was all I could say for sure.

We walked down onto the beach to gather around Franklin the retired adventuress. She glanced up at me, and grunted. "Shouldn't be surprised you felt it. Take a look."

She held up the telescope. I took it and looked. Well, that was definitely a dungeon. I couldn't see the shape of the island well, but I got the impression it was regular, geometric. Big, squared off arches, little more than rocks laid across two other rocks, go up stairs to the central building. That building was irregularly shaped, towering, and while I couldn't make out detail it shined with beautiful mixing colors. Tiny, tiny specks moved around the base of the stairs.

I lowered the telescope, and was about to offer it to Lisa when Yuki grabbed it with ravenous interest. As she took in the distant view, I told the old adventuress, "Either some people have already gone out there, or it's producing monsters."

"Monsters. The good news is, they're diving into the ocean, so there's probably not open to the ocean inside and the underground layers may not be flooded," she confirmed.

"I suppose the hopes of the soul cage being aboveground were always faint," I mused.

Franklin shrugged. Her dark leather jacket squeaked faintly.

With that neither confirmed nor denied, I continued, "Although it wouldn't last long in seawater."

"But no telling what it would spit out while destabilizing," she muttered. She wasn't tense. Her frown was sober, her tone a little resigned, a little exasperated. This was probably the amount of excitement a new dungeon actually deserved.

I nodded, because she was right.

Raising a grey eyebrow, she asked, "Can you tell me anything about the soul forge?"

Oh! That was a good question. I'd brought my stuff. The first, most obvious step was to take out my signature detector and slot my ID pendant into it, so I did that.

Rainbow lights ran around the rim in a constant circle.

Around and around, not stopping. Only two spots remained the same, the yellow spot behind me that marked my forge, and a sky-blue spot in the direction of the island.

I blinked, because everything was weird about this except the reading for my forge. Cautiously, I reported, "I think this means there's an ongoing breach. A hole to another world just... standing open."

The sour voice of the sour rift engineering professor warden guy said, "That is exactly what it means, Miss Forge."

He and the sheriff had come up behind us, the professor in his dark suit and white collar looking like a crow foretelling death, and the gangly, wrinkly sheriff in his denims looking like the world's friendliest vulture. The scowling rift engineer explained, "One of the original Breach's major portals opened up off the coast of Goblita. It was closed and locked centuries ago."

Yuki finally lowered the telescope, asking in her own echoey voice hypnotized with fascination, "What is on the other side?"

Me, I grabbed the telescope out of her hands before anyone else could, and passed it to Lisa.

Like any teacher, the priest-looking dimensional expert loved to lecture. He barely sounded unhappy at all. "I don't know. What it led to, how it was closed and locked, that is all lost. Most of my information comes from records of readings taken on dimensional pressure in the years since. Supposedly it was more than just a tear. It was a gate. That's why I needed the breach detonator the most, to bleed off pressure in an unstable area near such a dangerous point, and as an emergency method of closing the hole."

His bitterness was back, but who cared, because Yuki and I pounced on that last hint together. "Closing?"

"They're called 'detonators' for a reason," he snapped, but the urge to lecture was too powerful. His anger merely flickered as he continued, "The closest analogy I can give children is causing a cave-in to seal a tunnel. It will take at least two weeks for the replacement to arrive, and there is no telling what will come through during that time, or what further instabilities this will cause. All because my key was stolen in the first place."

Still sitting with her knees curled up against her chest, Franklin raised a hand. "No, Doc. Your breach key, maintenance, everything that came before became moot when the chimera's death released enough magic into the water to summon an earthmover. That was inevitable when I couldn't get support for a team large enough to track the beast down before it got too big. If anything, we're lucky."

She looked up at me with tired, but hard eyes. An expert's eyes. She asked, "Did you notice the order of events?"

I had, and they were interesting. "Fight, and about twelve hours later a god appears out of nowhere, then after that an earthmover attack at the same spot as the god. A portal opened some unidentified time during all that."

Franklin gave me a little nod, then looked out over the sea again. Maybe her face hardened just a touch, but the old woman radiated a grimly calm "been there, done that" like none other. Maybe she had. It matched her disapproving but unexcited tone of voice as she said, "The best way I can put it together is that the magic release broke the seal, opening a portal to one of the little universes that are just prisons or homes for a god."

The professor grunted, like someone who hated to do it but had to confirm those exist.

Needing no confirmation, the adventuress went on, "That saved a lot of lives. Instead of attacking at the site of the battle, where it would have destroyed the College and most of downtown and killed everyone having this conversation, the earthmover went for the portal. I don't recognize that architecture."

Yuki the dungeon obsessed teenager echoed, "Neither do I, except the gates."

Franklin went on, "I've never seen an ocean dungeon, but one thing earthmovers do is build prisons around gods. So that's what we're looking at. We need to remove the soul forge from that tower before monsters start crawling up on the beach, but that means gathering a team I don't have. After that, the dungeon and the portal become our solutions to each other. You'll have all the time you need to find a safe way to stabilize the ether or whatever it is you do."

Yuki said, "You have time to get your team."

The old woman raised her bushy eyebrow at the black-haired, white-skinned, besweatered young woman now.

Hands clasped in front of her, or at least one knit-enveloped hand clutching another knit-enveloped hand, Yuki told her, "If that is a prison, the monsters are guards. They want to keep us out, not use it as a base to attack us. If it is not a prison, they are still guards, but they are protecting the god from us."

Franklin stood up, slowly, with the heavy, creaky movements of her age, grumbling, "Still, it's going to take long enough to get a team together if I don't lollygag. Thanks again, Miss Forge. You two come with me. Monsters I can handle. I need all the help I can get fighting bureaucracy."

The sheriff spoke up for the first time, thumbs hooked into his belt. "I'll stop from killing any of them if that helps."

The professor guy handed the telescope back to Franklin. I was glad I hadn't noticed how it transferred from Lisa to anyone else.

Yuki grabbed my wrist and tugged. Leaning forward, big black glasses looming, she said, "We're late, but we need to tell Parsley about this. Come to school."

"I'll... I have to put my soul forge back together and do a safety check," I stammered, pointing my fingers in vague directions but most often back at my house, as if that would make anything more clear.

Lisa leaned past me, grinning her slightly fangy grin. "You want to hear this story." Her tone made it sound absolutely lurid.

I nodded repeatedly. "And I'll tell you later. As soon as I get done I'll be over, okay? Sooner started, sooner finished."

Yuki's other hand grabbed mine, and with both she gave me another tug before reluctantly taking a step back and letting go. "Even if it's after school, try. The Society will have a lot to talk about."

Chapter
Forty-Three

"I'm pretty sure school is over," Lisa told me, hands clasped behind her head and walking in stiff-legged marching steps.

Trundling along on my shorter, less hoofy legs as we walked up the street, I waved my hands between us and debated, "At least nothing was broken and the parts all fit back where they belong. Or are you telling me you don't think I should have done the full safety check?"

"I'm telling you we would know for sure if we got one of those little fancy wrist clocks. It would look great on me." Unhooking her arms, she held out her wrist and tapped it repeatedly instead.

Not that I thought she was serious, but I was when I shook my head. "Not yet. I don't think there's going to be a lot of expensive goblin transformations. I have to figure out a budget, and I have to cook when we get home, because all the meat we have left is raw. Being an adult is *hard!*"

The flame-haired demoness grinned so evilly it was

practically a leer. "We could invite Joe over to cook again."

Tempting, but... "I'm going to have to learn how to cook eventually."

The theatrical evil disappeared, or at least dropped to the tiniest hints behind a suddenly serious face. "Not just that. Wouldn't you like to have him over again before he leaves? I'm sure he wants to."

"Um," I said.

Up ahead, I could finally see the school approaching. At the same time, I heard its bell ring.

Jabbing my finger at Lisa, I crowed, "HA! School wasn't over!"

Unfazed, she poked her wrist again. "See? That's why I need a wrist clock!"

Kids rushed in a wave out of school, some scattering to their homes, some hanging around in the yard to talk or gather at the rock, some crossing the street to play ball on the sandy court.

Not just at the rock, but standing on it, Parsley raised an arm and waved at us. "Artifact, over here!"

I heard Emanuel's distant voice ask, "Artifact's here?"

I burst into a run towards the rock and that welcome voice, shouting, "Shouldn't I be asking you that?"

Everyone was here. Elvira, Emanuel, Lucky, Yuki, all gathered around the rock and its monarch Parsley. Even Joe hung around in back, watching us.

Elvira, in her usual long dress, this time dark grey, stood with her arms crossed and a pout on her lips. After a few seconds of that she put her hands on her hips instead. Then she crossed them again, and stared sulkily off to one side.

Emanuel slipped an arm around her shoulders and gave her a squeeze as he told me, "Our folks were keeping us out fishing to keep an eye on us."

Elvira sounded a lot less sullen than she looked. "That, but there really was something stirring up the fish, and they needed all hands with the sea near the coast being practically empty after the giant monster fight." Perking up, she bunched her fists together and gushed, "Which was the best. I've told everyone the story already."

"Five times!" declared Lucky. I patted him between his pointy ears.

Parsley started to say, "I could hear it again—"

Elvira interrupted her, and shoved herself past a couple of kids I didn't know to tell me, "I was going to say that you should tell them from your side."

I pointed a thumb at my pointy-eared, pink-eyed cousin by my side. "Lisa was right next to me the whole time and much less distracted."

Now it was Parsley who interrupted, raising her voice to declare, "—but *not right now!* We have the biggest thing ever to talk about."

Lucky bounced excitedly. "There's a dungeon right off the coast!"

Emanuel pointed at the presence I was constantly aware of in the distance. "And that. What *is* that?"

Now I looked at Yuki curiously. She was on the opposite side of the rock, bent over it with her hands holding her chin and her elbows all over the rock. Her limp black hair splayed all over the white-speckled grey surface. She chirped, or the closest her soft, echoey voice could get to that, "I was waiting for you!"

Holding out my hands, I checked off on my fingers, "There's a dungeon. It's built over an open interdimensional portal. Not just a breach, a gate. And there's a god inside. That's what, I mean—"

I faltered, trying to think of the best way to explain. Parsley took the issue out of my hands, standing up on the rock again, cupping her hands around her mouth, and shouting to the whole field, "If you know what I'm talking about, point at the god!"

Elvira, Emanuel, Parsley, Yuki, and Lisa pointed. Lucky and Joe didn't. To my complete lack of surprise the lead sports boy pointed, and so did all the kids with him. Overall, maybe a third of the kids hanging around the school yard did.

"Thanks, that's what I needed!" Parsley shouted, then dropped down to drape her legs across the rock again like a queen on her divan. Her own heavily braided golden hair coiled over her shoulder like a snake.

Okay, well, with that settled, I tried to pick up where I left off. "Anyway, the dungeon is probably a prison. That or it's guarding the gate from us."

Parsley frowned in concern. "Even with a dungeon around it, leaving a gate standing open like that doesn't sound safe."

Emanuel rubbed his currently stubbly chin. "I only know a little about rift engineering, but it's not. Lots of stuff could happen. It will certainly start altering how magic works locally, and that could make Goblita uninhabitable."

Lisa grabbed my bicep with both hands, squeezing it hard. Glaring at Emanuel, she demanded, "Could it make Artifact's soul forge go wrong?"

"Eventually," he said.

I held up my hands to Lisa, in the process dislodging her grip, and said in a soothing tone, "Adventurers will have dealt with things long before then. In a couple of weeks the College will have a new breach detonator and start closing the portal."

Parsley sat up straight now, declaring, "My parents work at the College, and it's going to take that long to get a team of adventurers able to deal with the new dungeon. That's what I want to talk to you all about. Elvira, tell everyone what you saw."

Elvira's scowl came back. She leaned a hand on the rock, and looked irritably away at the school, where no one was, as she grumbled, "There are monsters out around the new island. They talk, but it's not any language I've ever heard, and I'm pretty sure they're like that Shedu. It's just a warning to stay away. They're weird, too. They have arms and a human head, but the rest is like a mix of fish and snake, and they're cold. One of them actually used ice magic! And they wear blank masks that completely cover their face!"

My eyes went wide. "You encountered them? This morning, I guess?"

Now the bitterness in Elvira's voice turned thick and sarcastic. "Oh, we did. I had to fight them off when they got mad that we weren't leaving fast enough. That's why we're here. Can't have our little girl saving people from the monsters trying to drag their boats under the water. Better send her off to school where she can't help anybody!"

Ever the sympathetic and loving brother, dark and wiry muscled Emanuel slipped Elvira another hug. To the rest of us, just a little smug, he said, "She got to cast Magic Missile. Four hits on her first cast."

Parsley whistled, impressed.

Lucky squeaked, "There are adventure mages who never get past that!" and then went back to pressing the top of his head into Parsley's scratching hand.

Elvira's fuming deflated. Her head sagged down, then lifted enough to give us all an awkward, bashful grin. She scratched the back of her head, and did that head jiggle she did when she was happy. "Thanks, guys. I remembered the spell right first try, too. I can show it off any time anyone wants to see."

Parsley nodded with solemn majesty. "We'll set up a target for you to practice combat spells later. Joe, do you think Bonabelle would help?"

Joe grinned the biggest grin I could remember on his face. "If I ask her charmingly enough."

Parsley's gaze returned to the rest of us as she said, "But that's for later, because we're not done. Artifact, what do you make of that monster description?"

I shrugged. "It's not like anything I've ever heard of. They could be interdimensionals, not monsters. The way they acted, I'm guessing monsters. Dungeons on water are so rare, there aren't any records of what earthmovers build. There was one back at Lake Touhou, but it was tiny and old and never had a soul forge to begin with. This... it might be that no one has ever seen this type of dungeon before."

Parsley's expression changed. Normally calm, or at least passionate in a controlled, authoritative way, her grin turned suddenly feral. "*Exactly.*"

She got her self-control back. Sitting up, smoothing out her dress and arranging her braids that had slipped off her shoulder, Parsley explained, "We have an opportunity. Maybe an obligation. There is a new type of dungeon out there. One of a kind. Can we trust that adventurers aren't going to just blow it up to bury the portal? We have a fully fledged combat mage now. We have members who need treasure so that they can leave." She looked at Emanuel, Elvira, and finally Joe. "Or maybe so that they don't have to leave."

That hit all three. My friends' smiles disappeared. They stared down at the rock, thoughtful, maybe a touch haunted.

Emanuel recovered first, raising his eyes to look at us suspiciously with his face still tilted down. "You want us to clear the dungeon? As if we were adults?"

"Yes she does!" squeaked Lucky gleefully, the little orange cat boy bouncing around with glee.

Parsley's face tightened in a touch of bitter grimace, but her voice held only passionate purpose as she said, "Say the word, and you know I'll be at the head of the party, but what I'm thinking is that those of us who have the most ability and the most need do the clearing. They get first chance at treasure, and the rest of us go in after as a team to record everything. My tablet can take memory pictures. So can Yuki's. She'll be able to translate their language. Maybe she'll even be able to talk to the monsters and help get you to the soul forge without a fight."

I mused, "Shut that down, which I can do, and all that's left are traps. Most of those depend on the forge for power anyway."

Elvira flapped her hands around at shoulder height. "I can't do much against traps. I'm a simple, straightforward, blast-'em-in-the-face kind of girl."

Emanuel's mouth tightened on one side, and he reluctantly admitted, "I can't do enough about traps. It wouldn't be safe."

Her own smile predatory on her bloodlessly pallid face, Yuki pointed out, "We have someone who is good at stealth, at observation, at delicacy."

For a moment, everyone was quiet. What Yuki meant finally stole into my consciousness, and I was about to look at Joe when he raised his hands and got everyone's attention.

Slowly, hesitantly, he said, "You're right I need the money. That much money... I... it could make a big difference. But I have a plan that's safe and reliable. Elvira, nobody knows better than me how amazing you are, but if Emanuel and I handle the goofy dungeon puzzles, can you really keep us safe from the monsters?"

She stared for a second, and then her head sagged. She

deflated in defeat, and in the same begrudging tone said, "No. I like your plan, Parsley, but I've learned the hard way that I'm not enough. I need someone who can fight physically, who can hold off monsters and give me time to work."

Yuki, next to Joe, smiled up at the bulky wolf. "Someone big and strong?"

He shook his head, flat and serious. "I don't know anything about fighting."

Everyone looked stunned. Kids I didn't know who I wasn't sure if they were in the club looked stunned. Lucky said it first. "But you're huge!"

The big grey wolf nodded. "Right. So nobody picks a fight with me that I could have ever hoped to beat anyway. If you need a bruiser, it won't be me."

Now everybody sagged in disappointment. Lucky laid his head on Parsley's leg and mumbled, "Aw."

Parsley raised a warning finger, to Lucky, to everyone. "No one pressure him. Joe and Elvira have made their points, and I trust them. This was my idea, but if they say we don't have enough of a team, we don't. This only works if we can do it."

Scowling, folding her arms on the rock and resting her chin on them, Yuki said, "She's right."

And with that, the meeting broke up. Everyone spontaneously wandered away. With glum expressions at first, but as they clumped into little groups, they started smiling and chattering again.

Elvira and Emanuel only drifted away one slow step at a time. Elvira had her fists clenched and her arms straight down at her sides, glaring with bared teeth at the grass.

Her brother put both arms around her this time, lowering his dark tanned forehead to her identical forehead, murmuring, "If you can't, you can't. Tell me honestly. Can you?"

She quivered, squeezing her eyes shut, and in a hoarse voice said, "...no. I need a tank."

A pensive Yuki walked off towards town, although "stalked" might be a better word.

Joe started heading down the road running east. I burst into a run to intercept him.

Lisa leaped ahead of me, intercepting the tall wolf boy, grabbing his wrist in both hands, and pulling him to a halt. With open-mouthed glee, she demanded, "Come home and cook for us!"

Joe's smile came back, slyly amused. He put the back of one of his big hands to his forehead and orated, "Alas, if I must labor for my dinner and a comfortable couch to sleep on—"

"Actually, I had a different idea," I said as I caught up.

Lisa gave me a suspicious look.

Joe gave me an eager look.

We'd caught up with Joe fast, and Emanuel was within my arm's reach. I grabbed the sleeve of his shirt and gave it a little tug, getting the magical fishing siblings' attention as I told all my friends, "I was thinking about throwing a party."

Elvira's and Emanuel's depressed frowns disappeared instantly, replaced with blank curiosity. Lisa stared at me the same way. The only one who had been smiling, Joe kept smiling, but now intrigued as he asked, "A party?"

I smiled right back up to him, although a touch wistful about it. "A going away party. For you, and anyone else who needs one. If we're not getting together for that dungeon, we can still get together, right? I have a house to host a party in. I can spend the money I got for the goblin job on it."

Lisa stomped her hoof in the dirt. Hands on her hips, she protested, "Hey! You promised me we'd spend that on a clock! *Buuuuuut*, if it's for *Joe*, I *guess*..."

Joe gently took Lisa's sleek little hand with her sharp, red-painted nails in his fuzzy grey mitt with its short, harmless claws. Lifting her hand up above her head, he leaned down and kissed her knuckles softly. His eyes lifted to hers, and he said softly and theatrically, "You are a princess of beneficence."

She lifted her face and stuck out her chin. "I sure am."

Then she looked sharply over at me. "We'll still need food."

I waved my hands across each other. "I'm not going to make Joe cook for his own party. There must be... caterers? Bakers? people who you can buy food for parties from? Goblita has those, right?"

Elvira nodded, smiling wanly now. "Sure."

Emanuel rubbed his chin some more. He really did need to shave, and the stubble looked itchy. "I bet Mrs. Ballast would take an order, especially if the party isn't today and we can give her warning."

Lisa stomped her foot again, protesting, "Joe is a good cook!"

He still held her hand, and he gave it an affectionate pat. "But I'm not good at baking cakes."

The little pale-and-red demoness's eyes went wide and round. "Cakes," she whispered.

I added to the list. "And cookies. And cupcakes. A professional cook can make us a bunch of cupcakes with icing, right? Chocolate icing?"

Elvira, Emanuel, and Joe all nodded.

Lisa's whole body went tense, and a strangled, gurgling noise escaped her barely parted lips. I threaded my arm around hers at the elbow, and gave her arm a squeeze. Looking around at the others, I said, "And everything that was hanging over my head is fixed except my friends leaving, so I can celebrate that and get as much of you all as I can at the same time. I think a party is a great idea."

Having been dislodged from Lisa, Joe turned his permanent smile down at me instead and asked, "May I invite Bonabelle? You should meet her."

Elvira waved one hand sharply, her head tilting from side to side as she chattered, "If we throw this party without Parsley she'll chop our heads off, in a very serious, polite, responsible way."

That got a giggle out of her brother.

I thought about it. "I don't think we should invite too many people, but since this is partly a farewell party, you three should be able to invite the friends you want most to be there."

"Well we've got to invite Yuki, that's for sure," said Elvira.

Joe nodded emphatically. "Oh, yes."

Twisting half around, Elvira called out, "Hey, Yuki! ...where is Yuki?"

"She went home," said Parsley, still sitting on the rock, but now with her legs crossed as she scribbled away at school work.

Lucky pointed south, towards Goblita. "That way!"

"No, not that way." Parsley ruffled his head between his pointy ears, then pointed east, the way Joe had been going. "Yuki lives over there."

Lucky shrugged helplessly. "That's the way she went."

My brow furrowed, and I echoed, "I saw her going that way, too. But... the whole town is that way. She could be going anywhere."

My frown crept onto Parsley's face. She waggled her pencil in her fingers and speculated, "She might be sitting on the beach looking at the island. The whole dungeon crawl idea was hers. She doesn't like to burden other people, but I can tell she was disappointed."

Relieved, I nodded. "Right. She's just sitting on the beach."

"Right," agreed Emanuel, still looking and sounding worried.

Elvira nibbled her lower lip nervously, and awkwardly, haltingly suggested, "If there's a god out there, I know she's told you her thing about gods, but..."

Parsley set down her books and slid off the rock. She took a couple of steps towards us as she argued, "Yuki would love to talk to any god, but she wouldn't go crazy over it. She's looking for a specific one, that lives behind gates."

Right. Getting steadily more grim, I informed my friends, Yuki's friends, "There are big gates on the island. I know Yuki saw them through the telescope. They only look kind of like the ones she drew for me." My memory threw up another fact, and I slowed down as I recalled, "The picture on the plate I showed her looked a lot closer. The plate that might have come off the portal."

Anxious, Elvira looked up at the big wolf and pleaded, "Joe..."

The people watching boy nodded. "She's going to try to go to the island by herself. She'll think she can talk her way through the monsters to see the god. She speaks their language, and they'll listen to her because she's their kin. That's what she wants to believe."

Elvira grimaced. "I hope this is the first time you're wrong about something."

"She can't have gotten too far ahead," Parsley said.

I said, "I don't want to bet her life on it. Lisa, run, see if you can catch her and stop her. Either way, meet back at our house, okay?"

Lisa took off immediately, without any argument. Her hooves kicked up dust until she hit the street, where they merely rat-tat-tatted off the pavement at high speed.

"There's no way she can outrun Lisa," I tried to reassure myself.

"Unless she knows we'll come looking for her," Joe corrected, quiet and haunted.

Parsley became again the serious voice of reason and responsibility. One arm crossed under her chest, holding the other elbow in her palm, she said, "We have to assume she's going to get to the island before we can catch her, or at least to a boat. I don't want to sound like I'm pushing you four…"

Elvira bunched up her fists, pulled her head down to her shoulders, and whined, "I can't! I'm really good, but I'd be dragging you all to your deaths!"

An idea stirred. My whole body went still, trying to focus on an idea that wasn't concrete yet. I asked, "What exactly do you need someone to be able to do?"

Nodding a lot, hands on her hips, brow furrowed and frustrated, Elvira groused, "Someone who can fight physically would be nice, but mostly I just need someone tough and brave enough to keep the monsters' attention for a few seconds while I cast spells."

My voice stronger as my thoughts got more concrete, I echoed, "So, toughness. Really just someone stupidly brave but wearing a lot of armor. Strength would be nice."

"I'm serious. I can't do it," Joe declared.

I ignored him, talking to myself now. "I've always wanted to make a doll. They can't die. Working dolls often take a serious beating. They have spells to make them harder. It just depends on who's supplying the magic."

Hope suddenly back, Elvira raised her fists and gushed, "And if that's you, it will be indestructible. Can you really make one?"

Hmmm. "It's advanced bioengineering, but it doesn't take long, and I mean... I am a prodigy. The problem is, I need something to bring to life. I can't just make a statue move. It needs joints, like Herman has."

Joe was feeling the hope too. Pale blue eyes alight with inspiration, he said breathily, "You need a mannequin. A good one, with all the joints articulated, even the fingers."

Sweeping her head from side to side, Elvira declared, "There has to be one like that in a dressmaker shop, but finding it and buying it... Yuki is going to be at the island way ahead of us."

His permanent smile back where it belonged, Joe raised a finger and corrected her, "There is one a few blocks away, and I know the owner will give it to us if I ask her nicely. Come on. We need to hurry."

Chapter
Forty-Four

It really was just a few blocks away, in one of the spots more dense with houses on the edge of town.

Our destination was obvious as soon as it came into sight. Among all the small, wide homes, mostly pale and dingy, squatted a blocky house painted dull orange over brick, with a sign over the door. It swung gently from a pole, and looked like it was made of thin wood, with a copper silhouette of a cute, stylized rabbit head sticking out of a jug. No words.

We'd left Parsley and Lucky behind. It was just me, Joe, Emanuel, and Elvira now, and none of the other three looked surprised. Other than the color and the sign, the building's one other oddity was more subtle. There were no front windows.

Joe opened the front door and walked right in. Emanuel and Elvira followed close behind, all confident this was fine. I trailed in last.

Into a living room. A weird, wrong living room, but I couldn't put my finger on why. None of the details looked wrong. On the contrary, the room was practically picture perfect. Wooden panel walls made it feel cozy. Nice furniture sat far enough apart to not be cluttered, unlike my own crowded living room. Flower print clothes draped over a lot of the furniture kept the brown from being stifling, echoed by the floral print cushions on the couch. To give the whole thing a touch of individuality so it wasn't too perfect, shelves occupied the front wall, filled with pots, biggest on the bottom graduating to smallest up top, starting with rough clay on the left, through fine ceramic, glass, and finally fancy resin on the right.

Also, the building was filled with a wonderful fruit pie smell, which made me realized how much I'd gotten used to having Lisa's strawberry scent around.

I inhaled deeply, relishing that sweet bready, fruity, delicious aroma, and when I looked down I spotted my ID pendant sparkling. Just one or two tiny little glimmers amidst the normal dull glow, but continuous. That was it. The building felt weird because it was thick with magic. Now that I knew to look, I saw little formulae drawn in all the corners, floor and ceiling and in a few spots along the walls. Sealing spells like the ones I used to insulate my workshop floor.

Nervousness crawled up my spine. We were only twelve hours after an earthmover attack.

No, no. This was fine. Honestly fine. It wasn't about how magical a place was, or even how fast it released magic, but how that level of magic changed. This place felt steady, and that wasn't dangerous.

Gwenda, the brown rabbit pottery saleswoman, leaned out of a doorway in back. She had on a yellow and white flower print dress that made her look incredibly cheerful and motherly. She waved a hand covered in a blue flower print cooking mitten. "Hi, kids! All of you here to see Bonabelle at once? And isn't that little Artifact? Sweetheart, you brave little genius you, I heard about you saving us from that giant monster yesterday. I don't know why there isn't a parade in your honor, but if you'll wait around I'll make a pie all for you."

Solemn and respectful, Emanuel gave the plump rabbit furry a little bow and said, "We don't have much time, Miss Hoppity. A friend is in trouble and we need your daughter's help."

Gwenda put her mitten to her mouth. "Oh, gracious. Well, she's in her workshop. Hurry along, and Artifact, dumpling, you come back any time you want some sweets. I'm always happy to cook." She patted her undeniably round stomach.

Emanuel took hold of my hand and pulled me into another hall, and down it, until a girl stepped out of an open doorway.

She was also a furry, a brown rabbit like her mother. She looked like her mother in miniature, in more than one way. They both had that same basic figure, not round in total, but every part round. This girl wasn't as far down that road as her mother, and in particular had an only mildly plump stomach under a mud-splattered apron and a long, stained white linen smock.

The other way she was a miniature of her mother was literal. This girl was hardly an inch taller than me, but had to be at least a couple of years older, maybe more.

Joe bowed to her, one arm crossed over his chest reverently. It did not look even slightly mocking. The opposite. He radiated pride as he introduced, "Artifact, meet my girlfriend, Bonabelle."

Bonabelle put her round hands on her round hips, then reached up to tug on Joe's ear. A grin both amused and exasperated broke out on her face, and she tickled him under his jaw with her finger, then shoved him aside with her hips to address the rest of us. "Well, as I live and breathe. You must be Artifact, and you're as cute as Joe says. I heard about yesterday. Thank you so very much. What brings all of you together on a day Joe knows I'm working?"

Elvira leaned her head back, and tossed her dark hair back in a show of frustration. "I still wish you'd go to school with us."

Emanuel corrected her, "We don't have time. Bonabelle, Yuki is in trouble."

Which I guess made it my turn to be direct. Something about this completely not formal girl made me want to be formal, so I clasped my hands in front of me and said, "I need a mannequin. A human doll with lots of articulation. Joe said you could help."

Joe shrugged, grinning like he was bragging as he said, "I figured, why not go to the person who made all the mannequins in town?"

She bapped him on the nose with a pudgy finger. "Oh, shush, you flattering lunk. You know Mom did that. We only make them when ordered, and they're not fast to make, but... you really need one now? For Yuki? In a hurry? Will I get it back?"

"Yes, yes, yes, and it's possible but not likely," I answered honestly.

The brown bunny girl threw her hands up and declared, "Sakes alive. If Yuki is in trouble, I can't waste time debating this. You can have Bonnet. Come in."

She flounced through her bedroom to another door. She did flounce, moving with energetic hops from foot to foot that made her ears, skirt, and apron bounce. The bedroom itself reminded me of its owner, brown, comfortably furnished, and feminine, with simple furniture but lots of cushions in brown-and-white-checkerboard patterns with ruffled edges. Everything all tidy, exact, and brightly lit with sunshine from a spell-decorated glass skylight.

I only had a couple of seconds in the bedroom before I entered the workshop. It was the workshop of a mage. An accomplished mage. Thanks to that book I only got to browse at school, I at least knew this discipline was called Materials Magic.

Pots of all shapes and sizes sat on benches surrounded by painting supplies, and I discovered at that moment that there were a lot more kinds of painting supplies than I'd ever dreamed. A cylindrical kiln filled one corner, but not a regular kiln. This was covered in magical script, and no glow showed around the edges of the door. It trapped and concentrated magic, not heat. Shelves on the far side of the room were also covered in spells, black letters that glittered here and there with what looked a lot like soul fragments. In little hexagons sat small jars and boxes, a few made of bright, clear glass, a few of dull, grey resin, but mostly made of a weird sludgy stuff that might be on the way from the former into the latter.

There was more. A lot more, that I didn't recognize and didn't have time to study and figure out. For example, as we passed some gleaming, wet-looking glazed pots, Bonabelle pulled out her tablet and waved it over them. I couldn't even tell what the spell did, only that the pots looked sleeker now in a way I couldn't identify.

Stunned, I asked her, "Is this as advanced as it looks?"

She tilted her hips out to one side, and flapped a hand dismissively. "Well, I'm still learning, but—"

"Yes," Emanuel said, emphatic.

Somewhere above us, Joe purred, "You're not the only prodigy in town."

Bonabelle reached up and touched a fingertip to his lips. "Shush. I know your games, big boy. I just wish they didn't work on me."

Twirling around, she flounced over to a sheet-covered, human-sized thing in the back of the workshop. This corner alone held nothing obviously to do with pottery. Instead, it held sewing stuff. Piles of different colored cloths, boxes of needles and string, and so on. That was all I could say. It was a world more mysterious to me than Materials Magic.

The rabbit hauled the sheet off of the object it had covered, and declared, "Here you are. I suppose it's time to make a new— oh, you cad, get him out of here, honestly. This is between me and Artifact anyway."

The object was human-sized and human-shaped, because it was a mannequin. In fact, it was Bonabelle sized and Bonabelle shaped, almost eerily so. An exact duplicate, so exact it had to have been cast from a mold taken from life, or however you made copies like that. Only the complicated ball joints at some of the seams were different. The whole thing was made of fancy grey resin.

Joe leaned forward, gazing at it with an exaggerated leer that almost amounted to drooling. He theatrically didn't cooperate, but also didn't actually resist as Emanuel and Elvira grabbed his arms and hauled him out of the room and out of sight.

Bunny blew a puff of air up as if urging hair out of her eyes, and one of her ears that had been flopping straightened back up. She rolled her eyes and chuckled, "That impossible boy. I use her for adjusting my clothing. I'm sure I have something to make her acceptable in public. What do you need her for?"

She didn't wait for an answer, already bustling around the

room. When she didn't flounce, Bonabelle bustled, moving rapidly and with purpose, arms constantly in motion. She dragged out a bleached white burlap halter, tied it on the dummy, then put its feet through ragged denim shorts. It did indeed move perfectly. Being made of resin rather than ceramic resulted in smooth, even flexibility. Everything about the mannequin impressed me.

It would be perfect, so I told Bonabelle respectfully, "I need to make a fighting doll."

She tilted her head to the side and raised an eyebrow at me. "Is that as advanced as it sounds?"

"Yes." She was still dressing the doll, and I had to make some kind of conversation, so I asked, "Are you really Joe's girlfriend?"

She rolled her eyes again, with a lopsided smile and an airy tone, although both seemed to be common with Bonabelle. "Maybe slightly more than every other girl."

I didn't understand, and I hoped if I kept my mouth shut it would make sense before I looked stupid.

I wasn't sure if that worked, because Bonabelle's knowing glance saw something in my expression. She explained, "I have to keep him at arm's length. You know that rascal. If I let myself, I could fall in love, and I simply refuse to do that with a boy who's planning on leaving me."

Ouch. Right to the most awkward topic. Suddenly intensely aware she deserved to know, I asked, "Did he tell you he plans to... soon?"

She sighed. Her whole rounded body went up and down when she did that. Bonabelle did not make small gestures. "Joe tells me everything, whether he should or not. The tragic truth, honey hair, is he was ready to leave long ago, and he's been procrastinating because he doesn't want to leave me."

"So he's in love with you," I filled in.

"Pshaw!" she scoffed, waving a hand in aggressive skepticism. "I don't know if that would be better or worse. I'm his favorite, short stuff, no denying it, but Joe isn't looking for love. He's looking for playmates. That's not where I am. Maybe we both wish it was otherwise."

I nodded, but honestly, I was now even more lost. That had all been way, way beyond me. Not that I wasn't interested in boys and so on, but my policy was to not think about it. Anyone interested would figure it out for me.

I did panic when people surprised me by acting weird. I was good at bioengineering, okay? Having to understand anything else was the hardest part of living like an adult.

One thing I did understand. I could see why Joe was so besotted with this girl. Bonabelle was smart, sophisticated, complex, passionate, talented… a feast for someone whose joy in life was other people. All that, and I'd only known her sixty seconds.

With the mannequin properly modest, Bonabelle called, "Joe, get in here. Put those beautiful muscles to work doing something useful. All of you get out of here. Go save Yuki! Tell me from what when she's safe!"

Joe hurried in with downright desperate speed. From the moment he entered the room, his eyes never left the rabbit girl. He looked almost scared of her, if someone could be scared and adoring at the same time. Hoisting the mannequin over his shoulder, he ran back out, and Emanuel, Elvira, and I hurried to catch up.

Back on the street, we looked up towards the school. Grim again, Emanuel said, "I was hoping Lisa would have brought Yuki back by now."

Joe said, "We were right. She's headed to the island. She knew we'd follow, so she took a side road."

I pulled my hair back impatiently. "We won't catch her before she gets there, so let's get to my house as fast as we can."

ChapterForty-Five

W hich wasn't nearly fast enough, since I was by far in the worst shape of anyone in my group, and I slowed them down. By the time we actually reached my front door, I was tight with rising panic. Yuki had left school forever ago, and we were nowhere near actually on the way to rescue her yet.

I could only hope Yuki had been right, and her ability to speak their language would keep the monsters from murdering her. At least it might make them let her get away.

What would make me happiest is if the whole doll plan was useless. If I opened the door to my living room and saw Lisa sitting on Yuki, pinning her to the floor.

I opened the door to my living room and saw my living room. I did hear hooves smacking on wood, and Lisa ran in, holding a burrito wrap slathered in sorghum juice and with sticky yellow stuff smeared around her mouth. Swallowing, she reported breathlessly, "I never saw her. Maybe she's not headed to the island?"

"Do you believe that?" I asked.

Suddenly totally solemn, she answered, "No. I saw her expression when she walked away."

I trusted Lisa's judgment on this, and wished I didn't.

My plan remained the only plan. I beckoned with one hand to Joe, and said, "Bring the doll into the workshop."

Still subdued, Lisa asked, "So we're going to the island?"

Already following Joe, I said without looking back, "Yes."

Even on carpet, I could hear the little thumps of Lisa's hooves as she walked right behind me. Disapproval was creeping into her voice. "And you're about to do something crazy to help us."

I watched Joe lay Bonnet on top of the altar. The mannequin flopped limp, which was a very good thing. Imagine. This thing had been originally sculpted out of clay, and was now so mobile! One leg hung completely down off of the altar, since it wasn't big enough for even a small sized human. In this grey, concrete-walled room, the subtle purple in the doll's material stood out.

"Only a little. The only thing it risks is wasting time," I told Lisa.

She spun around so fast her tail should have made a whip crack, declaring huffily, "Then I'll make us food."

Joe stepped up next to her, putting a hand on her shoulder and suggesting, "I'll make us food. You guard your cousin."

She looked up at him with a wan smile, which disappeared like a shutter snapping shut as she stepped into the workshop, replaced by a suspicious glower. Planting her back against the wall, her whole body tilted back at an angle, she folded her arms and watched me like she expected me to stab myself with a knife any minute now.

And she was right, but not yet.

Anyway, that exchange was merely something I noticed as I flew to my benches and the shelves built into them, the shelves packed with stacks of paper mostly bound in string, with unbound stacks sitting on the desktops themselves. I knew exactly where the blueprints I need were, this time. Scooping out the rubber loop, I tied my hair back as I spread the formula-covered pages over the still-remaining wooden surface.

Elvira and Emanuel, being good friends, pushed the altar extensions into place. I straightened out Bonnet properly, locked and connected everything properly, and got to work.

Work consisted of drawing a lot of interconnecting diagrams

all over the mannequin. Thankfully, much less than there should be. Painting them on the outside like this they would last maybe a day, so I didn't need any of the long-term stability enchantments. We'd be going too far from my soul forge to reliably use it for power, so I could leave off all the spells that control how much power could go into the doll. Dolls powered by soul forges tended to melt or explode without serious regulators. I could leave out half of the remaining formulae, because I was planning on doing something that wasn't foolish or immoral, just... um, wildly unethical.

The only thing I had to copy completely and with scrupulous correctness were the control and behavior setup, a complicated web of symbols that I had no intention of trying to design fresh. I was sticking with something I knew had worked for multiple bioengineers in the past, thanks.

With all of that drawn, I went to my tools and picked up my sharpest knife. Sheesh. I scolded Elvira about black magic, and here I was about to do this.

Out loud, I warned, "Lisa, look at the wall. This isn't dangerous, but you won't like watching it."

She just glared harder.

I sliced the padded part of my palm in a long cut as shallow as I could manage. I just wanted blood, not to cut a muscle or anything.

Rrg. The pain made me wince, but the wound was perfect. Blood welled up along a line, but a shallow line.

I was too scared to look at Lisa's expression. I focused on my work, scooping blood up on my fingertips and bending back over the mannequin. Blood magic wasn't evil using your own blood, and using someone else's blood would be pointless. I wasn't superstitious about sacrifice, but an unwilling magical link? Ridiculous. Garbage.

I forced aside my worry about whether what I was doing was right or wrong, because I was busy fingerpainting blood over the glyphs that regulated power flow. I didn't need anything complicated if the source was always me.

Those painted, I took a step back. Emanuel immediately grabbed my hand, holding it up for Elvira's inspection. She held my medical kit, dabbed the wound with a clean cloth, and peered at the red line.

Elvira announced her judgment. "She'll be fine."

Emanuel, turning wondering eyes back to the almost-doll, asked, "Is it done already?"

"One more step. The jump start," I said, reaching into the soul forge's cage.

A very simple step. I grabbed the fragment in my left, non-bloody hand, because I didn't want to melt or turn into a lich. Then I followed the correct procedure: I jammed it hard into the central lead.

Yellow-green light swirled through all the symbols marked on the mannequin. Then the symbols painted with my blood turned back to red, glowing red, which crept out to replace the yellow-green everywhere. I took a deep breath from a moment of dizziness, and it cleared. The job here was way more strenuous.

My very first doll sat up, raised her arms, fists curled. She mimed flexing her biceps and crowed, "Ha! I'm back! Suck on that, losers!" in a buzzy voice that reminded me a little of Elvira.

The glow faded from the painted symbols as power dropped back to normal levels, but the regular symbols stood out sharper and blacker than I'd drawn them, and the blood-reinforced power symbols showed glaring crimson. Looking around, the doll pointed an index finger at me and babbled enthusiastically, "You're my new owner, huh? Wow, you didn't stint on the power, did you? I've got some brawn backing me this time. What's up? Revenge? Bodyguard? War? Experiment you didn't think would work?"

Boggled, staring, I said, "Dungeon dive."

The doll clapped her hands together, and that stuff like hard rubber she was made of boomed. "Best answer!"

Emanuel and Elvira had both taken a step back, their expressions identically lopsided and suspicious. Emanuel was the one who asked, "Is it supposed to have a personality?"

No. It absolutely was not supposed to have a personality. It was a fighting doll. Who would give that a personality? Granted, the control formula was ridiculously complex, but it would have to be just to handle basic fighting techniques and order taking and safety protocols. Not this... enthusiasm.

What I actually said was, "I copied the control pattern from one my dad gave me. So I guess... yes. It just didn't occur to me." Horrified guilt hit. "And I gave her a single day lifespan?"

The doll lifted a hand and rolled its eyes, smirking in unconcern. "Naah, boss, I've got continuity."

The expression was impressive. Only the eyes and eyelids were actually properly mobile, but the material flexed around the muzzle enough to pull into limited smiles and frowns. Similar dimpling moved the eyebrows, at least a little. The expressions might be kind of creepy, but the doll could emote. Her mouth didn't move when she talked, though.

I was still reeling from the fact she could talk at all.

Which I blame for my stumbling as I introduced, "Oh. Um, I'm Artifact, that's Elvira, Emanuel, Lisa, Joe will be here in a minute, and we're going to rescue Yuki. Right now. This took way too long."

And now I finally noticed the incredibly delicious smell of fried fish wafting around, as Joe stepped into the workshop with one of my dull brown grocery sacks over his shoulder. Its lumpiness and tempting odor suggested it already contained food.

"Ready!" he declared confidently. The talking doll didn't faze him at all.

I couldn't let it faze me. We'd been out of time half an hour ago. I grabbed my coat, goggles, and gloves. The gloves would shield my cut, and I might as well wear the closest to armor I owned.

Unlike Elvira, who had actual armor. She must have been carrying it, and switched into it while I worked. It reminded me of what Franklin wore, a suit of thick, stiff, padded leather. Gleaming, pure black in Elvira's case, unlike the faded, well-used armor of the much older adventuress.

It transformed her. I had never imagined someone could look so different just changing clothing. I had always assumed Elvira was pretty. The long dresses that exaggerated her already exaggerated shape had made that seem inevitable. The armor erased everything. It reshaped her into a block, hard and strong. Only now did I notice that her nose was long and sharp-edged, and the lines of her cheeks straight as razors. She wasn't ugly, but she wasn't classically beautiful. She was the person she wanted to be: A tough as nails adventuress. She always had been, but now it was obvious at a glance.

Her long hair had disappeared. I was pretty sure she'd tucked it down the back of the armor's high collar.

I scooped my detection equipment into my satchel, then remembered and added the hexagonal plate my monster dug up out of the sea.

Holding it up before dropping it in, I asked the group, "This has to be part of the seal. Right? Everyone agrees? With a signature just like a breach detonator? I wish we had the detonator. The professor said something about using it to blow up a gate."

Lisa jerked her thumb back towards the stairs, and asked me, "Do you want me to go get it?"

My brain crashed. Um. Um!? Face twisted in shock, I squeaked, "You know where it is?"

She gave a bland shrug, her own expression mild as she said, "I haven't looked in a couple of days, but sure, under my bed where it's been this whole time?"

I flapped my arms wildly. "You said you threw it in the ocean!"

She flapped her own arms. "You weren't supposed to believe me!"

My emotions rampaged inside me. Too many emotions. I couldn't make sense of them.

I could make sense of Lisa's expression. At least, in her outrage mimicking mine, I saw a pinched tension marring the theater, an uncertainty I rarely saw amid all her posing.

Walking over slowly, step by step, I wrapped my arms around her shoulders and hugged her. Leaning up on my tiptoes, I said quietly, "I am always going to believe you, so you'd better plan accordingly."

Her arms flapped again, but this time weak fluttering that barely left her side. She scowled as if I had just hit her, and sulked, "That really puts a cramp in my style, but ugh. Fine. I'll go get the detonator."

"Then let's go," I told my cousin, my friends, and my newly made doll.

Lisa zoomed up the stairs three at a time, and the rest of us were still crowding out the front door when she caught up.

Me, I stood in the doorway and realized something was missing. Leaning back inside, I yelled, "Bonnet, are you coming?"

"Is that my name this time?" she yelled back with eager curiosity.

"Yes!"

Both cheerful and guarded, she asked, "*Am* I coming? I don't decide what to do very well. It's part of the design. You can see why, right?"

"Follow me except when I give you other orders!" I shouted, to deal with that.

"Got it!" she answered, and came running out of the workshop, barely slowed down by turning a cartwheel on the carpet before trotting the last few steps up to me.

Lisa's raised eyebrows and smirking smile looked terribly amused as she moved aside to let the doll out the door, then locked that door behind us. She tossed the bulk detonator into my satchel, and it was the same oversize metal key that I remembered. Also as heavy as I remembered. As the only person without a physical job on this team, I wasn't going to complain.

We walked as a group down to the shore, and I asked the group one of the questions I'd been dreading. "How are we going to catch up with Yuki?"

Chapter Forty-Six

"We'll steal a fishing boat," answered Elvira simply.

Slightly more worried than before, I asked, "Won't that—"

Emanuel cut me off with a sweep of his arm. "Our problem."

I didn't like it, but this was an emergency. Yuki must be so far ahead that all I could hope for was that she was far ahead and alive.

I had to remember that we were not going to get to the island in time to catch her no matter what we did, and our hopes always rested on whether she could convince the monsters not to immediately kill her. If she'd managed that, this was the best plan for rescue.

So we walked down the ridge and then the beach to the fishing fleet docks. They weren't crowded, but there were plenty of fisherpeople around, doing fisherpeople things that I could not possibly understand. I didn't see Emanuel and Elvira's parents.

Emanuel and Elvira climbed into one of the boats, so the rest of us followed and settled into seats or the floor as best we could. A couple of fishermen wandered up to the dock next to us. One of them pointed at Bonnet and asked curiously, "What is that?"

Emanuel and Elvira already had the sails set and the rope untied from the dock. Joe started pulling at the oars. Without an answer, we sailed away.

Someone yelled angrily in the increasing distance, and I was pretty sure it was Emanuel and Elvira's parents. The siblings didn't look any more troubled than they already had by the seriousness of our mission.

We headed towards the island? Were we going fast? I couldn't tell. The constantly moving sea erased all hints, and the island still looked far away.

How could we know if Yuki was even there?

"I need a telescope," I grumbled.

Elvira suddenly whacked herself in the forehead with the heel of her palm, and declared in revelation, "So do I!"

Unable to contribute, I looked at the sea. Even at a time like this, it held a vast peace. Should the bouncing of the waves make me feel sick or uncomfortable? It didn't. It felt natural. It was hard to stand, so I stayed seated, but it was still a pleasant sensation.

My eyes turned down to the water right next to us, and a completely different emotion welled up in me. There was only this tiny, overloaded boat between myself and opaque water that went down, and down, perhaps forever, with who knew what in it. The idea chilled me.

But not enough to overcome the wonder of being on the sea's surface.

The island had become clearly visible, and not just to me, because Joe pointed and said, "There's a boat on the shore. We were right."

Water splashed. A strange, glittery person climbed up the side of the boat, clinging to the edge with one hand and the other draped arm.

It wasn't as strange as the monsters I'd made, but... it was strange. It had some mermaidness to it. The upper body was basically human shaped, with arms, shoulders, a chest, and a head on a neck. A mask completely covered the face. Completely, clinging to the monster's head like it was glued on, or just part of the body. The mask didn't have features of its own, just a blank, white, rounded surface, oval in shape. Below the chest, the body extended into a tail that disappeared under the waves.

Every inch was covered in a mottling of green and purple scales over slimy blue skin, and spines or little fishy fins stood out in erratic, asymmetrical, illogical places.

At least it didn't have claws.

Having no visible mouth didn't stop it from saying monster gibberish. If it was copying a human language, it was sure a weird language. There were syllables in there somewhere, stretched and slurred or too short, but I couldn't make out any of them and mostly it sounded like distorted musical notes.

Joe leaned over, gave it a friendly smile and said in a gentle, soothing tone, "We mean you no harm. It's okay."

It repeated the same monster gibberish as before.

Joe straightened up and sighed, his face and voice touched by honest grief. "It was worth a try."

It decided we weren't going to leave, or give the correct password, or whatever. The fishy, snaky thing leaned way back and tilted the boat a few inches down on its side.

Elvira grabbed one of its arms in both of hers. Declaring, "Bye, Felicia!" she hauled it into the air and flung it out over the water, where it landed yards away with an impressive splash. Its tail had been impressively long, and oddly bulgy.

Two more monsters reached up and grabbed the side of the boat.

Anxiety rising inside me, I ordered Bonnet, "Help her. Get rid of them!"

Elvira grabbed the next monster's arm and did her "Bye, Felicia" thing again. In sync with her, Bonnet grabbed the other monster and flung it the same way, and exactly the same distance.

"I can keep this up, but it's really slowing us down!" Elvira warned.

"On it," said her brother. Crouching down in the back of the boat, he got out a big pencil and started writing spell code on the back board.

For what felt like forever, monsters swam up, patiently and repeatedly grabbed the boat, tried to tip us over, and got thrown back over the sea by Elvira and Bonnet. A lot of them repeated the warning phrase, or whatever that monster talk had been. It was pure, mindless rote behavior—and thank goodness, because if they'd worked together we'd have been doomed.

Joe was rowing, but it looked like a strain.

Emanuel finished writing, and ran his hand over the spell. The boat kicked forward sharply, forcing me to cling desperately to my plank seat. Emanuel did it again and again, sending the boat ahead in uncomfortable jumps.

I had an idea. "Bonnet, take over the oars. We need to go fast."

"Got it!" The rabbit doll pushed Joe off his seat and grabbed the oar handles. She must have known something about rowing, because she did it at a different pace than him. Fast, yes, but with a rhythm rather than a spin. A very fast rhythm.

Between sail, Emanuel's spell, and Bonnet's magic-powered rowing, we were leaving the monsters behind and making lurchy progress. Occasionally I saw a masked head break the surface right behind us, look around, and dive again.

Suddenly the beach was in front of us, getting closer a lot faster than I expected.

Elvira shouted, "Hold on tight!"

I grabbed my seat with both hands. Lisa grabbed both me and the seat, including with her tail. Joe lay curled up at the bottom of the boat.

Thunk! We hit the beach, knocking everyone forward, but not actually toppling any of us over.

It wasn't a beach. A few feet of white sand spread around the base of the stairs with no sign of a... tide line? Was that what they were called? The marking as waves went in and out.

The tip of our boat actually rested on the lowest steps of those stairs, which were multiple body lengths wide, and went up and up and up at a stately angle. Overhead, at intervals, loomed three arches that looked like nothing except a gigantic, rough, oblong horizontal stone laying across two gigantic, rough, oblong, upright stones.

Off to the left and right, nowhere near but easily visible, were more staircases. From the angle, I got the impression this island was arranged in a five- or six-pointed star.

We'd landed right next to another boat, identical to ours to my ignorant land dweller eyes. That had to be Yuki's, which meant she'd gotten this far, and if she'd gotten this far, there was a good chance she was still alive.

There were no monsters on the stairs. There was nothing on the stairs, which rose evenly and seemed to be carved into one enormous pale rock that made up the whole island. Impressively made they might look, but they also looked ancient, scratched and worn and irregularly rounded by time.

"We might want to get away from those," said Joe.

Masks visible at the surface told us fishy, snaky monsters were headed for the beach and us.

Taking Joe's very sensible advice, we scurried up the stairs, with Elvira and Emanuel in front and Bonnet as rear guard. Almost immediately, Joe declared, "Hold up. The moment we passed that first arch, they stopped following."

"I hope that means this dungeon's monsters can't pass gates," Emanuel said.

Elvira answered, "I hope we don't need to find out." She sounded only slightly haunted. Her face was set in determination, and she stretched her shoulders like an athlete warming up as we climbed, now at an easier pace.

We got to the top, and wow. The tower was huge. It went up and up, twisty and shell-like, with slightly iridescent and colorful surfacing. Every color. Pink and white dominated, but I caught streaks of purple, and green, and blue... everything, all glittery in the sun. I had never seen a building nearly this tall, either. It was crazy, like something out of storybooks of the golden age.

The star of white rock around it might be more of a wheel, but with the spokes going out instead of in. A circle of plaza enveloped the base of the tower, and wide strips extended from the sides until they ended in stairs. I saw two strips on either side, and there was room for another beside the tower, so... yeah, six points.

A double doorway, arched to a point instead of flat-topped like the gateways on the stairs, dominated the front of the tower on this side. Well, no, it dominated the end of this strip running up to the tower. Despite being several times my height at least, it was just a little thing compared to that... well, towering building.

It wasn't undefended. Eight masked fish/snake people lined this spoke of the wheel, arranged in pairs one on each side of the walkway, with a big gap to the next pair. These had a lot less fins than the swimmy monsters, and held shiny blue-green spears in their right hands, and shiny blue-green shields in their left. Big, thick, ridged shields that reminded me of hexagonal turtle shells. They stood as straight as anything that blended into a tail rather than having legs could, stiff and motionless. Like the sea monsters, they wore blank masks over faces they might not even have.

The sheer motionlessness confirmed they were more mindless guard monsters.

They didn't react to our reaching the summit of the stairs, but another monster did. A single figure in a blue robe scurried up to us, with the way its robe flapped around the bottom as it moved suggesting there were legs under there.

It had a ways to go.

Everyone had been looking around except Elvira, who watched the monsters ahead of us like a hawk. Her brother Emanuel noted, "Doors face the shore. None on the other sides."

He was right. We'd at least have been able to see a pair of doors on the nearest spokes of the wheel, and the base of the tower remained smooth over there, or at least striated in a non-entrance way. The surface of the tower really did look like shell.

With the monsters ahead and one approach, something was going to happen. I murmured to Bonnet, "Up front with Elvira," and she bounced up to stand behind the dark teenage adventuress, the former's still competence contrasting to the latter's barely restrained power as the rabbit doll smacked a fist into her palm over and over.

We all moved forward, and met the robed character just ahead of the first pair of guards.

Only two things linked this monster to the fish things. It came in a color scheme of blue and white at least similar to the fish-snake scales, and it wore the same kind of blank white mask that completely covered the face. Otherwise this thing stood upright, human-sized if on the short side, in a loose robe that hid everything but the mask, furry white hands, and a long, fluffy white tail in back that seemed foxy to me. The face was too flat to be a furry, although again, there probably wasn't a face under that mask.

The robe was pretty. It looked like silk, or fine cotton, sky-blue but with white scroll work embroidered around the edges. The angular edged kind, not the curly kind.

To add slightly to the furry appearance, the robe's hood bulged in two little pointy triangular pockets that looked like they held animal ears. They might.

The masked fox-thing spoke, that same weird language full of musical, dragging sounds that contained letters or syllables without those being identifiable. At least, I couldn't pick them out. It sounded less slurred than the fish monsters, and it wasn't the same little speech.

Leaning out to the side past the twin shields of Elvira and Bonnet, I apologized, "Excuse us. Do you speak English?"

The thing yip-drawled some more. Again, new words, not a repeat. Did it sound frustrated? With the musical tone to its language, it was very hard to make out emotion.

I pointed past it at the tower. "Our friend came here. Is she inside? Um…"

Since it obviously couldn't understand me, I pulled out my hair, then mimed brushing it down even longer than it was, to my thighs. I curved my fingers into circles, and put them over my goggles to indicate even bigger glasses. Then I held my hand to the top of the head, and moved it to Yuki's height. Finally I pointed at the slightly open tower doors.

The fox-thing said something brief. Did it sound offended?

"This one is intelligent," said Joe. Someone had needed to say it out loud.

"It's in our way," replied Elvira, all icy and businesslike, and her business was danger now.

Already tickled by guilt, I asked, "Try not to kill it? It's going to disappear when the soul forge shuts down, but still…"

"Right," Elvira agreed, pushing the fox-thing aside with a leather-covered arm and stepping forward towards the tower. The rest of us fell in with her.

The fox-thing stumbled backwards, nearly falling on its fluffy-tailed butt. It shouted in yip-music, and ran for the front doors.

The snake-things lowered their spears to point at us, and slithered forwards.

Chapter
Forty-Seven

"Well, that was inevitable," Elvira muttered with dark amusement.

The snake-fish monsters moved much faster than their lack of legs had made me expect. Elvira cast a spell. Four thumps against its arm knocked the spear out of the hand of the monster on her side, but it held its shield up in front of it and kept sliding forward.

Elvira cast again, and Magic Missile hit the other snake in the face, knocking it onto its back. It started getting back up. The first snake with the shield reached us, and we all scattered apart, retreating towards the stairs.

Bonnet had stood there watching all this, intent, poised with fists raised, but not doing a thing.

Feeling like an idiot, I pointed at the shield snake and gave her an actual order. "Hit it as hard as you can!"

The resin at the corners of her short rabbit muzzle twisted into a smile, and the doll launched a punch at the shield, fast and straight. I got a glimpse of her fist speeding through the shield and the body behind it as if they were merely air.

Then dizziness hit me in a wave, and the world fell away in darkness. My legs didn't work, and I was vaguely aware I was falling over.

Arms caught me. Lisa's arms. I knew them and her strawberry smell by now. I heard the *thunk* and rattle of Bonnet hitting the stone platform's surface.

Then I heard a completely unexpected voice. Ruby, clipped and stern and somewhere close, said, "Drink this. All of it."

A container pressed to my mouth. It contained liquid that tasted harsh and stingy like vinegar. I swallowed it all.

My head immediately began to clear. I opened my eyes to see Bonnet climbing to her feet. Elvira was casting again, at the fish-snake-man she'd knocked over. They hit it in the face, four loud *whack*s that knocked its head back and broke something. It faded away like pure monsters did when they died.

The one Bonnet punched was already gone.

Well, I'd been incredibly stupid, I'd never owned a doll before, so maybe I could forgive myself. This time, I ordered Bonnet, "Hit the rest just hard enough to hurt them. In fact, just keep them away from Elvira."

She would have to do that immediately, because the next pair were almost here, and more slithered up behind them.

Bonnet flexed her beautifully flexible fingers, every joint working like a human's and each with its little painted control sigil. "Now we're talking. Come here and get your thumping, monsters!"

She leaped in the way of the next snake. It stabbed her in the chest with its spear, a short, sharp jab that bounced off with an audible *pok*. I felt a subtle poke in my own chest, feedback as my magic reinforced Bonnet's shell to resist the blow. Unharmed, the rabbit doll grabbed the spear in both hands, and used it to sling the fish-snake off its feet and into the air to crash into its fellow. The snake let go of the spear in mid-flight, and out of contact with the monster, the spear faded into nothing.

Bonnet stomped her foot and complained, "Aw! I hate monster weapons! Why didn't we bring a sledgehammer? Oh, wait, we did!" Raising her balled fists, she snarled gleefully, "Two of them!"

Leaping into the next pair of snakes that had just caught up, she punched the closer one in the shield.

I didn't have time to see more. My attention was diverted by the silhouette that faded silently into existence next to me, only to have blue and green and white solidity swirl into place at high speed. It took maybe a second, and a snake thing loomed over me, pulling its spear back to stab.

Ruby stabbed it first, the black-clad, pointy-hatted witch girl stepping forward to ram the point of her crude wooden broom in its stomach. Lisa leaped into the air, kicked the snake under its chin with a hoof, and then gave it a kick to the stomach where Ruby had just hit it. A hard kick rather than a fast one, shoving it back so far that its head and shoulders fell over the edge of the stone platform, and the rest followed like a noodle being sucked up.

"We're in trouble. There's a dungeon master!" I announced.

Alarmed, backing away from where the thing materialized, Joe said, "Are they supposed to be able to summon monsters just anywhere?"

"Theoretically, but it's not normal!" I shouted, even though he was only a few feet away. It's hard to whisper when snake monsters are attacking you from both sides.

"Advance! Get to the doors!" barked Elvira.

I crowded close behind her as she moved forward, with Bonnet driving the remaining monsters before her. I felt helpless, useless. Emanuel chanted Magic Missile too, although it took him at least twice as long to get through it. When his spell hit a snake it did so with the same four, devastating blows to the face as Elvira's casts.

Surprised and delighted, he declared, "You weren't kidding, sis. This is so easy to aim!"

"I know, right? Fast casting, accurate, best spell ever!" she called back, and cast it again.

I didn't know enough about fighting to understand what was going on. On the other hand, Bonnet seemed to understand just fine. Or at least, she was highly effective in punching and throwing things around, now that I'd given her permission. I could feel the constant drain of magic, as if I was doing exercise, but it wasn't bad. Like walking fast, not even jogging. I could keep this up awhile.

Which was good, because the snake-things on the other platforms had rounded the circle to ours.

Darkly amused and sincerely grateful, Elvira smirked. "Thank goodness they're stupid."

"Not all of them, remember," said Joe.

Which was a great time for the giant doors ahead of us to slam shut.

The crowd of monsters disappeared. More accurately, they'd been used up. There hadn't been that many, after all, just eight on each spoke, and they'd mindlessly attacked us in pairs, which Bonnet and Elvira disposed of fast and easily. So far Lisa and Emanuel had kept our backs free by hitting snakes as they materialized.

Which left the doors.

And the wall of coarse white ice, at least ten feet tall and twenty wide, that lurched up from nothing in front of them.

"Mage monsters. Not great," Emanuel observed.

"And I'd been thinking this is a weak dungeon," Elvira commented back, her tone sardonic.

A fox-thing stepped around the corner and blasted a line of icy mist at us. Everyone bolted out of the way automatically, but from the ice crystals the mist left on the ground, that mist would be deadly to get caught in. That the ice was melting rapidly in the Goblita afternoon sun didn't change that.

If the big wall was melting at all, I couldn't tell.

Elvira started a Magic Missile. The fox-thing was faster. It did have to use an incantation, a series of yips and squeaks somewhere between its language and the spell code I was used to. Actually, it sounded most like spell code sped up sharply with a little added squeak and buzz.

Ice mist lanced out again. Bonnet leaped in front of Elvira, taking the hit. Ice crystals sprung out all over her like knives, then cracked and fell off as she broke free.

It had only slowed down Bonnet a little, but I felt the exertion. Spells took a lot more shrugging off than spear points, apparently.

Magic Missile only took Elvira a few seconds to cast. The fox-thing ducked behind the ice wall after throwing its ice spell, but not fast enough. At least one of the magical blows hit its hip, and it went spinning out of sight behind the barrier.

I spotted something else as it did. This fox had three fluffy white tails it had been holding out stiff and straight in a triangle. It wasn't the original.

Emanuel had also been chanting spell code, but quietly. No rule said you had to shout it and be obvious. Now he swung his arm like throwing a ball, and a ball of fire did indeed leap out, hitting the ice wall. A flash of steam exploded out, and cleared to show a hole going right through the ice. Something blue and brown that I didn't get a good look at lurked behind the barrier, and with a *woosh*, a plug of ice not only blocked the hole but bulged out.

Elvira glanced at Bonnet long enough to say, "Circle around and shove everything behind the wall out."

Bonnet immediately looked back at me. I nodded. "Do it."

The plump rabbit doll took off towards the edge of the wall on the right, while on the left Elvira fired a series of Magic Missiles that rattled off the wall of the tower. After hers, Emanuel launched a set of his own, and the two kept shooting, peppering the area that the fox had been peeking out of, for the few seconds it took for Bonnet to round the corner.

I couldn't make sense of the noises on the other side. Bonnet was doing something that involved a lot of magic, because I had to take some deep breaths, and my body felt cold and burning hot at the same time from magical feedback.

I hunched forward, and Lisa put her arms around me, to hold me up if I needed it. I smiled and assured her, "It's not that bad." Unpleasant, but not more than I could keep up with.

Anyway, it didn't last long. The masked blue and white fox monster went flying out from behind the wall on the left side, tumbling across the stone. Bonnet emerged holding what looked like a blue and white snail with a brown shell over her head, a snail as big as a man. I didn't get a good look, because she threw it over the edge of the plaza and into the sea.

I took a few breaths to relax, but as soon as the doll threw the snail away I started to recover.

Elvira was casting. The fox began climbing to its feet, but before it got upright invisible blows pummeled it in the head. It fell, and lay still.

In the sudden, unexpected quiet, Emanuel asked, "Is it dead?"

"It didn't disappear," replied Elvira, quick and suspicious.

Merely thoughtful, her brother said, "But it's not moving. Do you think it's playing opossum?"

Quietly, I said, "I think it's not a monster. I think it's an interdimensional."

Lisa tapped me on the shoulder, then waved her hand over my head at everyone else. "Hey, we have a problem. You know how the monsters stopped zapping in?"

I hadn't known that, but the fuss of taking them down had stopped, so they must have.

Lisa pointed off to the left. "Turns out they were zapping in over there."

Spear and shield snakes advanced in an organized block around the edge of the building. At least it was a huge building, and staying together slowed the snakes down a lot. We still didn't have much time before they arrived this time not in easily disposed of pairs.

"I can help a bit," said Ruby, who had been standing quietly behind me. She had all that stuff on her belt, and I'd only ever recognized the potions, but witches did more than just make potions. Pulling off a little twiggy effigy off her belt, she kissed it and flung it in the direction of the snakes. She had a great arm, and it landed not far in front of them. They reacted with a group hiss. Were they slowing down? Did they not want to go past it?

I had other things to pay attention to.

Elvira was making plans. "We open the doors, get inside, close them again if we can. It will force them to come after us in a smaller pack. Bonnet can hold off one or two at a time forever."

I looked up at the glittery edifice above us. "How? The doors are huge."

"It's a dungeon. There will be a puzzle," Elvira said.

With a thoughtful frown, Emanuel said, "That looks like a magic formula on the door."

It did. The doors didn't have the rough, shell-like surfacing of the main tower. They were just as pretty, but smooth, except with intricate scrollwork depressions carved into the surface. The kind that looked like magic diagrams, although I couldn't see any meaning in this one.

"Ice magic," said Joe simply.

Emanuel snapped his head forward, sounding a touch disgusted with himself. "Of course!"

Elvira's mouth and eyes tightened. "No ice spells in the book. This is all you, Emanuel. Sorry about the rush."

Her brother nodded. The tall, dark, lean-muscled and hard young man stood still, scowling deeply. His lips moved silently. Very slowly, he nodded again. Holding up his outstretched arm, palm forward, he muttered something in spell code.

The spell cast. It was pathetic, a thin, twisty vine of ice springing from his hand to the door. Pathetic or not, the instant it hit it was sucked into the engravings, which all filled with ice. The door slid out smoothly.

Until it hit the ice barrier.

Elvira and Emanuel cast again, fast and confident this time. Elvira threw her fireball first, and Emanuel's launched a few seconds later, but they created a big enough hole for our group to run through and into the gap of the barely opened doors.

Which we did immediately, running and bumping into each other as a phalanx of faceless snake monsters closed in from the left side.

We got inside, spilling out into a loose group past the doors. I had time for a quick impression of an absolutely enormous chamber with shiny shell walls and a metal column going straight up the middle. Then my attention was drawn to the three tailed foxes standing on either side of us, tails splayed, with a man-sized snail next to each.

And in front of us, several yards away, a five-tailed fox. I could only see four tails stuck out, but from the angles, there had to be a fifth hidden behind its body.

Chapter
Forty-Eight

E lvira hissed, "Not good!"
      Elvira and Emanuel started to chant. Bonnet lurched forward.

The five-tailed fox shouted something, and held up a warning hand, palm out. The three-tails stopped cast. Half a second later, so did Emanuel and Elvira, which resulted in a brief, hissing air distortion in front of Elvira, and nothing else. Bonnet stood with one foot off the ground behind her, with suddenly nothing to protect Elvira from.

Everyone looked uncertain. The foxes had no faces, or if they did, those faces were completely hidden by the smooth, white masks. They stood twitchy and awkward, tails slumping, seeming as confused as us.

Five-tails beckoned with one white hand. We stepped forward. That was enough to completely clear the doors, and they slid ponderously shut behind us.

Five-tails spoke some more, that yipping interdimensional masked fox language, and pointed at us. We all looked around to try and figure out what she was pointing at specifically.

I worked it out, and squeaked, "Lisa? You want Lisa?"

My cousin stalked forward—no, strutted forward, with her most brazen demon walk, chin lifted so that her hair in its many shades of flame fell vividly behind her and her back-curved black horns prominently crowned her sinuous figure.

The five-tailed masked fox, its tails curled up rather than spread out in combat position, spread its arms like it was giving a particularly enthusiastic welcome, and jabbered at her. The three-tails visibly relaxed. A single-tailed fox, maybe the first we'd met outside, relaxed where it was peeking out behind the five-tails.

Lisa, with her usual subtlety, put one hand on her hip, flicked her fingertips vaguely, and told the five-tails, "You know I don't speak a word, right?"

Neither did I, but I guessed out loud, "I think they can tell you're also not from Earth, and that makes you… a friend, or one of them, or something." To my other friends, I said, "Let's see if they'll let us follow Lisa."

We all stepped forward, moving up behind my demon cousin with slow and completely unconvincing nonchalance. The foxes didn't get excited about it.

It was still hard to be sure with their weird, musical language and total lack of expression or anything to have an expression on, but five-tails sounded happy(?) as it yipped and mewed a speech at us.

Shrugging, I said, "I guess any friend of yours is a friend of theirs. I hope the dungeon master agrees."

Five-tails laid a hand on Lisa's shoulder, beckoning her to follow as the masked fox-thing strode towards the center of the room with the kind of straight-backed gait of someone in charge and proud of it.

I finally had a chance to take in the whole room. It was definitely big. It was the whole interior of the tower, at least for half a dozen floors. The walls had the same iridescent shell look as the outside of the tower, and weren't quite even, leaning subtly to one side and narrowing as they went up. I couldn't make out any details of the ceiling. It looked featureless metal, except from it hung half a dozen huge chains from which hung half a dozen huge, elongated crystals glowing white. Other than their size, just standard magical lights powered by the soul forge somewhere in the building.

The floor spread out in big tiles of interlocking blue-white and sky-blue. It was hard, and Bonnet's and Lisa's footsteps both echoed around the giant chamber.

A single metal column rose from what might not be quite the center of the tower. It was hard to tell, both because of the size of the room and the twisty tower shape. The actual center might be the pit ten feet in front of it, covered in a metal grating.

There was a bit more detail than that. Bulges in the walls reminded me of more columns, but wound up the walls instead of being straight and central. There were occasional signs posted on the walls, but the only ones I'd been close enough to read was the one by the front door and the one on the column, both of which showed the same symbol, of a ball with a bunch of circles around it, and a smaller ball embedded in each of those rings. I didn't know much about astronomy, but was that a stylized sun and planets design?

Aside from the sign, the column was marked only with a single closed and handle-less door in front, and a big yellow rectangle, at least six feet in either direction, painted on the floor in front of that door. Little black bars amidst the yellow painted no design I could make sense of.

Joe pointed at the grate. "Trapped. I guarantee it."

I peered closer as we rounded the pit, which was pretty big, I'd guess twenty feet across and completely blocked by the grating. That grate was made of twisty metal bars as thick as a finger, interlocking in a mesh even the smallest human could not hope to squeeze through. Right in the center, a hexagonal plate embedded in the mesh was engraved with a symbol of its own. It looked a bit like the gate Yuki had been looking for, with its two lines across the top instead of one, but inside the box that made hung a slanted, irregular star, with a crossbar that pierced the sides of the gate symbol.

Past the grate, I got a confused peek at descending spiral stairs and moving blue lights. Unlike the outer walls, everything

looked metal down there. Near the top—were those pipes,
turning to run underneath our floor?

Five-tails ignored the grate and the hole as she led us around
it. She had a lot to say in masked fox language, and I was at least
pretty sure she was being happy and friendly. She took us to
the column, where the door in front stood open to reveal a little
circular room with nothing in it.

Leading the way because she was the one five-tails had been
talking to, Lisa walked into the little room, looked around, and
asked, "This is it?"

Looking the column over, Emanuel said, "It's an elevator. It
goes up and down, so you don't need stairs. They had them in
the golden age, but they stopped working when magic changed.
Do these creatures have a working version?"

"If so, whatever the spells are printed on will be worth a lot
of money," Joe pointed out.

Fierce and suspicious, Elvira said, "It's a dungeon. The
power source will be the soul forge. I guess this place was made
to match the creatures out of the portal."

After Lisa, Elvira was in front, and stepped into the yellow
square first. It instantly turned red. A weird howling echoed
through the room, reminding me of the monster attack siren
yesterday (Only yesterday? Really?)

Most importantly, the door to the elevator slammed shut.

Elvira jumped back in alarm. The siren stopped, the square
turned yellow, and the elevator door slid open.

Inside the little room, Lisa grimaced with one hand planted
in the middle of her chest. "I thought I was trapped!"

Joe shook his head. "No, the building just doesn't like
humans."

Five-tails jabbered in a way that sounded apologetic, and
pointed down at the wall near where we'd come in. Was that a
door? Yes, I hadn't noticed it because it wasn't spectacular, just
a regular door made of the same shiny shell stuff as the wall.

Taking both of Lisa's hands in hers, the fox squeezed them
and then spun around and walked away, jabbering at the other
foxes now. As she walked off, five white tails curled upwards
like a fan, I wondered if what they really liked about Lisa was

the tail shiny blue shirt Lisa was wearing today. The demoness looked a lot more like them than any of us humans.

"I guess that means we have free run of the place," I said. At least whatever wasn't blocked by yellow marks to prevent humans entering.

No monsters appeared anywhere. The masked foxes with their different number of tails talked to each other energetically, but didn't seem angry. We all relaxed, stepping out into the room's open spaces and standing far enough apart from each other for comfortable conversation. Lisa did lurk close to me on my right side, and Ruby loomed with her tall, pointy hat on my left.

Her hard demeanor fading back into her usual perky cheer and little jiggly head movements, Elvira began, "Okay, I just want to say, we are a flawlessly coordinated dungeon butt-kicking machine. We don't just have the skills, we work together like that." She snapped her fingers.

Joe rubbed his forehead with his hand, and chuckled wearily, "It's fun, but as little fighting and danger as possible would be nice."

Undeterred, Elvira held out both hands to indicate Joe, and told the rest of us gleefully, "See? We have someone to remember that!"

Bonnet hunched forward disappointedly, ears sagging at the thought of less violence. "Aw."

"Also," I started, then spun around and clasped my gloved hands around Ruby's. "What are you doing here? And I mean that in the pleasant surprise way."

I was really glad that I'd added that last bit, because Ruby's eyes went wide like I'd hit her. It faded slowly back to her normal blankness after the correction, at least. Quite calmly, she explained, "I had news that will keep until we are safe, and I heard about the giant monster you summoned yesterday. Knowing how your work ethic drives you, I thought it best to bring you medicine for magic overuse."

Lisa slumped a little too, leaning to one side and gawking up at Ruby with open-mouthed relief so intense her words came out in a groan. "I could *kiss* you."

Ruby bowed to Lisa, deeply and formally, her whole body straight except where it bent at the hips. She stated, "Thank you, but my heart is set on another. I saw you all leaving Miss Forge's house, then saw you getting on a boat. I thought perhaps I should follow."

Her cat Sophie's voice came out of her spacious conical hat. "Once I pointed out you might need her help."

The bow ended. Holding up the broomstick that looked as much like a branch with bristles tied on as anything else, Ruby said, "Alas, while I am proud to have a broom at all, this one is quite slow, and you beat me here."

"So that stuff you gave me is medicine?" I asked.

With her usual detached, formal expression and tone, Ruby informed me, "A mana stabilizer. It will ease magical flow, while preventing you from using too much again. I have other medicines to apply as necessary, but I doubt we have time for a proper examination."

I shook my head. "No, we don't. Yuki is still here somewhere!"

Emanuel pointed at the column. "Well, we know they let her in, and tried to get her to take the elevator."

I pointed down, at the presence whose direction I constantly knew. "Yuki wants to go to the portal, and the god."

Looking over and past the rest of us like the human lighthouse he was, Joe stared at the distant robed and masked figures, saying, "I don't think these ice foxes want people going down there. If the barrier is trapped, and I'm sure it is, there are probably many more traps down there."

Elvira shrugged. "So we turn them off at the soul forge. You know how to do that, Artifact?"

I shrugged back. "It won't be hard to figure out. The problem is, we'd have to get past the traps to it."

I still had my satchel and a lot of detection equipment with me. Pulling out my signature detector, I slapped my ID pendant into it and took a look. The point on the wheel in the direction of the five-tailed fox flickered a little amid the whirling rainbow, suggesting she was much more powerful than I wanted to deal with. The blue signal was still there, nice and clear. It also zigged around the circle crazily, only settling down when I held the detector still.

Hmmm. I wobbled the disc a little. The blue dot slid from side to side a little. I tilted the detector down. The blue light swung to the back. I tilted it up instead. The blue light swung to the front. Either way, it was pointing...

I extended my finger towards the ceiling. "Up."

Getting scowly and businesslike again, Elvira said, "Top of the tower is as good as the bottom of the catacombs, for a dungeon."

"Either Yuki is up there, or we need to go there to get to her downstairs. How do we get up?" I asked, feeling a little helpless and desperate again.

"Stairs are over there," Lisa said, pointing at the door five-tails had indicated.

I blinked. "Of course. The masks want you to go up. That's... going to be a long climb." I shuddered just in anticipation.

"Yuki's no athlete either. We might catch up with her," suggested Elvira.

So we all shuffled across the long, open floor of the big, big room to the mostly regular door. It was surfaced in shell stuff and had a funny handle, like a bar stretched all the way across the front, but those were minor details. It was a door.

Joe stepped ahead, raising his hand. "Does anyone see a stick around that isn't a hard to replace, highly valuable flying broom?"

Fishing around in my satchel, I dug out the geodifferential stake. It was mostly wood, with line of metal going down about two thirds of the way to the point, and a hook at the top. It wasn't any use here, and I could make a new one. I held it out.

That door handle was pretty funny. Joe used the hook on the stake to pull on the bar, and it slid up like a lever until it clicked and the door opened. Not magically, just in response to Joe's pull, like any ordinary door.

"Good sign. They're not as paranoid about people going up as down," he said.

Elvira smirked, then grinned, her sour adventuress expression shattering. "'They' being the imaginary people the earthmover pretended built this place. I love dungeons. Eeeee, Emanuel, we're the first people into a new, living dungeon! Of a type nobody's seen before! Race you to the top!"

She bolted in, and up the stairs that I saw inside. Emanuel chased immediately after her, shouting, "That might not be wise!"

Joe laughed, watching them sprint up stairs that by leaning in I saw circled around the outer wall of the tower. The inside of the outer wall, walled off from both sides. I didn't see anything obviously glowing, but it was a pale, bland corridor featureless except for the pale, bland stairs.

He did shout up, voice echoing crazily, "Don't touch any doors, okay?"

I looked up those long, long, long stairs, and groaned in anticipation. "I don't think there are going to be any for a while." There was no room for them until we got past the ceiling of the entrance chamber, and that ceiling was hiiiiiigh.

Lisa slipped her arms around me, and with a minor grunt of effort picked me up off the floor like a baby. I protested, "I didn't say I can't!"

Ruby frowned with official medical disapproval. "No, she is correct. You have been straining yourself far too much as it is."

I pointed at my doll, who twitched from one position to another a lot as she looked around at everything with the blank default smile Bonabelle had molded in her mannequin. I protested, "Then Bonnet can carry me. You'd be okay with that, Bonnet?"

With perky and increasingly passionate good cheer, the doll said, "I'd be okay with unscrewing my own head if you tell me to. Someone will transfer me to a new doll eventually. Laughing at those meat muscled losers while I pass them by holding you sounds like five and a half hoots. Let's do it!"

A very large hand on a furry grey arm scooped me out of Lisa's arms, and Joe draped me over his shoulder. I hung there, with Lisa holding my satchel. Mild and amused, the big wolf said, "Or we could use the muscles of someone Artifact isn't spending her strength powering. In fact…"

Reaching out with his other arm, Joe scooped bonnet up

around her waist. He held her tucked against his own waist like that, tall enough that even if she dangled them, her hands and feet couldn't reach the floor.

Lisa gave me a viciously sharp grin. "Your friends respect you. No one promised dignity."

I sighed, and slumped over the big, muscular shoulder that promised discomfort but not burning leg pain or wheezing exhaustion on the stairs.

Joe wasn't just big. He was stupidly, ridiculously strong, because he climbed the stairs without showing any particular strain, carrying me, Bonnet, and his food sack. Bonnet folded her arms sullenly at first, then extended them and waved them and her feet, pretending she was swimming.

I guessed we had time for questions. I asked, "What was that thing you threw at the monsters, Ruby?"

Ruby could even climb stairs stiffly, but living at the top of a tower as she did, she showed no sign of strain either. She answered, "A magic sponge. I understand monsters are pure magic. I thought it might impair them."

I nodded. "Good thinking. I can think of all kinds of ways that might interfere. I'm happy to have you here, Ruby."

A thin, pink arm with a paw on the end extended from under Ruby's hat and whapped her several times on her face.

Possibly the only person in the world who could look dignified with that happening, Ruby said, "No, not now, Sophie. Thank you, Miss Forge. I would like to be as helpful to you as you have been to me."

"You know, I can climb stairs," I told the group, just in case anyone would listen.

Nope. Joe just said, "Your energy may save our lives. Mine won't."

We got far enough around the circle for me to see Elvira and Emanuel ahead. Emanuel had his hands on his knees, panting heavily. Elvira bent over him, her hands on her hips.

Bonnet pointed, shouting, "Ha! Losers! Loooooooseeeeers!"

Looking away from this spectacle to the merely amused face of my cousin, I told Lisa, "I had absolutely no idea a doll control program could grow a personality that transfers between incarnations. I'm starting to think Dad has been waiting thirteen years to laugh about this."

"I'd like to meet him," she said with a crooked, hopeful smile.

I nodded repeatedly. "That would be great! He's going to be so excited to find out Uncle Leonard had a daughter. I know losing my uncle is going to hurt, but knowing you exist, and especially when he gets to meet you, will really help."

Lisa stared up at me, so fiercely intent that it felt like an accusation.

Thinking a little more, I admitted, "Expect him to push really hard to make sure you're educated, though."

She made a disgusted, tongue-extended, unevenly slumped face. "Ugh, of course."

We made it a couple of steps below Elvira and Emanuel when Emanuel stood suddenly upright, and the two laughed, leaping back into a sprint and running way up the stairs ahead.

Bonnet waved her fists and feet uselessly. "Noooooo! Creator, order me to break free and go chase them down and kick their butts."

I shook my head, amused but definite. "No, but… in general, try to protect me and Lisa here, okay? Actually, all of the people in this group you have permission to protect from threats, but Lisa—"

"—and you—" Lisa reminded.

"—right, and me, I guess, are a particularly high priority. While we're in this dungeon fighting monsters, I mostly expect you to be keeping them off of Elvira so she can cast spells, but… just keep an eye out for my cousin, okay?" I finished.

The waving fists and feet turned into gleeful little fist pumps and miniature kicks as the doll squealed, "Potential contradictions and philosophical value judgments I am not mentally equipped to make! Yesssss, I love this incarnation! Cute body, too."

"I agree," drawled Joe, with a huge and shameless grin.

I spread my hands helplessly to Lisa. I liked Bonnet, but… well, I had no idea the control formula in my father's papers would result in this. Or even could.

Lisa's face fell suddenly, and she spent a few seconds in pensive silence before asking, "Can we still have the party?"

Because I had to be honest about my own predilections, I said, "I might need a day or two to recover."

Lisa snorted. "I might tie you to the bed for a day or two."

Ruby immediately interjected, "I'll be happy to help. With medical attention, of course. I'm sure Miss Forge needs no restraining. Medicine is not my specialty, but overuse of magic is a topic I know."

I nodded, enjoying a chance to actually talk to the erratic, mysterious teenage witch. "I bet you've done it to yourself a lot, huh? I didn't think I was that hard a worker, but maybe you and I are a lot alike."

Lisa swept her hair back, snarling in a strange mix of anger and relief. "YES. You're a lollipop and she's a popsicle, but you both won't bend an inch until you're eaten!"

Trying not to let my cousin interrupt this rare change, I asked, "If we do have a party, maybe you'd like to help decorate, Ruby? I suspect Lisa and I can use all the advice we can get."

"I'm afraid I have little experience with parties," the witch answered stiffly.

Lisa smirked. "That makes three of us."

I tried, "I don't know anything about party food either. What do you like to eat?"

"I fear we have hard business ahead of us and this conversation must wait," Ruby said, quiet and stony.

Inside her hat, Sophie let out a loud meow.

Pulling my hair back, I said, "You're right. It's just I'm hanging around."

Lisa giggled compulsively.

Which got my attention, and I told her, "But do remind me to find out what your favorite candies are."

"Oh, I will remind you," she promised, glowing eyes intense and open-mouthed grin hungry.

Emanuel and Elvira appeared around the bend above again. This time they weren't pretending to be tired. They stood on a landing instead, a short flat space before the stairs continued climbing. In front of them stood another door, with the same long bar handle as downstairs.

Excited, Elvira chattered, "Made it? We're above that big room downstairs! It looks like there are regular building floors on the upper part of the tower!" Pointing at the door, she continued, "Our best odds are this bottom floor, then something not at the top, but just below. I say we try this to see what we're in for anyway."

Chapter
Forty-Nine

She reached for the handle, but Joe was now close enough to nudge her gently aside with his shoulder. He put me and Bonnet back down at our feet, pulled the stake out of his belt, and tried the door. It pushed instead of pulled on this side, and opened easily and safely.

Echoey interdimensional fox language came out of nowhere. A monster formed. This one was squat, heavy, and covered in armor plates. Still shiny blue and green with an oval like a mask on the front of its wide bucket head.

Elvira cast Magic Missile. It only rocked the monster back a little.

"MY TURN!" bellowed Bonnet. She charged into the hallway on the other side of the door. Jumping up, she grabbed the thing's head in both hands. As she did, lightning shot out of a lump in the ceiling, flashing uncomfortably bright as it played over Bonnet's body. To my surprise, the strain to me from that felt like hardly more than a tingle.

Bending backwards, she kicked at the armored figure's

stomach, sending it pitching forward so she could slam its head into the blue-carpeted floor. She added a final twist to its flat-topped head, and the monster dissipated.

Emanuel was also casting. Slower than his sister, his Magic Missile fired now, and smacked into the blob on the ceiling, knocking it loose.

A few bits of metal covered in spell script fell and bounced off of Bonnet. The voice and the lightning both stopped.

The hallway stood silent. Another monster didn't seem to be forming.

Elvira's mouth tightened on one side. Fist on her hip, she commented, "You know, I really wish we'd brought Lucky. I never imagined wanting to talk to what I found in a dungeon."

"If we can find Yuki, she'll do that for us," I promised.

This whole hallway looked weirdly peaceful. The carpet, except for black charred sections where the lightning had hit, was thick and pretty and comfortable to stand on. The walls were metal, or at least metal-surfaced, but otherwise dull. White doors that could be made of anything were spaced regularly along those walls, with handles that were regular turnable latches. A couple of side halls branched off, one closer on the left and another farther on the right.

"Let me check a few rooms," Joe warned, stepping into the hall.

He did, pulling the handles with his stick. They weren't locked, and opened readily. He peeked inside.

After the second one, he asked us over his shoulder, "Dungeons mimic real buildings with real purposes, don't they?"

"Usually. In a distorted, dungeony way. Why?" Elvira replied.

Joe pushed the door further open. "Take a look. This looks like pictures I've seen of golden age buildings. These are all offices."

We filed over and looked. It was an odd little room. Certainly an office, with a weird, curvy chair with a hole in back that stood on a single fused leg that branched out into spider legs. The desk was completely covered in grey fabric, and blank papers covered in symbols that could be the same language as the one on the grating's plate were stuck to the fabric with pins. A sideways glass oval on a stand dominated the desk. It wasn't clear or opaque. It was lit up, showing an image of a masked fox person thumping its fist against a huge, bulbous... object. All in black, white, and grey, that was all I could understand of the moving image.

The office even had shelves, but they were bizarre, rickety things made of metal spiderweb, and one of the books had fallen off to reveal blank pages.

As we took it all in, Elvira said, "Almost. Interdimensional ice fox version of the golden age. A lot of the magic here works, and that old human magic doesn't anymore. We have to defang this place and bring Parsley in to document. We have to!" She ended in breathy, frustrated urgency, clenching her fists.

Joe turned his attention away from the room to the hallway, instructing, "Look out for those things in the ceiling, or if you see a room that looks weird and different—"

"Like if it has a soul cage in it," interrupted Elvira, with a smirk that could have been sarcastic or hungry, I couldn't tell which.

Joe resumed, "—but otherwise I don't think we need to worry about traps on this floor. Putting traps in your offices would be crazy. Security systems watching the halls, that's it."

Elvira waved fingers upwards, and promised, "Emanuel and I will go knock out any security things on the ceiling we can find. That means the rest of the rooms are safe to peek in."

Feeling like somebody should keep things on track to saving Yuki, I said, "But a soul forge would be in a special, obvious place, right? As soon as we know it's not here, we go back to the stairs."

I was talking to largely empty air, since everyone except Bonnet and Ruby had scattered, driven by curiosity. Who could blame them? This place was a chance to see simultaneously another world and a lost world of legend. I was very glad we'd be back after our responsibilities were done.

For the moment I just wanted to know if the soul forge was on this floor or not.

Bangs and clanks. I looked down a side corridor to see Emanuel standing over a little pile of magical devices that had been blasted off the ceiling. Both hallways looked pretty much the same, although at the end of Emanuel's I saw the curved door and yellow painted humans-stay-out square of the elevator.

More bangs from a hallway I couldn't see, and Elvira called out, "Looks like one trap in every hallway."

"On it!" shouted her brother, running around a corner.

More bangs and clunks.

Suddenly, Joe yelled, "Monsters!"

Of course. The dungeon master had realized that spawning them in front of us didn't work. They needed groups. They'd been building that group in a back corner.

I yelled at the top of my lungs, "Back to the stairs! The forge isn't on this level anyway! We'll search top down!"

They all came running. Lisa first, since she'd only been a few doors down sticking her head into an office. Joe next, then Emanuel, then Elvira. Everyone looked unharmed. As soon as Elvira bolted out of a side hall into ours, I started walking very fast backwards towards the stairwell door, watching with trembling nervousness for new and nastier monsters to come flooding in. Bonnet, knowing what I wanted now, retreated last, keeping her hard-to-destruct body between my friends and incoming danger.

The danger did not income fast enough, someone pushed the door open, and we tumbled out onto the blank, dimly but sufficiently lit, unthreatening stairs.

We didn't stop there, and with no further words hustled up the stairway until we were closer to the next door than the last one.

All hard again, Elvira glanced at Bonnet and Emanuel and said, "If they come out, we knock them down and let them fall."

"While we go up," I reminded her, then added, "One second."

I needed to take a few deep breaths. Excitement and running in panic weren't my skill set.

Ruby grabbed my chin in a strong, sure, exact hand, pulling me up straight so she could stare with searching eyes down at my face. Her stare snapped up to Joe, and Ruby ordered, "Feed her."

Joe opened up his fat shoulder bag and pulled out a burrito wrapped in thin cloth. It smelled heavenly, mouth-watering, of freshly cooked beef and beans and sharp cheese. Had I even bought cheese? I must have. Joe lifted me up to sit on his forearm, and as embarrassing as that was, I sat and ate.

Elvira had been throwing spells left and right, and she wasn't nearly this tired. Who was the prodigy here? Sheesh.

At least Joe threw a burrito to her next, and she bit into it ravenously.

Sitting on Joe's forearm was ridiculous. Okay, I fit, but just barely, and it put my head above his. I wasn't that tiny.

I took one bite, chewed for a little, then squeezed my eyes shut and thumped my head back against Joe's shoulder. Swallowing hard, I exclaimed, "I am such an idiot!"

Everyone stopped and stared at me. Elvira and Emanuel chorused, "What?"

"I'm carrying around a soul forge detector and we haven't been using it!" I wailed. Shame crawled over me. I'd literally been using it just a few minutes ago to tell we should go up the stairs at all.

I dug the signature detector back out of my satchel, stuck my ID pendant into it, and handed the whole thing to Emanuel. He held it vertically, and with a smile far too admiring given I should have thought of this when we walked in the building reported, "She's right. The blue dot is above us."

So we wouldn't have to search floor by floor by the top. Our party climbed the stairs, everyone but me alert. Nothing happened except that I gobbled down a burrito. The monsters from downstairs didn't follow.

"Does it seem like the monsters here are allergic to doorways?" I asked everyone and no one.

Elvira smirked. It was a hard smirk, but still a smirk. "Fine by me."

"This is it," Emanuel said.

We were at a stairwell with a door, identical to all the others. I held out my hand, and Emanuel passed me back my pendant so I could hang it around my neck again. Joe took position at the door, tilting me away from it as he used his other hand to hook the handle with the stick I'd given him, and tug.

This one barely moved. It was locked.

Bonnet smacked her fist into her palm, her favorite form of punctuation, and declared hungrily, "I'll get rid of it."

Emanuel brushed that off immediately. "Easier if I do it."

Easier because it would save me a tiny bit of magic, of course. I scowled, and complained to the ceiling, "Why is everyone treating me like an invalid today?"

Lisa glared at me, and pink glowing eyes can really glare. Fists on her hips, her words dripping both sarcasm and outrage, she answered, "Because you think you can do anything and keep pushing yourself until you literally collapse."

I tried to scowl back and be crabby and disapproving, but… a tightness lurked around her eyes. She let her concern and pleading peek through.

Unable to fight with that, I sighed in exasperated defeat. "Okay, but I can stand. I just needed that snack for some energy."

Elvira extended her arms above her head, one hand gripping the other elbow, stretching out her whole body. Amidst a groan, she said, "Boy, me too. It really helped. Ready, Emanuel?"

He nodded, all serious, a finger already pointed at the door where the lock should be. "Ready."

Joe stepped off the stairwell and up onto the stairs, warning us quietly, "What's on the other side will be heavily defended."

Elvira listened to that, gave him a grim nod, and also got out of the way before telling Emanuel, "Hit it."

ChapterFifty

Emanuel cast Magic Missile, and I was learning to recognize the spell by the sound. When it went off with its four loud smacks, the door lock broke and the door itself slammed open.

A blob of white stuff shot out. Thank goodness none of us were standing in front of the door. The blob hit the wall, scattering ice crystals in a six-pointed star around it. The crystals were all so cold I could feel it several feet away.

Peeking the barest bit around the edge I saw another snail thing near the back of a short, narrow hallway. I wasn't sure if it was the same type snail as the one that made walls. I ducked back just before it spat out another couple of blasts.

The food really had helped, and anyway, nobody flesh and blood should walk into that doorway. Snapping my fingers, I said, "This is my turn," and looked right at Bonnet. "Clear it out."

"HA!" she barked in glee, and charged into the hallway, dove under the ice ball, was hit by lightning from a ceiling turret, kicked hard enough to dig a divot out of the snail and disintegrate it, got hit by another lightning turret, stood up, reached out past counters I hadn't even noticed on either side of the hall, yanked out a couple of foxes, slammed them mask-first together, and threw them back into their cubbies. At that point, Elvira and Emanuel destroyed the turrets.

The lightning blasts hadn't hurt much this time, either, but I still wouldn't want to be a flesh and blood human hit by one, thanks.

Stuffing a few escaped locks of hair back into her jacket, Elvira flashed a sparkly, evil grin. "Joe, I like your paranoia even more than your cooking."

He brushed both hands back over his ears as if he had head hair—although he did have a short, spiky mane—and puffed out his chest in pride. "This is nothing. You should see me when I don't have other people who can do my fighting for me—and win."

Bonnet trotted back to us, dusting off her hands and radiating satisfaction despite not having much expression. "Hey, I left those," and she said a weird word that sounded like fox language, "alive, just knocked out. That's what you wanted, right? You give the vaguest orders. It's fun getting to use my own discretion, but don't blame me if I get it wrong!"

I took one of her hands in both of mine, squeezing the very slightly bendable surface, made of stuff that felt somewhere between fine ceramic and rubber. "You're doing great. I... look, this is the dumbest time and place, but it's the time and place we are. I told you I didn't make you with a long lifespan. It didn't occur to me you'd be so alive. I'm sorry. I'm really, really sorry."

She lolled her head back and to the side, the corners of her muzzle turning up and at least giving the impression of a big smile. "Naah, no big deal. Self-preservation is for losers and meat bags! Someone will incarnate me again, I'll remember a lot of this, and I've had some creators who got really existential about this but that's not my bag. I just wish you'd let me break stuff. You made me stupid crazy ridiculous total excess strong, and all you want is for me to give a few monsters love taps!"

I gestured at the charred, battered room she'd just left. "Well, you can go first down this hall. Whoever pretend-made this place did not want anyone getting to the soul forge."

Joe gave me an approving nod.

"Sure!" the doll squeaked. She strutted back down the metal hall to the door at the other end, one of those otherwise normal cross bar doors. Nothing attacked her.

"Open it," I ordered.

She pushed on the bar, and the door opened neatly. I saw blue light inside, what looked like a spiderweb of magical instrumentation, and a figure with long, black hair bent over a floating ball.

"Yuki!" I yelled, darting forward.

I got one step into the hall, red stripes lit up the floor on either end, and the siren wailed. A metal plate slammed down, covering the door to the soul forge room.

Emanuel turned a wry grimace up to Joe. "You were right. They were determined not to let any humans in, weren't they?"

Me, I gave my wry grimace to my worried and protective demon cousin. "Sorry, Lisa. Bonnet, you asked, you get your wish. Break it down."

"I'll try to be gentle," she promised.

That this might be Bonnet's idea of "gentle" was scary. The grey metal door blocker looked like steel, and not thin steel, either. Bonnet punched it, then punched it again, and again, and I immediately felt my heart race up and I started breathing hard. I didn't know what required more magic, powering those blows or keeping them from crumpling Bonnet's fists on impact. Deep, knuckle-print dents showed in the metal. The whole thing warped. On the fifth punch something snapped. The seal flew inward, breaking the door behind it off its hinges and sending them both skidding into the other room to the foot of the dais inside.

Me, I saw the long-haired figure bent over what was definitely a soul forge inside, and stopped caring about safety. I leaped forward, arms extended, yelling, "Yuki!"

I was well into the room when Joe caught up and shouldered me aside, then Ruby sprang up and grabbed his arm.

The young witch shrieked, "Don't touch her! No one touch her until Artifact says so! Look at her. It's possessed her somehow."

I stopped, and now that I wasn't focused solely on Yuki, I took in the room around me.

Here, near the top of the tower, this one circular room was made of the same shell-like material that coated the tower's exterior. It all had that same curving, psuedo-alive look that seashells did, flowing up in a curve from the floor and down from the ceiling, with flattened spaces covered in magical diagrams, all of which looked activatable. No two consoles were the same size or angle, and metal cables, mostly copper, ran like vines embedded in the floor from the central pedestal to the various spells. A lot of stuff glowed pale blue, a lot didn't.

The most dominant feature of the room I'd missed only because it was behind me, facing the soul forge. Like the crystal plates in the office, oval or rounded-off rectangular sheets hung on the upper half of the walls, arranged in a semi-circle. Each showed a black, white, and grey image of some part of the tower, inside or outside.

Meanwhile, the forge itself stood in the center of the room, the focus of everything around it. A low, organically uneven circular dais held the knee-high pillar at the center, and above that floated a soul cage that looked like it was made of an ominous, charcoal-grey version of the shell stuff. Spherical, too. There was no reason they couldn't be round, but other soul forges, even wild ones, were always cubes. This had only two layers, cobwebs of shell connecting irregular plates engraved with magical symbols. Spikes studded the inner shell, pointing at the soul gem suspended at the core.

The soul gem. I gawked. My mind went blank for a second, then filled with the frustration and regret that none of my friends would understand why this amazed me so much. Powering this odd, spherical cage floated a complete soul gem. Not a soul fragment, like my forge, like practically all forges. Not a glowing, yellow-green, jagged shard of crystal. This was beautifully light blue, a flattish rectangle maybe the size of my hand with my fingers extended and pressed together. The edges were all rounded by a glittering array of precise facets, and it resembled nothing so much as a sapphire from a piece of jewelry. It also barely glowed.

These were so rare, I couldn't describe it to a non-bioengineer. The Dollmaker probably had a soul forge with a recovered soul gem. Nobody else I'd ever heard of did.

Since the soul forge and its gem were no more than a tool to the others, they all looked around the room full of other curiosities, until Emanuel and Elvira got our attention by pointing to one of the picture screens simultaneously.

Emanuel was the one who said, "I bet that's the top floor. Look at it."

I did. In a domed room whose walls were lined with shell-stuff, whose rounded ceiling had a few triangular windows here and there, lurked a crowd of monsters. They came in way more variety than we'd seen so far, and the floating mask, this one with seven eyes rather than faceless, looked particularly threatening.

Softly, Elvira said, "She heard us say we would go top down, and set a trap."

Joe was still looking at Yuki. She stood there, hunched over the forge with both hands on it, her shockingly long, limp black hair draped over the sphere's sides and almost hiding her face. The dark glasses hid the rest. She didn't move, just stood there, with only barely perceptible breathing revealing she was alive.

Brows pressed together in worry, Joe asked, "If she's the dungeon master, why isn't she responding to us now? Yuki? Yuki, can you hear me?"

I looked up at the picture screens. I saw the little security corridor. I saw the outside plazas. I saw lots of internal hallways. I saw something underwater I couldn't identify. I saw a big room we hadn't seen, with lots of cables attached to a flat-topped metal arch like the ones outside. The interior of this arch shone pure white, and the room around it contained stuff that made so little sense my eyes couldn't work out the shapes.

The portal room.

But just this second, the portal room wasn't important. I gave my professional judgment, and I gave it in a grave hush. "It's a proto-lich link. She's been taken over by the soul forge, or rather, by this room. It's one enormous spell that runs the dungeon. She can only see what the room sees. Does this happen?"

I only knew it was possible. Elvira, who knew dungeons, reported, "I've heard of it, but it's not normal. Parsley is going to have a fit that she didn't get to see this. I hope we don't have to destroy it to save Yuki, which we had better do now."

"Agreed," said her brother.

The rest of us nodded.

Finding Yuki intact and merely frozen had taken the edge of panic off my concern, but she needed saving even if every second no longer counted.

And as the bioengineer, this was my job.

"Alright. Get ready to grab her. Don't let her touch it again," I instructed my friends, stepping up to the soul forge, my eyes on its webbing and its gaps.

"Is this another—" Lisa started to ask.

I didn't let her finish, because I knew she would try to stop me. I plunged my arm through the spaces in the outer and inner cage, wrapped my gloved fist around the soul gem, and yanked it entirely out of the forge.

Lights all over the room winked out. The screens slowly faded. Yuki shook her head, like someone who'd zoned out for a moment, and Joe grabbed her shoulders and pulled her out of arm's reach of the empty soul cages.

Lisa screeched, arms in shimmering blue sleeves extended as she leaped towards me.

Extending my left arm to ward her off, I stammered, "Wait wait it's fine!"

Lisa grabbed the lapels of my lab coat, trembling, her face twisted in shock and horror and voice hoarse as she demanded, "No it's not! Soul fragments explode when you do that! Why aren't you dead?"

She'd been paying attention. It was more than a little gratifying, and I felt a little joy at lecturing mix with my urgency to comfort my cousin. "Fragments don't technically explode, they ground themselves through the holder and— that's not important. This isn't a soul fragment. It's a soul gem. It's complete. I think… it had to be all the horseshoe crab blood the chimera ate, and then the earthmover ate. It's even the same color. I don't know. Nobody knows how earthmovers make any soul forge, and soul gems are incredibly rare."

"You're babbling, Artifact. It's doing something to you," Lisa insisted, glaring into my eyes, or maybe watching them, analyzing them.

"Wait, one second," I said, as non-confrontationally as possible.

Leaning down, I slid my right arm back into the cages, which now sat in a rounded basin on the pedestal, victims of gravity like the rest of us. When my hand reached the center, I let go of the soul gem and carefully pulled my arm back.

The gem floated. The spheres floated up and back into place. Lights flickered back on. The screens, which hadn't quite gone completely dark yet, surged back to life. Literal life, since they must be reporting what a specialized monster somewhere saw.

None of the images now showed any monsters. All but the ones operating the screens had turned back into vapor without the soul forge's power.

Confused, very confused, but alert, Yuki asked, "What's going on?"

Elvira squealed in joy. She and Emanuel flung themselves on Yuki from either side, cocooning the already sweater-enveloped girl in a hug. I wished I knew Yuki that well, because it was such a relief to see her unharmed and back with us.

Joe contented himself with kissing the top of Yuki's head.

Elvira shivered, and commented, "You're colder than usual. A lot colder," but didn't let go.

Yuki frowned, looking at a blank-ish space of wall rather than at anyone, but even with her magically resonant, echoey voice she didn't sound vague, just like someone sorting through confusing facts. "You Young and Old were so friendly. I remember that. And the monsters thought I was one of the Young and Old, and ignored me. They said they'd accidentally activated some security when they opened the front doors to look at our world, and the gate closed, so now they couldn't get back and no other explorers could get in. They weren't allowed to reopen the gate, but I could. The symbols in here, they all make so much sense, but I touched it and… I don't know. I remember a voice, but not what it was saying. Which is weird, because I remember it so well, it's like I can almost hear it now, like when you wake up from a dream."

"How did you even get up here?" Elvira asked. Yuki wasn't much more physically fit than me, if at all. Bioengineering did involve lifting a lot of heavy things.

Joe, smile tight and amused, suggested to Elvira, "Look behind her."

Because the tower wasn't perfectly straight, and the elevator tube was embedded in the back wall of this chamber. It blended into the rainbow-touched, pink-and-white-shell surfacing of the rest of the weird room, but the yellow security stripe on the floor and the protruding, rectangular gate shape around the door frame were obvious enough if you knew to look.

One fist on her hip and the other still holding my lapel, her voice thick with angry sarcasm, Lisa declared, "This is great and Yuki is great and all, but my cousin just did something even stupider than usual and I need to know why she's still alive before I kill her."

Both hands available now, I held them up between us and swore, "I was safe! Complete soul gems are special. Look, none of you know or care about the technical stuff anyway, okay? But it's a lot more stable than a soul fragment, especially a big, soul forge level fragment."

Watching me with his head tilted a little and eyes thoughtful, Joe said, "It sounds powerful."

I waggled my hands vaguely. "I guess? Maybe slightly more than my forge. Not enough to care about. The differences are stability and technical. You can do things with a gem that you can't with a fragment because it won't overload. Not that you can't cause one to devolve or short out, but it can survive outside the cage, which means—"

Lisa lunged forward, throwing her arms around my head, and squeezed me to her tight. "Please don't do that again," she begged, very quiet, into my hair.

Her hands clasped around her diagonally held broom, Ruby said solemnly, "I trust your expertise, but a warning would be appreciated. I know what a mere fragment would have done if you took it out, and was quite alarmed."

Looking around at my friends, she added, "And please, no one but Miss Forge touch the gem, or the forge. I am sure there are things we do not know. Many things."

Patting my cousin's shoulder, I told the witch, "Well… yeah. You know I'm safe, so can we get back to Yuki? I'm glad we saved you, too!"

Clasping her hands in front of her belly, Yuki turned her face from side to side, looking at all of us and bouncing a little as she enthused, "I'm sorry to scare you, but he's down there. Can't you feel him? Can't you hear him? Almost, I mean?"

Lisa tilted her head sharply, squinting, and now she looked a touch confused. "Uh… yeah, I think so. It's really annoying, like a bug buzzing at your ear. Is that why I've been so crabby since we got here?"

"No, you've been worried about Artifact, and with good reason," Joe corrected, beaming affection at us.

This conversation was so chaotic, with so many people talking, I was starting to have trouble following it. I cut it down to the important thing, and said, "Okay, team. We have Yuki. The monsters have all been dismissed, and those masked mages—"

"The Young and Old," Yuki supplied.

I gave her a nod of acknowledgment and continue, "They can't use the soul forge. Wait, it's probably got an automatic setting. Yes, there it goes, look."

To an expert eye, the construction of this wild soul cage was interesting. It was designed to make specific monsters. Connections snaked between aspects and containment patterns, so you could make one of its monster designs with a touch of your hand. It also worked in reverse. The curious prongs—yes, there it went. Blue light arced to one of those prongs, flowed up through a tightly packed design on the inner cage, and then up to specific points on the outer cage. On a screen overlooking the outside, a spear-carrying snake-fish materialized, and slithered to its guard post.

"I can fix that. Hold on," I said.

The easiest way to do that would be to take out the gem, have Bonnet break those inner prongs, and put the gem back.

What side effects would that have, though? Anyway, I'd hate to damage something that so much bioengineering could be learned from. For example, what told the soul cage that a monster needed replacing?

I looked down at the pedestal underneath the floating orb, and found my answer. Wow. What an incredibly complex spell diagram. I saw tiny monster symbols. Was this a layout of where every monster was supposed to be?

Well, sorry, future explorers, but I didn't need that.

Pointing at the diagram, I told Bonnet, "Erase that, would you? Try not to damage anything else."

She dug her fingertips into the pedestal, and clawed deep furrows around the monster map. When it was thoroughly ruined, I said, "That's enough," and returned to the forge.

Let's see. A few negation symbols despawned the existing monsters. I still couldn't see why it had taken over Yuki. She hadn't tried to lich herself. There was nothing visible in its spells to control its user. It was a weird forge, but it still worked by regular bioengineering.

"Remember the traps," Joe murmured over my head. I was briefly aware of his towering presence behind me before my focus shifted to that puzzle.

"Right. Yuki, you said you can read this? Help me find them. I've never done this, but… they'll probably be some of the glowing symbols?" I scanned those, working out roughly what each one meant.

Her wonderful language talent could do that even faster than me. She pointed. "Yes. Those, and those, and… none of the others look like traps."

Hmmm. Yes, those aspect-heavy glowing formulas with rings of cables around them did look like they were powering destruction spells. Oh, and that third thing was the front door, right? I swiped my hand over it, and saw the front door on the image screen close. Another swipe reopened it.

Still looking at all those consoles, I asked Yuki, "You said something about an emergency lockdown, right? Oh, wait, maybe there's an easy way."

I put my foot on the yellow strip by the elevator. It hooted and turned red. I took my foot off. It went back to yellow. One of the tangled wires running through the floor had lit up as I did. I followed it to... yes, this looked like a whole set of remote controls all bound together in a group. I swiped them, all, turning them on and activating the siren in the process, then swiped again, turning them all off.

Pulling a little chisel out of my satchel, I carved a tiny lock symbol, and swiped that. It glowed, so hopefully that worked. Those emergency lockdown spells couldn't activate now.

I looked up from the console, and saw one thing changed. There was exactly one screen for that big, central room, and all it focused on was the elevator and the pit going underground. The grating covering that pit was gone.

The soul forge was neutralized, the traps deactivated, the doors open. We should take our win and go, but... "I already know Parsley would never forgive us if she couldn't get down to see the portal. There might be something I missed between us and it. First, let's see if I did what I think I did. Cross your fingers, all..."

I walked across the room and set my foot on the yellow stripe. It stayed yellow.

Throwing up my fists triumphantly, I squealed, "YES! I think we can use the elevator!"

Everyone groaned in relief. Emanuel muttered, "Oh, thank goodness."

I frowned, looking at the shell-decorated tube. "The door isn't opening, though, and I don't see a control."

Lisa, who the tower did like, stepped up onto the stripe next to me and knocked on the door. Nothing happened. She suggested, "Maybe you just shut it off?"

"*Where is Yuki!?*" shrieked Elvira.

Chapter Fifty-One

My head snapped up. On the image screen showing the pit, the elevator door opened. Yuki stepped out. Two of the fox things took her hands, and led her down the staircase.

The elevator door on the screen closed.

I pounded my fist on the door in front of me, the sound of flesh on shell a faint clonk. "Hurry up!" I yelled at it uselessly.

Turning around, I fell against the door, leaning my back on it, and grabbed my forehead. "I'm such an idiot. *Again.* She told us she was still hearing voices! No wonder the foxes are nice to her. They wanted us to open the basement so their god could lure her down there!"

I looked around at my friends. Joe, his smile gone, standing straight at his full height, furry grey face revealing nothing. Ruby staring at me, her frown as concerned as if I was the one in trouble. Elvira and Emanuel, hands clasped, rigid and horrified. Bonnet, sitting on the soul forge but with her hand over her face as if she was a mirror of my emotions.

Only Lisa looked suspicious as well as worried. Her scowl deep and puzzled, she asked, "They'd have been nice to you even without me, wouldn't they? If that's what they wanted?"

Right now, even a little uncertainty felt like an improvement. I nodded over and over, trying to calm my pounding heart, stop my panic, force back my guilt. "You're right. You're right." Swinging around, I pounded my fist into the elevator door several times, shouting, "Why is this thing taking so long!? It only took her seconds to get down there!"

"At least we have backup," said Elvira, throaty with hope.

I followed her gaze. On the image screen looking out past the front door of the building, four little figures had just climbed the stairs in a tight group. The tall scarecrow-looking one in front was probably the sheriff. The short, blockier one next to him had to be Franklin, the adventuress.

My own relief seized up as it started, covered in a new chill of dread. My voice haunted, I asked Elvira, "How are the foxes going to react to her?"

That gave Elvira pause. Thinking hard now, she answered, "If we get down there to greet them, I... think the foxes won't attack?"

I asked the next unwanted question. "How will she react to them?"

Horror crept back into her look of concentration. "I'm not sure, but... probably..."

"Monsters to be cleared out so the dungeon is safe?" I guessed. How else would someone who had spent decades cleaning out dungeons for loot and to protect people react?

Elvira nodded, mouth twisted in the pained grimace of wishing she could change the truth.

"How will she react to that?" I asked, quiet now, as I pointed at a different image screen.

In the portal room, five-tails pulled Yuki by her hand over to the huge, glowing white portal itself. I couldn't see the details, but it looked like Yuki reached inside the white glow and pulled out a masked fox. And another. And another.

Elvira stared for two seconds, then cringed and looked away. "Not well," she muttered.

The elevator (FINALLY) dinged and slid open. I pointed at it. "Go rescue Yuki. I'll hold them off."

Hurrying over to the globe floating in the center of the room,

I looked the cage around the soul gem over. Monster formulas and aspects I could use to upgrade them. Right. I bet those markings on the floor with cables leading to different screens were what Yuki used to place monsters.

"You really think you can hold off her," Elvira asked behind me, stunned and disbelieving.

"I do," I answered. Let's see, where was…

I found the upgrade symbol I was looking for, and drew a path back to the monster emblem with all the metal aspects. That would be the big, armored guard, I was positive. That would be the perfect beginning.

"Without killing her?" Elvira pressed.

More than half my thoughts on making the right connections and looking for the symbols I would use next, I said, "I can handle it. I'm not just any regular dungeon master."

Dry and amused, Emanuel said, "She's a prodigy."

"That's what I've heard," echoed Joe in the same tone.

"I trust her," Ruby said simply.

Sour, but maybe a touch relieved, Elvira said, "So do I."

I pointed behind me at the elevator. "So go rescue Yuki!"

They all piled inside, except Lisa and Bonnet.

Lisa, arms folded and face set in determination, pointed a finger at me and then at the floor. "Where you go, I stay."

Inside the elevator, Ruby's expression turned strained. I gave her a smile, and said, "Yuki is going to need medical help. I know I can rely on you for that. Bonnet, I bet they'll need your strength. You're within my range. Obey and protect my friends, okay? Elvira is in charge."

Bonnet, who had gotten out of my way so I could use the soul forge, threw herself backwards off her feet into the elevator, and was caught in the many arms of my friends. She started talking in midair, chattering, "Sounds good to me. I like smacking things. Can I break that big trilithon?"

Elvira touched something inside the elevator, next to the door. I looked into her eyes, and said, "Good luck."

"You too," she answered solemnly.

The door slid shut.

Back to work. I put my foot on the indicator for the plaza,

and when its wire lit up, swiped the guard symbol. To my satisfaction, the monster that looked like an overly wide suit of armor coalesced in front of the doors, finishing appearing in time for a crossbow bolt to bounce off its armor.

Controls. There were mood aspects. I should have made it aggressive. No matter, the attack got the monster's attention and it lumbered forward to fight.

I was sure Franklin had fought and triumphed over much worse, although I'd bet its upgraded armor was unbreakable by any force the adventuress had brought with her. Its job was to slow her down to give my real plan to work.

Yuki's idea of summoning groups of monsters too far away to be destroyed as they appeared was good, but she didn't have my experience with a soul forge. I started summoning the basic, unarmed fish things off to the side of the tower, and set them to aggressive. I swirled my fingers around the monster symbols, summoning them faster than Yuki would have known how to, but...

I yanked my gloves off and threw them aside. They were in the way of magical contact between my skin and the cage, slowing down my casting. I still had an ugly scab running up the side of my palm, with a little still-wet blood around the edges because I'd been irritating it, but the tiny pains of that wound were the last thing on my priority list today.

I needed to cast fast, because I needed a mob of these things. Why? Because their design was to pull things down that got too close. If they couldn't pass the gates on the stairs, they'd push visitors off the plaza but nothing else. Which was perfect.

I had half a dozen already, glanced up at the image screen, and saw the armored guard dueling with the old woman. Its clumsy attempts to hit her weren't connecting, but I hadn't wanted them to. The upgrade I'd given it had probably slowed it down, even. That was definitely the sheriff behind her, because he stood back holding his pistol in his hands. No sound came from these screens, but he must have fired, because her monster staggered back. The old woman cast a spell while the armored guard recoiled. A flash, and the guard staggered more, but didn't fall. Still perfect.

I went back to summoning pushing fish, lots of pushing fish, on the other side of the building. I needed lots. They weren't exactly tough, and Franklin would carve them apart three at a time, not to mention the ones she'd get with spells before they reached her.

So I summoned lots, on either side of the building. They stood there waiting. I'd figure out how to trigger then when the guard died and they were needed.

The numbers were starting to look good when I looked up at the screen again.

The guard was just lying there on its back on the plaza, like it was dead. Except if it was dead, it would have disappeared. What was going on?

Franklin was equally unsure. She hung back, watching it. That was good. More delays. The old woman was methodical, which is what I needed. All I wanted was to slow her down.

Without sound, at a distance, I couldn't make out what Franklin actually did, but when she ran forward towards the guard, it twitched and couldn't seem to get up. She jumped on it, stuck her knife between armor joints, and the armored monster disappeared.

It had done its job wonderfully. Especially that clever playing dead trick.

Sure the trick didn't work, but it was smart, and it delayed Franklin long enough for me to summon another dozen fish-snakes.

A smart trick. That meant the guard had been thinking. It hadn't been just an automatic spell playing it's formula, like the pushing fish things. It had a mind.

Which meant I'd made a thinking creature just to die.

Horror, revulsion, welled up in me. My eyes stung with tears. My heart knotted in my chest. I shuddered. What a disgusting thing I'd done.

Should I even send the mindless fish things? It probably wasn't morally wrong, but… I couldn't do it.

One more sacrifice. I could make one more mindless sacrifice, even if I felt like the real monster doing it. I had an idea.

The ice aspect was already part of most of these designs,

but I activated it again, and again, and again, and again, as fast as I could, layering it madly on top of itself. Half a dozen times would have to do. I transferred that to one of the snail things we'd seen at the start of this adventure, and spawned it in front of the door.

Not the spitting snail. The wall snail. I set it on aggressive as I materialized it, and true to its spell, it spat out a wall of ice right in front of itself the instant it became real.

A gigantic wall of ice. It exploded upwards, outwards, so tall and so broad that it blocked a lot of the screen's vision. I felt sorry for the snail buried in that, but this would delay Franklin for a long time. Even if she had good fire magic, the front doors were not opening with that blocking them, not any time soon.

Could the adventuress find another way in? Probably. But the goal of slowing her down was achieved.

Uncharacteristically gentle, Lisa tapped me on the shoulder, and murmured, "I think you need to look at this window."

My eyes followed her pointing arm to the screen showing the portal room. The angle was terrible. It was hard to make out anything for sure. The room contained maybe two dozen foxes now. Where were my friends?

In the row of shimmering magical cages.

Except for Yuki, who now appeared to be wrestling physically with the five-tailed fox.

"Lisa, get the elevator!" I shouted.

She took a couple of steps to the side, standing between me and it, her arms folded. Flatly, she said, "Unless you've learned some spells, I don't think we can do anything."

Shocked, I squealed, "This is an emergency!"

Her lips trembled. She stayed just as stiff, just as warding, but her voice trembled as she said, "Tell me what we can do. Tell me what we can do, and we'll go do it."

I… couldn't think of anything.

Yes, I had a lot of power, although I'd been using it pretty hard today. The spells I knew were the little domestic ones on my tablet, and I could activate and power magical devices remotely. Otherwise, I wasn't even all that fit. A little strong, but not very. No agility. No endurance.

Lisa was in great physical shape, but in the same boat magically, except she didn't have my useless raw power.

I was a bioengineer. I could spawn a bunch of monsters down there, and get two dozen ice mages destroying everything they could see, maybe killing my friends. My magic was slow, it took calculation rather than strength, and this soul forge could only do a few specific things.

One of those was powering the entire building. After all, magic had to come from somewhere.

I reached into the soul cage, grabbed the soul gem, and pulled it out.

With my right hand. That fact leaped to my mind as the traces of blood on my hand touched the crystals surface. A shock ran through me, turning my skin ice cold, yet damp with sweat.

Fear. The shock was only fear, because if I'd touched a regular forge's soul fragment with my blood I'd be... absorbed, a lich, melt... dead, one way or another.

Instead, I felt refreshed. All the magic I'd used today was full again, and I was wide awake and alert, as if I'd just hopped out of bed. No, as if I'd just bathed and breakfasted in the morning.

A soul gem was stable enough that its power didn't hit me, it was just available.

How much was Ruby's power limiting potion responsible for my being alive and human right now?

How much could I use this power without it infecting me and turning me into a lich?

A lich with—I shut down that thought. Sufficient unto the day.

Which might be right now, because the lights were going out everywhere in the room. The image screens were barely grey now. All the controls for the building had gone dark. The serpent things outside would have faded into nothing already. Poor things. Maybe they were less alive than ants, but I shouldn't have been so irresponsible with what little they had.

I snapped my fingers. The screens flared back to life. One showed the pit, grating still open. Outside windows showed the giant ice wall outside still intact, and it was huge, so big I couldn't see the humans on the other side.

The masked fish monsters were indeed gone.

The cages down in the portal room were also gone. The only light down there came from the portal itself, although lots of that. My finger snap hadn't extended to the basement. Nothing else looked like it had changed. Were my friends all on the ground, unconscious?

Something small moved by the portal, and smacked into the five-tailed fox. Sophie?

Something bigger moved. Bonnet. A burst of white, powerful ice magic hit her. I had to take a deep breath again, but the power of the soul gem refilled me instantly.

Anxiety trickled up my spine. My humanity was on the line every time I used this power, but it had saved my friends. The fox was down. Bonnet had it pinned. Yuki was free, and stepped up to the portal, reaching her hand out to touch the shining surface.

I remembered, too late, that it wasn't the foxes that whispered to Yuki and took over her mind.

The screen went blank, flickered white and dark grey for several seconds, then came back on. Nothing seemed to have changed. The masked foxes hadn't even moved.

In fact, they hadn't moved during the struggle. They all stood as still as statues.

Yuki pulled something out of the portal with both hands. It seemed to take effort, but after a second it came free. A little white blob. A mask. She turned around the room, lifted her glasses, and put the mask over her face. Then she rose slowly into the air.

"Lisa, the elevator!" I shrieked.

The elevator dinged. Lisa was standing on the yellow stripe already. The door opened. I hadn't thought to ask if my finger snap powered it, and now I had the answer, thank goodness.

I heard fox yipping, and spun around again, now to face the door to the stairs.

Two masked foxes, each with only one tail, stood in the doorway from the security corridor. Barely. One had the arm around the other, and they leaned against each other, with even the one holding up the other none too steady.

Bonnet had knocked out two foxes while going through the hall. They weren't monsters, so they didn't evaporate. They hadn't died. So, eventually, they'd woken up.

Together they held a strange device, each holding their side in one shaky hand. It was a weird thing, like a metal circle with a hexagonal plate of blue material in it. That plate had a big hole in its middle, and spell script around the edges.

A weapon. It had to be.

Lisa leaped in front of me, yelling, "Hey! She's my friend! That's what you need to be worried about!"

She pointed at the portal room screen. They looked. They immediately turned and ran down the stairs, or at least shuffled with desperate, clumsy urgency.

I grabbed Lisa in a tight hug and yanked her into the elevator. Symbols lined up along the side, and I swiped the one on the bottom.

ChapterFifty-Two

The door closed. The room went down. Boy, was that a weird sensation, like falling, but less so.

I adjusted the satchel on my shoulder with my left hand. In the sudden waiting, the thing I usually didn't even notice weighed down on me, heavy and uncomfortable. I couldn't possibly have left it behind. The weird plate and the breach detonator were both in there.

My right hand flexed my fingers around the soul gem, warm but not intrusive in my grip.

The waiting dragged, and yet it felt too soon, too sudden when the door opened.

The main hall was empty. The front doors remained closed. It was also utterly dark, with all the lights having run out of power.

Lisa pulled out her tablet, flicked it with her thumb, and it lit up. I didn't dare try that with mine, not while holding the soul gem, and I didn't dare put the gem down anywhere.

The grating was still open. The stairs still waited inside the pit, running down in a circle.

We descended a dark, strange passage. The walls were

metal again, with lots of tubes, some laid next to the wall, some bulging out. It didn't go down very far. When the tunnel ended the staircase continued, becoming a weird metal mesh that led down to a platform made of the same mesh over a huge room lit by the portal. Not as big as the main hall of the tower, but really big.

Still barely big enough to contain all the weird stuff in it. Cables and pipes, running out of bulgy devices of unknown purpose. Blocky devices of unknown purpose. Pillars, squared off but narrowing as they went up. A few hung from the ceiling, narrowing as they went down. Really, really weird devices, like the giant white arms ending in bowl shapes with prongs and rings sticking out, which loomed over my unconscious friends' bodies and pointed down at them.

More staircases and ramps of metal mesh, with chain link railings, split off this platform, winding down erratically to the floor, all carefully distant from the portal.

The portal. It was big. It was the shape of the gates over the stairs outside, one horizontal slab laid over two vertical slabs. Unlike those crude stone things, these were metal, precisely and evenly shaped, engraved with symbols I didn't recognize. At least, the parts I could see were. Barnacles, encrusted rock, and limply hanging seaweed concealed most of its surface. This thing had sat under the ocean for a long time.

A hexagonal divot showed right in the front and middle of the upper slab, with some of the encrusted stone broken off where it would have crossed over the middle of that hexagon. The place where the sealing mechanism plate goes. Would putting the plate back save Yuki? Would it lock whatever the thing was that had her on Earth with them?

Yuki still floated a couple of feet off the floor, and in front of her floated the fox Bonnet had tackled. Definitely that one, because its robe was ripped around the edges. In the little window in the control room, I'd been wrong about one thing. This wasn't the five-tailed fox. It had seven tails. I didn't want to think about how powerful a mage it must be.

Maybe stronger than Ramona.

I was not going to lose any more friends here.

The fox wasn't nearly powerful enough. It writhed helplessly as Yuki spun it around and pushed it towards the portal. Her turning around revealed she had spectral tails, ghostly white outlines, too many to count. More than seven, definitely. The fox yelped spell work, and hexagonal blue lights sprung up in front of her. They might be some kind of shield, but they only slowed down her being pushed to the portal.

At the top of my lungs, I yelled, "Yuki! Snap out of it!"

My friends, who'd been lying down in a line spaced a body's length from each other, stirred and sat up. How much could they see, in a room full of frozen foxes?

Because seriously, none of the other foxed moved at all. Not a tail flick, not a sign of breathing, no matter how awkward a position they stood in.

Yuki's echoey whisper filled the room, and I wasn't sure all the words in all the echoes were the same. "My body says you can only understand these words. You are Artifact. My body respects you. Do not worry, Artifact. I have no interest in you or your world. How could I? I am only reclaiming what is mine."

I'd expected to be overwhelmed in a god's presence, but this room felt only uncomfortable itch. More like the awareness had gotten much stronger, at every moment, that it was...

... not quite where Yuki was. The presence was behind the portal. Maybe it was the portal.

Maybe there was no god at all.

After all, none of us had stopped and asked what it's like to have a fully open dimensional gate around, right? That was the kind of thing that might stand out to the magically sensitive.

I couldn't see much through the gate. It wasn't blank. What I saw on the other side was... snow? A driving snowstorm on a snowy surface, all so bright that the light poured out and partly illuminated this bizarre room. As nonsensical as a lot of the massive devices scattered around were, being highlighted rather than properly lit made them even less understandable.

As I climbed down the winding staircase to the floor, I discovered another source of light, although a pathetic one. Opposite the portal, out of my sight originally, a bank of image screens like the ones in the control room were mounted above a board of magical symbols. Certainly controls. Not regular magical symbols like in the control room, but the kind of symbols on the portal. Fox magic?

My friends were all sitting up now, groggy but alive, thank goodness. On the far side of the room, Bonnet hopped to her feet and waved. Pointing at Yuki, she called out, "Hey, this one is your friend and I'm not supposed to hit her, right?"

"Right! Not even if she hurts me!" I shouted back.

Bonnet tilted her head to the side and spread her hands. "Weird order, but okay. Should I break this big square thing?"

Cupping my hands next to my mouth to make it easier, I called back, "Not yet, and I don't think you can!"

"Oh, now it's a challenge!" I could hear the grin her face couldn't put on and I wouldn't have been able to see at this distance, and she smacked her fist into the opposite palm.

"Please, Bonnet, be quiet for now," I shouted.

Obediently, she didn't answer.

Yuki's voice slithered out of everywhere. "Again, you are in no danger. However, there are too many distractions in this room, and my people are being difficult. Let me sort them so we can talk."

My friends made soft, annoyed noises as they were scooped out of their places by an invisible force. The foxes, a few at a time, turned and marched stiffly into the just abandoned spots. As much as they'd looked like a crowd from above, I figured there had to be two dozen total, because it only took half a dozen rounds of that before the foxes were all standing in little groups.

Yuki snapped her fingers. Ironic, that the mask was using the same spell the same way I did. The results were far beyond what I could do. Magic symbols lit up the huge pipes curving up to the ceilings, and the obelisks around the portal. More lights played over the control panel, and the bizarre shapes around the room hummed and pulsed.

That is, far beyond what I could do if I wasn't holding a soul gem in my hand, bonded to me by blood.

Jittery blue domes formed around the foxes. They regained the ability to move, for all the good that did them. I couldn't hear anything they might be saying. Silent bursts of ice magic flowered on the inner walls of the blue domes, doing no good.

Yuki's sourceless voice said, "Your tension is obvious. Everything is under control. Once the Oldest has been returned, the others will resist less."

"Returned?" I asked. It was a lot easier to hold a conversation without a crowd of robed, masked foxes in the way, that was true enough.

The seven-tailed fox Yuki—no, the thing possessing Yuki— had called "the Oldest" yipped desperately and kicked its feet. It was almost to the surface of the portal, but had paused as Yuki's floating body, and the mask controlling it, faced me.

"You're... taking them back across the portal? They're... criminals? Prisoners?" I guessed.

The mask said in Yuki's echoing voice, "My body can't translate what you are saying, despite its useful gift. I am taking them back because they are mine. That is where they belong. They accepted my touch, and now they are trying to run away."

I was suddenly very much on the foxes' side. Could I even make myself choose between saving them and saving my friends? That looked ominously like the choice in front of me.

"So you'll make them go back across the gate, and then you'll let Yuki go and close the gate and that will be all?" I clarified.

Yuki's voice answered serenely, "I will put them back where they belong, which is not in this world. I cannot close the gate. My body was already touched from the outside, and belongs to me."

I gawked. "What? No she doesn't!"

"She does," it insisted, although that hardly described such a calm statement of fact.

"Why?" I demanded.

"Because I have decided she does," said Yuki's voices.

My friends were fully awake, and climbing to their feet. Elvira warned, "I can't hit it. I'll be hitting Yuki."

Joe stepped forward towards Yuki's floating body, his hands spread out to the side in a show of harmlessness, and offered, "Can we make a trade? Negotiate? Is there something you want? I'll go."

The big, brilliant furry lunk. Whether he meant it or not,

just offering was an incredible, sacrificial risk, and admiration flared inside me.

Ruby stepped up next to me, and slipped a tiny jar into my left hand, big enough I could hide it completely in my grip. She whispered one word. "Sedative."

The mask hadn't responded to Joe, so I asked, "Does Yuki want to go with you? Did you talk to her? Did you answer her questions? What about the foxes?"

It certainly was looking at me, with its blank, eyeless face that covered Yuki's. It otherwise didn't move, hanging in the air, arms and feet dangling, but not clearly held up anywhere. It said, with maybe a touch of frustration now, "I have told you, you are not at any risk. You are not mine. I want only what is mine back. Do not worry about my body. Hurting it will not hurt me. I will keep enough of it animate to maintain my reach here until what belongs to me is where it should be again."

Was this what gods were like? I still wasn't sure it was a god, despite its power.

I needed to keep it talking while I looked for a way to use the sedative, to do anything useful at all. If I could get the sealing plate back onto the gate, it sounded like this thing wouldn't be able to touch Earth anymore. That was my best plan.

Except I hadn't the slightest idea how to do that. It wasn't small and easily hidden like Ruby's vial. Maybe Elvira had a precise object-moving spell, but she seemed more interested in destruction magic. Emanuel probably knew one, but it wouldn't be fast, and it would be incredibly obvious.

"So you're the god of that world?" I asked, as my brain raced and spat up nothing.

Well, my questions were making it sound surprised, at least. "A god? No. I am merely taking back what is mine."

Okay, next question. "So what are you? You're the most powerful of the foxes? These are your... children?"

Yuki's omnipresent voice went calm again. "No. I am—" and she made some of those musically yipping interdimensional fox noises.

I had an idea. "Let Yuki concentrate. She can say it in English."

Just give Yuki a chance to resist. Even a couple of seconds might be enough.

The floating, lumpy figure in her enveloping orange sweaters regarded me with her white-masked face. It didn't sound suspicious. Maybe exaggeratedly patient. "There is no good language to identify me that you know. I am the other side of the portal. The Young and Old belong with me. You can see now why I have no interest in your world. It cannot belong to me, and my body is the only one that can hear me, so I know that none of you belong on the other side with me."

It... was the other side of the portal? An entire intelligent universe? I couldn't compete with that kind of power, even with a soul gem! Nothing could!

But maybe with the soul gem I could compete with the amount of power it could bring outside itself, through Yuki.

"Bonnet, hold her still!" I ordered.

"Hot diggity!" the doll squealed. She leaped to her feet by pushing herself up with her arms, then flipping forward in midair. Extending her arms, she charged the floating Yuki. Not fast, and every step slowed, more and more. I felt the strain of the magic pushing her forward, but the soul gem refilled me instantly, constantly.

The thing inside Yuki was not all powerful. It had to extend an arm towards Bonnet before the doll stopped completely, and keep that arm there as the doll quivered. The seven-tailed fox, the Oldest, yelped louder and struggled more where she hovered by the portal, arms at her sides like she was gripped in a giant, invisible hand. The yipping didn't sound like fox language, it sounded like fox spells.

It was. White frost and ice crystals sprang up out of the portal frame, then fell away. They made a lot of clatter, and not much else.

I walked closer, right up in front of Yuki, maybe two arm's lengths away. The portal behind her transformed her into a dark silhouette with only the white mask visible, and that as a pale shadow on darkness.

Pulling out my tablet, I thumbed the tidying up spell, and pointed it at the mask.

The spell dutifully attempted to drag the mask back to wherever it was before it was put on Yuki's face.

It didn't succeed. The thing possessing Yuki resisted. The mask vibrated, pulled by my prodigy strength and its alien universe strength. I let the tablet use everything I had, with the soul gem constantly refreshing me. Right now, what that would do to me didn't matter. Saving Yuki and the Young and Old did.

This was more power than the tablet could process. The metal heated up.

Yuki's echoing, everywhere voice sounded confused now. Not angry, just baffled. "Stop this. I will not hurt you. You are not mine. This strength will not convince me that you are mine."

Bonnet started moving again, but slowly, very slowly. The thing in the mask was having to use so much power against me, it couldn't completely keep up with all its other burdens.

Bonnet wasn't moving nearly fast enough. I heard a *crack* from my tablet. It would shatter in a few seconds. Both my hands were full, and I wouldn't be able to use Ruby's potion until it was too late. I didn't know what to do!

Lisa jumped down from the top of the gate, next to the floating Oldest. With all the magic that fox was throwing around, Lisa's hooves hitting the floor was just one more noise. Jumping up into the air, the demoness slammed her head and those back-curved black horns of hers against the back of Yuki's head, reached around, and yanked the mask off.

Yuki fell to the ground, on her knees, curled forward with only her sweater-concealed hands over her face between that face and the floor.

Me, I fell back onto my butt from sheer surprise.

Tossing the mask aside disdainfully, Lisa took a couple of steps forward, held out her hand to me, and asked sardonically, "Have you ever considered solving problems with something other than magic, cousin?"

I grabbed the hand, pulled myself up, and threw my arms around her. Squeezing the strawberry-scented demoness in a ferocious hug, I said, "Nope. Never."

Her echoey voice coming from her body instead of

everywhere, Yuki complained, "My glasses. You can't see me without my glasses."

That this was now her biggest worry filled me with incredible relief.

"I already have them," Joe assured. He did. Crouching down, one arm holding the food bag over his shoulder, he slipped the other and Yuki's dark glasses under her face.

The Oldest floated to the ground. The moment its feet, hidden by the robe, touched the floor, it ran to the cages holding its people. It jabbered a lot.

"They'll be free in a second. Look," I said. It couldn't understand me, but it wouldn't need to for long. With the powering presence gone, the lights around the room were shutting down.

Yuki stood up, eyes and much of her face hidden by her huge black glasses again. She turned her head from side to side, brow pinched, and whispered, "It's talking to me."

"Joe," I began to order.

"Got that too," he assured me, scooping Yuki up under his right arm like he'd held Bonnet earlier.

Sophie padded out of the shadows up to Ruby, her skinny, wrinkly pink cat body moving with sinuous grace despite how uncatlike her lack of fur made her seem. Airily proud, she told the young witch, "That's a good idea. Pick me up. Now would be a good time to tell her, but since you're going to, *again*, you can talk about me instead. It's always a good time to tell me I'm a kitty."

I dug the hexagonal plate out of my satchel, and held it out in both hands. "We have to close the portal. Here. I... couldn't figure out a way to put it in sooner. I'm sorry." I wasn't sure who I was talking to or apologizing too. I just hoped someone could fix this.

Lisa glanced between the plate and the huge portal. "Hmmm. It's a little high to jump. I'll climb up onto the top again."

Yuki spoke to the Oldest in fox language. It yipped in fox magic. Stairs of ice thrust up leading to the top of the arch. The spell had been so fast and casual, not to mention strong. That creature was one scary mage, and I was glad we were now officially on the same side.

Looking up at me from where she dangled in Joe's grip, Yuki put on a wan smile. "The Young and Old are very nice. They said they used to be human. They were tricked into leaving Earth hundreds of years ago, and were adapted by that... thing they were sent to. It's a tiny little world and it wouldn't let them change anything. They never imagined escaping until the gate opened, and then they all wanted to."

"I hope they like Earth." What else could I say?

I handed the hexagon to Lisa, then turned to Ruby.

Okay, now I could let myself be scared, and I was. I was scared. My voice fluttered as I requested, "Lich infection check, please?"

"Drop the gem," she told me, her arms full of familiar.

I let go, relieved that yes, of course it would be that simple and easy to check. Then I heard the clatter of the gem hitting the floor, and winced in a new flash of horror. But... no, it didn't break, there was no disaster, and I felt just fine. The gem hadn't become part of me.

But I might be a part of it. "Co-opt check?" I asked weakly.

Yes, Ruby knew the term. She lifted her cat, which slipped back underneath her big, pointy hat with the grace of an eel. The burgundy-haired teenage witch took my cut hand in one of hers, and lifted it close to her face. She touched it to her cheek, then leaned close and ran her fingers through my hair as she peered at the orange fluff.

After that she let me go and stepped back abruptly, for which I was very grateful. It was nice that Ruby had also thought that was weird and had been so totally professional.

"No signs, but it may not be visible. When we get home I can run more tests," she reported.

I bent down and picked the soul gem up carefully. Not something to leave lying around. Besides, it was more valuable than the whole rest of the dungeon combined. It was so valuable that selling it for any amount of money would be a waste. Could I replace my forge's fragment with it? I definitely had to get this gem home and put it in a proper containment so it didn't rupture, or overload, or...

Well, "more stable than a forge soul fragment" was still dangerously unstable.

The portal still shone bright and white, with all the rest of the room's lights out. I looked up at Lisa, who stood at the top of the ice stairs, holding the hexagon in its slot. Trying the obvious thing, I asked, "Did you line it up with the encrusted bits?"

"I did! Nothing is happening!" she yelled back, audibly frustrated.

With Lisa no longer by my side, I noticed something odd. The portal room had the strangest smell. A little metallic, a little dusty, and a lot like the acid smell of powerful magic being used.

Okay, maybe there was nothing strange about that smell, under the circumstances. It just wasn't one I was used to.

Emanuel, the magic expert, stood watching the portal and Lisa's efforts, and said, "I suspect the plate is a lock that holds the gate closed. It doesn't close it. Once it's open, it's open."

I swept a hand sharply horizontal. "We have to close it. I don't care if it doesn't want to hurt regular humans, that thing is evil and a disaster waiting to happen. Not to mention whatever the breach itself is doing to our universe."

Hopping down the ice stairs one at a time, Lisa suggested, "The breach detonator. The old guy said it can close a rip in an emergency, right? Blow it up?"

"Yes, but I don't know how," I told her.

Still, I pulled the heavy, key-shaped detonator out of my satchel with my left, non-soul-gem hand. Without the detonator or plate, the satchel was much lighter. Holding the detonator by the ring part at what I thought was the back, I walked over to the barrier between our world and falling snow, and jabbed the other end into the dividing line.

It stopped, blocked as if it had run into a wall.

I'd only wanted to see what would happen, but now I said, "It must work. The thing on the other side doesn't want to let it in." I was not going to test if it would reject my flesh the same way.

"Try pushing harder!" Lisa suggested.

I did. Nothing except hissing and sparks at the tip where the metal hit the dividing line. Not even a lot of hissing or sparks. No sense of give, none at all.

I sagged, lowering the key, and stared across the border of worlds at an icy waste that was utterly evil despite not seeming to understand what malice was. Shaking my head in defeat, I said, "We can't do it. There's supposed to be a ritual. I saw the diagrams in that book. This is a precision magical device."

"If you can't manage precision, brute force often works," Emanuel said in a sly drawl.

"A fact I live my life by!" agreed Elvira. I glanced back, and saw her holding Yuki's hands, and Emanuel patting the back of Yuki's head. Yuki dangled face-down in Joe's arm, not able to do much else. It was a sweet and charming scene that gave me hope and new purpose.

Turning back to the portal, I told the world, "Well, I am a prodigy."

I shoved the detonator against the portal hard, and tried to activate it. I held back nothing, pouring power in. I knew I wasn't holding back, because I felt the exertion, and sparks sprayed in a furious stream. Was that the slightest sensation of the barrier bending?

If so, only the slightest.

Stepping back, I said, bleak and resigned, "I'm not powerful enough, but… I know what is." Looking down at the soul gem in my right hand, aching with regret, I added, "And we have to close this. No matter what."

Nobody else showed any sign they understood why I was upset, which was just as well.

Chapter
Fifty-Three

Emanuel at least understood my plan, because he protested, "Artifact, if you try to channel the soul gem's full power into the key you'll burn to a crisp, and it still won't work. Nobody can handle that kind of power. I know you did the giant monster, but that was a fraction of your forge's full strength."

His sister argued, "If it does work, the gem will blow up and take you with it, and I'm not willing to risk that. Emanuel, go get her."

"My job!" declared Lisa sharply.

"Wait!" I shouted, holding up my soul gem hand.

"Not debatable, cousin!" she shouted back, stalking towards me with her hooves stomping and her arms swinging straight at her side.

"No, I have another way," I promised. When Lisa paused, glaring at me skeptically but not actually coming to drag me off, I turned to call out, "Bonnet? I'm sorry. Come here."

The grey rabbit doll, in Bonabelle's cast-off halter and shorts, its visible surface covered in black and red magical symbols, skipped across the room to stand in front of me. Downright enthusiastic, she asked, "Time for me to sacrifice myself to save everyone else?"

Ugh. "Yes, but... no, I can't." I hung my head. I couldn't. Asking one of my magical creations, one so alive and thinking, to die for me, was awful.

Bonnet leaned so far to the side that she could look up even at my lowered face. Amused, she asked, "You know I've done this before, right? Well, not blown up a soul forge to close a portal to an evil dimension, but sacrificed myself for my creator. It's written into my spell! It's always sweet when a creator feels bad about it."

Emanuel, face pinched and puzzled, watched me and asked, "How...?"

I put the ring part of the key in Bonnet's grip. I wedged the blue soul gem between the metal ring and Bonnet's fingers. Rubbing at my scab until it cracked, I rubbed blood in a trail from the key to the gem to one of the crimson power symbols on Bonnet's wrist.

Emanuel nodded, surrendering. "That will do it."

The room's power finally faded completely. The cages, the last thing functioning, unlit. Emanuel got out his tablet and lit it up. Lisa lit hers. Sophie peeked out from under Ruby's hat, and lit the tablet hanging from her collar, which left the light shining from Ruby's forehead.

All of that was unnecessary, because the foxes—the Young and Old—raised their hands and each one summoned a wobbly ball of blue light.

"So I just push this against the portal like you were doing until it activates?" Bonnet asked, doing just that. The knobby end of the metal key pressed against the barrier between worlds, and flicked the occasional spark.

"Yes. Let us get out of range, because..." I broke down, my voice hoarse, and put my arms around Bonnet's shoulders, pressing my cheek to hers. "I'm still sorry, Bonnet. Even with most of the power going through the gate, there will be an explosion. A big explosion. Too big for me to shield you."

She pulled her head away to give me what might have been

a skeptically amused stare. "I told you, it's my purpose! You might want to hurry, though. The thing on the other side is maaaaaad. I wish I could punch it."

Yuki started to struggle in Joe's grip, but that was useless against the big wolf's muscles. The Oldest might not know English, but she knew plenty about magic. She (I didn't know why she and the earlier five-tail seemed female to me) pointed at Bonnet, jabbered at her foxes, and they all rushed up the stairs.

I ran up and grabbed the Oldest by the shoulders, turning the seven-tailed fox to the image screens, which were still on. I pointed at the one showing the front plaza. The ice wall had sagged and broken in several spots, but it was still there, blocking the doors from opening.

The robed, mask-faced fox nodded, jabbered some of its weird, yowling, musical language, and ran for the stairs herself.

"If she thinks she can handle it, let's get out of here," I told my friends.

We did. As fast as we could, leaping up the metal mesh stairs two and three at a time. The slowest and thus last, I paused at the edge of the tunnel mouth and shouted down, "Thank you, Bonnet!"

Those words weren't enough, but no others would do.

"See you in my next incarnation!" she yelled back happily.

We hurried up the tunnel, in back of a big line of foxes. Their floating blue lights lit up the main chamber almost as well as the ceiling lights had, and I saw the pair of one-tailed foxes from upstairs stagger out the stairwell door as we arrived. Some other foxes hurried up to grab them, supporting the injured pair and bringing them back to the group.

The Oldest stood facing the front doors. She clasped her hands together. Her tails spread out like a star behind her. Three five-tail and half a dozen three-tails lined up on either side of her, doing the same. They all chanted in their twisted version of spell code.

Whatever they'd done to the ice wall, the door started to open. A big puddle of water poured in harmlessly around our feet.

I ran ahead of everyone as soon as I saw the first sliver of light running up the middle of the doors. Spreading my arms, I shouted at the people outside, "Don't fight, they're friendly! Just let them escape! We all have to get out of here *now*!"

"Trust her!" shouted Elvira behind me.

Foxes streamed out the door. Franklin, Sheriff Westlake, and behind them Emanuel and Elvira's parents stood at a safe distance, past the puddle that used to be an ice wall. Franklin looked solemn. The others just looked confused.

At least, for half a second. Then the fisherman and fisherwoman parents shouted, "Emanuel! Elvira!" and threw open their arms.

The magical teen siblings ran into their parents' embrace. The whole group hugged each other so tight I couldn't tell whose arms were whose.

Bent over his son's head, Emanuel's father husked, "When we saw you go to the dungeon, we were so scared. Nothing we've been fighting over is worth losing you."

Jogging up to Franklin, I told her urgently, "We really do need to get out of here. A soul forge is about to break."

She snapped her fingers at Emanuel and Elvira's parents, and barked, "No time for apologies. Back to the boats. Hurry!"

Everyone ran down towards the end of the plaza except the Young and Old, who made ice stairs with magic and ran right out over the water on ice rafts.

I could affect Bonnet from a big range, but I wasn't sure how big. About halfway down the stone plaza to the stairs, I turned, looked back, and snapped my own fingers.

It felt like a gut punch. I heard booming, and more booming. The island shook. The sense of something I could point at stopped. The portal had closed.

Lisa must have been waiting for this, because she crouched down, hoisted me up piggyback, and ran to the end of the plaza. Despite the shaking ground, despite her burden, she beat everyone else to the stairs.

Lisa let me slide down off her back, and we scrambled down the quivering stairs to three waiting boats. My friends and I climbed into ours. The adults got into theirs. Ruby already hovered away from us towards land on her broom. She'd been right, it flew slow and shaky, but it did fly and that made her safer than all of us already.

Elvira rowed away from the island as Emanuel set the sails.

We weren't far off when the tower cracked, and fell in jagged pieces down into its own base.

Dust floated up around the island. We stared at the wreckage, which had stopped shaking and making noises. The regular ocean sounds of moving water and offended seagulls replaced the sounds of catastrophe. Sea breeze, fresh and yet carrying the faint stink of rot, blew away the sandy smell of the dungeon.

Eventually, Yuki said, "Parsley will kill us."

My friends all doubled over laughing.

Elvira and Emanuel didn't steer us towards the docks. We headed straight for the white, sandy, inviting beach, and the town stretching off behind it. Waves tossed the boat up and down unpleasantly, but nothing obviously dangerous happened. I took some deep breaths, but felt fine. I'd only provided the spark for that cataclysm. The explosion was all the soul gem. The pain I'd felt would have been Bonnet blowing up.

I had to bring Bonnet back some day, but I knew that if I didn't, someone else would inherit the formula and she would rise and break things again.

The priest-looking rift engineer from the college stood on the sands, waiting for us.

Our boat hit the beach with a jarring thump. A very jarring thump, that sent me stumbling out of the boat, splashing through a few inches of surf, and not quite falling on my face on the beach itself. Lisa handled that a little more elegantly, her leaping steps a much prettier and slightly more controlled version of staggering. Yuki didn't fall out only because she fell against Joe.

Okay, the rift engineer wasn't waiting for us. He was waiting for the adults, whose boat slid up a bit more neatly, and they stepped out with more grace as it tilted to the side.

The sour-faced College professor addressed Franklin. "You did it. The gate is closed. I came out to look as soon as my instruments registered the change."

She looked at him hard, and demanded, "You're sure? The threat is over?"

"Long enough for my new breach detonator to arrive. I'm sure of that," he answered.

Lisa reared up straight, and the funny bend in her legs let her gain at least two inches when she wanted to. "Okay, great, I'm taking Artifact home and tucking her in," she declared.

Ruby fluttered down, hopping off her broom and standing between Lisa and the rift engineer. "I will come along in case she needs medical attention."

Joe hefted the food sack farther up on his shoulder, and said cheerfully, "I'll come along because I like her."

We started walking as fast as possible away from the adults.

After we crossed the ridge from sand to spiky grass, and we couldn't see any of the adults, or Emanuel, Elvira, or Yuki anymore, Ruby pulled three little clay pots off her belt. She held them out to me, and I deposited in my satchel automatically. With prim authority, the burgundy-haired witch instructed, "One of these a day, and no magic for the next two days. Not even with a tablet."

I held up mine, with the visible crack running down its underside. "That won't be a problem. I have to get a new one."

Fervent and determined, Lisa promised, or maybe threatened, "I'll make sure she takes her potions, and that she doesn't work."

Ruby looked over at Lisa, her face flickering in momentary surprise, and then she nodded her head deeply. "Thank you. I will leave Miss Forge in your responsible hands."

Sophie's leg extended from the pointy hat, and her paw smacked Ruby's face repeatedly. *Bap bap bap bap bap.*

Ruby's head rose back up, and she stated, "Yes. As Sophie reminds me, I have something to tell you, Miss Forge."

"Finally!" yowled the cat in the hat.

Hands clasped around her broom, Ruby told me, "Word has come from Sin Fortress. Not merely word. Mistress Flora's friend has been thinking about moving to Goblita, and is on her way to set up a shop here. I will be staying in town, and I hope to work with you more in the future."

"*And?*" demanded the slightly muffled cat.

Ruby bobbed a bow maybe two inches deep, without missing a step. "Yes, Sophie. I should get back to see if she has arrived. Thank you for taking care of Miss Forge, Lisa."

The witch climbed onto her broom, and it floated up into the air and turned away over the houses towards the witchcraft school. In the increasing distance, I heard Sophie yowl in anger and frustration.

That left me, Lisa, and Joe. Joe looked around, but the street was remarkably empty for a warm, sunny, late Goblita afternoon. Then again, how would people know yet that the dungeon had collapsed? Maybe the people who felt the portal go away were curious, but that had happened several minutes ago, and they'd moved on.

Sliding the sack off his shoulder, Joe reached into it and said, "Here, you should have your food back." He pulled a few cloth-wrapped bundles out, and set them in Lisa's arms.

My demon cousin said what I was thinking. "Why is that bag still full?"

Grinning in a tooth and unconvincing display of sheepishness, Joe opened the mouth of the sack wide, and held it low enough for us to peek in. His voice too mild and too casual, he explained, "Everyone else seemed to forget about loot. I didn't."

Boy, he hadn't. I didn't recognize the stuff inside, but there was a lot of it. Some of it gleamed like silver. A lot of it was weirdly shaped and had magic script on it. I would bet most of it was magic, more valuable than mere precious metals. On the top of the pile lay one of the weapons like those security foxes had, and a blank white mask that I suspected had been the one the snow universe forced Yuki to wear.

And there, next to it… was that round, glittery thing a necklace encrusted with soul fragments instead of jewels? Who would wear that?

Didn't matter. It was very valuable. Joe had successfully plundered the dungeon for serious profit, if he could find buyers for this stuff.

As we gawked, Joe leaned down and kissed my forehead.

Soft and sincere now, he said, "Thank you. With this... I don't know how long I can stay, but I'll be able to rent a room. I'll have time to... maybe figure something out."

"More time to spend with Bonabelle, at least," I added, enjoying being the sly, teasing one for once.

He sighed blissfully. "Yes. In fact, if you girls don't mind, I'm going to go tell her now."

He walked off down the street towards the Northern hills, leaving us behind with his long, long legs.

We reached my front door. Its brown wooden rectangle on the brown wooden building that was my house looked shockingly normal after a dungeon dive, but the normality was broken up by a gleaming black little creature like a bird with long, skinny legs standing in front of the door. It reminded me of a roadrunner dragon, but covered in black spikes of what looked like obsidian. It must have been a roadrunner dragon, because it had a scroll case tied around its neck.

I unlocked the living room door. Lisa dumped the pile of food on the table next to the door, dragged me inside with both hands gripping my lab coat, and pushed me into the comfy chair.

The comfy chair. "Okay, this feels good," I whimpered, sinking into its blissful softness. Thick cushions, a pleasant chill, the faint scent of dust and wood and strawberries, clutter and an excess of furniture all around me—it was good to be home.

The dragon hopped up into my lap. I pulled open its scroll case, and drew out the letter. Lifting my goggles so I could read easily, I discovered I was wearing no goggles. How long had they been gone? Where did I leave them? Oh, well, it didn't matter now. I settled down to read.

My eyes widened. As they moved over the text, I said aloud, "Lisa, it's from my dad. He says... he's sorry he hasn't written. He knows I must be worried out of my mind. None of my letters have gotten to him, because one of his experiments got loose and has been eating messenger dragons. He had to make this special dragon that he's sure will get through. If I send this dragon back, a letter of mine will reach him. He loves me and hopes everything is well!"

The relief was incredible. Incredible. I leaned back and laughed, and laughed, and laughed. When that ran down, my voice giddy and squeaky, I said, "I'll write the letter back tomorrow. I should be sad having to tell him about Uncle Leonard, but after all that… I can handle it. I'll figure out what to tell him so he'll let me stay and run the forge, and course I'll tell him about you. I know he'll be proud of me. It's all okay."

It was all okay. Wow. Just saying it, just thinking it.

Lisa sat down on the couch opposite me, elbows on her knees, pink, slit-pupil eyes watching me with searching intensity. Solemn but otherwise carefully blank, she asked, "Everything? Are we finally safe?"

I leaned my head back into the chair's plush, and groaned happily, "Can you think of anything? The chimera is dead. The portal is closed. There's not going to be another earthmover attack. They don't care about wild forges breaking. Nobody's worried about the breach detonator. My parents aren't suspicious of anything. Nobody is suspicious of anything. My friends aren't leaving town. The biggest problems I have now are writing a letter and wondering what's a good school schedule."

I took a few more deep breaths, just for the pleasure of relaxing. With one more sigh, voice weak and croaking, I asked, "What's it been, a week? I've lost track. Disaster after disaster. But it's all done. We're safe and happy. It really is over."

We sat in silence for at least a minute. My dust-eating horseshoe crab hovered past. New disaster failed to rain down.

Raising one eyebrow, folded hands under her chin, Lisa asked archly, "Did you learn any lessons from all that?"

"Friends are great?" I offered, then grinned, and corrected, "That doesn't count, I learned it immediately. All my problems were caused by my ego, my belief that I can do anything. They were all solved by my ego, my belief I can do anything."

I sat there and thought for a minute, in the quiet, with the dragon on my lap looking around with brainless, birdlike curiosity.

Finally, I admitted, "No. I don't think I learned any lessons at all."

Lisa leaped over the coffee table, her flame-colored hair streaming across her as she bounded across the room. Flinging herself into the comfy chair next to me, she sent us bouncing an inch upwards as it recoiled. The dragon screeched and ran upstairs. As we settled back into the cushion, Lisa threw her arms around my shoulders and gave me a ferocious squeeze.

"Welcome to my world, cousin!"

About the Author

Richard Roberts is drawn to dark, strange fairy tales, which of course is why he got famous for his perky middle school supervillain stories instead.

That presents the two halves of his work, the fun and crazy, and the dark and weird. In both cases, he does his best to entertain, to look at old ideas to see how strange they are if you think them through, and to make a story where his characters earn their happy endings.

Bibliography

Please Don't Tell My Parents Series

Book 1: *Please Don't Tell My Parents I'm a Supervillain*
Book 2: *Please Don't Tell My Parents I Blew Up the Moon*
Book 3: *Please Don't Tell My Parents I've Got Henchmen*
Book 4: *Please Don't Tell My Parents I Have a Nemesis*
Book 5: *Please Don't Tell My Parents You Believe Her*
Book 6: *Please Don't Tell My Parents I Work for a Supervillain*
Book 7: *Please Don't Tell My Parents I'm a Giant Monster*
Book 8: *Please Don't Tell My Parents I Saved the World AGAIN*

Stand Alone Novels

You Can be a Cyborg When You Grow Up
Quite Contrary
Sweet Dreams are Made of Teeth
Wild Children
A Spaceship Repair Girl Supposedly Named Rachel

Curious about other Crossroad Press books?
Stop by our site:
www.crossroadpress.com
We offer quality writing
in digital, audio, and print formats.

www.ingramcontent.com/pod-product-compliance
Lightning Source LLC
Chambersburg PA
CBHW030930020726
47498CB00001B/190